little
boy
blue

also by edward bunker

No Beast So Fierce
Animal Factory
Dog Eat Dog

edward bunker

little
boy
blue

st. martin's
press
new york

This novel is a work of fiction. All of the events, characters, names, and places depicted in this novel are entirely fictitious or are used fictitiously. No representation that any statement made in this novel is true or that any incident depicted in this novel actually occurred is intended or should be inferred by the reader.

Design by Bryanna Millis

Bunker, Edward, 1933–
    Little Boy Blue / Edward Bunker.—1st St. Martin's Press ed.
        p.   cm.
    ISBN 0-312-16907-8
        1. Young men—United States—Fiction.   2. Criminals—United States—
Fiction.   I. Title.
    PS3552.U47L5   1997
    813'.54—dc21   97-16103
                                                                                                              CIP

Previously published by The Viking Press

First St. Martin's Press Edition: September 1997

10   9   8   7   6   5   4   3   2   1

To my beloved Jennifer, and to Dustin,
who carried me for six months

little
boy
blue

1

in the

summer of 1943, a plain black Ford sedan carried three
people through the Cahuenga Pass from Los Angeles into the San Fernando Valley. A middle-aged female social worker was driving. An
eleven-year-old boy was in the middle, and the boy's father was on the
right. All of them stared through the windshield with somber faces. The
social worker looked stern, but it was really a practiced stoicism insu-
lating her emotions from the pain of sympathy. The father was silently
determined, but his determination was furrowed with worry; his jaw
muscles pulsed as he sucked on a cigarette. The boy's lips were curled in
until almost hidden, and occasionally he bit them inside to stifle the
smoldering tantrum. He was both working himself up and restraining
himself. Rebellion was coming, but this particular moment was too
soon.

Beyond Cahuenga Pass the large highway curved to follow the base
of the hills dotted with white houses buried in green slopes. The social
worker turned off onto a narrow, straight road through endless orange
groves. Every so often there was a flash of white as the car passed a
neat frame house set back from the road. The day was hot and the air
dusty, and many insects splattered against the windshield. Once they
passed two bare-legged girls riding bareback on a fat mare. In 1943, the
San Fernando Valley was still the countryside—without smog and without tract homes—where a few small communities were separated by
miles of citrus and alfalfa.

The boy stared ahead, as if transfixed by the white line in the black
road that disappeared in shimmering heat waves. Actually he saw nothing and heard nothing. He was thinking of how many identical trips
he'd taken since he was four years old, to yet another place to be ruled
by strangers. It was nearly all he could remember—boarding schools,
military schools, foster homes—those places and snatches of ugly
scenes, tumult, and tears, the police coming to keep the peace. Whenever
he thought of his mother it was with her face contorted in tears. He
knew he disliked her without knowing why. He remembered the day
when his father walked out, and he had run after him, dragging a toy In-

dian headdress, tugging at the car door and begging to go along. His father had driven away, leaving him sprawled in tears in the dirt, and his mother had come with a wooden coat hanger to make him scream even louder.

He remembered being in a courtroom but nothing about what happened. Then his mother was gone, never seen again, never mentioned. After that began the foster homes and military schools. He couldn't even remember the first one, except that he'd been caught trying to run away on a rainy Sunday morning. His memory images grew clearer concerning later places; he remembered other runaways, one lasting six days, and fights and temper tantrums. He'd been to so many different places because each one threw him out.

At first his rebellion had been blind, a reflex response to pain—the pain of loneliness and no love, though he had no names for these things, not even now. Something in him went out of kilter when he confronted authority, and he was prone to violent tantrums on slight provocation. Favored boys, especially in military school, looked down on him and provoked the rages, which brought punishment that caused him to run away. One by one the boy's homes and military schools told his father that the boy would have to go. Some people thought he was epileptic or psychotic, but an electroencephalogram proved negative, and a psychiatrist doing volunteer work for the Community Chest found him normal. Whenever he was thrown out of a place, he got to stay in his father's furnished room for a few days or a week, sleeping on a foldup cot. He was happy during these interludes. Rebellion and chaos served a purpose—they got him away from torment. The time between arrival and explosion got shorter and shorter.

Now, as the tires consumed the dusty road, the boy worked himself up, anticipating what he would do. Tears and pleas had been futile, his father not deaf to them but helpless to change things. He too had no choice. He was in his fifties, worn and thin, his skin red and leathered from alcohol and laboring in the sun. He wasn't an alcoholic, but in recent years he drank a lot because of his wife, his son, and the Depression. A good carpenter, he was proud of his craft, but work had been impossible for nearly a decade. Only with the start of the war had he been working steadily. He would have been happy except for his son. Why couldn't the boy accept the situation, the necessity of boarding him out? The man had told the boy that the law required someone to look after him. If only there were a family—aunts, uncles, cousins, friends—but both the man and his former wife were orphans who had come here from southern Ohio, thinking that they'd build a new life in sunny southern California. The man had an older sister who lived in Louisville, but he hadn't seen her for twenty years.

The man felt guilty about his son and salved his conscience by paying more than he could afford on the military schools and boarding homes. He scrimped on his own meals, lived in a cheap room. The boy didn't seem to notice the sacrifices. The man wondered if the boy was crazy.

The man flipped his spent cigarette through the window and suddenly felt angry. He'd spoiled his son. That was the trouble. Only a spoiled boy would run away, fight, steal, throw tantrums. The man had done his best. He knew he'd done his best.

The social worker kept her hands firmly on the wheel, her no-nonsense shoes on the gas and clutch. Traffic lights were gauged early to shift down the gears. She'd learned to drive when she was forty, having grown up where automobiles were not part of the landscape, and she was always conscious of what she was doing. But with an empty road and moderate speed, she had room to think. She could feel the boy beside her, his body well known to the welfare agencies. Eleven years old and he'd already accumulated a file. A bright boy, in the top two percent in intelligence, though his chaotic behavior and emotional problems kept him from being a good student. The boy had potential, but it would be wasted. Years ago the situation would have agonized her, but for her own peace of mind she'd developed a protective shell around her feelings. She did all she could to help but didn't invest her soul in a case. Too many cases failed, as if divorces and foster homes were precursors to Juvenile Hall, reform school, and prison. This boy's chances for a successful life were very slim, made worse by his tempestuous nature. His unique potential would develop into unique destructiveness. What a pity, she thought, that there's no direct relationship between the intellect and the spirit. This boy needed a home and love for salvation, and nobody could provide them, certainly no agency or institution.

"We're early," she said. "We could stop for a bite somewhere."

For a moment the man didn't respond, and then, as the words filtered through his reverie, he seemed startled. He looked down at his son—a boy with a head too big for his body and eyes too big for his head. "You hungry, Alex?"

Alex shook his head, not wanting to speak and break his gathering emotions. He needed everything for the looming conflict.

The man, Clem Hammond, flushed. He too had a temper. He

shrugged an apology to the woman for his son's churlishness, thinking what his own father would have done faced with such a snotty attitude: the stern farmer would have cut a switch and raised welts. Times had surely changed, and not necessarily for the better. Yet Clem could understand Alex's misery, and he was sorry for being angry with the boy. "We could stop and get some airplane magazines." Then to the social worker he added with pride, "Alex doesn't like comic books."

"I don't want 'em," Alex said, without looking around. His hands were pressed between his legs, clenched into white-knuckled fists. Acid burned in his stomach, and tears pressed behind his eyes. I don't want to go there, he moaned inside . . . don't . . . don't . . . just take me home, Pop. I'll sleep on the floor and I won't be any trouble . . . please, Pop . . . please, God. . . .

The silent prayer didn't slow the Ford. The orange groves fell behind, and now alfalfa fields glowed in the sun. Whirling sprinklers threw off necklaces of sparkling water. The low foothills that were the northern border of the San Fernando Valley grew larger. The Valley Home for Boys was nestled at the base, shaded by eucalyptus, pepper, and oak.

SCHOOL ZONE   DRIVE SLOWLY

Alex's feet pressed the floorboard, his body rigid, as if he could restrain their forward progress by willpower.

VALLEY HOME FOR BOYS

A narrow road coated with fallen leaves was behind the sign.

"I don't like it," Alex said through tight jaws.

"How can you say that? You haven't seen it." Clem was holding back his own anger. Hadn't he done all he could? He also saw the hints of a tantrum.

"It's dirty," Alex said.

The Ford went through sunlight mottled by the overhead foliage. Stillness filled the grounds, a hush broken by occasional trilling birds. But all living things were hiding from the August heat.

Everyone was tense. Alex's eyes roved like those of a small, trapped animal, and his breathing was thick, but he held back the tantrum, waiting.

The road widened into a parking lot. Around it were several two-story buildings with yellow tile roofs; near the eaves the yellow was streaked. These were the dormitories. The administration building was white-washed frame that had seen better days. The parking lot was nearly empty.

The social worker parked and turned off the motor. Nobody spoke or moved. Finally Clem unlatched the door, the sound sharp. He stepped out and beckoned to his son. "C'mon."

The woman got out the other side, but the boy stared straight ahead and didn't move.

Clem flushed. "No, no, I'll have none of your shenanigans today, young man. Just get out of the car.'"

The boy shook his head without looking around. His breathing was audible.

Each of them knew the script. The man would be more determined because he'd seen other tantrums, and the boy's fury was greater through practice. Long ago a display of tears and thrashings brought conciliation. Now each of them had a tolerance.

The boy needed to behave insanely, even though that would probably not change things. His rage was simultaneously blind and planned, berserk irrationality as a means to an end.

"Get out or I'll drag you out," Clem said.

Alex didn't move a muscle.

The social worker was a worried spectator, sweating in the heat.

Clem leaned inside, one knee braced on the seat, a hand on top of it. "Come on."

Alex's breathing became a hoarse rasp, a choked cry, like someone having a seizure.

"Knock it off," Clem said, his anger rising.

The gasping intensified, and the boy's face purpled. The man leaned in further, reaching to grab the boy's elbow. At his touch the boy yelped and jerked away, sliding down to the floorboard in the corner, banging his head on the dashboard and wrapping his arms around the steering post. Tears poured down his face, and he gave wheezing sobs of futile rage, his body too small to consummate his fury.

Clem kneeled down on the seat and reached for the boy's locked arms. He jerked one hand loose, muttering curses. As he went for the other, the first one fastened again. The boy's breathing now contained coughs and animal sounds. A discharge of adrenaline flooded the boy's nervous system, giving him additional strength.

Infuriated, Clem moved in closer on his knees on the seat and tried to reach down and slap his son across the face. The steering wheel and narrow space made this ineffectual.

The social worker stood watching in the hot glare. She was horrified. She'd seen many rebellious children, but this was like watching a soul begin to die. The woman stood helpless while the cries cut through her and the summer afternoon.

Clem backed up, his rump jutting out, and grabbed a foot. The boy thrashed, kicking, twisting, and screaming. Clem couldn't pull him straight out; the leverage was insufficient, and the boy's arms were locked too tightly around the steering post. The man was sweating now, puffing from exertion. In sudden fury he wrenched his son's leg, pulling him loose in one swift move, dragging him out so that he flopped on his side on the hot macadam. The fall jerked Clem's hands loose, and the boy lunged for the bumper, fighting for every inch. But Clem pried his fingers loose and hauled him to his feet, cuffing him across the back of his head.

The woman assisted Clem now, taking an arm to help restrain the child. They dragged Alex, kicking and screaming, toward the administration building.

Thelma Cavendish stood peering from a dormitory window, attracted by the uproar. She knew the boy was being assigned to her cottage. Her stern, fat face reflected sharp disapproval of such rebellion.

As the trio struggled up the walk, a school bus jammed with the younger boys of the Valley Home pulled in. The boys leaned from the windows, yelling, then spilled out of the door.

Despite his flaming brain, Alex was aware of the new arrivals, and his fury was redoubled for their benefit, sensing that it further discomfited his father.

The two dozen boys came over to Alex like filings to a magnet, forming an audience, falling silent and serious. None seemed particularly sympathetic to the newcomer.

Clem tripped on a step and fell momentarily to one knee. "You're gonna be sorry," he muttered between clenched teeth, wishing he could thrash the boy but afraid that the Valley Home might refuse to take him. Already Alex had been thrown out of half the boarding schools in southern California.

The sweating social worker was encumbered by her purse and had to release the boy to reach for the screen door. Alex turned on his father, clawing for Clem's face.

A young man from the bus—the athletics coach—pushed through the crowd of boys, scattering them. He wrapped his arms around Alex, pinning him. The boy collapsed, and the coach carried him inside. Alex had not willfully surrendered, but the ferocity of his resistance had sucked all his strength away. His brain fogged near a faint, and if the young man had not been holding him up, he would have collapsed on the floor. His body tingled as if charged with electricity. His eyes fluttered and nearly rolled back into his head. The woman and the young man were frightened by the boy's paleness and the blue tint to his lips. Neither had had any experience with such behavior. Clem, however, had seen this stupor that followed the tantrum many times.

"Is there any hot water around here?" Clem asked, scanning the waiting room, which was furnished with an empty desk and stuffed furniture, the masonite floor scarred by years of young feet. The coach waved toward a short corridor where a frosted-glass door at the end opened into a washroom. It was too small for more than Clem and Alex. The father shut the door and turned on the hot water, waiting until steam rose from the bowl; then he shoved his son's hands under the water. For nearly half a minute Alex remained limp and oblivious, until the pain got through to his stupefied brain and the scalding water made him squirm. His hands turned scarlet.

Alex tried to pull his hands away. "It's okay, Pop. I'm okay."

Clem turned him loose, knowing the episode was over, the rebellion spent. "Wash your face," he said quietly, ashamed at having lost his own temper, aching and sad at the whole situation.

Alex turned on the cold water and used cupped hands to splash it on his face, mindless that it dampened his cuffs and collar.

Clem Hammond lit a cigarette and sat on the toilet and waited.

Outside the washroom the young coach, Mike Macrae, listened as the woman told him about the boy's history. The young coach was awed and for some reason felt guilty. He was just ten years older than Alex, and he wondered if he could befriend the boy. In his whole life Mike Macrae hadn't experienced as much anguish as he'd seen the boy go through in just a few minutes. Maybe he could take a special interest in the newcomer, straighten out the warp. The social worker sighed.

Inside the washroom Alex Hammond patted his face dry with a paper towel. Clem dropped his cigarette butt into the toilet. "Hey," the man said, "look here." The boy's eyes were downcast. The man searched hard for words, and words came hard.

"You've got to act like a man," he began, then halted. After a pause he said, "Remember the poem you learned last year . . . by Kiping?"

"It was Kip*ling*, Pop."

"I don't remember . . . but I remember what it said . . . about taking what happens and holding your head up and being a man. It isn't my fault you have to be in these places. What do you want me to do?"

"Let me stay with you." The boy's head was still down; he shuffled a foot.

"If I could, I would. I've got to work, and there's nobody to look after you."

"Pop, I can look after myself. I won't get in trouble, I promise."

Clem fought down the wetness in his eyes. "You can't live in a furnished room."

"We can get a small place."

Clem shook his head. He wanted to hug the boy, but such gestures had stopped. Maybe . . . maybe, he thought, we can rent a place and have a woman come in to help. "I can't make any promises," he said, "but maybe we can work something out."

"Oh, Pop, please."

"Remember, it's not a promise . . . but I'll see what I can arrange."

The tears welled in the boy's eyes, triggering a similar response in the man, and he gathered his son in his arms. Please God, Alex pleaded silently, let it be so. I won't do anything wrong.

Clem held his son at arm's length, hands on his shoulders. "Okay, I'll work on it, but you be good here. Don't give them any trouble. I've got to work out of town this week, but I'll be here to see you a week from Sunday."

"Promise, Pop?"

"Promise. You can go horseback riding at Griffith Park if you want."

"Oh, yes!"

"I talked to the superintendent. He's a nice man and he tells me the housemother, Mrs. Cavendish, is a fine person. Show me you can stay out of trouble so I can leave you alone while I work." He tapped the boy's arm with a clenched fist.

Alex nodded rapidly, his face glowing.

"You'll have to apologize for causing the lady all that trouble. Then we'll see about getting you settled."

The glow faded from the boy's eyes. Suddenly he was embarrassed by what he'd done and pricked by the reality that he had to stay while his father left.

2

thelma cavendish, a widow, lived in three cluttered rooms of the cottage—the cottage being the lower floor of the two-story dormitory. The upper floor was for boys aged fourteen to sixteen. The clutter of Thelma's quarters was in contrast to the strict neatness she insisted on for the boys on her floor. She was sixty-five years old and healthy as a bull elephant, despite more than two hundred pounds on a five-foot-five frame. She'd raised her own three children into good, successful Christians, and a thousand other boys had come under her wing during twenty-two years as a housemother. Her stamina was evidenced by her being in charge of thirty boys, ages eleven and twelve, five and a half days a week. Other housemothers had a college student to assist them, but Thelma Cavendish ran her cottage alone. If she had Victorian strictness, she could also clamp a homesick boy to her bosom. If excessive strictness had occasionally harmed a forming personality, the balance sheet was still in her favor. She lacked patience with interfering parents. They'd turned over to her a job they couldn't handle. Most of the boys came from broken homes; many had alcoholic parents, some had been abused, and a few were en route to full-blown delinquency and institutions.

Thelma Cavendish told Alex to make his bed, put his clothes away, and then come to see her.

The room had two double bunks. A bottom bunk was empty, and Alex put his duffel bag and cardboard box on top of it. He ignored the two boys watching him silently from their bunks. Alex didn't unpack anything but instead went back down the hallway to Mrs. Cavendish's rooms. The door was open, and he could see the woman darning socks from a large basket, her fingers flying. Alex knocked on the doorframe, and she beckoned him in with a head gesture. She nodded toward a wicker chair, the only place to sit not piled with clothes.

"I saw that display in the parking lot and I'm not going to stand for anything like that, you understand?"

"Yes, ma'am. I'm not going to be here very long anyway."

The woman's fingers paused as she looked closely at the youth. "I talked with your father. He didn't mention that you weren't staying."

"When did you talk with him?"

"Last week. We had a long talk about your problems."

"Well, he just told me."

"Are you sure you're telling the truth? That it isn't something you're imagining because you want it to be true?"

"No, it's true."

The woman's lips pressed tighter. "Well, be that as it may, while you're here you're going to have to follow my rules. If you do, we'll get along fine. If you don't, we won't get along at all."

Alex said nothing. He resented her authority and the threat it represented.

"I can't tell you all that's expected in one session," she said. "But the boys get up at six and clean their rooms. Breakfast is at seven. We all go together. The school bus leaves at seven forty-five. When the bus brings you home, you check with me before you go out. You get back to the cottage by five. Study hall is from seven to eight for junior high school.

"One place my boys don't go—behind the kitchen. That's the smoking area for high school boys. I don't approve of it, but Mr. Trepesanti is the superintendent, and he lets them smoke there."

Alex said, "Yes, ma'am," whenever it was appropriate; he was glad when she let him go back to his room.

When he reentered the room, a fat little boy was searching through Alex's box. When he saw Alex he wheeled around, flushing wildly, obviously frightened. Alex had long ago learned how boys steal in boarding homes. He'd done it himself. Usually he would have started a fight, but today he was too drained. The fat boy had nothing in his hands, so Alex simply warned him to never do it again. The boy's name, he later learned, was an appropriate "Porky."

No sooner had Alex put his property on the floor and started to make his bed when an olive-skinned boy came in. He slept on the bunk above Alex. His name was Sammy Macias. His father was Mexican, but his reddish hair came from his Irish mother. She'd died in an automobile wreck two years ago, which was how Sammy had gotten into the Valley Home for Boys. He was also constantly in trouble.

When they finished putting Alex's things away, Sammy offered to show Alex the grounds.

"We can go swimming after supper," Sammy said.

Much of the Valley Home's ten acres was trees and underbrush, wild as a forest and more green than most of the area because a trickle of the Los Angeles River bordered one side of the property. In the shadows of the greenery, where their feet crunched on fallen leaves, the heat was less intense. Streaks of dazzling light broke through the trees. When they were through exploring there, Sammy showed him the barns and pastures. The Valley Home bought its milk, but there was a small herd of steers. Sammy picked up a dirt clod and threw it at them, trying to make them move. Alex told him not to. "Why hurt helpless animals?" he said.

"That won't hurt them."

"Well, don't do it."

Sammy dropped the second clod of dirt. The steers, Sammy explained, were owned by some of the high school boys, who bought them as calves, raised and fattened them, and sold them for a profit. The younger boys weren't allowed such enterprise, though many of them worked for various motion picture celebrities who had homes in the area. The Valley Home for Boys had friends.

As they wandered around the grounds, several boys passed them, the older ones ignoring them, and those their own age greeting Sammy and eyeing the newcomer shyly. Once Alex glanced back and saw the three boys they'd just passed with their heads together, the motions of one of them indicating he was describing Alex's struggle when the bus drove up. Alex looked away quickly, his eye muscles twitching.

The swimming pool was Olympic-sized and filled with lithe young bodies cutting the pale chlorinated water. Their suntans were deep and their eyes red. Even the youngest ones swam like fish. They were hurrying, diving, laughing. Alex could swim, but not like these boys.

A whistle bleated, and the boys began to pull themselves from the pool grudgingly. "Come on," a voice called. "It'll be open after supper." A tow-headed boy, hair plastered to his head, dove back into the water, and when his head bobbed up, the voice called, "Billy Boyd, if you're not out in ten seconds you won't swim for the rest of the week."

The boy scrambled up, grinning.

Only then did Alex recognize the voice of control as that of the young coach from the administration building. He was coming over to where Alex and Sammy stood behind a low wall. Usually Alex wouldn't have recalled a name from such a frenzied episode, but this time he remembered. Mike.

"Hi, Alex," the coach said. "You look better."

The boy blushed, looked down, and circled a foot in the dry grass.

"What're you guys doing?" Mike asked.

"I'm just showing him around," Sammy said.

The coach nodded. Then to Alex, "Seen the gym yet?"

"No, it's locked."

"Come on."

"I got to call my father," Sammy said. "I call him collect every Wednesday."

Alex went with the coach. He wasn't interested in sports, but he yearned for some attention and dreaded meeting the other boys in his cottage. He remembered how they'd first seen him. He wanted to belong and be liked—and in most places he was, but only by the outcasts and troublemakers.

The gym was ten years old, gift of a fraternal organization. It had a polished hardwood floor with a basketball court and signs that said no street shoes were allowed on it. There were collapsible bleachers and a storeroom of folding chairs, so it could double as an auditorium if necessary. The shower room was cluttered with towels, discarded basketball jerseys, and soap that had turned soft from being left on a wet floor.

Mike told Alex that the boys at the Valley Home got fifty cents an hour for any work they did, and if Alex cleaned the shower room, Mike would put in an hour voucher. Alex was surprised. He'd never heard of being paid in any of the other places he'd been. He accepted quickly, not so much because of the money but because he wanted Mike's friendship. It took him half an hour to fill the laundry hamper, sweep and mop the floor, and put everything away.

Alex had been gone from the cottage for two hours; it was late afternoon when he finally walked back in. The long center corridor from which the room doors opened was full of boys moving up and down from a community washroom. They formed a line beside the washroom doorway, towels over their shoulders, toothbrushes, combs, and other things in their hands. When a boy finished and left the washroom, the next boy in line entered. They went in with tousled hair and dirty faces, and came back scrubbed clean, with hair soaked but combed flat.

Thelma Cavendish stood in the middle of the hallway where she could watch both the traffic and the washroom.

Alex's room was beyond it, and he walked nonchalantly toward the woman, though inside he was very tense. He saw the boys glancing at him, and more than one conversation stopped at his approach.

Thelma Cavendish seemed not to see Alex—until he started to pass her. Then a hand reached out and snatched his earlobe, holding him frozen.

"*Where* have you been?" she demanded. An anonymous giggle made her glance around wrathfully for a moment, in futile search of the culprit. Alex's eyes also searched, for he wanted someone to vent his humiliation upon.

"Don't look away when I talk to you," she said, shaking him by the ear. She let him go. "Didn't I tell you the schedule?"

"Yes, ma'am. I was with the coach at the gym. I didn't notice—"

"The coach! The coach doesn't have anything to do with my cottage." She noticed two vacancies in the washroom—the first two boys in line were more interested in Alex's predicament than in washing—and motioned the two to go in.

Alex was swollen with indignation. He'd done nothing wrong. He wanted to scream at her, but nothing came through the wall of control but wet eyes. When she turned her gaze back to him, the sternness was gone. She was strict but not cruel. "I talked to Mr. Trepesanti about you this morning, Alex. I know you're a brilliant boy with a lot of troubles. Whatever trouble you've been in elsewhere doesn't matter—just what you do here. You did wrong by not coming in. I could've thought you'd run away, but Sammy told me where you were. Still, you've got to remember that old Cavendish runs things."

He hated people who "ran things," who expected obedience simply because of who they were rather than because what they ordered was right and just. The woman went on about what a good man Mr. Trepesanti was, how he loved all the boys, and although this wasn't as good as a regular home with a mother and father, it was as good as the staff could make it. "If you have a problem, my door is always open. It doesn't matter if it's midnight. Mrs. C. loves all her boys. Even when I have to make them mind or punish them, it's for their own good. We live in a world of rules and orders, and we've got to learn to follow them."

She waited for a response. He stared silently at the floor. He already hated the place.

"It's almost time for supper," she said. "Get yourself washed up. And this evening bring your clothes so we can mark them for the laundry."

"Yes, ma'am," Alex said.

"All right. Go on now."

Sammy wasn't in the room, but the other two roommates were, both in T-shirts and blue jeans. One was roly-poly, with carefully parted lank blond hair. The other boy was thin, with a butch haircut. Both were tanned, and the slender boy, who had freckles, was peeling. He had white salve on his nose.

Alex nodded as a greeting, and the chubby boy broke the ice. "Boy, that was some fight you put up in the parking lot," he said.

Alex didn't know what to say, so he tossed a shoulder and looked at the freckled boy, whose legs dangled over the edge of an upper bunk.

"My name's Freddy Wilson," he said, jumping down and extending a hand.

"I'm Alex Hammond. How long have you been here?"

"Two years."

It seemed an eternity to Alex—a fifth of the boy's life, perhaps a third of what he remembered of life.

"It's okay, though," the boy said, as if sensing Alex's thoughts. "I haven't been in any other homes, but it's better than being with my mother."

"What about your father?"

"He took off when she was going to have another baby. Then she started drinking, and when she got mad at me she'd burn me with cigarettes."

"I don't like it here," Alex said. "I don't like any of these places, and I've been in plenty."

"Me too," the fat boy said. "This is okay, as far as they go . . . even if Mrs. C. is always giving me swats."

Suddenly it was time to eat. Sammy Macias appeared in the doorway. He took it for granted that Alex and he would buddy up.

The boys gathered inside the front door and went out together and down the walk in a loose group, their noisy voices raised in the perpetual excitation of the very young.

Alex walked with the crowd, but he was thinking of his father and of getting out of there. Outside he could be alone to read, walk to school by himself, go alone to weekend matinees. His father would be the only authority. He and Clem could do things together all the time instead of just a few hours on the weekend.

Other groups of boys from other cottages were straggling along the walks. Thelma Cavendish waved to another housemother; they were hens shooing in their brood. The last sun was filtering through the trees, turning the leaves gold and red before black. A faint breeze had risen, taking the edge from the day's heat. It was the hue of twilight before the night.

3

the city of Los Angeles had no breeze. Clem Hammond sat dripping sweat on the edge of his bed in the furnished room. He leaned forward, elbows on knees, a cigarette smoldering between his fingers. In the dusk the objects in the room were colorless silhouettes. Clem looked around. The room was no place to raise a boy, even if Mrs. Griffin would let him. The big rooming house was dreary, the tenants elderly, the neighborhood bad. Alex had already displayed delinquent tendencies, such as the theft in the military school (they'd broken into the kitchen, stuffed themselves, and vandalized the place, with Alex as ringleader). And once Alex had stolen money from Clem's wallet. The boy also had a tendency to roam, and the neighborhood was fertile for trouble.

Clem felt the cigarette burn his fingers. He mashed it out and continued thinking. Could he afford a small house and a woman to come in a couple times a week? Alex *was* getting old enough to care for himself most of the time. Work was steadier, the Depression seeming to recede. It could be managed if work was regular. Two years ago it would have been unthinkable. Now it was possible. Barely possible. Certainly something had to be done. The psychologist was wrong—Alex simply needed a home. Clem would pick up the classified section of the newspaper after he went to eat.

Clem glanced at his heavy pocket watch. It was nearly seven, and the traffic would be clear. He took a sweater, gulped a shot of bourbon from a bottle he kept in the drawer, and went out. He was conscious of the narrow, dark hallway and stairs with the frayed carpet. It was the wrong place for an energetic eleven-year-old.

The landlady had an apartment on the bottom floor, and her door was open to stir a breeze. Fibber McGee and Molly were on her radio; though he couldn't hear the words he recognized the voices. He'd have to get a radio, maybe a used one.

Clem's mailbox was empty, as he'd expected. His only relative, his sister in Louisville, wrote about once a year, and he usually sent her a Christmas card.

Near the rooming house was an early version of a shopping center,

a market bordered by small shops and a café that catered to the neighborhood. Clem always ate his evening meal there; the waitresses knew
him. He always left a tip, not large but something. He always joked
lightly with the waitresses. They were plain girls—such prettiness as
they possessed came entirely from their youth. It was the most fleeting
kind of prettiness, especially in their world of arid poverty.

It was still a hot night. Clem ate a cold ham sandwich and a salad.
Tonight his conversation with the girls, though never lengthy, was close
to silence. He was still preoccupied with the problem of his son. Increasingly Clem was feeling the necessity of getting Alex away from the
boys' homes, the military schools—with having him live at home. Then,
too, there was the boy's potential. Clem had been told that Alex's I.Q. was
in the very superior range. Alex should go to college. How did a man who
sometimes couldn't find work send a boy through college?

I'll worry about that when the time comes, he thought. Right now
I've got to get him out of that place.

Clem didn't have to buy the evening paper. One was on the counter.
He was the sole customer left, and he asked the girls for the classified advertising section; they told him he could take the whole newspaper.

■

At the Valley Home for Boys, Alex learned about his new environment
as he waited for the time when he would leave. It was still two weeks
until the new school semester. The boys from the Home attended public school and, Alex found out, ran both the junior high school and high
school because they more or less stuck together. The area was generally
affluent, and the progeny thereof weren't conditioned to violence.

"I should be gone from here right after school starts," he told
Sammy.

"Yeah, they've been telling me that too."

"My pop promised, and he doesn't lie when he promises." Alex's
face was flushed. Then he saw that his anger left Sammy hurt and surprised. "Forget it," Alex said. "Let's go swimming."

Alex spent a week exploring the grounds, some of which, down by
the nearby dry riverbed, were out of bounds. He found a soft place of
rich green grass against the bole of a tree. It was hidden, except the side
facing the river. He preferred being there, alone with his books, to being
around the rest of the boys. He went to the pool in the evening, when it
was cooler and less crowded.

Many of the boys had bicycles, some given by parents, some by the
local police department when they couldn't find owners; some were vir-

tually handmade, created by cannibalizing from a basement of broken bicycles and parts. Alex tried to put one together, but even with the help of Sammy he couldn't do it. Some key parts were in short supply, and resourceful as he was, his mechanical aptitude was nil.

"We could steal one when we go to the movies Saturday," Sammy said. "Bring it back and change it around. Maybe paint it."

"Oh no," Alex said. "I don't want to take any chances. Not now. I'm getting ready to go home and be with my dad. What if I got sent to Juvenile Hall?"

The large recreation hall had full bookshelves along two walls, mostly donations—an eclectic collection. Few boys in the home were interested in reading, but Alex was at the shelves nearly every day. He'd already devoured Edgar Rice Burroughs and the Tom Swift books. Now it was Westerns. Reading was impossible, however, in a room with three other boys and their friends slamming in and out. Alex loved solitude. In addition to the patch of grass by the river, he found another secret place under the gymnasium stage. It was a dark area, where the gym mats were stored, but enough light came in through a hole to read by. There he hid and studied books on ancient history and prehistory. He fantasized himself into a world of giant lizards and other strange creatures.

Occasionally some of the older boys baited him, in the hope of arousing another rage to entertain them, but he managed to control himself. What they did was less painful and humiliating than it had been in military school, where the cadet officers had authority. Alex had smashed one of them over the eye with a large rock, bringing forth a torrent of blood and another expulsion.

Sammy Macias was his only buddy, but Sammy was always in trouble, usually for stealing. He was an outcast. Most of the boys had an insatiable craving for adult approval, and they were afraid to be tainted by association with Sammy. It was one reason Alex became his friend.

Sammy's background was more somber than the average boy's at the Home. His father had gone wild after the accident when Sammy's mother was killed, turning to booze and bad checks; he was now in jail. Sammy was aggressive and impulsive, nominally the leader because he was bigger and stronger. Alex was too young to see that his friend wasn't very bright. They roamed the grounds together, throwing rocks at blackbirds and trying to catch gophers, for which the Home paid a quarter bounty. In the evenings they went swimming.

The days were easy enough for Alex, and he was able to avoid Thelma Cavendish's wrath. But after lights-out he thought of Clem's promise and felt both lonely and excited.

On Saturdays the younger boys were taken to the movies. The bus carried them fifteen miles into Hollywood, then dropped them off near a group of theaters on Hollywood Boulevard.

One time Hollywood Boulevard's traffic swallowed the disintegrated group, and Alex and Sammy walked off together toward the row of marquees, which were nearly side by side. One that specialized in Westerns had a facade of logs and a hitching post.

They were looking at the posters in the outer lobbies when Sammy said, "Let's not go. I've got two dollars. . . ."

"Two dollars! Where . . . ?"

"I found it."

"You found it?"

"Well . . . a visitor left her purse in her car with the window down." He grinned, shrugged a shoulder. "What could I do? She had twenty dollars and I just took two. Anyway, hell, we could hitchhike to Griffith Park and go horseback riding."

"No, my father's coming tomorrow to take me horseback riding."

"What about running away? It's still summer and not too cold at night."

Alex shook his head, pursing his mouth for emphasis. "I'm not chicken. I ran away for six days about four months ago. I was sleeping under a shoeshine stand, and the colored guy who ran it brought me food every morning."

"How'd they catch you?"

"I went to the movies during a weekday, and they look through them for truants."

"I like running away. Nobody to tell you anything. You just go where you want and do what you want—like an explorer. The only bad thing is if you get hungry or can't find a place to sleep when it's cold."

"If you want to run away, go ahead. You can have my sixty cents."

"It's no fun alone. Anyway, let's not go to a movie. Let's just fool around here."

Alex hesitated, needled by a premonition of disaster, then nodded agreement. Crossing the street, they went back up the other side, ducking through alleys, wandering through a department store, playing. At a hot-dog stand they bought hamburgers and milk shakes. When they reached the end of the business area, they turned off along a tree-shaded residential street and walked down to Sunset Boulevard. As much as anything they were roaming.

On Sunset they stopped at the window of a huge store called

"Builder's and Sportsmen's Emporium." A gleaming Schwinn bicycle made them stop and stare.

"Let's go in and look around," Sammy said, beckoning to his friend and walking toward the door. Alex trotted behind.

The vast store had many aisles and departments, selling everything from bolts to boats—tires, shotguns, hinges, outboard motors, rakes, shovels. They were wandering around when suddenly Sammy touched Alex's sleeve and motioned to a counter laden with sheath knives in leather scabbards. Sammy picked one up, unsheathed it, returned it.

The counter had no clerk. Nobody was paying them any attention. Sammy picked it up again. "Two dollars," he said.

Alex sensed what was going to happen. Sammy was glancing around; then he lifted his shirt and stuck the knife down into his waistband. Alex held his breath, looking around in fright, remembering his promise to his father.

They were pushing at the door, blinking at the glare outdoors, when the man came up behind them. "Hold it, boys," he said, reaching for Sammy. Alex could have run but didn't.

∎

The punishment was left to Thelma Cavendish. The assistant superintendent of the Home came to the store, thanked the manager for not calling the police, and drove the boys back to the cottage. He walked them to the housemother's open door. She was in her chair, and a boy was in the doorway, but when she saw the new arrivals she told the boy to step out and close the door. The assistant superintendent also left.

The culprits stared down at their shoetops while the woman, immobile as a statue except for her breathing, glared at them with contempt. Alex's panic in the store and worry during the silent ride back slowly dissolved in resentment. He hadn't stolen anything. This was persecution. Instead of nervous fear he had anger, and instead of looking down in guilt he met her eyes, until it was she who looked away.

Finally she spoke: "Well, let's hear what you've got to say."

Neither one answered. Sammy moved his feet and kept looking down. Alex stared at her. The challenge was so open that she had to meet it.

"Sneak thieves . . . dirty little sneaks. You steal small things now and get off light, you'll steal bigger things later." Her voice rose with the fervor of her simplistic convictions. "Believe me, I'm going to teach you . . . both of you." But her eyes were on Alex. She rose from her chair and waddled, shaking with tension, to a cluttered table, where she picked up a paddle. It was like a table tennis paddle, except the handle was extended, and it had holes the size of quarters in it. "Five swats apiece," she adjudged. "Drop your pants, Alex."

Alex's breath was coming faster, and the fever was rising in his brain. "No," he said, tears of fury starting. "You're not going to hit me with that."

The intensity froze her, but just momentarily. She was a determined woman, and her authority was the focus of her life. Rebellion was sacrilege; she flushed under layers of face powder.

"Don't try that with me," she said. "Take your pants down and bend over." She loomed above him; he could smell the decay beneath the scene of flowers. Her bulk was intimidating, but his brain was frozen on refusal to submit to injustice. He felt smothered. Oh, God, I wish my father—The thought was unfinished as tears flowed.

"You're the smart one. Sammy's a follower. I'm going to teach you who's boss."

She reached for him with a liver-spotted hand with purple fingernails. At her touch he leaped forward, butting her with his head, pushing and clawing but not using his fists. The charge surprised her, driving her back a pace.

"Oh you . . . little bastard," she said, fending him off and reaching for his hair. As she forced his head away, he grabbed the top of her dress. The cloth ripped away, exposing the fish-white flab above her slip. She dropped the paddle and pulled the cloth up to cover herself.

Alex stepped back, at bay. Then he stopped crying, for Thelma Cavendish had tears in her eyes too. It was unbelievable.

"You'll get it now," she said, her voice shrill. "Now you're in real trouble. You're going to reform school for that."

Alex was no longer furious. Tears started again, but they were from the ache. It was all wrong. He wanted to tell her the whole thing was a mistake. He was even ready to blame Sammy, something he wouldn't have done a minute earlier. "Mrs. Cavendish . . . I'm sorry, but . . ."

"Go to your room while I have the superintendent call the police. We don't have a place for heathens like you."

Alex's heart pounded with fear, and he stumbled out—Thelma Cavendish following him to the door—and down the hallway to his room. Nobody was there. He stood trembling in the middle of the room.

Sammy came in, staring at him. Their relationship had changed. Sammy was afraid of him. Anyone who would do what he'd done—attack Mrs. Cavendish—was capable of anything.

Alex conjured up an image of Juvenile Hall, one based on movies with the Dead End Kids. He had no reason to doubt that the superintendent could call the police and have him taken away. It had happened last week to a boy, though Alex didn't think that the boy had set a brush fire in a vacant lot, which had burned down a garage.

Suddenly he knew the answer: he'd run away. He wouldn't wait for either the superintendent or the police. He opened a closet and grabbed his windbreaker. From a dresser drawer he took a rolled pair of clean socks. One of the room's missing residents had a piggy bank in a different drawer. Without hesitation, Alex took it and put it in the pocket of the windbreaker.

"What're you doing?" Sammy asked.

"Getting away from here."

"The superintendent is coming," Sammy said. He was by the window.

"Are you coming with me?"

"Where?"

"Running, you ninny."

Sammy's face churned, shaded with inner confusion.

"You wanted to today," Alex said. "What happened to your guts since then?"

"Let me think . . ."

"The guy's coming," Alex said, heading for the door. "I'm going."

"Let me get a coat," Sammy said.

"Hurry!"

The cottage had two doors. The back door was swinging shut behind Sammy as the superintendent opened the front door.

The boys skirted the building and ran toward a line of trees beyond the lawn. Within the trees it was already night.

4

clem hunted for a place for himself and his son. Every day he marked the classified section of the *Times*, and after work he made telephone calls or drove to look various places over. None was satisfactory. Those he could afford were dilapidated and in bad neighborhoods, nor was there anyone there to look after an eleven-year-old boy. The nice places in private homes where he and Alex could have room and board cost too much and didn't provide enough privacy. He'd been confident at the beginning, but as days passed and the time neared when he would see Alex, he began to worry. He found himself awake in the middle of the night, squirming mentally.

He was awake after midnight when the landlady knocked on the door and told him the superintendent of the Valley Home for Boys was on the telephone downstairs. Ten minutes later, when he had the news that Alex had run away again, he sat on the edge of the bed, smoking a cigarette and wondering what he would do. It couldn't go on like this. Alex had also attacked the housemother. The boy was getting worse.

Clem knew there was nothing he could do. He turned off the lights and tried to sleep. It was impossible. He kept wondering where his son was, though after half a dozen runaways he wasn't as worried as he once had been.

■

The two boys left the grounds by following the nearly dry riverbed for a mile, and then began crossing through orange groves on dirt roads until they reached the railroad track paralleling the highway toward Los Angeles. The odd shadows of night and the strange sounds made them tingle with excited fear. Alex was thrilled at the freedom, to be able to go wherever his whims dictated.

As midnight neared, the warmth of the day left the air, replaced by a chill. They were on the outskirts of San Fernando and knew they couldn't walk the downtown streets at this hour without attracting attention from the first passing prowl car. Between the railroad right-of-way and the highway was a large auto wrecking yard stuffed with gutted, truncated vehicles. The yard had a sagging board fence that shivered as they climbed it. They found the hull of a bus and used it to spend the night. Sammy lay on the floor, on shards of glass from a broken window, trembling with the cold, hands between his thighs. Alex sat up, watching the traffic on the highway, the growling diesel trucks outlined in lights, more relentless than the darting automobiles. He thought of Clem, imagining the pain he was causing his father, and yet he was not sorry for running away. Mrs. Cavendish had been wrong, and he'd *had* to fight back. He had no goal. Once when he ran away he'd gone to Clem's room, and his father had immediately taken him back to the military school. Alex wouldn't make that mistake again. They would head toward the ocean and then south toward San Diego.

He didn't realize that he'd been dozing until he woke up, shivering. The sky was lighter in the east. He touched Sammy's shoulder, and they left the junkyard, still following the railroad tracks. Sammy wanted to hitchhike, but Alex knew it was still too early, and they were still too close to the Valley Home for Boys.

Hunger drove them to cross a field to the highway and enter a small café, where they spent half their money on pancakes and milk.

Beside the café was a trailer set on blocks and settled to rest. It had a dirt yard and a rope swing hanging from a tree. The yard was cluttered with rusting things, but leaning against the trailer, near the door, was a shiny red bicycle. The blank wall of the café blocked the people there from seeing it, and the trailer was dark and silent.

"Look at that!" Alex said, grabbing Sammy's arm.

"It's sure nice."

"Let's steal it. We can go a lot faster riding than walking."

Sammy stared at the mobile home. "What if somebody comes out?"

"If they come out . . ." He shrugged. "But they're still asleep."

Sammy said nothing, but his face registered his fear.

"I'll get it," Alex said. "You keep walking along the road, and I'll pick you up." Alex's young voice contained the hint of a sneer.

Sammy hesitated, but one fear overcame another and he began trudging along the highway shoulder. Alex waited until Sammy was about a hundred yards away, then moved quietly across the yard. When he reached the side of the trailer he froze, listening for signs of someone moving. All was silent. He took the bicycle by the handlebars and walked it across to the highway, where he mounted and began to pedal. Up the road Sammy was walking, looking back over his shoulder. When he saw Alex, Sammy waited. A minute later they were on their way.

◼

It took all day to cross the city of Los Angeles. Late in the morning they stole a second bicycle from a park playground, and thereafter they played follow-the-leader, weaving on sidewalks and down alleys and around automobiles. The day was warm but bleak and overcast until early afternoon. They wandered down side streets in both middle-class and slum neighborhoods. It was an exploration of uncharted land where they might meet any adventure. They stopped to rest and play in places as diverse as a huge gravel pit (they were coated with white dust when they left) and a small park with a public swimming pool. Once they had to walk the bicycles up a long grade, but they raced wildly down several miles on the other side, laughing at the wind in their faces. By late afternoon they'd traveled almost fifty miles from where they started and were in Long Beach. Dinner was milk and sweet rolls shoplifted from a small market, gulped on the beach in the shadow of the immense amusement pier. Night arrived, and the gala lights, smells of hot dogs and onions and candy apples, and carnival sounds beckoned to them. They wandered around the amusement pier, which overflowed onto a wide boardwalk. They had no money for rides nor for what was giving off good smells, but they wandered with the crowd and poked their noses wherever they could, forgetting temporarily that they were still hungry. Movie theaters were numerous and cheap. One was showing a Boris Karloff double feature—*The Mummy* and *Frankenstein*—and they couldn't resist the lure of being frightened. Alex bought one ticket for twenty cents—leaving them another twenty-five cents—went inside, then opened an exit door so Sammy could slip in. They stayed through two shows—until the lights went on as the theater closed.

The amusement park was going to sleep. Half the concessions were shut down, and the crowd was reduced to a few clots of moving people. The temperature had dropped, and a wind was up from the sea. They spent their last money on a hot dog and orange drink that they shared, standing in the mouth of an alley—two ragamuffins. An occasional passerby stared at them. They looked forlorn and began to feel so.

"Let's turn ourselves in," Sammy said. "I'm tired and hungry."

"Not me," Alex said. "They've got to catch me."

Sammy's face screwed up, close to tears. "It isn't fun anymore," he said. "It's going to be cold tonight."

Alex felt hot anger. "You wanted to run away yesterday morning. You wanted to steal that knife. Go if you want to. You can turn yourself in."

Sammy hesitated, and Alex turned into the darkness of the alley. It was the way back to the bicycles. Seconds later Alex heard running footsteps as Sammy caught up with him.

On the coast highway the white brilliance of the headlights flashed across the two boys on bicycles. The wind of passing vehicles beat upon them. About five miles outside of Long Beach Alex saw the small grocery store, on the seaward side of the highway. There was a small frame bungalow across a driveway from it but the mingling roar of the highway and the nearby surf would erase any sound. The bungalow's lights were out, and there was no car in the driveway.

The idea of breaking into the store came full-blown to Alex. He turned into the driveway and Sammy followed. They were in the dark shadow of the store wall.

"What'd you stop for?" Sammy asked.

"You're hungry, aren't you?"

"Sure I'm hungry."

"There's some food in here. We're gonna break in and get it."

"Oh, man, that's really serious. If they catch us—"

"Shut up, dammit! Turn yourself in if you can't take it."

Head bowed, Sammy followed Alex. They went to the rear and found a door that was half glass. The lock could be opened by hand from the inside. "Find a rock," Alex said, excitement beginning to pound in his throat as he bent over the moon-whitened ground, the dirt mingled with sand. The beach was only a few feet away, and beyond that the ocean glistened silver and black. The boys were shadows. Alex found a small piece of concrete and told Sammy, "Go out front and see if you hear anything. Keep a lookout until I call you."

Sammy disappeared down the driveway. Alex waited a minute, then stood a couple of feet from the door and hurled the concrete through the glass. The velocity punched a hole slightly larger than the missile itself. The rock rattled around inside for a second after the tinkling glass was silent. Alex had ducked around the corner of the building, heart pounding, his ears tuned to hear any sound breaking the rhythm of the night.

Nothing had changed; nobody had been aroused. He reached through the hole and unfastened the lock, then pushed the door open. He was in a small storeroom, and a lighter shadow ahead indicated an arch. Through the front window he could see the passing traffic and make out silhouettes against the background of the lights. He went and got Sammy.

"What if somebody comes?" Sammy said as they entered again.

"Nobody's coming. Get some snacks."

"Where are they?"

"Probably by the counter."

"This is robbery. They'll really send us to reform school if they catch us."

"Catch us! Catch us! You're always scared. You shouldn't have run away if you're so chicken."

"This isn't stealing small stuff."

For a few minutes they were furtive, and then they became confident.

In the meat locker they found wieners roped together and took a long strand. Alex opened a quart of chocolate milk, guzzled part of it, and spilled the rest on the floor. He took several raw eggs and hurled them up against the wall. But it was not his nature to take pleasure in vandalism, and he was immediately sorry.

Sammy was gathering packages of bologna and several loaves of bread. He took quarts of milk and large bottles of root beer and boxes of candy bars.

Meanwhile, Alex was behind the counter. The open cash register had two rolls of pennies, which he pocketed. He felt under the counter and found the long barrel of a revolver. As he held it up in the shadows, an electric thrill shot through him, both fright and excitement. It was the first firearm he'd ever had. He put it in the sagging waistband of his jeans. On shelves behind the counter were bottles of wine. He unscrewed a bottle-top and took a swig. It was sweet and distasteful, but he swallowed it down; then he did it again, wondering how it would feel. When a minute passed without his feeling anything, he took several more gulps. Suddenly the warmth and the giddiness crept through him. He felt dizzy and disliked it. He turned the remainder of the bottle upside down and let it gurgle into a pool on the floor. Then he filled his pockets with packets of chewing gum and grabbed a paper bag filled with packaged pastries.

Sammy, meanwhile, had been in the freezer but came out without taking anything. He was already carrying a large sack filled with food. Now his fear was gone. "We've got plenty—"

At that moment headlights flashed across the front window. Not headlights going by but headlights turning into the driveway. Alex dropped to the floor. They could hear the car engine outside the building.

The engine went silent. Car doors opened and slammed shut. Alex visualized the leaning bicycles framed in the headlights' glare, while, simultaneously, the wine spread intoxication from his belly through his brain.

"Oh Jesus . . . oh Jesus," Sammy whispered, clutching Alex.

"Get the sacks," Alex said. "We'll go out the front when they come in the back. Forget the bikes. Just run across the highway."

"Look what you've got us into."

Alex felt the fire of anger. He wanted to punch Sammy. Instead he grabbed Sammy's sleeve and pulled him toward the front of the store. His elbow brushed the half-empty wine bottle on the counter, knocking it to the floor with a crash that seemed like thunder.

Voices from outside could be heard in snatches, in between the wind and surf. Alex visualized the bicycles illuminated in the automobile headlights. A giveaway.

He reached the front door. It was the accordion-type, folding back from the center during business hours. Now it was closed—and there was a padlock. Glancing back, he could see down the aisles and through the arch into the storeroom; a flashlight beam was probing around the open back door. He ducked away from Sammy and into an aisle. His fear was growing. He had nowhere to go. The store had no windows.

A silhouette behind the flashlight beam filled the back door, moving slowly through the storeroom, sweeping the beam over the shelves, lighting Pillsbury sacks and cans of Crisco.

Alex hunkered at the end of the aisle so he could go either way when the intruder entered. If the man came down one aisle, Alex would take the other. He might be able to get out by the rear. He'd forgotten Sammy—

"I give up, Mister," Sammy said, his shadow rising. Then he was framed in the flashlight beam.

"Sally, I caught one—a goddamn kid, just like I thought."

"Be careful," a female voice called. Alex could make out her figure in the doorway.

"I'm sorry! I'm sorry," Sammy whined, going toward the man.

"Where's the other one?" the man asked.

Alex, on hands and knees, moved behind the counter. It would take him near the arch. Maybe he could just run by the woman. His heart was squeezing in his chest. He barely breathed. The flashlight swept over the countertop, but he was hidden. He was tempted to crawl onto a counter shelf and hide, but he knew they would find him eventually.

The man held Sammy's wrist in one hand and the flashlight in the other.

The woman hovered outside, alternately asking what was happening and advising the man to watch out.

"You take care of this one," the man said. "He's just a kid who should get a switch across his ass."

Suddenly, without warning, the alcohol and fear worked on Alex's stomach, and he retched. The rich food he'd just gulped down spewed from his mouth, followed by a reflexive cough. The sounds were a magnet. The footsteps grew loud; the light was coming. It struck Alex in his eyes. He came out of his crouch, turning and running pell-mell, crashing into displays. He plowed into a glass cabinet, his foot going through it. It sliced through his pants and cut his ankle.

The light and the man followed him relentlessly. Alex ran down an aisle and reached a dead end—trapped. He whirled, hearing the grunted breathing; the light was in his eyes now, with a giant shadow behind it.

"Little cocksucker," the man said, closing in on him slowly.

Alex pulled the revolver from his waistband, not thinking. "Stay away," he said, his voice quaking—and at the same instant the revolver exploded in his hand, sparks leaping from the muzzle, the sound deafening in the close quarters. The flashlight somersaulted and hit the floor, spinning its beam in a circle. The man went down, yelping in shock. Then he said, quite clearly, "Well, I'll be damned . . ." He lurched into the shelf, and it toppled, spilling cans and loaves of bread.

The man moaned and writhed.

"Phil! Phil!" the woman bleated, each call more shrill. Then she began to scream when there was no answer.

Alex scrambled over the fallen shelf, stumbling as he stepped on things, the revolver still in his hand.

The woman was in the back doorway, but she ducked out of the way when the small figure came hurtling toward her.

Alex bolted into the fresh air, running in a straight line toward the beach. He reached the sand and it seemed to clutch at his ankles. The woman was still screaming somewhere behind him. He never saw Sammy. He ran until the soft dry sand turned hard near the water. Twice he stumbled, his panic overrunning his legs. The second time he paused and hurled the revolver into the foaming surf. It sank without a splash, and he began running again. The ocean was ahead of him, so he turned left, staying on the hard sand just above the surf, which occasionally splashed his ankles. The beach was empty for miles, bordered by an occasional house and the highway.

A swath of moonlight—like a path across the sea to the moon—

raced beside him, but the lights that intersected him were behind. He was half a mile away when the blinking red light turned in the driveway. His lungs burned and his legs ached. He could run no farther along the beach. He turned toward the moving lights on the highway, looking back toward the house where three blinking red lights were gathered now.

A house faced the highway where he approached, a big old house with a yard and a dog. The dog began to bark. Normally a dog would have frightened Alex, but he was beyond that now. His dilemma was how to get across the eight lanes of highway without being spotted. He flopped on his stomach on the slope beside the roadway, waiting for a break in the traffic and a lessening of the pain in his side.

Another blinking red light came speeding along the highway toward the store. The surf drowned the siren until the light was close.

It was an ambulance.

The highway was empty.

Alex rose up and ran—it felt like slow motion, as if he were running in a dream. Would the highway never end? Then he was on the other side, scrambling through bushes up an embankment, falling once as he went down the other side.

Looming everywhere were oil wells, a forest of them, their pumps in silhouette like prehistoric birds scavenging the earth.

Now he walked, driven by the blind instinct to flee, not thinking rationally of his predicament but rather suffused with it. He was in mental shock that insulated him from emotions, though flashes of panic, pain, and guilty horror cut in for a second or two, pushed out before a whole thought could form. The sense of destroyed hope was intense. What would happen to him now? His wrongdoing was beyond what he could conceive.

As he trudged through the forest of oil derricks and wells, he sensed the extremity of his isolation. He saw again the looming figure behind the flashlight and remembered his own fear; then the explosion, the darting tongue of fire, the scent of burnt gunpowder. For the rest of his life he would have flashbacks and dreams. He thought of the screaming woman and caught his breath. He'd taken her love away, and he knew what it was to be alone.

The oilfield was on softly rolling hills. At the summit of the first he took a last look back toward the highway. The traffic flowed slowly past the cluster of lights at the store—curious yet oblivious. For the first time Alex sensed how alone everyone really is.

He stood for a long time, but nothing moved below. The sea wind was growing. Sudden shivers went through him, and goose bumps rose.

He began walking again, without destination, the smell of oil and ocean in his nostrils, despair in his mind. He never should have run away. If God gave him mercy this time, he would never do anything wrong again as long as he lived.

He had nowhere to go, so he headed toward the glow of Los Angeles. He'd go to his father's room. If nothing else, he would be fed and given a bath before being turned in. He thought that maybe his father would stick by him this time, help him hide out.

An hour later the air was muggy and he was perspiring. Suddenly the sky rippled with light, followed by a clap of thunder. It happened a couple of times, and then a sprinkling rain began. Alex was soaked before he could find a place to hide, in an unfinished tract home. At dawn he was walking, clothes dry but caked with dirt. He was coughing green phlegm now and had a fever and chills. He was sick and going home to his father, no matter what happened afterward. He still had the two dollars in pennies from the cash register, so he would get something to eat and catch a bus for downtown Los Angeles. From there he knew his way to the furnished room.

He came upon the railroad tracks where they cut through a barrio on the outskirts of Santa Ana, an impoverished place of sagging fences, mongrel dogs, and olive-skinned women and children. The women hanging clothes on backyard lines looked at him silently, without curiosity or judgment.

A passenger train went by, and he stood beside the tracks and watched the faces stare out.

The populated area fell behind, and now there were orange groves and avocado orchards. As the tracks crossed a rural boulevard Alex saw another market a quarter of a mile away. It was a converted house with signs on its walls. He took the wrappers off the pennies and let them drift away. The pennies weighted his pocket down.

The store had a screen door and a bell that tinkled when he entered. An old woman came from the back room. He went to the freezer and got a quart of milk, then took two prepackaged cupcakes and two candy bars. He piled everything on the counter and saw the woman look away quickly when he turned to her. He realized how he must look, covered with everything from dry mud to cockleburs. His hands and face were gray with a film of dust.

"Sixty-four cents," the woman said.

Alex plunked the pile of pennies down and began pushing them across with a forefinger, counting them out one by one.

"Where'd you get all these pennies?" she asked.

"What?"

"The pennies. Where'd you get so many?"

"I saved them in my bank."

"I haven't seen you around here before. Where do you live?"

"Just a couple of miles away." He jerked a thumb to indicate a direction. The woman's false teeth clicked as she started to speak, then decided against it. She rang up the sale.

Carrying his breakfast in a paper bag, Alex hurried down the road to the tracks, glancing back occasionally. He thought he saw her behind the screen door but couldn't be sure.

He climbed up the embankment and walked in the dust for half a mile, looking for a shady place to eat. Both sides of the tracks had thick foliage, but it was low and dry and ugly as well as uncomfortable. Finally there was a tree, and the earth was cool beneath it. He ate the cupcakes and gulped the milk. He could see an overpass a mile away, and suddenly a black-and-white police car was there, halting long enough for its occupants to scrutinize both ways. Alex was hidden by the shadows and shrubbery. The woman had called the police. They were closing in. He dropped the unfinished milk container, darted around the tree, and went into the brush. The dry foliage was thick, a cousin to cactus without spines, but it had many sharp branches that tore at his clothes and scratched his hands. He struggled for fifty yards until he reached the edge of a plowed field. It stretched for a mile before there was a fence and a road. Moving slowly down the road was a police car. He backed into the shrubbery, keeping out of sight while heading toward the road with the overpass. The railroad right-of-way seemed to be fifty yards on each side, and then there were flat fields, either freshly plowed or with low-growing beets.

Ten minutes went by, many heartbeats for the hunted, and he crawled back to the edge of the bushes. The police car had a twin now, and they were parked three hundred yards apart; one policeman was outside, holding up binoculars. He heard dogs baying. He began to run blindly, the shrubbery whipping and scratching at his face and hands. Before long his lungs were on fire, he felt a searing pain in his side, and his legs weighed fifty pounds each. He kept running entirely on instinct. He did veer toward the railroad tracks, where the brush was thinner. The baying sounds were relentless, but he couldn't tell if they were louder or falling back. He ran without hope, but he wouldn't surrender.

The end came when another dusty road cut across the tracks. The shrubbery thinned and he saw the police car, the two patrolmen in leather puttees and wide-brimmed Stetsons. He had no strength and nowhere to go. He was surrounded, and the dogs were getting even louder.

He sat down in the dirt, legs crossed, chest heaving. He was empty of fear, empty of all feeling and all strength—a sponge squeezed dry.

5

it was alex's first time in handcuffs, the first time he'd ever felt the blows of policemen. They threw him face-down in the dirt, jerked his hands behind him, and fastened the cuffs. Anyone with a pistol aroused fear and anger in the police. An eleven-year-old boy could pull a trigger, he'd proved that. They dragged and shoved him to the car. No tears were shed, not of sorrow nor anger. He refused to speak. They threw him face-down on the rear floorboards, and one sat over him, a thick crepe sole planted firmly on the boy's neck.

When the three cars in the retinue pulled into the rear parking area of the substation, where the signs said SHERIFF CARS ONLY, he was hauled out by the scruff of the neck. They called him "punk" and pushed him through a back door. He wasn't afraid, but he realized that back there in the bushes, *they* had been afraid.

Inside the substation's main room, a place of several cluttered desks and a counter, they made him sit under a desk, in the niche where someone's knees would fit. Nobody spoke to him, but they talked about him. The store owner, he learned, was a former officer, and the police took his being shot very personally. They were furious that Alex didn't have the revolver. The victim was alive and would be all right.

Two hundred deputy sheriffs, highway patrolmen, and city police had been in on the search. Alex was captured less than a dozen miles from the crime.

The substation was small, serving the small town of Norwalk, just inside the county line of Los Angeles. The three cells were occupied, and someone wanted to use the desk.

"Where'll we put him?" a turnkey asked a grizzled sergeant.

"Put the little asshole in the deep six. The juveniles will be here for him later on."

The turnkey beckoned. Alex crawled from under the desk and followed the man down a short hall, passing cells with bars, to a door of solid steel. At eye level was a slot that could be pulled open to peek in. The turnkey opened the door, motioned Alex inside, then locked it. The darkness was total, but in the seconds before the door closed Alex could see it was less than four feet wide and perhaps six feet long. A hole at the rear served as a toilet, and there was a nauseating odor coming from it; he nearly vomited. He sat beside the door, his nose pressed to the crack to capture whatever fresh air seeped in.

The juvenile detectives were coming. He'd go to Juvenile Hall and then to reform school until he was twenty-one. Boys in various homes had talked about Juvenile Hall. A few had been there. There were also stories about reform school, though none of the boys he'd talked to had been there yet. Quite a few would wind up there, though, for there seemed to be a connecting line between foster homes and military schools, and the juvenile courts and delinquency.

He thought about his father and began to cry. He remembered his father yelling, "I wish you'd been lost in a condom." And he remembered his father crying in torment, taking the blame for Alex's misdeeds on himself. The tears hurt Alex worse than the rage, and they had both cried. Now there was no telling what his father would do, this was so much worse than anything before.

The peephole opened every so often, shooting a shaft of light in, followed in seconds by an eyeball. From the conversations he could tell he was being shown off.

Once the door opened and a uniformed fat man with lieutenant's bars stood outside with the turnkey. The fat man's porcine face squirted from a tight uniform collar, his marble eyes hostile. Alex felt fear. He'd seen angry eyes before, but they'd always reflected that he was a little boy. These eyes held unadulterated hostility. Alex trembled, and the first electricity of fear became indignation.

"Get a good look," he said, his child's voice shrill.

The challenge reddened the fat man's face, as if it were a slap. Then he paled before turning a splotchy crimson. "You little . . . piece of shit. I wanted to see a junior scumbag. You shot a good man."

"I wish I'd killed him," Alex said, meaning it as he said it but not meaning it deep inside.

The fat man sprang forward with surprising agility, his hand lashing out with a slap that knocked Alex on his ass inside the dark room. He drew up his legs to kick if the man came after him, but the fat man halted at the door.

"You didn't kill him," the fat man said. "But you killed your father."

Alex uncoiled and sat up, certain of the words yet disbelieving his ears.

"A preacher was supposed to tell you," the fat man said, obviously savoring the moment. "Whenever they found out if you were Catholic, Protestant, or kike—but your father's dead."

"Liar! Fuckin' liar!"

"He was driving down to help search for you and ran under the rear of a truck in the fog."

"Liar! Liar!" Alex denied what he simultaneously knew was true and was unable to comprehend.

"Get the newspaper on the desk," the fat man said to the turnkey, whose face was pale and wrinkled in discomfort. The turnkey looked at Alex and, with tears, nodded confirmation. Then he faced the fat man. "He's just a kid . . . a goddamn kid, and you—"

"He's a criminal."

Alex's wail of absolute despair blotted out conversation. His mind was blind. He was unaware of the darkness brought by the closing door. He abandoned himself to sobbing that strained his throat while he was oblivious to it. Death was beyond his grasp, but it was enough that he would never see Clem again. The pain suffused his entire being. He began rocking back and forth, his forehead banging into the steel door, at first accidentally; then the anguish was so complete that he wanted the pain, so he began butting his forehead into the steel, trying to knock himself unconscious while still sobbing.

■

The juvenile detectives came in the afternoon—big Irishmen with booze-reddened complexions, Sen-Sen on their breaths, and after-shave on their razor-polished jaws. They were a matched pair.

"C'mon, kid," one of them said when the steel door opened, spilling light within. "We're taking you downtown and then to Juvenile Hall. Who put you in here, anyway?" The detective indicated the hole.

Alex ignored the question. He heard what was said, but the words meant nothing that he cared about.

The detective knew the boy had been told about his father, but the big Irishman didn't know what to say. It was beyond the realm of police work. And the boy had shot a man, nearly paralyzed him. The detective had once felt sorry for straying boys, but he'd seen too many go from delinquency to hard crime, from reform school to prison. Now they were acorns to trees he could anticipate.

"C'mon, lad, let's put the show on the road."

Absolutely nothing mattered to Alex. The man's tone said they would drag him out if they had to, and Alex was indifferent to that, too.

Still, he got up and came out. The handcuffs appeared, making a clicking *whirr* as they opened.

"Behind him?" the second detective asked, cuffs poised.

"Naw, he's not going to give us any shit, are you, kid?"

Alex said nothing. The cuffs went in front. Now the detectives were
quick, getting on each side while the turnkey led them out.

The white light of the sun on concrete hurt Alex's eyes. Blinking,
held by the elbows and rushed down the stairs to a NO PARKING zone, he
couldn't believe the waiting crowd was for him. Nearly a dozen reporters
and cameramen were there, the latter retreating with cameras clicking.
The reporters came as close as the detectives would let them and tried
to ask questions: Where was his mother? How did he feel? Where was
the gun?

The cluster reached the car and he was pushed in the back seat, one
detective beside him while the other rushed to the driver's seat. The men
with cameras photographed him through the glass.

The car lurched away.

"First time I've seen such a blowup for a kid," one detective said.

"It's one helluva human-interest story."

The car moved quickly through the light traffic, and then came to a
two-lane highway.

The detective in the back seat glanced down at the boy, who was
staring ahead blindly, eyes level with the top of the front seat.

"City Hall first," the driver said. "Then Juvie?"

"That's the schedule."

Alex didn't even move his eyes.

"The district attorney's office wants to talk to you, Alex," the back
seat detective said.

Alex didn't reply. The detective shrugged and dug around in a pocket
for a pack of cigarettes.

The interrogation at the district attorney's office was brief. A young
man with ambition gleaming from behind his horn-rimmed glasses sat
on his desk, legs dangling, and tried to question Alex, expecting that any
eleven-year-old would pour out all that had happened and, certainly, tell
where the revolver was. Actually, without a statement they had no case.
No identifiable fingerprints had been found. The victim and his wife
couldn't identify Alex. They'd seen nothing but shadows. Under California law Alex could not be found guilty solely on Sammy's testimony, for
Sammy was an accomplice, and an accomplice's testimony had to be
corroborated by something independent: a confession, the missing gun,
something. . . . The deputy district attorney's infectious smile and man-

to-man demeanor cracked into perspiring worry when Alex sat absolutely silent before sympathy, cajolery, and, finally, threats.

"Please let us get that pistol before it hurts someone else. You don't want that, do you? We know you were just scared, that you didn't intend to hurt the man. . . ."

Alex's hazel eyes stared blankly into space. He didn't open his mouth, except to eat a hamburger and drink a Coke. The bribe failed, and in exasperation the deputy district attorney slapped the empty cup away from him, scattering ice around the room.

Alex's thoughts behind the impassiveness stormed with guilt. He saw his father disappearing into the ground—it was all he could see.

"Get him out of here," the deputy district attorney said. "I'll get an order for a psycho exam. I think he's loony."

■

Juvenile Hall's front door was innocent in appearance but really impregnable to anything short of a bazooka. It could be opened only by an electric buzzer from inside a glass booth.

The detective handed his papers to a female receptionist. The reception area was roomy, with dark hard-backed benches along one pale-green wall, on which glass-framed prints of Norman Rockwell's visions of America were hung. The prints and the drapes covering the wire-mesh windows were the total decor. The half-glass control booth, with a periscope view of the outside, had a six-foot bulletin board, black, with removable white lettering and numbers giving the count by unit and then the total: 476 males, 53 females. Now the count would be increasing by four. A very pregnant black girl, her hair askew, sat weeping on a bench. Two young teenaged Mexicans in dirty jeans and maroon sport shirts buttoned to the throat sat on the other bench. Both wore upswept ducktails. When Alex had started to load his hair with pomade and comb a ducktail, Clem immediately took him for a haircut, saying, "We'll have no *pachucos* in this family."

The receptionist pressed the intercom switch and told the other end that three males were waiting. Minutes later a huge black woman entered, her eyes sweeping over the room. She was six-foot-three but perfectly proportioned; she wore her hair in a natural, unpopular in 1943. Her white uniform said she was a nurse.

"Sorry to keep you waiting," she said. "We stop for lunch, too." She took the papers from the receptionist and waved them at the boys, beckoning them to follow her long strides up the corridor to a large room that combined a medical dispensary with a clothing storeroom. One corner was piled with cardboard boxes. She waved in their direction. "Get one and put your clothes in it, except for your shoes. They'll be washed for you when you go out." She walked past Alex, saw his glum face. "Cheer up, pretty eyes. It can't be that bad."

The simple words touched him, made him smile, but then he wanted to cry. She was trying to be helpful, but she didn't know. . . .

They went into a community shower with three shower heads. The front had a tile wall, shoulder-high, so they could be seen but still have some privacy. The nurse went to a desk across the room and began to fill out papers. She called Alex's name. He felt so good in the water that he was ashamed.

"What's your birthdate, Hammond?" she asked.

"March tenth, 1932," he said.

She was standing bent over the desk so her rump jutted out. She asked him the routine questions of a medical history—mumps, measles, et cetera. He answered mindlessly, oblivious to the two older Mexicans standing beside him. They talked in Spanish, half whispering.

Then a hand reached out and stroked his ass. Alex jerked erect and turned abruptly, not understanding the grins confronting him, twisted grins beneath evil eyes. Homosexuality had existed in some of the military schools he'd been in, but it hadn't affected him.

Prior awareness was unnecessary, however. The bitter-looking Mexican had a semi-erection protruding from a shadow of pubic hair. "Touch it," he said, meaning his penis, and he seemed to be half laughing.

The nurse was paying no attention. The wall hid the shower area. Alex felt distaste. He shook his head.

"You better . . . if you know what's good for you." He dropped his eyes to his penis to emphasize his meaning. The other Mexican was out of the water, standing beside Alex. Their postures held threats of violence. It puzzled Alex, for he'd done nothing to them. He shook his head, smiled to show he was friendly, and went back to his shower, quickly washing off the brown laundry soap that burned his skin.

They were drying off when the nurse left the room. Alex had already forgotten the momentary episode in the shower, so he never expected or saw the punch. It was a flashing pain, exploding lights in his eyes. He felt his feet go out on the wet floor as his rump hit the tiles and his head snapped back into the wall.

He was sitting naked on the floor, one hand to his mouth, blood seeping through his fingers. My father just died and they won't leave me alone, he thought.

"Don't rat on us," one Mexican hissed.

Alex frowned; it would never enter his mind to snitch. The ethos of boys' homes included that rule, though it was often ignored by the smaller boys.

But fury was welling up in him. He held up the hand with the blood.

"Tell 'em you fell down," one of the Mexicans said.

"Why'd you hit me?" Alex asked. "I didn't do anything to you."

"To show you."

"Show me what?"

"What you want, your ass kicked good."

Alex came up in an explosion, surprising them enough so that they didn't move. They tensed for a direct attack, but instead he sprang to a shelf where jars of saline sat in a row. He snatched one, whirled, and half swung, half hurled the bottle. The distance was only three feet, but he had telegraphed the attack and the Mexican ducked, so the heavy missile missed by inches. It shattered against a wall. Alex grabbed another.

"Man, cool it . . . don't get us busted!"

The older boys had split apart, half wary and half afraid, ready to duck. Alex faked a throw, the Mexican ducked, and then Alex let go. Again he missed, but he ran to the desk and snatched up a letter opener.

The door flew open and the black nurse rushed in, two men in blue shirts and gray pants at her heels, their heavy keyrings jangling as they moved. One man wrapped his arms around Alex, lifting the boy off his feet and hauling him backward. "Ho, boy, dammit!" the man said. "Knock this shit off."

The second man interposed himself between Alex and the Mexicans, spreading his arms as if to hold them back, but it was unnecessary.

"Get him out of here," the nurse said, nodding toward Alex. Blood was dripping from his nose to his chest. The man carried him in the same grip out of the room. Alex wanted to cry in mortification.

Twenty minutes later the bleeding had stopped and he was dressed in faded, unpressed green khakis. The shirtsleeves hung to his fingertips, and his pants were both rolled up at the bottom and folded at the waist beneath the web belt. The man and the nurse asked him what had happened, but he hung his head and pressed his lips together. They knew he hadn't started the fight because of the odds against him, the differences in size and age as well as numbers. The men wanted to lock all three of them in "seclusion," but the nurse made both sides swear that the fight was over, and then she decided to let the matter drop. She outranked both of the men.

"He can go," the nurse said, patting the boy's head. "Take it easy, kid." She smiled, her good white teeth contrasting with the mahogany of her skin.

One man had already disappeared; the other got off his perch on a table and motioned to Alex. "Time to go to bed," he said.

Still shivering slightly, his energy spent from the fight, Alex followed the man. He was afraid of this place, having heard wild stories in the military schools and boarding homes; it was the threat the housemothers always used. The man led him down enclosed stairs, along a narrow corridor where the concrete walls shone dully from light striking enamel, then through a steel door that the man opened with a big key. It clanged shut, and they were in another, even wider corridor. The masonite floor was waxed, the green-enameled walls immaculate, and the corridor seemed to stretch into infinity, though actually it was only a hundred yards or so. The lights were dim and his escort's leather heels reverberated in the stillness. They passed a nurse at a desk in an alcove. She looked up at them without expression. Now they were at a gate of bars like a grille, beyond which another corridor formed a T. At the juncture was another desk, a hooded lamp fastened to its side so the beam of light hit the green blotter but shadowed the face of the man in the chair.

"See we got a baby this time," the faceless man said.

"Yeah, pretty young," Alex's escort said, handing over a sheet of paper. "Not too young to pull a trigger . . . or fight. He's already had a tiff with a couple of Mexicans in Receiving—they'll be down pretty soon. Better put 'em in a different dorm."

The man behind the desk grunted; he was looking at the paper. "Attempted murder," he said, then "humphed" disparagingly. "Shit, they're never too young anymore." He made a sucking sound with his teeth while he opened a battered loose-leaf binder and inserted the paper in proper alphabetical order with fifty other identical papers. Each sheet was a log for an individual boy. The man opened the drawer and shoved a small brown-paper sack across the desk. It was stapled at the top. "Take it," he said to Alex. "It's a comb, toothbrush, and—but you won't need the razor blades."

"You got him?" the escort said. "It's my lunch hour."

"You can go. I'll have him tucked in bed in a minute."

The gate clanged shut behind the escort, and the sound of his footsteps grew fainter as Alex waited. The man behind the desk swiveled his chair around and looked at a huge board that covered the wall. It had slots for tags, grouped according to dorms, and most of the slots were filled. The man wrote Alex's name on a tag and inserted it in an empty slot.

"Come on, Hammond," the man said, unwinding his legs from under the desk and startling the eleven-year-old with his six-foot-six height. He took a flashlight from a drawer and led Alex down a hallway. The dormitory door was a frame of heavy wire mesh. The man used the flashlight to judge the keyhole. "Third bed on the left," he said, locking the door behind Alex without waiting to see if the boy could find it.

Along each wall were ten beds, the blanket-covered mounds illuminated by a floodlight outside the windows. The glare was sliced into elongated rectangles by the bars on the windows.

Alex was surprised at the hospital bed, expecting a cot. He undressed quickly. A hospital stand was between each bed, but he didn't know which one went with his bed, so he dropped the ill-fitting clothes on the floor and got quickly under the sheets. He felt conspicuous and didn't want anyone to wake up and question him. The cool, clean sheets felt surprisingly good, making him remember the preceding night, spent shivering and wet in the house beside the railroad tracks. From that recollection jumped the image of the man looming over him and the fang of fire leaping from his own hand. Then suddenly, always there in the background, was the stabbing memory that his father was dead. He had no visual recollection or impression, but the thought suffused him in total anguish. All he had—the one person—now gone forever. Crying out to God was useless. Death was as mysterious to Alex as to everyone, and because of his age less frightening, but he was old enough to know that his father was going under the earth forever. And Alex felt responsible, not merely for shooting the man in the market but also, even worse, for having in times of fury wished Clem dead. Then it had been just a word, "dead," but now he was damned by the reality. He trembled with stifled sobs, wanting to purge the hurt in long, loud, and exhausting tears. Instead he bit his lips while streaks of tears ran down his cheeks. He couldn't let go; he'd wake up the others and they would see his torment. Children were cruel to a child who cried, and these kids would be more callous than most. He stared at the lighted windows, at the bars, and he quaked in silence. He was rigid, holding back, but eventually the accumulated exhaustion of nearly two sleepless nights overcame everything else, and he fell into a troubled sleep, emitting moans that disturbed nobody.

6

the lights went on while it was still dark outside. The hard glare seared through Alex's eyelids and brought him awake with a start, while against his ears pounded the clatter of metal banging metal. A man in the doorway was whacking a large key on the doorframe, yelling, "Reveille . . . reveille! Up an' at 'em!"

Boys were rising, some with alacrity, others indolently. Alex raised himself up on his elbows and looked around, his eyes gritty, feeling out of place but not afraid. More than half the boys were black or Chicano; the youngest were around his age (only a couple of them) while the others ranged up to fourteen or fifteen. Talk was minimal. Everyone ignored everyone else. There was no chatter and no horseplay, unlike other places he'd been.

"Best hurry," a voice said, and Alex turned to look into the pale-yellow, freckled face of a black boy. The face had a wizened look, and kinky hair exploded from it like hundreds of tiny watch springs. The pale black boy began tugging his own bed together quite inexpertly. It was something he had obviously had no experience with.

Alex got up from the bed, put on his clothes, and joined the hurrying. He straightened the bed, making neat square corners as he'd been taught in military school. Some of the others knew how, but many fumbled and tugged, and some tried to slap the rippled blankets down without tightening the sheets beneath. The freckled black boy was exasperatedly saying, "Sh . . . sh . . . shit," in jerky phrases, nodding his head in quick emphasis. He backed into Alex between the bunks and turned with his lips pursed pugnaciously. Then he saw Alex's neat bed.

"Man, you done been here before?" he asked.

Alex shook his head.

"How the fuck you make that bed so cool?"

"I'll help you." Alex did so, first pulling the sheets tight so the wrinkles disappeared, while the black boy cocked his head and blinked his eyes, looking angry that Alex could do something he found so frustrating.

The key banged again on the door, triggering the boys to a final burst of activity. Then they all took positions beside the foots of the beds and folded their arms. Alex followed their example.

The man in the doorway—short and gimp-legged, wearing a cheap, shapeless sweater—now stalked down the aisle. Where the beds failed to meet his standards, he grabbed the blanket and tore the bedding to the floor. Nothing was said until he reached the freckled black boy's bed. Then the man smiled mirthlessly, showing yellow-stained teeth. "Seemed to have learned, eh, Chester? Guess you wanna start eating breakfast."

"Yassah," the boy said, grinning.

"What's funny, Chester?"

The boy's face went blank in an instant. "Nothing, Mr. Barnes."

Mr. Barnes grunted, stalked back to the door, and whacked it with his key. The boys whose beds had passed inspection formed a line in front of him. The others had to stay behind.

In columns of two the boys going to breakfast marched down the long corridor of the night before, the leading pair stopping at pre-arranged places so the column and the gimpy man didn't straggle. The twenty boys from Alex's dorm were joined by those of two others, making a group of about sixty. Alex saw the two Mexicans he'd fought with, but they ignored him. Absolute silence was required, and the boys also had to walk with their arms folded across their chests, to stop grab-assing. Three older boys swaggered beside the column, each with a blue kerchief folded into a rectangle and pinned at the shoulfertop as a badge of authority. They were "monitors," and each was of a different race. A thin Mexican with kinky hair started whispering to another boy and was seen by a black monitor, who trotted forward and kicked him in the butt, using the flat side of his foot against the soft flesh. It arced the victim upward, humiliating more than hurting. Alex's cheeks turned red in sympathy. Mr. Barnes saw the kick and said nothing. The company was at a stop when it happened, and he simply waved them forward.

Silence prevailed in the mess hall, too. Ten boys sat at each table, with a monitor at the head. The monitor filled the bowls with oatmeal and did the same with the milk. He used the sugar shaker first and watched to make sure nobody took more than his share.

While the meal was being eaten, Alex's eyes roamed furtively over the faces, all of which were engrossed in getting down the plain but wholesome fare: oatmeal, bread, prunes, and milk. Except for the numerous olive and brown skins, the faces were no different from those at military schools and other places he'd been. He'd expected them to be . . . different. He couldn't remember details, but he recalled the stories about Juvenile Hall, all frightening. He expected tough kids and faces that showed it. He felt less out of place than he'd expected. Nobody was paying him any attention—that was part of it—but it was also that the other places had, in their regimented atmospheres, somewhat prepared him for this. He did notice that most whites and Chicanos had ducktail hairdos that shone with grease, and he saw a few boys sneak the white margarine into pieces of paper and slip the packages into shirt pockets.

When they went back through the corridor it was to a large room with straight-backed wooden benches and a waxed floor. The benches were covered with names gouged in the soft pine, so that ensuing layers of lacquer didn't erase them. He was to learn that the Los Angeles gangs took their names either from neighborhood streets or from some landmark in the neighborhood: Chapo de Temple (street), Alfie de Forence (street), Topo de Dogtown (dog pound), Sonny de Hazard (park). "De" meant "of."

The boys sat in arms-folded silence, except for the monitors. They sprawled in a corner at the front of the room and played Monopoly, though even they didn't get loud. Mr. Barnes sat in a chair tilted back against the wall beside the door, a clipboard cradled in his hand. He nodded affirmatively when a boy asked to go to the bathroom. They had to ask by holding up a hand, extending one finger as a request to urinate, two to defecate, and three to get a drink of water. It was done one at a time, so that when one boy returned, half a dozen arms shot up.

One boy that Alex thought was Mexican, except for his slanted eyes, was passing the time by forming bubbles on the tip of his tongue and blowing them into the air. None lasted more than a few seconds, but it fascinated Alex, and he worked his mouth in futile imitation, unable to form a bubble much less blow it into the air.

Half an hour later the company trudged outdoors. Juvenile Hall was larger than Alex had thought, larger than any military school he'd been in. Buildings blocked his view for half a mile, mostly two-story brick, though others were simply concrete covered with paint. Other columns of boys were emerging from the buildings, and these seemed to be grouped according to age. The youngest group was seven or eight years old and wore bib overalls, whereas the oldest was sixteen or seventeen and wore khakis. The company marched along a road underneath a fifteen-foot wall topped with barbed wire. Alex looked up, and the weight of imprisonment pressed on his young mind.

Across a hundred and fifty yards of lawn, surrounded by pepper trees, was a building that stood all alone. A group of girls in denim dresses emerged, surprising Alex. What could girls do to break the law?

The companies met in a paved square outside the school building and went through the ritual of raising the flag and pledging allegiance. Only the dozen teachers clustered near the doorway seemed sincere. Most of the boys watched silently.

When the ritual was over the companies splintered to organize in small clusters around each teacher. Five new arrivals remained, Alex and the two Mexicans he'd fought among them. A skinny old man in a shabby black suit and wire pince nez, wearing a hearing aid, came over. He knew one of the Mexicans.

"Back again, Cisneros? What's it this time? You're getting a little old for bicycles."

The Chicano, a boy of thirteen with Indian cheekbones and raven hair that jutted out like porcupine quills—except for the ducktail—smiled affably, showing good, even teeth. "No, joyriding a car this time."

"Glad to see you're moving up. Don't worry. You'll make the big time yet. Just like your brother. You said he's in San Quentin?"

"He got out last week. He sent you his regards."

"How'd he know . . . I mean, you just came in last night."

"He came down to the precinct yesterday."

"Oh . . . well, go on to Mrs. Glantz's class. You haven't gotten any smarter in three months, have you?"

Cisneros, still smiling, shook his head.

"You probably didn't even get near a school," the man added, an ironic twang in his voice. The man didn't know the second Mexican, who had pale skin and green eyes. "Bet they call you *huero*," he said.

The boy nodded but didn't smile. He wasn't comfortable.

"What grade are you in?"

"B seven."

"Spell 'personal.' "

The boy's face, already expressionless, went completely blank.

"Go to Mr. Beck's class." He pointed to a group of twelve-year-olds seated around a squat figure in a tweed jacket with elbow patches, a stubby pipe clenched in his teeth, a man sartorially the apotheosis of the country pedagogue.

When Alex claimed to be in the seventh grade, the black-suited man's rheumy eyes narrowed suspiciously. "Spell 'observation,' " the man said.

Alex did so. Since he was eight he'd been a constant winner in spelling bees.

"What parts of grammar are required for a complete sentence?"

"A subject and a predicate."

"I'll bet you can even *read*," the man said, again with an ironic tone.

When Alex didn't reply, the man gestured toward where Cisneros was checking in with a schoolteacher. "You can go to Mrs. Glantz's, too."

A score of boys were loosely gathered in front of the fortyish woman, who reeked of scent and wore layers of makeup that nearly, if not completely, subdued acne craters. Her clothes were fluffs and flounces. She formed them into the inevitable double column, counted heads, and led them into the building and up the stairs.

Alex was now directly in front of Cisneros; he was very conscious of the bigger boy's proximity, almost as if they were touching.

The column stopped as Mrs. Glantz looked for her key.

"Hey, Paddy," the voice behind him said softly but clearly. A finger patted Alex's shoulder. He turned, wary, wondering if they were going to fight. "I'm sorry we fucked with you, *ese*. For a Paddy you've got lots of guts. My name's Lulu."

The surge of bodies as the door opened amputated their conversation, though Alex didn't know what to say anyway. He was still suspicious.

Mrs. Glantz made no attempt to teach. Nearly all the boys had been raised in slums and disliked school. They didn't want to learn. Book learning had no value in their lives. Mrs. Glantz was happy if they didn't fight or sabotage the room. Some did jigsaw puzzles, while others cut photos from a magazine for a collage that would eventually cover one wall. Some leafed through magazines of all kinds from huge cardboard boxes—the overflow of donations to the county medical center—not reading but looking at the photos and jokes. Even if the class wanted to learn, none of them would be in Juvenile Hall for more than two months (two weeks was average), and it was impossible to develop a curriculum when the class lacked continuity. Indeed, Mrs. Glantz saw so many come and go that she seldom bothered to learn a name. When she noticed Alex standing respectfully before her she knew he was a newcomer. She told him to find something to occupy himself with.

Lulu was at a desk in the rear, a pile of books stacked in front of him. Alex went by, hoping to receive an acknowledgment, but Lulu was engrossed in writing his name in a curlicued holograph, LULU DE TEMPLE, on the blank front and rear pages and the empty spaces where chapters ended. He wrote relentlessly, over and over.

Taking several *Life* magazines, Alex slipped behind a desk near Lulu, hoping not to be noticed, and quickly lost himself in the words and pictures, mostly about the war.

At midmorning the class went out to the softball diamond for a long recess. Lulu and a muscular black youth were told to pick teams. Alex, younger and smaller than any of the others but appearing probably superior to a very fat towhead with floppy ears, was chosen next to last by the black.

Before he could take the field, Mrs. Glantz called his name, not knowing who he was by sight. She was on a bench, and beside her was a monitor with the blue kerchief on his shoulder.

"Go with him," Mrs. Glantz said. "Dr. Noble wants to see you."

As Alex followed the older boy toward the administration building, which was also the Receiving company and the hospital, he asked, "Who's Dr. Noble?"

"A lady doctor. She's the one you see when they think you might be nuts."

Alex flushed, insulted. The monitor was fourteen, much too big for Alex to challenge, and so he swallowed his retort resentfully. Indeed, Alex himself often wondered if he was crazy; he obviously did things that were very different from other boys.

The monitor left him waiting on a hallway bench on the second floor. From an open door he could hear radio music, boogie-woogie and swing. He was just beginning to listen to music, realizing that it made him feel good most of the time. Now it filled his mind to pass the time.

A girl not much older than Alex came by, walking with a nurse. The girl shuffled along in floppy canvas slippers, and her gown was stretched far in front from advanced pregnancy. Alex was stunned that so young a girl could have a baby. She was nearly a baby herself.

A head of gray hair packed into a bun poked out of an office door. "Alex Hammond," the woman said.

"Yes, ma'am."

"Come on in."

As Alex stepped into the office, his first impression was of books. A floor-to-ceiling bookcase lined one wall, and a typewriter stand was stacked high with them. Others were piled on the floor beside it. Then he looked to the desk with the large window behind it. The drapes were half open, exposing the bars and, beyond them, the roofs of the houses across the street.

The petite woman in the pale blue suit—its severe lines broken by a fluffy lace shirtwaist jutting from the bosom—wore her forty-plus years gracefully. Her blue eyes were both intent and warm, and her mouth seemed near a smile even in repose.

"I'm Dr. Noble," she said, extending a hand.

Alex blushed as he took it. Very few times had he shaken hands with an adult.

"Sit down," she said, waiting until he'd done so before going behind her desk. "I hope you don't mind answering some questions. It's routine when a boy is accused of doing something violent."

"Okay."

"Do you know the date?"

"September twenty-third, 1943."

"Who's the President of the United States?"

"Franklin Delano Roosevelt."

Dr. Noble marked something on a form, dropped the yellow pencil, and looked up. "All right, I'm going to tell you a saying. You tell me what it means. Okay?"

"Sure."

"What does it mean when I say, 'A rolling stone gathers no moss'?"

"I guess it means that if you want to go . . . get things like a family . . . a home . . . you've got to settle down. Wanderers don't have things."

"Good, Alex. Now what does it mean when I say, 'People who live in glass houses shouldn't throw stones'?"

"It means you shouldn't criticize people unless you're so perfect that nobody can criticize you. I think it kind of means you should be kind to people if you want them to be kind to you."

"That's good, too. Next week we might have you take some tests. Probation is filing a petition with the juvenile court, and they want some reports. You'll go to court when the petition and the reports are ready."

"Is the man okay? I didn't mean to—"

"He'll be all right, but you could have killed him. How do you feel about that?"

Alex looked inside himself, at his feelings, a rare thing for an eleven-year-old, and tossed a shoulder. "I'm sorry I hurt him, I was scared . . . I think I tripped. I didn't mean to shoot him, but it's unreal, too. I didn't know him . . . never even saw his face . . ."

"Do you ever feel really sorry just because you've done something, even something you've gotten away with?"

"Sometimes. In one foster home the lady had a parakeet, and I used to duck it under water because I liked to see it flap its feathers to get the water off. One day it drowned. They didn't know I did it, but I cried for a long time. I prayed for the bird to come back, but it wouldn't. Another time I hit a boy who had that sickness where he won't stop bleeding if he gets cut—hemo something—and he bled inside under the skin, and they took him to the hospital. He didn't tell on me, but I felt so bad that I went to the superintendent. I wanted him to punish me. That *is* crazy, isn't it?"

"No, Alex, that's more human than you think."

"I'm sorry about shooting the man because of my dad."

"How's that?"

"He came to look for me and . . . got killed." Tears welled up in the boy's eyes. The ache had never left but somehow had been held below consciousness. He'd had no time to think, and his mind had resolutely looked away from so painful a sight. Now he sniffled but tried to stifle it.

"I didn't know . . . you poor boy." The professional distance was shattered. She wondered how the police report had missed such a thing. "If you don't want to talk we can do it some other time."

The words of warmth splintered the last of his control, and his eleven-year-old body suddenly quaked with the force of his sobbing. It was the first real purge of his pain. The cries in the darkness of the sub-station hole had been adulterated with fury, but this was pure pain. Dr. Noble leaned forward, as if she wanted to go around and gather him up in her arms, but her years of training in detachment held her back. She ached in silent sympathy, watching his ferocity expend itself. He was no longer just another boy in trouble. When the sobbing diminished she gave him Kleenex to blow his nose. Another appointment was waiting, but she stepped to the door and cancelled it.

"I didn't know about your father or I wouldn't have asked you those petty questions."

Sniffling still, he nodded, not caring about the questions. Dr. Noble, whose job was handling distraught persons, was at a loss for words. She decided to talk to him as she would an adult in similar circumstances.

"What about the funeral?" she asked.

He hadn't thought about the funeral. "I don't know if there'll be one. He always said he wanted to be cremated, and he'd already paid for all that . . . when the divorce . . . 'cause there wasn't nobody to take care of it. I heard him say it lots of times—he'd made arrangements so nobody would be bothered."

"There'll be some kind of service. I'll find out." She was thinking of where she'd telephone. "If you want to go, I'll see about that, too." She didn't know how such trips were arranged, but she was sure it could be done.

"Yes, ma'am. I want to go."

"I imagine someone will have to go with you, and the county will charge for their salary. Your mother should be willing to do that much."

Before she could finish the sentence Alex shook his head. "They're divorced and I don't know where she is . . . don't want to."

"Oh," Dr. Noble said, momentarily disconcerted. By itself the hostility wasn't so strange, but it was unexpected with so much sadness. "What about an aunt or—"

Again he shook his head. "There's nobody. It was me and my dad." The tears welled again, and he choked them down, swallowing. "He had a sister in Louisville. Her name is Ava something . . . Swedish. . . . They had some kind of fight. . . . He stopped talking to her. He was sorry, but he couldn't bring himself to apologize. I know he wanted to."

"I'll take you if that's the only way," she said.

Alex looked up, studying her face. "Is that a promise?"

"It's a promise. But we'll have to find out when it is and how to go about it."

A lull ensued. The electric wall clock said that twenty minutes remained.

"Your father must have been stubborn sometimes. Are you like him?"

"Sometimes, I guess . . . when I know I'm right."

"Do you hate it when someone tells you what to do?"

"I hate it when they think I should do what they say just because they say it. A social worker said I'll always be in trouble as long as I hate authority."

"Do you really hate authority?"

He shrugged. "Sometimes. It depends on . . ." He shrugged again.

"What do you think should be done with you now?"

Alex frowned. He was being carried along without having any idea where he was going.

"What do you want?"

"I don't know. I want things to go back, but I—"

"What about when you grow up? What do you want?"

"I want to be somebody. I want people to respect me."

"You'll have to work to get that."

"They have to give me a chance . . . and I wish they'd leave me alone."

"You like to be alone?"

"Sometimes. I like to read a lot."

"What do you like?"

"Tarzan, Zane Grey, and those books about collies by Albert Payson Terhune."

"Have you ever had a dog?"

Alex shook his head.

A light knock on the door interrupted them. Dr. Noble glanced at her watch. "I've got to go, Alex. This afternoon I'll see about taking you to the funeral. It's probably tomorrow."

Clem's death had been forgotten for a few minutes. The reminder brought the pain and tears again, but they were quieter. He fought them back, not wanting his red eyes to be seen by the other boys. Dr. Noble waited until he had composed himself, wondering how she could possibly help him.

■

After supper it was still daylight, and the company went outdoors to the recreation yard until dark. Each company had its own area, and mingling was forbidden. Receiving company had a space where two basketball hoops were suspended over a dirt court. But this evening a monitor carried two pairs of 12-ounce boxing gloves, the reddish leather scuffed from endless use, and instead of the basketball area, the company went to a patch of scrubby lawn in the shadow of a building. There they broke ranks to form a circle, squatting on the ground.

The supervisor was the tall man who'd been on duty when Alex came in. A boy had carried in the man's own chair so he could prop it against a wall and watch the fight in comfort. He took the gloves and stood in the circle. "Any grudges to settle?" he asked.

For a moment there was silence; then a tall, yellow-skinned black with curly rather than kinky hair stood up. He was about fifteen years old. "Yeah, Ah wanna kick off in Miles's ass. He think he's somepin' an' he ain't shit."

Miles was the black monitor who fawned over the Man and was cruel to weaker boys. He'd kicked Chester for unfolding his arms in the line. Now he came to his feet, his flat nose distended even more than usual. He was shorter, huskier than the others.

"Remember, there's no rounds in a grudge fight," the Man said. "You go until somebody's out or quits or I stop it."

The two black youths glared at each other. Both had supporters, though the monitor had more. He'd been in Juvenile Hall longer and had power over the boys. They stripped to the waist, took off their shoes, and were helped into the gloves. Their faces were somber, and the jaw muscles of the light-skinned youth throbbed as he clenched his teeth.

The Man called them to the center. "No kicking. No hitting below the belt, no wrestling, and no hitting if someone goes down." He motioned them to separate, and then he stepped clear. "Time," he said, finding his chair to watch.

Alex sat cross-legged in the front row, fascinated. He expected the combatants to rush at each other and begin flailing, like the boys in military school. (Those who didn't hide behind their gloves and quit at the first blow, that is.) But instead these boys came out slowly and circled each other. The taller boy seemed to dance, moving his long arms in a motion that vaguely resembled someone running—so strange a "guard" that Miles, who had one hand cocked by his chin and the other down low, was made nervous, jerking back his head at every motion. Suddenly the taller boy swung a punch like a whip, with much velocity but little power. It splatted loud on Miles's body, and he charged to retaliate. Then the poor charade of "boxing" disintegrated. Miles pumped his punches up from the floor, most of them landing in the body. He was stronger than the taller boy, who was swinging with both hands at the head. Everything landed. For thirty seconds they beat each other up. Miles's nose was bleeding. Without warning, he lowered his head and shoulders and drove in, pushing the taller boy back until they both crashed into the front rank of the crowd. Alex tried to scramble away but couldn't. They tripped over him and went down grunting, still trying to pound each other but not getting much leverage.

The spectators broke from the seated circle and jammed in tight for a view of the fighters rolling on the ground. The boys yelped encouragement, their bodies jerking and jumping in spasms of empathy.

Alex had untangled his legs and scooted clear on his rump as the supervisor waded through the boys, yelling at them to sit down, shoving them aside. His already sunburned face was even darker with a flush of anger. "Get the hell up," he snarled, looming over the black youths, who had frozen their struggle at his arrival. The taller boy was now on top, his arm headlocked around Miles's neck. The supervisor had hands to match his great height. He leaned over, wrapped his fingers through the taller boy's web belt, and hoisted him to his feet.

"You're supposed to box, goddammit! Not roll around in the dirt like animals."

"That motherfucker started it. Ah was kickin' his ass."

Miles had scrambled up again, blotches of dirt sticking to his sweaty ebony skin and a film of white foam under his armpits. Now blood trickled from his lip to join the blood from his nose. To Alex the fight had seemed even, but Miles had all the bruises, and he was breathing harder, exhausted.

"Ah'm gettin' yo' ass, you half-white nigger," Miles said.

"Fuck you . . . you kiss-ass motherfucker."

Miles suddenly spit at the taller boy, and even before it landed, the other youth kicked out, his toe hooking up into Miles's crotch, bringing forth a yelp of pain. Miles froze momentarily, then doubled over, clutching his groin with gloved hands. At the same moment the supervisor swung the taller boy away by the belt, half-throwing and half-slapping him down. "Okay . . . you like to kick, huh? Like to kick, huh?"

"He spit on—"

The words ran together and ended as the man began kicking the boy in the legs, still muttering, "Like to kick, huh? Like to kick, huh?"

Alex watched with horror and fury. Even an eleven-year-old could see the injustice. Miles had started the wrestling; Miles had spit. But Miles was the man's pet, and a monitor too.

The sixty boys watched with somber expressions that boys did not usually wear. The taller boy rolled away from the kicks, the man following—and in ten seconds the man stopped, his contorted face turning blank as he realized what he'd been doing. "Get up," he said. "Get those gloves off. You too, Miles." Then the man looked around defiantly, embarrassed by his loss of temper. "Anybody else have a grudge to settle?"

7

half the company was being showered while the other half filled the dayroom with bodies and bedlam. This was the recreation hour before bedtime and lights-out. The supervisor was at the shower room, and the dayroom door was locked. A few boys lay on the floor writing letters (there were no tables), sharpening their pencils by rubbing them sideways on the cement. One group in a corner was playing Monopoly, complete with kibitzers, and beside them was a poker game in which ten markers had the value of one contraband cigarette. The biggest crowd was near the window where a radio sat on the ledge. Half a dozen youths, nearly all Chicano or black, stood as if at a street corner hot-dog stand. They were all in their mid-teens and ready to graduate from delinquency to crime. Their shirt collars were turned up, and so were their sleeves. Their shoes all had double soles and horseshoe taps on the heels; it was both style and a weapon. Finally, their pants were pulled precariously low on their hips and rolled up at the bottom, making their legs look ridiculous short and their torsos freakishly long. Some silently mimed the singers on the radio, dusky black voices doing rhythm and blues, backed by syrupy saxophones. Lulu was there, completely at ease, one hand braced inside the front of his waistband, his olive features haughty. Alex thought Lulu looked cool, that they all did, and now he, Alex, could start combing his hair in a ducktail and maybe get some double-soled shoes. He was stretched out on a bench, alone and friendless and feeling it. He wanted to go over to the crowd, but the boys there were older, and he was afraid of rebuff. It didn't cross his mind that he was white and they were brown and black; he was still too young to think about race.

A shadow passed over him, and when he looked up it was Chester's face. "What you doin'?" Chester asked.

"Nothing."

"Wanna play some checkers?"

"No, thank you anyway."

"Hey, how come you be saying' 'no thank you'? Can' you say jes' 'no' like everybody else? You say 'yes, sir,' and 'excuse me' like some kind of sissy. Or some rich white boy. You ain' no rich white boy, are you?"

"No, I ain' no rich white boy."

"Don't be makin' fun of me, motherfucker!"

The quick threatening anger was unexpected. Alex hadn't intended to make fun of Chester, certainly not maliciously, and the angry command was like an open-handed slap, stinging and igniting anger in response.

"Don't call me a motherfucker," he said. "I don't call you names."

"Fuck you, Paddy . . . scared-ass motherfucker."

"I told you—"

"So what're you gonna do about it? If you get mad, then you can scratch your ass and get glad."

The freckled black boy was already standing, leaning a little forward in readiness. At the first heated words Alex swung his feet down to the floor, but he was still seated and at a disadvantage. Chester could hit him the instant he moved. He was heavier than Chester, whose body was like a skeleton draped in clothes, but Chester was older, his reflexes more developed. Alex had no fear; he had known a fight was unavoidable the instant Chester cursed him. That had been a challenge. Maybe a fight would burn away his vague bad feelings of helplessness, futility, anxiety. It would not alter reality, but it would alter how he felt.

"What're you gonna do, *mo-ther-fuck-er?*" The words were deliberately slow and exaggerated, a style that copied many challenges Chester had seen in his neighborhood, one that radiated contempt far beyond his twelve years.

"Let me up."

"Sheeit!"

As Chester sneered, Alex ducked his head and dove forward, feeling a fist graze his cheek a moment before his forehead rammed into Chester's chest. He clutched blindly at Chester's clothes. A fist hit him in the kidney and Chester's foot kicked up but landed no higher than his knee.

The two boys went down in a tangle, and Alex got an arm around Chester's neck in a headlock. Alex was more or less on top and had control. Chester couldn't break the hold.

At the first blow every head in the room had turned to see, and then everyone rushed to watch the fight, standing jammed up so close that the fight was at their feet.

"Lemme up an' fight, motherfucker," Chester demanded shrilly. "Fuck this wrestling bullshit."

Though not really hurting Chester, Alex had an advantage. They stayed immobile for half a minute. The crowd was quiet; the action was too frozen to arouse them, though at the outset a couple of older black youths had encouraged Chester to "kick that Paddy's ass."

"Lemme up," Chester demanded again.

Alex squeezed harder.

"Let him up, motherfucker," said a fourteen-year-old black with red, processed hair, emphasizing the order with a kick to Alex's hip. Alex looked up. The boy's face was high above him, and he was frightened. Fighting Chester was one thing; fighting a fourteen-year-old was another.

"Hey, *ese*, they're having a fair fight. Leave 'em alone." Lulu Cisneros had spoken. "It's none of your business, *que no?*"

The older black's head came up in haughty disdain. "My business ain' none of your business either."

"I might make it my business."

Seeing that Lulu was serious, the black youth shrugged and backed up from his position. "That's a Paddy. How come you're gettin' involved?"

"No, I ain't involved . . . 'less somebody gets me involved. I just say to let them fight it out."

"They ain't doin' much fightin'."

The silence in the room brought the man from the shower room down the hall. The boys scattered when the key hit the door. But Alex and Chester didn't have time. When the man saw them, Alex was pulling his arm from around Chester's neck. When he reached them, they were on their feet.

The man's half-smile was more frightening than an angry scowl would have been. "Having a little fight, eh?" he said.

"No, *sir*," Chester said—and as Alex heard "sir," he giggled without thinking.

The man looked at Alex. "Something funny, Hammond?"

Frightened, Alex shook his head.

"Jus' horseplayin', Mr. Fitzgerald," Chester said. "That's all." Chester put his arm around Alex's shoulder. "We friends, Mr. Fitzgerald. See . . . ?"

"That's bullshit!" Mr. Fitzgerald said. "I know what I saw . . . and that's why we had the gloves out this afternoon . . . to get it out of your systems. All you little bastards wanna do is fight."

"We're not mad at each other, are we, Alex?"

Alex shook his head; he was only mad at the man, and he kept his eyes averted because of the rage building up within him.

"You know the rule on fights, Nelson . . . isolation until the chief supervisor talks to you and decides what to do. Gotta make sure you *can't* start again when my back's turned."

"Mr. Fitzgerald," Chester wailed. No matter how tough the ghetto and how precociously tough the child raised on its mean streets, Chester was still barely twelve years old. "Don't put me in isolation."

"I don't make the rules. I just follow them."

Alex didn't know what isolation was, but he wanted to cry, the ache of sadness and rage eating him. However he just blinked and remained silent. Tears would accomplish nothing, and he would look bad.

"Let's go to the desk while I call an escort," Fitzgerald said, motioning the boys to precede him.

Alex watched the eyes of the others in the company as he marched by. Every face was impassive except Lulu's; the Chicano winked at him.

■

A solid door from the corridor led to an alcove where there were two barred gates—one to the right and one to the left. Each opened into an isolation room.

The light was out when Alex stepped in and the gate was locked behind him, but powerful floodlights on the grounds came through two layers of wire mesh and one set of bars strongly enough to illuminate the cell's vacantness. A bare striped mattress was on the floor, with a washbowl and toilet—the former above the latter—making a single facility on the wall.

"You'll get a blanket later," the escorting supervisor said.

"Is Chester Nelson coming in here?"

"I'm getting him now. He'll be right across the way."

When the man left, Alex went to the sink for a drink of water, discovering that it lacked buttons or handles. The toilet was the same. They had to be operated from outside the cell.

The window was open, and a chilly breeze was coming in. Alex poked his fingers through the wire mesh but couldn't touch the window, much less close it. The frame had a padlock.

The corridor door was open, light spilling inside, and Alex heard Chester's voice without deciphering the words.

"You'll probably get out tomorrow," the Man said.

"Say, Mister," Alex said. "Can I get this window closed? It's cold in here."

"I haven't got the key."

"Well, don't forget the blanket."

"Don't worry."

"I need one too," Chester added, as his cell door was closed and locked.

"I said don't worry," the man said irritably. "This ain't a hotel."

The Man slammed and locked the door; the click of the lock sounded emphatic.

"Jive-ass motherfucker," Chester said, the salty words incongruous in his piping child's voice. "Ah best get me some blankets or ain' nobody sleepin' in this buildin' tonight. What you bet?" His bravado sounded thin.

The slamming door had been like a slap, and Alex also seethed. The blankets were the focus of a wider indignation. It was slowly being etched into his young mind that those with authority didn't care about right and wrong, good and evil—only about subservience.

From somewhere in the city's night beyond the wall came the sound of a siren rising and falling, a lament for human misery. From somewhere else came a terse screech of brakes followed by the bleat of an automobile horn, reflecting the driver's anguish. The sounds were sharp in the stillness, carried on the crystalline night air. Alex hooked his fingers on the wire mesh and stared out at the grounds of Juvenile Hall. The glare of the floodlights—not merely bright but other-worldly—bleached out colors so that the trees and bushes were in stark silhouette, casting impenetrable black shadows, a surreal landscape. Inwardly Alex felt quiet, cleansed, as if the fight had sweated out angers and drained away bad things that he'd felt vaguely without realizing them. His father's death already seemed to have happened long ago, the heavy pain slowly melting. Clem had been the most important person in his life, and yet Alex had been conditioned to live without a father. Seldom had he seen Clem more than a couple of hours a week, and even then a barrier had existed between them, so they talked little. It wasn't as if something fundamental to his daily existence had been taken. His anguish was less for a lost reality than for a lost hope. Clem had been his one chance to get away from *this*, and now Alex had no idea what his future would be. Right now things were unraveling too quickly to do more than deal with the moment, but whenever he had a premonition of his tomorrows, it was bleak. He wasn't going home, no matter what; home had no place, even in a dream. An eleven-year-old could see that much.

He lay down on the bare mattress, sighing, his hands tucked between his legs, and emotional exhaustion put him to sleep very quickly.

Not for long, however.

The electricity of fright flew through him as he jerked up suddenly.

A rhythmic, crashing sound had awakened him—so loud and so close that he thought it was inside the cell itself. Then he heard Chester's screaming voice and realized the freckled black youth was making an uproar. Alex went to the gate and saw Chester crouching down in the shadows, with both hands on the bars, rattling them against the steel doorframe.

Chester paused when Alex appeared. "Motherfucker never brought no blankets. Ah tol' him nobody's gonna sleep. I'll wake this whole motherfucker up. C'mon and help."

Alex fell to, making it a duet of din. From the second floor, where the girls' hospital ward was located, came answering voices screaming in foul language, but whether in opprobrium or support couldn't be understood.

The light in the alcove went on, and then the door opened. At the light Chester had stopped, but Alex kept on until the door started moving. He still had both hands on the bars when a fat man stepped in. His physique made his trousers sag below his belly, and the heavy keyring hanging on his belt increased this tendency, so that the pants staying up seemed to defy gravity. Remaining in the doorway was the man who had slammed and locked the door.

"What's wrong here?" the fat man asked. He had a flashlight and waved the beam to look over the two boys. "Somebody got a problem?"

"We need some blankets," Alex said. "It's cold in here."

"You haven't got any blankets?"

"*No!*" Chester yelped. "We ain't got shit."

"I told them I'd bring a blanket apiece," the second man said.

"That was two hours ago," Chester said.

"This isn't a hotel, and I'm not a maid. I've got other things to do . . . like count."

"You're just countin' now," Chester said. "Bringin' a couple blankets wouldn't take a hot minute."

The fat man had been nibbling at a fingernail. "You didn't have to wake up the whole institution. You'd have gotten a blanket in due time." As if to emphasize his words, from upstairs came another burst of screaming and obscenity. "Listen to that," he said angrily.

"If he'd brought us some blankets—" Alex began.

"You don't run a goddamn thing here, kid," the fat man said. "And raising all this hell sure isn't the way to get anything."

"It got you down here," Chester piped in. "Ah know we wasn't gonna see you till morning . . . what you bet?"

"You're not going to get any blankets—not tonight—and if you keep making noise we'll take the mattress."

"Why don't you come in and whip us?" Chester asked.

"Believe me, I'd like to, but little turds like you aren't worth my job. It's probably what you little punks need."

"It's what your mother needs," Chester yelped, then stuttered in search of other curses without finding them.

"Keep your shit up and *I'll* come in there," said the man in the doorway. "Lemme hear those gates again. You punks think you can get away with it because you're kids."

The haughty contempt enraged Alex out of proportion to the threat. They acted as if he was nothing and they could do whatever they wanted. It was only a blanket apiece—that was all. He began to tremble, and his breathing became audible.

The fat man heard the gasps and turned the flashlight on him. "What the hell's wrong with you?" The question dripped challenge.

Alex cried out and leaped at the bars, trying to claw the man's face, missing and then spitting on him. The suddenness of the attack, even by an eleven-year-old behind bars, startled the man so that he flinched backward a step, the flashlight beam tilting crazily. He wiped the spray from his cheek.

Chester laughed. "Scared-ass motherfucker!" he sneered.

"Okay, little cocksucker," the man said. "Now you've done it."

Alex didn't hear. He was blind with fury, spinning around in the cell like a dervish, seeking anything to smash or tear. He grabbed the toilet-washbowl fixture and tried to get it loose, but that was futile. Then he saw the mattress. That he could destroy.

It had no holes he could get his fingers into, so he knelt and began biting the striped material, wanting to get an opening so he could tear it apart and throw its innards around the cell. He had just started to gnaw when the cell gate opened and the light came on.

The fat man came first, his round face livid. Alex scrambled to his feet, the absolute blankness of moments before now cracked so he could see enough of reality not to attack. Yet he was still too furious to be afraid.

The open palm slapped him off his feet, dropping him sideways so that his head whacked into the wall. He lay stunned for a moment and then, sobbing with fury, came up and started at the man again, who simply grabbed him by a sleeve and slapped him again, sending lights flashing through his brain. "Oh, you bastard! Bastard!" cursed Alex through tears, his fury increased by helplessness. The man grabbed the boy's hand in such a way that the wrist could be twisted, forcing Alex down on the concrete.

The second man was in the cell now, tugging out the mattress. "We oughta make him do it," he said, having to turn the ungainly object sideways to get it out the door.

"Just get it out," the fat man said, his temper dissipated somewhat. "Settle down, kid," he said. He thought to himself, This one is crazy as a loon.

Chester was at his bars, yelling: "Brave motherfuckers! Sure are brave . . . you motherfuckers!"

The second man had the mattress out and stepped back in. "Lemme go in there on that pipsqueak nigger," he said to the fat man.

"Not yet," he said, releasing Alex and going out the door. When it was locked, he announced: "You two better stop raising hell or you'll wind up in straitjackets. Take it for what it's worth."

"Fuck you!" Chester said.

Alex said nothing; he was too frustrated by his helplessness. Someday he'd get even with them—all of them. He looked around the empty cage, wanting to destroy something. Again all he saw was the toilet-washbasin fixture, and it was mounted too well for him to tear it off the wall.

The alcove light went out and the corridor door closed.

"Hey, man," Chester called, but Alex was too overwrought to answer. He knew his voice would be choked, so he remained silent. "Hey, white boy! You think they're fakin' 'bout straitjackets?" The worry Chester felt was obvious. Alex was sitting against the wall in the darkness, fighting to compose himself, the quaking sobs slowly diminishing. But the fury in his brain ate deep into the core. Even when he calmed down, there was an abscess in his soul.

8

elizabeth noble

came to see him at eight-thirty A.M. He re-
mained seated when he heard the outer door open, and he smelled her
perfume before he heard her voice. He went to the bars slowly. She was
still wearing her hat and carrying her purse. Her dress was black.

"Alex, what happened?" she asked plaintively.

He shrugged and looked down.

"The superintendent sent for me when I walked in. Yesterday afternoon he gave me permission to take you . . . the funeral's this morning.
Now he changed his mind. He got a report that you'd been fighting and
causing a lot of trouble. Now he's afraid you'll do something bizarre out
there."

"That's okay," he said softly, his voice hoarse from all the sobbing
and screaming. He'd expended too much emotion to feel pain now.
"What difference does it make?"

The woman opened her mouth; then her teeth clicked, for she
didn't know what to say. The pendulum movements of his emotions
were confusing, even to a psychiatrist. The sad fatalism of "What difference does it make?" was shocking from a eleven-year-old—especially
a boy who, at other times, had no control whatsoever, and to whom
trivial matters were critical. She decided at that moment to recommend that he go to Camarillo State Hospital for ninety days of observation. That had already been her tentative decision, because she could
think of nothing better. She wanted to save him from reform school,
where the repressive atmosphere would almost certainly suffocate his
good characteristics and exacerbate his inner furies. Alternatives to reform school were meager. Shooting someone was serious, even when it
was a semi-accident committed by an eleven-year-old. Few foster homes
would accept a child with a history of violence. And he'd been through
so many similar places already that the judge would hesitate to send
him to another, though it was really up to the probation department;
the judge just rubber-stamped the recommendation ninety-five percent
of the time. If Alex went to a foster home, it would be a matter of weeks

before he was back before the judge, no doubt of that. The state hospital idea had been in lieu of anything better, for his emotional problems were severe enough to justify it. Now she was even more justified, for this sudden lack of affect coupled with the volatile explosions raised the specter of incipient psychosis. It was unlikely, but it was possible—and in a way it would be better if he was psychotic. *That* could be cured, whereas the psychopathic delinquent had to burn out, which seldom took place until youth was long gone—often not until the person neared forty years of age. By then many were buried in prison, while many others were in the grave. The literature was full of case histories, and the prisons were filled with persons the histories were based upon.

"We've got you scheduled for a test at the general hospital tomorrow," she said, turning her thoughts away from these complexities before she got bogged down in the morass. "They'll fasten some wires to your head, but you don't feel anything."

"Wires! What's it for?"

"It's called an E.E.G. Your brain gives off electrical impulses, and it measures them to see if you have epilepsy or a tumor. Sometimes people with a temper like yours have something wrong with them, and we can give them pills to help them."

Alex nodded but seemed uninterested. "Where's my father . . . going to be?"

"In Sunland. It's called Valhalla."

"Valhalla. I read about that. It's a sort of heaven, isn't it?"

"Norse mythology. I think it's where warriors go. Something like that." She looked at her wristwatch. "Someone's waiting at my office for me. I've got to go. Is there anything I can do for you?"

"Can I get something to read?"

"If you're allowed to have books in here. What do you want?"

"I really liked some books about collie dogs by a man named Albert Payson Terhune . . . but I've read most of them. I like Westerns, and Tarzan. I think he wrote about Mars, too."

"If you can have them I'll bring some by this afternoon. Most of the companies have big bookshelves full of things—donations—and not many kids here are interested in reading."

"I'd rather read than do anything else. It's like I'm in another world."

"And you don't like this one," she said wistfully, a comment both on his outlook and on his real condition. If he wished to escape reality he had a good reason. If his few yesterdays were dismal, his many tomorrows threatened to be worse, unless something miraculous happened. Not only was the miraculous unlikely, she didn't even know what it might be.

■

Dr. Noble didn't bring the books, but in the afternoon, when everyone except a monitor was at school, Alex and Chester were taken out for a shower. Alex spotted a bookcase en route, and on the way back he snatched a book and wrapped it in a towel without seeing the title. Back in the cell he was disappointed by the title, *Arrowsmith*, and he wouldn't remember it or the author, Sinclair Lewis, for many years, until he began reading it again and realized it was the same story that had enthralled him so long ago. He started reading it because he had nothing else to do except lie on the stained mattress, which had been given back at supper, or look out the window at night in Juvenile Hall. Without knowing there was such a thing as literature—a book was a book—he was suddenly immersed in life born on paper. Some of the words were beyond his vocabulary, but that didn't matter. The cell faded from consciousness, his troubles were forgotten, and he thrilled and ached and struggled with Dr. Martin Arrowsmith, M.D. When the lights went out at nine-thirty he tried to read from the glow coming through the wire mesh, but it wasn't enough. As he rolled up his clothes for a pillow and got under the gray blanket, his mind still overflowed with feelings about the book. He didn't realize that the evening hours in isolation in Juvenile Hall were happier than any he'd known in many months. Erased was Clem's death, the missed funeral—and also the nagging worry about his fate, though he had realized that his control over it was the same as that of a chip of wood on a river.

The next morning the deputy superintendent came to see if Chester and Alex were through fighting and ready to go back out with other boys, though to a regular company rather than Receiving company. Chester was ready to promise anything, and Alex went along with the attitude expected of him, although he was really content to stay indefinitely where he was—as long as he had enough to read.

■

"B" Company was in its dayroom when the escort brought Alex in before supper. The boys sat in silence, arms folded, on hard benches around three sides of the long room, while the counselor and monitors were in chairs on a landing up three steps, as if onstage. The proscenium was the frame of the bars and the grille gate, beyond which was the rest of the company quarters.

All the watching eyes burned into Alex from faces already trained in hardened repose, and he colored and looked along the floor. It was concrete, but waxed and buffed to gleam like varnished maple. No human blemishes marred its surface. Alex saw that every boy except himself was in stocking feet.

The seated counselor was speaking to him, and he could see a yellow nicotine stain at the base of the man's lower teeth, but he couldn't see his eyes—they were hidden behind wire-framed, tinted glasses, and they caught the sunlight through the window. The man was swarthy and his name was Miranda, that much Alex understood from the words. A pointed finger told him to remove his shoes, and one of the monitors, fetching him a folded rag of gray blanket, told him to buff away the marks he'd made.

The shoes encumbered him, but he didn't know what to do with them. His face flamed, and he knew he looked like a fool.

"Put them down, dummy," Mr. Miranda said, his voice cutting through the silence, eliciting a few snorts and snickers before his glance stifled them.

Just as Alex got on his knees and his rump jutted up, someone made a loud farting sound. Laughter followed, and although Alex was embarrassed to the point of pain, he managed a lopsided, cemetery grin to convey camaraderie.

"It's funny, yes?" Mr. Miranda asked. "Someone makes a foul sound with their mouth, and you young heathens think it's hilarious."

Alex had raised himself upright, though still on his knees.

"Nobody told you to stop," Mr. Miranda said, flicking a hand and dismissing him back to work.

Alex kept at it until the company went to eat supper.

After supper they stayed outdoors until dark. They had the softball diamond area, but a vote switched the game to dodgeball instead. The forty boys became a herd, and Mr. Miranda hurled a white volleyball into it. The boy it hit came out and threw, and then a second boy joined him. At first it was impossible to miss, and those hit slowly formed a large circle. As more came out, those who remained had more room to dodge, leaping, ducking, feinting one way and jumping another, running from one side of the circle to the other. The boys yelled in triumph and dismay. Alex was caught up in the game, enjoying himself immensely. He was still in the circle when just five others remained, more because others threw at their friends than because of his agility. Finally, a ball missed everyone, and before he could scurry to the far side, he tripped and fell down just four feet from the boy with the ball. Moments later he was a member of the circle.

It wasn't until shower time, just before bed, that he realized how few of the boys were white—not more than half a dozen among forty. Nearly every torso and pair of legs was olive or brown. He wondered why it was, but otherwise he had no feelings about it. During the fight with Chester, when he had been getting the better of it, he hadn't attached any significance to the grumbling blacks, and if asked what it meant, he would have answered that they simply knew and liked Chester. Clem had always used "nigger" and "kike," and because these were said so easily by the father, the son didn't know they were offensive.

He learned otherwise on Sunday morning. The boys had to attend church, Catholic or Protestant, and since he wasn't Catholic he went to the other, which was really just fervent volunteers in shiny, cheap suits, poor sinners who had found Jesus and were offering him to these troubled children. There was much praising the Lord and singing of "The Old Rugged Cross" and "Onward, Christian Soldiers." On the way out the boys were each given a candy bar. Alex didn't want his, and two boys immediately clamored for it. "Eenie, meenie, minie, moe," he said, the timeworn child's litany, thoughtless and without malice. "Catch a nigger by the toe. . . ." Suddenly looming in front of Alex was a whipcord-lean thirteen-year-old with chocolate features twisted in anger, fists clenched in challenge. Alex stood his ground and put his hands up, because he knew no other way. A bony black fist whacked into his nose, knocking him on the seat of his pants and bringing forth a stream of blood. When he was getting up, puzzled and afraid because he was overmatched, the counselor ran over between them. This time it was a different counselor, one who liked the black youth, so he sent Alex to the washroom to stanch the blood and afterward made Alex apologize for using the word. Alex never again used "nigger," except—very rarely—as a curse of hate directed at a specific individual. He never used it just with whites, feeling it was wrong to be two-faced.

The following week he was fully impressed with the differences and divisions of race when a husky white fourteen-year-old called "Okie" got into a scrap with a Mexican in the schoolhouse latrine. Okie was big and strong, but as he rammed the Mexican youth against a wall, four other Chicanos leaped at him. One white youth came to Okie's aid, and both took a beating before the uproar brought an adult to the rescue. All involved were older boys, on a different level than a eleven-year-old, so Alex just watched, but finally he understood. Thereafter he was conscious of race, self-conscious whenever skin color was different, until he'd had some sign about attitudes. One part of innocence was over.

Days drifted into weeks of routine in a world similar to the schools he'd known, but it was different, too—tougher, crueler, and a greater challenge. All the boys spoke atrocious English laced with vulgarity, and his own precise grammar stood out, though it began to change slightly, like a bright leaf with the first dot of brown mold at its edge. His vocabulary was extensive for his age, and often the other boys couldn't understand a word he used. So instead of using the vocabulary he'd been proud of, it became a habit to use simpler words. Sometimes he had to think consciously of an easier word, and it gave him a sort of hesitant stutter. The boys used the word "motherfucker," which he'd never heard previously. "Fuck" had been rare and daring, and "motherfucker" slapped him for a while.

A probation officer called him to the front office for an interview. A clinical psychologist summoned him to the hospital, and he took tests, saying what he saw in ink blots, putting blocks together, reciting numbers backward and forward, figuring out puzzles.

He didn't think about his future. The world of Juvenile Hall pressed lives too closely together for him to dream as he used to. The hours were scheduled tightly, from lights-on to lights-out. Only on Sunday evening did he feel his lonely condition. On Sunday afternoons the boys had visitors, and nearly every boy had someone, usually a whole family. Families could leave bags of candy, cookies, and magazines. After supper the bags were distributed. While the bags were being passed out, he sat alone, sunk into himself, shaking his head if someone offered him something. In his pain was bitter anger, a way of coping with it.

He had no friends in the company and was pretty much ignored. He'd established that he would fight if bothered, so he was left alone. The half dozen other whites were older and from different backgrounds, nearly all of them affecting ducktails and low pants. Two were cousins and bragged that they had been charged with murder. They had shot a hobo walking along the railroad grade behind their house with a .22 rifle stolen from a neighbor's bedroom. No newspapers were allowed, so the claim was unverified. True or not, it was their prestige in a world where rank depended on skill at violence. The toughest boys were the most respected, even if the toughest were slobbering cretins. Most of the adolescents had committed some crime—broken into a house or got caught rifling glove compartments. A few had stolen cars, and one twelve-year-old black, Lewis—he seemed much older—had been caught burglarizing gas stations for ration stamps which he then peddled lucratively in his neighborhood. This boy seemed always ready to smile in a warm but superior way, and when the company was seated on the benches and forbidden to talk, which was for hour-long periods several times a day, Lewis always read a book. Nobody else did so except Alex, though it was the one activity Mr. Miranda allowed.

Books were sneered at, but nobody sneered at Lewis. On boxing day nobody would put the gloves on with him. Although Alex couldn't call him a friend, Lewis was the first to notice that he had no visitors and to offer cookies from what his own family left. Once when an older black crowded in front of Alex at the sink in the washroom, Alex pushed back, and before the uneven fight could start, Lewis stepped in and stopped it. He didn't make the black give back the sink but instead gave Alex his own.

At the school, Alex had Lulu, who was friendly when they were in the classroom. But during recess, when the boys withdrew into groups, Lulu ignored him, though he sometimes picked Alex for his softball team ahead of boys with more ability. He was from Temple Street, and there were several boys from his neighborhood gang in Juvenile Hall. He hung out with them and had time for Alex only when they weren't around.

Only to Chester did Alex talk very much, as if the fight and being in seclusion had cemented the friendship. Chester had four brothers and two sisters, and his father was in the army; his mother worked as a cleaning woman in a hotel, and the children were pretty much on their own. He wanted to be a professional baseball player. This was his third trip to Juvenile Hall, and he was waiting to go to a county camp for six months. He planned to run away as soon as he got there.

■

One morning, without warning, Alex was among a score of boys taken to court in a battered gray bus with wire mesh on the windows. The juvenile court was in the Hall of Justice, and the bus pulled into a tunnel beneath the tall building, parking near a sign of a red arrow with CORO-NER and MORGUE above it. They rode a freight elevator to the eighth floor and went down a tunnel to a windowless room with walls defaced by graffiti—some in pencil, some gouged into the paint. They were mostly names, but some were crude drawings of immense phalluses or female breasts and crotch, the last merely a dark triangle. No matter how crude and distorted the drawings, Alex looked at them with curiosity, wondering how closely they approached reality.

Most of the boys were pensive while waiting to be called, though one who had already been in reform school and knew he was going back was angry and contemptuous. Among the first half dozen to be called, four were put on probation and two were committed to county camps. One of the two broke into tears—he'd expected to go home—and the reform-school graduate began kicking him in the shins, spitting on him and telling him to shut up. This cruelty elicited nervous snickers from the others. Alex had neither fear nor hope of what was going to happen, but he would never show any feelings that might bring ridicule. Everyone looked up to the reform-school boy and looked down on the crybaby.

A key turned in the lock, and a uniformed bailiff called Alex's name. In the hallway the boy was startled by the crowd. Somehow he'd expected the corridor to be empty and silent, an image garnered from the movies. Instead it was packed. Theater-style chairs with foldup seats lined one wall, and each seat was filled with a body. Many people stood up, and the bailiff held his arm and led him in a weaving route through the press of bodies. The crowd was mostly frazzled-looking women, poor and prematurely worn. For each woman there was a sullen boy—plus toddlers and babies. The few men there were also grizzled and seamed, looking stiff and uncomfortable in their ill-fitting Sunday clothes. As in Juvenile Hall, most of the faces were chocolate or olive, and the voices maimed diction or rattled in Spanish.

The brass doorplate read: HARRINGTON P. WYMORE, REFEREE. Alex had only a moment to read it before the bailiff opened the door. The light filtering through immense Venetian blinds struck his eyes, momentarily dazing him as they entered, so he heard a rattle of polite, dry laughter to some previous quip before he could see faces emerging from the glare. He was in an aisle with two rows of empty chairs on each side, facing a long, wide, and highly polished table. One man in a dark suit sat in the middle; another was at the end, a pile of folders in front of him. A middle-aged woman, whose corpulent body seemed to consume the chair she spilled over, was next to the window, pencil in hand, seated at the table.

The man in the middle, who seemed dwarfed by the table, had his head bent forward, exposing thinning gray hair on a narrow skull, but his eyes and features were hidden. One bony hand was turning typewritten pages, until he paused and finally looked up. For the first time Alex was afraid—not the tight knot of physical fear before he got into a fight or did something dangerous, but the dull hollowness that sucks strength because one understands powerlessness when confronted by power. It wasn't fear of what the narrow-visaged old man might do but a sense that nothing could be done about it. When the judge looked up, it seemed like a signal for the others to do the same, focusing their eyes on him as if they could tell something about him by his face in repose. The judge glanced to the stenographer to make sure her pencil was ready.

"The number here is A, five, five, zero, four, zero," the judge intoned, "on a petition *In loco parentis* filed by the probation department on behalf of Alexander Hammond, a juvenile." He paused and looked into the boy's eyes. "I'm very sorry about your father."

For a few seconds Alex screwed up his face in perplexity, not understanding what the man meant. Sorry about what? It wasn't that Alex had stopped thinking about his father's death, though emotional wounds turn quickly to scar tissue in an eleven-year-old. Rather, this expression of sympathy was so far from what Alex had expected that he didn't know what the words referred to. His puzzlement showed, and the judge blinked rapidly, taken aback.

"Your father," he said, as if to clarify or remind.

"My father's dead, sir."

"That's why I was saying I was sorry."

"Oh."

The judge flushed red blotches through his gray skin, then pushed his glasses higher up on his nose, as if this would let him observe better this strange boy sitting primly with hands folded in his lap. The psychiatric report mentioned a lack of "affect," and the off-kilter reply seemed to confirm it.

"You know why you're here, Alex, don't you?"

"Yes, sir."

"We're not here to punish you . . . but to help you. How do you feel about what you did?"

Feel? Alex wished he hadn't shot the man, was sorry about his condition, but there was nothing to *feel*. Yet he instinctively knew that the judge wanted to hear something different. "I'm sorry, sir," he said. Then he added, "I didn't *think* when I did it. I was . . . scared . . . and it just happened." He tossed a shoulder.

"But you were in the man's store."

"We were hungry, sir. I didn't think—"

"You know it's wrong to steal, don't you?"

"Yes, sir."

"But you've stolen before. You ran away from the Valley Home for Boys because you were caught shoplifting."

"I wasn't," Alex said quickly, his body stiffening and voice rising. "They said I did but I didn't."

"Why would they lie?"

"I don't know."

"I can't imagine, either. . . . Then there's this temper of yours. You've been in several fights in the last three weeks, and you attacked the woman at the Valley Home the evening you ran away. . . . And those tantrums. Now you're just a little boy, but if you can't train your temper by the time you grow up . . . when you weigh a hundred and eighty pounds you'll be dangerous."

The judge stopped to sip some water from a glass beside a carafe. Alex watched his Adam's apple bob and tried—unsuccessfully—to imagine weighing a hundred and eighty pounds.

"I don't know what to do with you, son. You're a smart boy, and although you haven't had a happy childhood, it couldn't very well be described as deprived. You've always had enough to eat. . . . Committing you to the Youth Authority and sending you to a state school is what the probation officer recommends, but that's the final alternative. We can always do that if we can't help you any other way. You're too young for our county camps, and I don't know if that would be any good for you anyway. You've got emotional problems. A foster home isn't the answer . . . you've been through them. So I'm going to order that you go to the state hospital at Camarillo for a ninety-day observation period. If the staff there needs more time we can extend it. Maybe they can help you, or tell me what to do for you. You're a troubled child and—"

The closing words faded out of the boy's consciousness. He was going to a *nuthouse!* Maybe I *am* crazy, he thought. I don't feel crazy . . . but how does a crazy person feel? They must know *something* about what they're doing. The thought frightened him so that he had to fight back tears.

He didn't tell the other boys where he was going when he got back in the room. He told them that he was going to the Youth Authority.

9

the waxed *deep* red of the dayroom floor sparkled from the yellow winter sunlight, sliced into squares by the flat bars of the windows. Inexpensive wicker-framed chairs with removable cushions ran along all walls and in back-to-back rows around the room. Most of the chairs were occupied, and most of the occupants wore grossly ill-fitting, rumpled state denim, the pants cuffs either high above skinny ankles or drooping low enough to be walked upon, either too small to be buttoned or so large they were held up by string or shoelaces. The more ragged the clothes, the crazier the person, or so it seemed. Some talked to themselves, some to Christ and whoever else came to mind and sight. The ward population was over one hundred, but less than half were in the room. The sitters were unusually placid this Saturday morning, for most had been given shock treatments yesterday and were still trying to sift facts from the ashes of memory. The really berserk patients were strapped to cots in small, dim rooms along a corridor (one of two) leading from the dayroom. They, too, were temporarily quieted from electricity applied to the brain.

This ward was the infirmary as well as a receiving and processing unit, and had many slightly corroded minds, including alcoholics and a few addicts taking the cure. Most of these were off the ward this time of day, working in the kitchen or loose on the vast semidesert acreage of hospital property; like most of southern California, what wasn't desert was farm. They all had grounds parole cards.

The sane who remained on the ward wore civilian clothes—or at least shirts—and were involved in the nearly perpetual ward poker game. Today the locked wicker cabinet with the radio had been moved close to the table, and the gamblers half-listened to the Notre Dame announcer sadly describe a slaughter by the great Army team led by Blanchard and Davis, a pair of All-America backs in tandem, while Notre Dame players who might have stopped them were at Guadalcanal and North Africa. "Now for the half-time statistics," the announcer said.

The poker game was five patients and an attendant, the last a young man in crisp whites who stood at a corner of the table, following the regulation that he wasn't to sit down on the job except in the office during coffee breaks. Three white patients were playing, two of them alcoholics and the third an ex-con trying to avoid a forgery sentence to San Quentin by claiming he heard voices. The two blacks ("colored," then) in the game were junkie confidence men, partners in crime and time, taking a cure because their supply of narcotics had been cut off by the war; they'd been reduced to paregoric and trying to talk doctors into writing morphine prescriptions. One of them was ebony-black, square-jawed and heavy-shouldered, with the flat nose and scarred eyebrows of an unproductive prizefight career. He was know as First Choice Floyd.

The largest pile of money was in front of the other black, who was lighter-skinned than the average Sicilian. His partner Floyd sometimes joshed him as "you ol' shit-colored nigger," and indeed, his name was Red Barzo. His reddish hair was processed to stiffness and had a pompadour in front. He looked younger than his thirty-eight years. He was thin and voluble, chattering far more than a poker player is supposed to, continually counting his coins in stacks between hands, counting and arranging, knowing full well that a new hand would erase his count and his neatness and he'd have to start over. He was fidgety, and occasionally his eyes wandered to a wall clock. "I'm gonna have to start gettin' the funk off my body and get dressed pretty soon, so Clarice don' be waitin'."

Alex Hammond stood just behind Red Barzo's right shoulder, sometimes shifting his weight from one foot to the other but otherwise expressionless, which were the conditions under which he was allowed to watch. His wise young eyes burned with concentration. If Red stayed a winner, he would let Alex play for him when he left to get ready for the visit.

"Last hand for me," Red said, shuffling and dealing smoothly but without excessive flourish. Only Alex, standing behind him, could see him squeeze back and view the bottom card when he retrieved the cut. The man could ease it off so smoothly that the eye couldn't tell, though there would be a telltale popping sound that he covered with a cough. Red wasn't a good poker player—he was too prone to gamble and bluff— but he could cheat pretty good and usually won.

The down cards spun low across the blanket so there was no chance for exposure. As he turned up the second card, Red chanted the values: "Jack . . . Ace . . . ten . . . Ace . . . another ten . . . and a cocksuckin' low-ass seven to the dealer." Alex was fascinated by the exposure of mysteries, by something he sensed but could not articulate, that this had meaning or metaphor beyond itself. "First Ace bets," Barzo said.

First Choice Floyd had the Ace and dropped a quarter into the middle of the bare blanket. The next player dropped. The second Ace called and so did the second ten. Red pinched up his hole card so Alex could see: a King. He pushed out two quarters. "Small raise," he said. Alex, who had been watching and studying the techniques of the game for weeks, was surprised by the raise. He could understand it if Red had another seven in the hole (then it would be a bigger raise), or an Ace with no Aces showing. But the King couldn't beat what was showing.

"Two sevens," said the next man, the alcoholic with the exposed Jack. "You wouldn't raise with an Ace, not with two showing."

"Sho' nuff glad you can read my hand," Barzo said. "But whatcha gonna do?"

"I call."

"Then throw in another quarter."

The man did so. His face was full of tiny blue-red veins, giving a purple cast to his face.

First Choice flipped up the four of hearts. "Gotta go," he said, throwing in his hand. The other two called. It made Red the focus of their attention. They thought he had either the Joker or another seven.

"Cards comin'," Red said, leaving the deck on the blanket and turning each card with one hand so there would be no question of trickery. "No pair," he said. "Ace still bets."

"Check to the raiser."

Those in between also tapped the blanket or said "check."

Red had a wilted dollar bill ready and dropped it in, a substantial but not enormous second-card bet in this game. The next man, he of the Jack and the quip, looked at the nine beside Red's seven and then at his own six. He put a dollar in the pot. The Ace had added a Queen and called. The other two folded. "Naw," the attendant said. "You can't have but sevens, but if I draw out on you, one of them is liable to draw out on me." He tapped the blanket with the back of his knuckles and was turning over as Red spun the fourth round. "Jacks a pair . . . a trey to the Ace-Queen, and a King to the dealer. Jacks bet."

"Five dollars," the alcoholic said.

The Ace-Queen was face-down before the bill landed.

"I call," Red said.

"Gonna try and draw out," the alcoholic said, as certain now as if the cards were face-up that Red had another seven in the hole. The last thing in the world that he expected was another King from the way the hand had played.

"Last card," Red said. The pair of Jacks caught a three, and Red had a five.

"Beat the Jacks," the alcoholic said, his voice assured. It meant he didn't have anything more than the Jacks. Two pair was a cinch, and it was forbidden to check a cinch in five-card stud.

Now Red had the man in the crosshairs. "How much you got?" he asked, eye-gesturing toward the pile of money. "Whatever it is, that's what I bet."

"Oh no, Mr. Slick Barzo. You can't run me this time. Just cause you got all the money on the ward." He was quickly counting the dimes, quarters, and half-dollars. "Fourteen dollars," he said.

"Put it in," Red said, dropping three five-dollar bills into the pot. The other man didn't hesitate.

Red turned up the hidden King.

The alcoholic's face was already red, and now it blotched. "I can't go for that bullshit. Not with you dealin'."

"Sheeit," First Choice said. "Talkin' like a fool. Nobody gotta cheat you. An' if you're gonna be a sucker, be a quiet one."

"Right," the young attendant said. He was the voice of authority. "If you can't lose quietly, don't play."

Red stacked the coins and watched the play of emotions. A good confidence man reads human nature unerringly, understanding beyond the wildest hopes of the psychologist. A con man *must* be right to prevail, where the psychologist depends upon his diploma for a living. Deciding the man was no actual threat, he cooled him off. "I didn't know a King was coming. I put a chickenshit two bits in the pot as a raise *to make you think* I had the Joker or a pair of sevens. It was a setup for just what happened, that I catch a pair of Kings and someone would be able to beat the sevens but not the Kings. If nobody paired, I run the bluff all the way through. If somebody made Aces, or could beat the Kings, I fold up . . . with a dollar-fifty invested. The trap got set, and you fell for it. Don't feel bad—*good* poker players get nailed in that one, and you ain' too good." He extended three one-dollar bills to the man.

Alex hadn't needed the explanation. It was analogous to a chess gambit, offering the poisoned pawn. Chess was another game Alex had learned with ridiculous ease. First Choice had taught him how the pieces moved and the purpose, and in two weeks Alex won regularly. Now the other poker players were digesting the information. First Choice caught Alex's eye and winked. Although Alex was around Red more, Red being more voluble, he was more comfortable with First Choice. The black man also showed him boxing rudiments: how to stand, how to stick out straight left jabs instead of the head-lowered wild roundhouses natural to young boys. Minds were too sick with other things to be sick about racism in the state hospital, so nobody thought anything about the boy hanging out with black confidence men. And Alex liked being around them; they made him laugh and were obviously fond of him. They told him stories of prison, where the "code" of violence was similar to that of the Old West, and for Alex it had a similar fascination. They told him about hustling, too, and about things an eleven-year-old doesn't usually learn: how to spot a card mechanic (his hands were too small, actually, to learn how to do anything), "short" con games such as "The Match" and "The Strap," the ethics of criminality, and tales about hustling and thieving. He remembered one story about a crap game in the parking lot of Churchill Downs at Derby time, where they'd switched in "Ace-Trey-Fives," dice with only those numbers and consequently unable to "7," giving them into a mooch. The mooch was shooting twenty dollars, while they made side bets of a hundred and two hundred. After five passes, when they'd trimmed off two thousand, they walked away, leaving the square with the dice. Now they laughed in recollection, conjecturing what might have happened if the others had found the square shooting phony dice.

"Wanna play for me, Alex?" Red asked. "I'm gonna take a shit, shave an' shower, an' get ready for my woman."

This was precisely what Alex had been waiting for for the last three hours. Whenever Red won, he pocketed his investment and some of his winnings, then left the remainder for the boy. The first time, thanks to strict instructions to play only cinches, and also thanks to the other players never believing an eleven-year-old, he won thirty dollars. The next three times he lost, but only small amounts, once less than a dollar. Now he grinned, and Red tousled the boy's hair while turning over the seat. Red picked up the currency, but the remaining stacks of coins equaled what most of the other players had before them. The tightness was already in the boy's stomach, the quickened heartbeat and utter concentration on the falling of the cards. Red paused a moment to watch; Alex had a Jack in the hole and a nine up, and he folded the hand. Red patted him on the back and left. In all previous sessions, Alex had been allowed to play only an Ace or a King in the hole or a pair back to back, and he had to be able to beat whatever he could see, with no bluffs. Now Red had told him to keep playing that way, but if he had a King in the hole and had an Ace up, he could bluff, if that pair would beat whatever else someone might have. As the cards came, he felt a glorious fear—glorious because it was equal parts hope.

Two hands later he won with a pair of eights back to back, catching the third eight on the last card to the attendant's two Aces. It was a fairly good pot. Because he was ahead, he decided to bluff at the first chance, and because it was more fear and hope than batting a cinch hand. The chance came two deals later. He had a King in the hole and an Ace exposed and didn't pair either. Another player paired tens on the last card and checked. Alex shoved out ten dollars, delicious terror spreading from his stomach to his throat and limbs. The pair of tens hesitated, while Alex wondered if his face was showing his fear. The tens turned over, flinging the cards angrily to the next dealer. "Fuckin' kid sleeps with Aces and Kings. . . ."

Playing the Joker in the hole, Alex caught a Queen-high straight on the next hand, trapping the attendant with two big pair and another player with three of a kind. It was a huge pot for an institution, nearly fifty dollars. The attendant slammed the cards down and quit. First Choice was short of money, and Alex gave him twenty dollars.

On weekends the game always lasted until supper and started again after the weekend movie on Saturday night. On Sunday there were fresh players, since patients got visits and money. But this was Saturday, and the game ended at one-thirty. The last player with three sixes ran into Alex with three Aces. In a fury, the man tore up his cards and threw them into the air; then he kicked his chair over as he stood up. First Choice leaned back, grinning, but there was no doubt what would happen if the losing man tried to strike the boy. Alex couldn't help but flinch in the face of a furious adult.

The crashing chair brought attendants into the room; they were keyed to psychotic assaults and explosions. When they saw the man slowly picking up the chair, they relaxed.

Just one player besides First Choice remained in the game, and now he claimed a headache. Alex had nearly all the money in the game, and had already squirreled away two twenty-dollar bills, which were contraband in the institution. Nobody was supposed to have anything of a larger denomination than a ten-dollar bill, and a total of twenty-five dollars—but Red had a huge bankroll and First Choice Floyd also had several hundred. Now Alex's shirt pocket was stuffed with bills, and his jeans pocket bulged with coins that pulled them dangerously low. "I wanna catch Red before his visit," he said, glowing.

"It ain't always gonna be gravy," First Choice said. "Believe me, boy."

"I bet I won over a hundred dollars!" To an eleven-year-old it was an immense amount.

"So you're a poker prodigy, young'un," Floyd said. "An' sho' nuff a lucky young motherfucker." He was folding up the card table blanket.

Alex started across the dayroom, glowing and bouncing, paying no attention to the minds full of unreality around him. Then his eyes focused on a grossly obese man (a round circle of a body topped with a round circle of a head) who was beardless as a eunuch, and whose cheek flesh was wrinkled in infinite tiny creases rather than seams. Red had said the man was a hermaphrodite, and when Alex learned what the word meant he thought Red was joshing him. Alex never did find out for sure, though he peeked at the man's penis in the shower and it was no bigger than a pencil. The other part he couldn't see. But since then he had talked to the poor demented creature and couldn't help teasing him. Now he looked around the dayroom for attendants (they'd warned him already), and he saw none. Probably drinking coffee in the office, he thought, flopping down in an empty chair beside the man. The beardless blob didn't even glance around.

"Look here," Alex said, tugging at his sleeve.

The round dome turned slowly, the eyes blinked slowly, and the stubby, nicotine-brown index finger and thumb (from butts pinched to the last puff) came slowly to the mouth. "Gimme Ol' Gold. Please. Ol' Gold."

"Fuck you and Old Gold, too, queer old cocksucker. Tell me what you're gonna do about it."

One hand stayed gesturing at the mouth, while the other came ponderously up and patted the immense belly. "Ol' Gold . . . Ol' Gold."

Alex's eyes shifted to the corridor, again seeing no attendant. He bit his lip and quickly slapped him—a whiplike flip of the fingernails—across his flat snout. The round head jerked back like a turtle's. A shadow passed over his face, and a redness suffused it. "Bad boy, bad boy . . ."

"Tell me what the fuck you're gonna do."

"Stick a stake in your ass, bad boy. Stick pins in your eyes, naughty boy. Put you on a big ship with a frying pan in the hold, and put you on there, so when the ship rolls in the sea you slide back and forth and sizzle. . . ."

"Hey, kid! Goddammit to hell!"

Alex jumped before looking around. The attendant in charge of the ward, a redhaired man in his forties, thin and sourpussed, was just inside the dayroom from the corridor. "I've goddamn told you not to tease Benny. Someday he's gonna backhand you across the room. He'll stop talkin' and make it real as hell."

"I thought he had one of those brain operations where he can't."

"That's what they say. Anyway, you don't fuck with him anymore. Christ, I'll be glad when they send you to the juvenile ward. Get away from him."

The fat, lobotomized, hermaphrodite schizophrenic was still chanting a litany of grotesque tortures when Alex scurried away from the man in white. The boy headed toward the other wide corridor, down which was the big ward restroom, dormitory, showers, and clothing room, all the places the light-skinned black man might be unless he'd already gone on his visit. While Alex walked, the words of the attendant went through his mind, making him wonder why he hadn't been sent to the juvenile ward. Nearly all new patients were sent to permanent wards in two weeks, and juveniles usually sooner, most of them to the regular juvenile ward and a few to the electric-shock ward. Just one juvenile that Alex knew about had been kept in Receiving during his entire observation commitment, though he'd left before Alex arrived. The other boy had killed his father, sneaking up behind him with a .22 rifle while the man was in a chair. Alex had seen the juveniles but kept away from them. They had their own courtyard for recreation, but it was too small for softball so they came to the main yard once or twice a week. It was big enough for four softball diamonds, all formed by the surrounding buildings. All the male patients sane enough to find their way back to the wards were let into it during the day. When the juveniles were out in it, they kept to one area, and Alex kept away from them. Now as he looked for Red, he realized that they must think his case was serious, like the other boy's; otherwise they would have moved him. It didn't matter. He preferred being right where he was.

As he kept looking for Red, Alex was still excited about his triumph in the game. He pushed through the restroom door and was met with a cloud of thick tobacco smoke. This was the one place on the ward where smoking was allowed. Inside was a crowded foyer of puffing men, most of them with hand-rolled cigarettes made of awful-tasting, sweet-smelling state tobacco packaged at San Quentin and nicknamed "Duffy," after the famous warden of the prison.

Alex walked by unconcernedly, barely glancing at the cadaverous, swollen, fierce-eyed, vacant-eyed faces. Then he went through a second door into a much larger but less crowded room with huge semicircular washbowls on the right and urinals and toilets on the left. Butts and streamers of toilet paper littered the floor. Red wasn't here.

"Hey, kid," a toothless black man with scaly gray skin and hair like wild watch springs said. His teeth were huge and yellow, and some were missing. But he didn't faze the boy, for Alex knew that, frightening as he appeared, he was harmless. Alex reached into his jeans and picked out a cigarette without extracting the pack. Exposing it would have invited a crowd of beggars. Factory-made cigarettes were at a premium, and the mentally ill were the world's most unabashed beggars. Alex had started smoking three weeks earlier and had been inhaling for the past week; he was proud of himself.

Red had to be in either the clothing room or the dormitory, though the last was out of bounds during the day. Red, however, had an attendant who accepted ten-dollar bills slipped into his pocket with a wink. He also brought Red bottles of whiskey and cough syrup laced with codeine, which Red hid in a locker under his bunk. Once late at night Alex had found him and First Choice Floyd in the small dormitory restroom, huddled over a spoon with matches flaming under it. Red had told him quickly, "Get the fuck outa here," and he left, red-faced. The next morning Floyd told him to forget what he'd seen.

Barzo was in the clothing room—actually two rooms: one a place to get dressed next to the showers, and the other for storage of civilian clothes. He'd shaved and changed into a zoot suit of hound's-tooth check, with a yellow shirt and maroon tie, the era's epitome of sharpness. His processed red hair was slicked down stiff, and he smelled of cologne. Somehow First Choice Floyd had found Red first; the dark-skinned black man was propped on one elbow on a bench next to the wall.

Red looked around at the sound of the door opening. "How do I look, boy?"

"C'mon, niggah," Floyd said, slurring the last word. "You know you look pretty. But hurry your ass up an' don' keep that broad waitin'.'"

Red turned back to the full-length mirror, making a final check of how his clothes hung. He looked at Alex in the mirror. "Heard you won a bundle. Took you a while gettin' heah. How much you steal?"

Alex's face crimsoned and he stuttered a denial, realizing, as Red burst out laughing, that the accusation was a joke. "Well, young'un, you shoulda took a little end. That's what I'da done. How much you got?"

"A hundred and twenty dollars."

"The boy is a poker-playin' genius. Sheeit! I might 'dopt you, sho' nuff."

Alex was digging out the roll of bills.

"Take twenty in green and the change," Red said. "Coins fuck up the hang of my rag."

When that was done, Alex sat down while Red finished his ablutions. "Boy," Red said when he was ready to go, "ain' no doubt you headin' dead for San Quentin, 'cause you got the devil in you. Ain' no stoppin' it, so it's good you fuckin' with me 'n Floyd 'n gettin' schooled. You gotta decide if you wanna be a pimp, a player, or a gangster."

"What's the difference?"

"One's slick and the other's tough."

"I think I'd like to be a little bit of both."

The two black men burst out laughing. Alex couldn't help another blush, but his embarrassment was mixed with pleasure.

10

the ward doctor was an infrequently seen god. When he did appear, it was seldom to talk directly to patients. He disappeared with the senior attendants behind the office door, looked at charts, sometimes wrote on them, listened to what the attendants had to say, and drank coffee. Occasionally he toured the corridor of lockup rooms, peered through the window slots, and looked at each occupant strapped to a bed. Then he swept out, followed by a retinue of white suits until he went through the door.

Alex never talked to the doctor or knew his name—or cared. He was happier here in the state hospital than in any of the foster homes or boys' schools or anywhere else. His initial fear of being among the insane quickly went away. The joy of this place was that he lived a virtually unstructured existence. He was too young for work, and there was no school. Within the vast confines of the institution he was free to roam until sunset, and during the evening the ward itself had the poker game or something else to pass the time. He had no hunger to escape from his surroundings into books. What went on around him was more stimulating, especially the huge yard surrounded by the buildings. The institution was both circus and menagerie, a multitude of the insane thrown into the sunlight across two walled acres. Alice found beyond the looking glass no weirder conversations than Alex found here. One old man cruised relentless as a shark, searching for cigarette or cigar butts. They didn't even need to be discarded—if someone set one down, he grabbed it. During a softball game the charge attendant of the juvenile ward, a cigar addict, set his stogie on the bench while he went to bat. He took a third strike—bat on his shoulder, mouth agape, and eyes wide—as he watched the shark scoop up his cigar and stroll off, puffing. Alex began giving the shark whole cigarettes, which only prompted gestures for a match. The shark was known to be able to talk, but nobody had ever heard him say a word. Alex wondered how they knew he was crazy.

Another character, nicknamed "the Flusher," stood in one place, muttering curses to himself, working himself to a frenzy; whereupon he put his index finger knuckle between his teeth, contorted his face, and meanwhile raised his right hand and jerked down, as if ringing a train whistle or pulling the chain on an old-fashioned toilet. Alex made friends with the chain-puller through bribes of cigarettes and discovered what he was really doing. The Flusher was in charge of all executions throughout the world, and when he cursed he was passing judgment. When he pumped his raised arm, another trap on another gibbet somewhere sprung on some poor wretch.

One afternoon Alex was waiting in the yard for an attendant to open a gate so he could go back to the ward when he noticed an immense black man with gray hair, standing pressed against a nearby wall. The man was looking around wildly, and he focused on Alex's glance as swiftly as radar. The flicking eyes kept coming back to the boy, and the huge body began to tremble. Now Alex's attention was laced with anxiety because of the unpredictable fear he saw. The boy watched the man, who suddenly began moaning, "Abe bad, boss . . . easy, boss . . . no, boss . . . no . . ." And while he spoke the huge hands began rending his own garments. He tore new denim as if it were paper, his protestations of guilt and fear growing more and more feverish until foamy spittle flew from his mouth. Alex was somewhat afraid, yet he wondered what could have implanted such fear in so powerful a man. The boy started to step forward to soothe the man, but the yipping cry and the ripping cloth stopped him short. By then shredded rags hung on the giant ebony body. Seeing that Alex might approach, the giant fell to the ground and began groveling in utter terror. Across his whale-sized back were hard lines, the silky scars of black skin. Alex turned away, ignoring the crazy man because he couldn't think of anything more appropriate. It was easier to force himself to forget the man, and Alex was glad when the attendant finally came with the key.

Later, First Choice told the boy that Abe had gotten those scars on a Louisiana chain gang, in the thirties. Abe had been a professional thief, booster, and con man, one who crossroaded around the country; he had been caught shoplifting three Hickey-Freeman suits and got a one-year sentence on each. An educated man, he'd lacked the syruped burr of northern blacks and the hat-in-hand demeanor of southern blacks. These things had marked him to redneck guards, and his worst mistake had been to meet the focused repression with head-on rebellion. "Fool-ass niggah didn' know how to jeff to live. They fucked him over bad—stuck sweat boxes to him, clubbed him, whipped him. They didn't kill his body, but they got his mind. When he finished that trey they sent him back here. You gotta be a man an' say 'no' an' fight sometimes, even

if they kills you . . . but suicide ain' nuthin', an' he committed it sure as
he used a gun."

"I'd make them kill me if they did that," Alex said, the words intense
but strange in his childish voice.

"They'll damn sure do that. They don't care if you white—sheeit, you
a white nigger, boy. You can *pass* sometimes, but if they knew 'bout you
they'd sho' nuff treat you like a nigger." First Choice rumpled the youth's
head. "You got a lot of fool in you, white boy."

■

A few days later, in another part of the yard, Alex walked close to a potbellied little Syrian, a demented creature with hooked nose and beady
eyes beneath a hairless pate. His nickname was "Abraham," which never
failed to bring vociferous protest; the words were nearly unintelligible
because his passion exaggerated his accent. But his claim to fame was
that he spent every day masturbating. He stood near a corner where
two buildings came together; he'd worn the lawn down to bare earth in
a four-foot-zone. But his penis remained healthy, though it was a miracle when he got an erection. Indeed, it was on such an occasion that Alex
first saw Abraham. A small crowd had gathered, and they were egging
him on. His tongue flapped out of his mouth, and sweat broke on his
forehead from the effort. Someone watching said it was the first time
Abraham had gotten it up in six months. Alex laughed and shook his
head, blushing because he too was beginning to masturbate, in great privacy and unsuccessfully.

Now, as Abraham was flailing away, Alex stood closer to him than
ever before. The man called out, "Boy, eh now!" He faced Alex, clenched
his fists beside his pelvis, and rolled himself suggestively, jerking his
head toward a stairwell doorway.

Prior warnings—half in jest and half serious—from both Red and
First Choice had made Alex sensitive to homosexual overtures. And this
gesture from the Syrian was definitely obscene. The boy's rage flared,
and his eyes swept the ground for a rock. He snatched one up—it was
the size of an egg—and hurled it with all his strength at the man's head.
The distance was short, but the Syrian barely managed to duck away.
The potbellied degenerate was also a coward, and he stood there, cow-
ering behind his hands. Alex grabbed another rock and threw it at the
man's still-exposed genitals, hitting him on the thigh. The man yelped
and trotted off. Alex kept throwing, and the man kept circling away,
ducking most throws, yipping when struck. On seeing the Syrian's fear,

Alex's indignation turned into something crueler: enjoyment at causing torment, a sense of power. When he tired of it he quit, but he was back the next day, and the day after that. The moment Abraham saw the boy coming he began to moan and put out his hands. A couple of times he was goaded into charging, but Alex was too nimble, and the pursuit never lasted more than a few steps.

The patients in the yard paid no attention; they were filled with their own problems and delusions. No adults were on hand to pass judgments born of love that nurture seedling consciences. Alex knew what he was doing was wrong, but his *feeling* of wrongness was lacking. Red Barzo saw the stoning from across the yard, and that evening, when they were in the mess hall, the black con man–junkie admonished him: "Best freeze on that shit, boy. White folks runnin' this camp will get in your young ass if they catch you teasin' the nutty motherfucker. Ain' no money in it, anyway. You can' go wrong in life, un'erstan', if before you do somepin', un'erstan', you say, 'any money made here?' That ain' no bullshit. That's the best way to look at the fast life, can you dig it?" The frequently interjected question wasn't really a question but a rhetorical pause. Yet the advice was intended seriously, and the sincere tone impressed the content on Alex. He would always remember and quote it, even if he didn't always follow it.

This time, however, he did follow it, and he stopped harassing the man, both because Red's approval was important and because he found other things to do. Mainly he found a way to get out of the yard by squeezing through wrought-iron bars into a tunnel walkway, and then through other bars into a courtyard with an open gate. Outside the gate was a road that went around the sprawling institution's buildings.

Among the six thousand patients, nearly a thousand had "grounds paroles," meaning they were allowed to roam the vast grounds, much of it alfalfa fields, orange groves, and walnut orchards, and some of it rocky desert like most of southern California. Many male juveniles (not females) had grounds paroles, so one more boy walking around didn't attract attention, though Alex did stay away from the administration buildings, where he might run into a staff member who knew him.

The first few days when he squeezed out, he hurried straight into the rugged low hills behind the hospital. Dotting the rugged terrain were little shacks—perhaps half a dozen over a square mile—built by long-term patients. Most were actually roofed pits with stoves and makeshift cots, a chair and table—and maybe a footlocker where someone kept cigarettes, coffee, and other things of small but important value. The cabins all had a tribe of cats; the scrawny felines were half-wild, but they came running when the man from their particular cabin came up the hill carrying food scraps wrapped in newspaper. The scraps were easy to get from the kitchen, and the cats mewed loud and tangled themselves in the men's feet, providing them with a facsimile of needed affection; they frequently talked to the cats as they spread the scraps on the ground.

Alex watched one of these men feeding his cat from a distance, wanting to be invited. But the man turned away, as if the boy weren't there, so Alex went on with his explorations, following narrow paths upward to high rocks halfway to the summit of a mountain; they provided a view of the hospital grounds and the flat land stretching west. He could even see the glimmer of the sea in the distance. It was about five miles away. To the right the hospital property stretched for three miles, mostly cultivated fields, some just rows of turned earth waiting seed, others gleaming emerald, the geometric lines framed by the dirt roads and windbreaks of tall, swaying eucalyptus. There, too, were the farm buildings, and someone told him of a large melon patch.

After a week of exploring the nearer side, of digging into holes and dislodging hordes of red ants (he put flaming twigs into their holes), of tearing thick green wrappings from unripe walnuts, he decided to circle the buildings, staying out of sight, and head toward the melon patch and dairy.

He trudged through the soft, dry earth beneath the walnut trees, then went along an irrigation ditch, staying off the hospital roads. Finally he was in a dry wash; it became a shallow, swift stream in winter but was now empty and smooth. From his earlier pinnacle view, Alex knew it came close to the melon patch and the farm buildings beyond. He trudged along, his feet sinking into the soft earth. It would have exhausted the average adult, but youth isn't so conscious of physical exhaustion. Ahead was a concrete bridge, the main road leading into the hospital, traveled by many vehicles. Before getting too close, Alex turned off the main road. But the dry shrubbery on the banks offered no path, so he plunged in, holding his hands up to keep the thin, scratchy branches away from his face. It was a hot day, and in seconds he was sweating; the sweat attracted a swarm of gnats that clustered about his face. The earlier thrill of adventure was gone, replaced by a kind of desperation. The barrier of wild shrubbery wasn't the few feet he'd expected; he'd gone fifteen yards and it was still solid in front of him.

He burst through after thirty yards, his hands and forearms itchy and irritated. He wondered from his itching face if he'd run into poison oak or poison ivy; he'd heard about the torture of itching, of scratching until the flesh was stripped (the horror stories told by little boys to each other), and right now he certainly felt as if he could scratch that much.

Finally he was on a dusty road beside the field of melons. Two boys were already there; one of them, who looked older than Alex, was hunkered down, chopping a striped watermelon open with a rusted garden trowel. The ground around him was littered with half a dozen split melons, their meat pale pink rather than succulent red, unripe except to the swarms of flies they attracted.

Both boys were in profile to Alex, facing each other and not seeing the new arrival. Their voices but not their words came across the twenty yards of heat-shimmering air. The younger boy's voice had a sibilance higher than most, making Alex think of a girl, and in profile his chest had the twin jutting configuration of budding breasts. Alex's hostility toward these interlopers in a territory he was hunting broke into confusion. He'd seen this rosy-cheeked young boy with the other juveniles, that was certain, and that meant he wasn't a girl even if he had a girl's breasts, voice, and complexion. Later Alex would learn that a hormone imbalance caused these things, and in turn these had caused a nervous breakdown. The boy was getting hormone shots for one problem and psychotherapy for the other.

The older boy saw Alex first. He stood up from the split watermelon, trowel in hand. "Whaddya want?" he demanded.

"Nuthin'," Alex said, taken off balance and ashamed because his response wasn't equally challenging.

"What're you doin', watchin' us?"

"I'm not watching you. I didn't even know you were here."

"You could see us from half a mile if you came down the road. Where *did* you come from?"

Alex waved at the thick wall of foliage.

"Through *that!* Why didn't you just walk?"

Before Alex could answer or even decide if he was going to (he resented the tone of the interrogation and had answered only because the other boy had momentum), the rosy-cheeked boy touched the other's arm and talked too softly for Alex to hear. The older boy grimaced and nodded, indicating that he understood what was happening. Then Alex noticed that the older boy had extremely bad acne; it had scarred him so, his face had lost most of its flexibility. He turned to Alex. "You haven't even got a grounds parole. You're on Ward Fourteen. You killed somebody and now you're running off. That's right, huh?" The boy had piercing green eyes, old for his years.

"No, it's wrong. I didn't kill anybody and I'm not running away. But what's it to you? Are you a cop?"

"Hell no, I ain't no fuckin' cop."

"Well," said Rosy Cheeks. "I know you're on Fourteen and I know you had to do something serious or you'd be with us. And you can't get a grounds parole on Fourteen . . . at least no juvenile can."

Alex's feet suddenly felt hot in his tennis shoes. He wondered if they would snitch on him, doubting that the older one would, for in youth Alex equated physical toughness with strength of character. But he was uncertain of the pretty boy. Years from now he would learn the impossibility of determining who would snitch from mannerisms. Actually, there was nothing he could do now—except run away—and he might have to chance it. These boys weren't clean either; half a dozen watermelons were smashed open and thick with flies.

"We don't care what you're doing," Acne said. "Are you escaping?"

Alex shook his head. "Just messing around."

"Did you really shoot somebody?" Rosy Cheeks asked.

Alex nodded, the thread of awe in the boy's voice making him view that never-forgotten but time-dimmed memory in a new way. In some places with some persons it was an accomplishment to have shot a man.

"None of these fuckers are ripe," Acne said, chopping the trowel into the mottled green shell of yet another melon.

His manner signed acceptance, so Alex came down the row. "I'm Alex," he said.

"I'm Raymond Taylor," Acne said. "But everybody calls me 'Scabs.' I don't know why." He grinned. "This is Pat."

Alex shook hands with Pat. Alex wanted to ask him if he was a boy or a girl but thought it would be impolite. Now he was part of the group, and it was taken for granted that they would spend the afternoons together, at play, smashing watermelons on the grounds of Camarillo State Hospital.

Leaving the smashed watermelons to the flies and the birds, they went toward the cluster of yellow frame farm buildings surrounded by trees that provided shade and a windbreak, an oasis of coolness amid the glare and weighted heat. Scabs assured Alex that nobody would pay them any attention, that he'd been here many times and the free personnel and patient workers were used to boys wandering around.

Scabs's prediction was accurate. Nobody gave the three boys more than a glance. The area was more like a model farm than a real one. The frame walls had fresh yellow paint, and the windows gleamed. The gravel-paved roadways and square were raked clean and smooth, so the handful of leaves fallen on them from overhanging trees were like pimples on flawless skin. Weeds were nonexistent; the flowerbeds were tended; the lawns were manicured. The many trees gave shade and coolness.

The exploring trio, like all boys, instinctively sought out the animals. First the cows, the boys marveling at them as they came into the milking barn on their own, turning into their stalls, chewing placidly and waiting for the patients to arrive and hook their swollen udders to the machines. Alex wanted to squeeze one, to follow what someone had once told him about rolling the fingertips from top to bottom. Cows were harmless, everyone said, and he wasn't really afraid, but he was from the city and a cow was, after all, awfully big. He slipped past a fly-slapping tail and along the road flank. "Easy, Bossy," he said, patting the cow, then leaned forward to grasp the pinkish-white nipple, pulling and squeezing, surprised by the force of the squirting stream. The cow sounded and shifted its bulk, its flank banging into Alex's head and pushing him back because of his ungainly posture. It also frightened him— a flash fright that made him leap out to the aisle and brought laughter from Scabs and a grin from Pat.

Alex blushed, embarrassed, angry at himself, vowing to erase their laughter by doing something recklessly wild and brave.

Cows are less interesting than dogs and horses, especially the latter. The State Hospital had a flock of sheep and a pair of black-and-white sheepdogs. The boys watched them in action, their mouths seemingly stuck half-open in amazement, since the dogs were incredibly swift and often seemed to anticipate which way a ewe, who seemed to be leader, was going to break as they were being moved from one pasture to another. When the shepherd, an elderly Mexican who was a patient, closed the gate behind the last piece of wool on the hoof, the boys tried to call the dogs, who were trotting at the old man's heels. With lolling tongues and brambles in their fur, the dogs looked at the suplicants but didn't even falter in their prancing stride. Alex suddenly wished he had a dog that loved him as these two did the old man.

Beyond a line of trees was a back pasture holding three horses. All were fat and all were grazing, their necks arched down to the short grass. The boys were on a dirt road going beside the pasture.

"Let's take a dip," Pat said.

"Where's a place to do that?" Alex asked.

"An irrigation cistern. I guess you call it a cistern," Scabs said. "But it's really cold and feels good as a motherfucker on a hot day . . . even if you can't really swim."

Alex nodded, but he was looking toward the pasture. "That's fine . . . but we should go horseback riding first."

"Oh, no!" Pat said. "You know better, Scabs. Tell him how mad they'll get."

"It doesn't matter," Alex said. "We're not going to get spotted out here."

"If we do—"

"We're not hurtin' 'em. And horses are *for riding,* or doing something."

"How you gonna steer him?" Scabs asked.

"I'm going to put a belt around his neck and hope he's well trained. If that doesn't work, I'll just hold on."

"We'll keep a lookout, just in case. I know a lot 'bout cars, but about horses I don't know shit from Shinola."

■

Putting a hand on a fence post, Alex climbed the wire and dropped down. Twenty yards away the horse looked up, but his long tail kept slapping rhythmically at flies. The knot in Alex's stomach began to unravel a little as he came up beside the horse and patted its flank without getting kicked or snarled at—or whatever it is horses do to threaten. He saw that he couldn't swing onto the horse's back from the ground, even with a firm grip on the long mane. He put the belt around the horse's neck and led him to the fence. The horse came easily. Scabs held him while Alex got up awkwardly on a fence post and half-fell across the animal's back. The horse held firm, conditioned to suffer fools and the ungainly. Alex swung a leg over and found himself astride. He got the belt around the big neck so it vaguely resembled a short bridle. "C'mon, giddup," he said, spurring the horse's sides—and the horse followed instructions.

Alex was conscious of Scabs and Pat standing on the road outside the fence, and he knew that they were impressed by this scene; they might even be envious.

Using just the belt, the "reins" were short, so he leaned forward along the horse's neck, accustoming himself to the roll and sway of horseback. Then suddenly he wanted the horse to run. He wanted to be the racing, free figure on horseback that he'd seen so often in movies. "Hah!" he exclaimed, shaking the reins and kicking his heels into the horse's sides. The horse lunged into a trot—a gait it was unaccustomed to. It was better but still insufficiently exhilarating, so he urged the horse to greater speed, feeling the hard bounces whenever the hooves thumped into the earth, sending up puffs of dust. At the end of the pasture he pulled the belt to the right, wanting to ride up to his friends. The horse turned obediently, slowing down. Now Alex was facing the road.

Scabs and Pat were gone. And where they'd stood was a green pickup truck with the State of California seal on its open door. Its driver was bent over, coming through the fence—it was the farm foreman. When he came erect he brandished a clenched fist at Alex, yelling angrily.

"Stupid-ass kid!" came through the hot air as Alex pulled up and half fell off the horse. He hit the ground running and heard the voice saying, "If that mare has a miscarriage . . ."

He hit the fence, glancing back. The man was running across the pasture, but his feet were sinking into the earth and he wasn't moving very fast. The ground Alex was on, beyond the fence, was packed hard, and his feet were flying. The man gave up before he reached the fence. Alex ducked into a cornfield, then cut across at an angle that brought him beside the devastated melon patch en route to the creek bed, though this time he went to the bridge and down into it instead of fighting the brush.

Minutes later, as he followed his opposite-direction footsteps in the smooth dirt, the fear was gone. Now he felt a pang of remorse; he hoped the horse would be all right. No harm had been intended; he hadn't known the mare was pregnant. Yet he also begged fate to let it be, that nothing would come of it, that he wouldn't be found out.

■

That night Pat snitched on him. The horse was all right, but the foreman had found the litter of gutted watermelons and the tracks of the same trio he'd chased from the pasture. He'd gone to the juvenile ward, picking Scabs out. The attendants then told him that if Scabs was one, Pat had to be the other. Scabs denied everything until Pat burst into tears and confessed, telling who was with them.

Alex had no idea—no forewarning. He was playing chess with First Choice Floyd when he saw the evening supervisor and the farm foreman come onto the ward; they went into the office with the ward's charge attendant. At precisely that moment, Alex ceased to be able to see how the pieces moved or their relationships. His mind flooded with dread. Floyd took his queen and chortled happily.

The charge attendant came out, spotted Alex in the dayroom of the insane, and beckoned him over with head and hand gestures. Alex pointed a finger at himself in silent question. The man nodded. Alex swallowed back his fear and got up. "They want me," he said to Floyd. "I think I've gotten into a mess."

"What'd you do?"

"Not much, but they think it's serious."

"Hold your mud like we taught you."

Alex nodded and walked toward the closed door of varnished wood.

Moments later, as the door closed behind him, Alex knew what his trouble was. Two of the three waiting men wore white, but the other was in khakis and brogans. It was about riding the horse. Alex was unable to tell if this was the man from the truck, but he thought it likely because of how the man's eyes narrowed, studying him.

Next to the farm employee, perched on a reversed straight-backed chair, his chin resting on crossed forearms, was the nightwatch supervisor. After four P.M. he was in charge of the institution—so long as things remained fairly routine. A major problem put him on the telephone. Now he was irked. He'd been called from the mess hall/auditorium where the women's wards were seeing a movie. His duties included seeing the movie, and if this interruption was frivolous . . .

"Sit down, lad," the nightwatch supervisor said.

Alex looked around. "No seats," he said.

"Well, guess you'll stand up. This won't take long anyway."

Alex suddenly decided that he would deny guilt no matter how much evidence or how many witnesses were against him. His brain locked into place.

The room was silent, with each adult waiting for the other to speak. It was the farm foreman, coloring as he did, who spoke first: "You're lucky you're in an institution. If you were my kid I'd blister your ass for you. That's what you need. But that's a *no no* because you're a *patient.* I think you just need to learn better than to violate society's rules . . . and respect things. Do you know how many good watermelons you destroyed? Ruining food when people in China are starving? . . ."

"Exactly what happened, Jeff?" asked the nightwatch supervisor.

"This kid and a couple of others from the juvenile ward—they admit they did it, and one of them said this one was with them—tore up a watermelon patch, vandalized it, and then started riding mares ready to foal. Wonder they didn't cause a miscarriage."

The nightwatch supervisor looked at Alex, cocking an eyebrow, no hostility evident. "How come you did some shit like that?"

"I didn't do nuthin'," Alex said emphatically. "I don't know what you're talking about."

The foreman flushed in livid spots. "We oughta put him in a side-room in straps," he said to the other two men. "That'd teach the punk."

The supervisor popped the gum he was chewing and let his eyes float momentarily toward the ceiling, as if mildly bored or bemused at the vengeful words but unwilling to argue the point.

"What's the use of denyin' it?" the supervisor asked Alex. "Nothin's gonna happen to you except take your grounds parole for a month. That's no way to treat a privilege."

"I don't have a grounds parole card," Alex said. "I wasn't out there."

The supervisor was suddenly alive, rising up and looking at the ward attendant, who hadn't spoken since summoning Alex. "That's right," the ward attendant said. "He doesn't have a grounds parole card. He goes out to the main recreation yard, but that's all. He's no relation to Harry Houdini."

The supervisor looked at the foreman, now questioning him without words, waiting for an explanation. Now the coloring was of discomfiture and confusion. "I dunno. I just know there was three of 'em . . . and that other kid said it was this one." He punctuated the sentence with a lame shrug.

"Maybe he *did* do it," the supervisor said. "Little Orphan Annie could get out of here in ten minutes. But all we've got is the word of a schizophrenic youngster. . . . So"—he turned to Alex—"you get the benefit of the doubt this time. But if it was you out there fuckin' things up, better think about it. Some people around here would see that as a sign that something's wrong with your brain, and the way to fix it is with a dozen electric-shock treatments. I guarantee that would stop you for a while."

Alex had seen the treatments, given to dozens twice a week in an assembly-line process: the oiled temples, the small electrodes, the seconds of convulsions, and the hours of deep sleep with foam running from the corners of mouths; and after awakening the slow return of memory, men never knowing where they were or what was happening. They were indeed unlikely to do anything wrong or have a wrong thought—or much of any thoughts. The patients on shock treatments, with rare exceptions, were diffident, wearing perpetual semi-smiles. They all said they couldn't remember feeling anything, but all of them were frightened of the black box—and so was Alex. In the mental hospital all misbehavior was considered a symptom of mental illness. It was *treated* instead of punished—and Alex was terrified of such treatment.

Afterward, when he stood alone in the dayroom, Alex was incredulous—so much so that his relief was edged with fear. It had been too easy to get out of the trouble; the supervisor had been too friendly. It was unnatural.

That night in the dormitory's darkness—amid snores, coughs, and muttered words from psychotic dreams—Alex was too keyed up to sleep. He was elated at having found a friend of Scabs's stature, an older boy who had respect and status in the juvenile hierarchy. Alex was mildly angry at Pat and knew the boy's snitching would make Scabs drop him, but it would be a couple more years before Alex looked on all snitches with unmitigated hate. Now he would have someone to pal around with. It was a good thought. Then once again he recalled the scene in the room with the men. In the past he'd been punished for things he hadn't done (and things he had, too), and now he'd gotten out of something he was really guilty of—after he'd been caught. It seemed to prove that right didn't always overcome wrong, nor the other way either. Sometimes it was even hard to know the difference. He hadn't felt wrong in riding the horse . . . but he did feel a little wrong in smashing the watermelons, destroying things for no good reason. . . . They hadn't been as upset about the melons as the horse. . . .

Alex fell asleep wondering how he'd contact Scabs in the morning.

■

For the next few weeks things happened as Alex had anticipated. Scabs, his cruel nature finding moral indignation to justify tormenting his former friend, slapped and kicked the sobbing Pat. Scabs spat on him and chased him away, first ordering him to lower his head and drop his eyes whenever he or Alex approached. A few days later three older boys on the juvenile ward slapped Pat around, then buggered him, tearing his rectum. "You got tits like a girl, voice like a girl, you cry like a girl, and you're a snitch—so you're gonna be a girl."

That night Pat sliced himself up with a razor blade, up and down both arms, his neck, and his cheeks. It took a hundred forty-two stitches to sew him up. He was transferred to a "closed" ward and put on shock treatments twice a week for ten weeks. Alex never saw him again, though a decade later he would learn of a Californian with Pat's identical name and description, unique as it was with the breasts, who was electrocuted in Texas for an especially gory rape-murder.

Alex and Scabs became friends and constant companions. It was taken for granted that the older boy was the leader, and Alex went along with him unquestioningly. Just once did Alex assert himself, and he did so without thinking, the red haze of anger glowing in his skull. Scabs had referred to Red Barzo and First Choice Floyd as "those buck niggers." It was his tone more than the words that caused Alex to snap in reflex, his voice sharp. "Don't call 'em that. They're my friends . . . and they're both sharp cats. Call 'em colored or Negro."

The words were an order, and Scabs's teeth clicked shut, his eyes hooding and cheeks reddening, for an *order* by a peer was insult and challenge. He was older, tougher, and Alex shouldn't—While his ire was developing, he saw something in Alex's face—the distended nostrils and the eyes, especially the eyes—and decided Alex's statement wasn't intended as an insult and was, in fact, actually right. He shrugged and said he didn't mean anything derogatory by the word, but he'd check himself from now on.

Late that night in the darkness, waiting for sleep, which was invariably when he reviewed the events of the day and thought of tomorrow's, Alex suddenly flinched, seeing Scabs's face in memory, not having really seen it at the time. It had nearly been trouble, and Scabs could surely kick his ass. Even worse, their friendship would cease, and replacing the good feeling would be the hollow pain of loneliness spreading from his stomach through every corner of his being. He was glad it fizzled before it lighted.

Scabs had long since explored every cranny of the grounds, and he spent a few days showing Alex everything there was to see. Legitimate activities for young boys were nonexistent, and those for older patients (weaving, art, and so forth) were excruciatingly boring. So they turned to delinquency. Scabs came up with the idea of breaking into the various hillside shacks, and Alex agreed without thinking of right and wrong, or even about the chances of being caught, or the consequences.

They spent a whole day—a swift, exciting day—prowling the barren hills, watching each shack until the owner left, then breaking in. For three such "burglaries" they got twelve packs of Camels and half a bottle of contraband wine, enough to make Alex feel really good and not enough to get him drunk.

Next Scabs led him off the property to break into a cabin in a canyon. They could take nothing with them, so they vandalized it, splattering eggs against the walls. Actually, Alex went along with the vandalism halfheartedly, feeling bad about it.

They also prowled the hospital's parking lot, rifling the glove compartments of unlocked cars, which was most of them, despite a sign telling people to lock their vehicles.

Scabs knew how to drive a car, and Alex wanted to learn. They were planning to take a car from the lot (eventually someone would leave keys in the ignition), joyride around, and have Alex learn how to shift gears.

At this point Scabs was suddenly told to pack his belongings. He was being discharged to his parents. They were leaving the state in a few weeks and would take him with them.

The next morning Alex met Scabs's mother and stepfather as he helped carry his friend's belongings to the car. They brusquely acknowledged the introduction, then turned away. Scabs, too, was brusque, anxious to get into the car and be gone from the nuthouse.

Several times that morning Alex's eyes got wet as loneliness flashed up through him. The next day the sharp hurt of losing someone had gone away. Now the ache was dull; he just moped around and watched the sun change the colors of the world. . . .

■

One week after Scabs's departure, Alex was walking beside one of the roads near the administration building. He heard a car motor but didn't turn until the brakes squealed and the horn bleated.

Scabs was behind the wheel of a 1936 Ford coupe, the absolute heppest car of the era. He was grinning, beckoning Alex over to the passenger door. A great surge of joy went through Alex; he'd been lonesome since Scabs had gone. Without reflecting on what he was doing, yet looking around to make sure that nobody saw him (nobody was in sight except two patients weeding a flowerbed), he slid into the open door and slid down so that just his eyes were visible.

"Atta boy," Scabs said, poking him in the ribs. "You still have all the guts in the world." Scabs was still grinning, but the joy of meeting turned to momentary consternation when he released the clutch unevenly and the car spasmed forward until the motor died. "Goddamn Fords," Scabs cursed. He got under way again, more careful now, and turned on to a little-used dirt road that eventually left the hospital property for a two-lane highway toward the ocean and coast route four miles away.

Now Alex sat erect, almost stiff, leaning slightly forward in tense anticipation of each new sight; he knew he was embarking on a course of adventure. Minutes before he'd had misgivings in some compartment of his mind, and for another moment he'd thought of having Scabs take him back before the institution count found him missing, but he slammed the lid on the idea without really viewing it. Like most people, Alex could highlight justification for what he wanted and minimize the contrary realities. So now he overflowed with joy at the imminent possibilities for adventure without envisioning the probable repercussions. Why doubt? he thought; it was already too late. He was committed to the unknown.

The few miles until the seacoast highway were fields of emerald alfalfa in undulant waves made by the breeze; there were also unbelievably neat and uniform orange groves. A white frame house sat at the edge of a lemon orchard, picture postcard-pretty, and several boys around Alex's age were tossing a football. A pang of envy's cousin went through him, as it always did when he saw boys leading normal lives, but this time it went away quickly. They were playing football but he was riding around in a car, could go anywhere, because he was utterly free— or so he felt. Everything was so beautiful. He looked over at Scabs, whose damaged face was rigidly expressionless as he concentrated on the road; he wasn't *that* at ease behind the wheel, and the road curled and had lots of traffic.

"Where'd you get this?" Alex asked.

"I stole it, dummy. Whaddya think, Eleanor Roosevelt come down and give it to me?" The chiding rebuke was intended as humor, for there was whimsy in Scabs's voice and eyes. Nevertheless, Alex blushed for a moment. Scabs glanced over, reached out his arm, and tugged the younger boy's earlobe. "Take it easy. This is the day you learn how to drive."

"Aw, man, really! No jive?"

"N'no jive. Anyway, you'll learn to shift gears, and after that it's just practice mostly."

Alex nodded, grinning yet suddenly apprehensive too. Would he make a fool of himself, run into something? Would he get stupid and clumsy at a critical moment? His hands sweated. Yet he had to learn. It was a rite of passage.

"You gonna teach me how to hotwire it, too?"

"Sure. That's easy. You just—forget it till we get there."

"Where?"

"I know a huge parking lot they don't use since the war started. It's got grass coming up through the cracks, but it's still a good place for this. Say, you got any money?"

Alex felt the handful of change in his pants pocket. "A little over a dollar."

"I'm hungry. You gonna buy me a hamburger?"

"Sure, Scabs. Glad to."

■

Abundant refreshment stands served the hundred miles of beach.

"Get that one," Alex said. "They've got twelve centers."

Scabs started to pull right but then straightened and kept going past the stand.

"What happened?" Alex asked.

"There's a highway patrol car in the lot. I'll bet he'd want to see my driver's license if he spotted me."

"Yeah, that's right. I didn't think. I didn't even look. I will now, though."

Scabs grunted, obviously liking the role of mentor. His marred face brought him a dozen jeers for every sign of respect, and Alex instinctively knew how to make his friend feel good.

Scabs parked on the highway shoulder, one hundred yards from the next hot-dog stand. Sweating beachgoers seeking cool refreshment gave the stand a lot of business, so the boys had to wait to be served. The sun was hot on Alex's cheeks, but the sweat brought by the sun was cooled by a soft sea breeze. He had been away from the free world enough months for its sights, especially normal people, to appear strange, ever so slightly out of focus. The abnormal had become the norm for him. And he felt a new sensation, too, as he looked at women's bodies in tight one-piece bathing suits. He'd never before given any attention to female legs and asses; now they fascinated him—some more than others—and he got hard and felt a wonderful sensation spreading from his crotch through his lower stomach. To a much lesser extent he'd felt this when masturbating in hiding, envious of Scabs having an orgasm while he couldn't. Now, however, he was sure he could have one, except this wasn't exactly the time or place to masturbate.

While they ate the hamburgers, their mouths too full for much conversation, Alex also watched the other customers. Two little girls, perhaps sisters, tried to bite delicately through the surface of a candy apple. Alex felt much older than they. Silliness was in their eyes, gawkiness in their movements. It amused him to feel wise and mature, and he could see them glancing at him, too, in a way that was entirely new but that he recognized instinctively. All were too young, getting ready for when they wouldn't be.

Scabs gave no heed to his surroundings. His hamburger was collapsing, so he was bent forward at the waist to avoid the drippings, try-ing to stuff the end of it, but not the paper, into his mouth. He'd gotten most of it when a bold seagull banked in swiftly, making its foul noise, and zoomed by just four feet away.

"Aw, shit!" Scabs said, throwing what remained into the air behind the gull. That one didn't get it, but another had a fat neck within a sec-ond after it landed on the sand. Almost immediately a young man, sun-tanned to the marrow and wearing a lifeguard patch, was on them. "Don't feed the birds, boys," he said.

It was time for them to go. When they were in the car, Scabs said he wished the lifeguard hadn't noticed them. "The beach is a good place to steal," he said. "People leave their wallets in their cars, or in their clothes on the sand when they hit the water."

The teeming beach, where it was hard to know who was watching what, made Alex hope that Scabs wouldn't want to steal from clothes. The cars were bad, too, but Alex could crank up enough nerve for that. Scabs, however, kept on talking while starting the motor, watching the highway in the mirror and pulling into the river of cars.

"Don't people lock their cars?" Alex asked.

"Sure, but you can get in with a coat hanger quicker than with a key. You straighten it out, put it through the windwing, and pop the lock on the door."

"Is that right?"

"I'll show you when we stop."

Scabs seemed to know everything, and Alex was insatiable to learn about anything. Alex was already more intelligent and better educated, since Scabs didn't read books except for an occasional Captain Marvel Comic. But Scabs was an encyclopedia of delinquency; actually, he knew more than many adult criminals, and had been in Juvenile Hall a dozen times. They would have sent him to the Youth Authority and reform school, except that they thought his problems were psychological—a re-action against his blemished flesh. Scabs didn't see it that way, and after getting accustomed to the pitted face Alex forgot it, though he could see it bothered Scabs whenever women were around. How much depended on the attractiveness of the girl.

"Say, Scabs," Alex asked.

"Huh?"

"I think I can come when I jack off now."

Scabs jerked and turned his head. "So."

"I dunno," Alex said, shrugging. "I don't know when I'm gonna get a chance to fuck—and I don't know what to do." He waited, hoping his talkative friend would offer information about that. Scabs, for once, had nothing to say. "Do I just stick it in?"

"Yeah, but not *just* . . ."

"What's that mean?"

"There's more to it than just that."

"Well, tell me, Scabs. Would ya?"

"No! I won't! Quit buggin' me."

Taken aback, Alex knew the shrill response came from more than the question; he had touched a nerve. Scabs had claimed that he'd been with girls and gone all the way, but in everything else he was vociferous in giving details and embellishments, while now he snapped and stifled conversation. To Alex it was a revelation—not just that Scabs lied, for lying was as common as truth everywhere. Alex's revelation was that people unwittingly exposed themselves by word, gesture, and attitude, that deep chambers were unintentionally opened if the right button was pushed. It wasn't lying, not exactly; it was that their view of themselves, or of things, was sometimes more pleasurable than truthful.

Alex would have to think about it more at a later time.

■

It was afternoon when they reached the empty asphalt acres of Santa Anita Racetrack, now closed in its off-season. The stands were nearly a mile from the street entrance where they turned in.

"You can't hit nothin' here," Scabs said. They cruised slowly across the endless white lines.

"Won't somebody say something?"

"Nope. People use it all the time for this. It's where my uncle taught my mother. And if the police come, we can see 'em when they turn in, go around the other side, and jump out into miles of orange groves and countryside. So it's really cool."

For no particular reason Scabs came close to the entrance gates before stopping, turning off the engine and getting ready to start the lesson. A statue of a horse was there, slightly pigeon-stained. The plaque said SEABISCUIT, and an ache went through Alex; he remembered being a very little boy in the car with his father and some neighbors, listening to a portable radio (nobody had car radios then) tuned to the Santa Anita Handicap. Clem had nearly run into a car at a light as he pounded his hands on the wheel and urged Seabiscuit to victory. Then he'd head-locked his son and kissed him on the forehead. The flash memory made

Alex hurt now, almost to wet eyes, and then to mute anger at life itself. It wasn't right; he'd had nobody but a father. Others had mothers or aunts and uncles or brothers—or somebody. . . .

"Damn, Alex. C'mon, quit daydreaming," Scabs said. He had come around the car and had the door open. "Slide on over."

For a fourteen-year-old, Scabs was a good teacher. He started from the beginning: have the gear in neutral and the emergency brake on, or have the clutch pressed down before starting the motor.

Alex's tenseness and total concentration made things harder, at least the most important thing of releasing the clutch in conjunction with feeding the gas for a smooth start. Again and again the car lurched forward and died, or gave lots of bounce-jerks before dying or keeping on. When the latter happened, the subsequent shifts were also bad, but not so completely.

It was when tenseness and concentration seemed to have drained him that things smoothed out. All of a sudden he had the knack of it, and he was exalted. The jerks in reverse were gone in half a dozen tries. Then Scabs taught him arm signals.

"You got most of it now," he said. "All you need is practice."

"I don't know where I'll get that," Alex said.

"Steal cars," Scabs said, then burst into laughter. "My mother taught me how to shift. She thought it was cute. Now she curses herself. She pulls her hair and says, 'A monster I made.'"

"How many cars you stole?"

"They know about over twenty. I must've stolen twice that. But I don't hurt 'em, just drive 'em for a few hours until they run out of gas."

"Didn't you wreck one?"

"Oh yeah, one. But it wasn't my fault. That old lady slammed on the brakes to miss a cat, and I was getting ready to pass her. Bet she don't go nuts for a fuckin' cat no more."

Neither of the boys had a watch, but the boulevard traffic had grown heavy and then thinned. The sun softened, shadows lengthened, and a breeze began stirring things.

"Well, I gotta go home, Alex," Scabs announced.

Throughout the afternoon, Alex's thoughts had flicked to this moment. He'd hoped it wouldn't come, that Scabs would run away. And now he momentarily regretted getting into the car in the first place, but he immediately ridiculed the regret. His black, junkie pals had taught him about the futility of regret. He didn't articulate the thing that worried him, but it was the dread of loneliness. The night would come and he would be alone with no place to go.

Scabs glanced over at the younger boy while following a homeward course on residential side streets. "Less liable to meet a prowl car that sees how old we are," he explained. When they were near where he lived, one of the first tracts in southern California, which was also one of the last constructed before the war ended the building trade for the duration, his guilt at leaving Alex came out obliquely. "You wait with the car around the corner. I'll go in and get some money for you."

"Okay. Thanks," Alex said unenthusiastically, barely nodding and continuing to stare from the window.

"Keep the car, too. It's got half a tank of gas and it won't be on the hot sheet until tomorrow. As long as you don't get stopped for something, you'll be okay."

"Yeah, thanks," Alex said.

"Come by tomorrow morning and we'll go fuck around together."

"What time?"

"Early. Seven-thirty—when they leave for work. We can make breakfast. I cook pretty good . . ."

Alex replied with a noncommittal grunt this time, and for the first time saw the flaws in Scabs. The older boy was obviously discomfited, afraid—not physically, but of losing his young follower.

"Wait now," he said after parking around the corner. "I'll be right back."

Scabs was gone about fifteen minutes, and when he returned a blanket was tucked under one arm along with a shopping bag. He slid inside.

"Here's some socks and underwear and stuff in here."

"Thanks."

"All I could get was eight bucks. My mom just had fifteen in her purse."

"That's fine. Look, man, I'd better get going."

"What time tomorrow?"

"Huh? Tomorrow?"

"When'll you get here?"

Alex snorted and shrugged. "Who knows? I don't even know where I am . . . or where I'm going now. I wish I hadn't—" He stifled the last words. Saying it aloud would make it worse, like tearing a scab from a fresh sore.

"All right," Alex said, trying to shift without depressing the clutch. "Jesus!" But he quickly did it right and got under way without a jump. He stayed on side streets, mainly residential, avoiding boulevards with traffic where anyone who saw him would know he wasn't supposed to be driving an automobile. The only way someone his age could get a car was to steal it, and if a cop saw him . . . In the residential streets the darkness hid him; drivers were shadows, traffic an occasional pair of yellow orbs. At first he was so concentrated on the automobile that he dripped sweat; his hands were so slippery that he couldn't hold the wheel unless he wiped them off on his pants. From the outset he was lost, but now he didn't even know north from south, or anywhere else. Not that it mattered. He had no destination. He was driving for practice and pleasure, and soon he was running the speedometer up to sixty between stop signs, braking in squeals. Now he was having fun, troubles forgotten.

Scabs's parents lived in Culver City, one of several incorporated "cities" within the endless sprawl of Los Angeles. It was about five miles from the Pacific Coast Highway. Alex didn't know which direction he'd gone from there after dropping Scabs, nor whereabouts he'd emerge along the coast, but heading west would bring him there eventually, and from there he could find his way, although he had nowhere to go except back to Scabs in the morning.

The side streets disappeared in the direction he was going. He tried to appear taller, and if someone at a traffic light glanced his way, he turned his head. He was at a light when the engine coughed twice and fell silent.

Repeatedly he jammed down on the starter button, uselessly grinding the small motor to an ugly sound that made him frantic. Then he saw the fuel gauge on *empty*. He would go no farther in this car. His trying to gas it up would bring a chuckle and a grip around his collar.

Two large boulevards intersected here, but the blackness was absolute until lights speckled the hillsides miles away. He had no idea where he was, which increased his dread. The traffic lights went through their cycle; as a red got ready to change, headlights flashed into the stolen car from the rear. Brakes squealed when Alex's car didn't move. The car behind pulled around and stopped, a window coming down. The male voice came from the featureless shadow of a face.

"What's that car doin' out there in the middle of the street?"

"It just stopped," Alex said; his voice squeaked in fear.

"Hey, who's drivin' over there?"

"My father," Alex said, still squeaking.

"Where the hell is he? Leavin' a car in the middle of an intersection is inviting trouble."

"He went . . . to get help . . . call somebody."

"Why didn't you push it to the side?"

Alex was stumped for long seconds; then in a stronger voice he said, "He's got a heart condition."

"Uh-huh, I get it. Well, we can't leave it there." The man pulled to the curb and came over. As he lumbered forward, a big man in checked mackinaw, Alex reached for the door, primed to bolt. But he'd never out-run the man. The odds were better to brazen it out.

The man slipped the cap from a flare and scratched it until it fired. He dropped it behind the car and told Alex to get out and help.

"How long's your pa been gone?" the man asked.

"Twenty minutes, maybe."

"I got time. I better stay here with you—damn boondocks out here. There's bums back in the beach canyons."

"I'll be okay," Alex said. "I'll lock myself in."

"No, that's okay. I got off work early an' the old lady'd think I got fired if she hears the car come in now."

Minutes ticked away, and Alex sat physically quiet in the front passenger seat, feet outside on the curb. His mind was spinning. The man paced on the other side, out of Alex's sight but not out of his consciousness.

The black-and-white highway patrol car came from the other direction; its driver looked over at the two parked vehicles. The man stopped pacing and watched the cruiser go along the highway divider to a place for a U-turn. Alex watched in the mirror. As the headlights began to turn, he made sure the man wasn't looking; then he crouched down, using the stolen car as a shield, and ran awkwardly toward the darkness. He saw the waist-high ditch two steps ahead, so he only half-fell into the soft, damp dirt.

The prowl car headlights lighted up the route he traveled, but car and ditch hid him enough—until he was far enough away where he could scramble up and duck into the wild bushes. He halted there, looked back, and now a flashlight beam was playing across the bushes nearest the car.

It was much like the last hunt, he thought, momentarily dismayed as he recalled the ending of that one. Then dismay disappeared into excitement, and the excitement made him feel alive. The exhaustion of having to run went away. He was oblivious to the scratching twigs and shrubs. He would avoid getting boxed in.

Another hundred yards ahead, he crept back to the roadside and looked at the starting point. A fourth set of headlights was there, another highway patrol cruiser. He was beyond the range of their lights. Bunching himself, he ran bent over across the highway and through another wall of bushes. But then he was on smooth lawn with occasional silhouettes of trees. Minutes later the grass was manicured, and he saw a flag in a hole. He was on a golf course. He could walk without worrying that he'd run into a wire and cut his head off. However trivial and temporary the escape—victory—elated him. He'd gotten away, and he felt a form of exaltation. Tired as he was, he walked jauntily through the night.

11

morning found him under the boardwalk of the beach near the Venice Amusement Pier. He'd trudged for three hours, first following a westward railway right-of-way, then keeping as much to alleys as possible. When he was forced onto regular streets he sprang into bushes or whatever cranny was available the instant headlights appeared. Every police officer would stop to question a child wandering the city at three A.M., especially when there was a call about the stolen car. A couple of times he detoured around gas stations or passed open cafés, their windows misted from the warmth within. He was afraid to enter because most adults would be as curious as a policeman. So he walked until he reached the beach, the sea glimmering in the moonlight a hundred yards away, and then curled into a niche to wait, shivering, for dawn, wishing that he'd never gotten into the car with Scabs, sad and angry at having done so. But he would never give up. He would postpone the consequences of his behavior as long as possible.

When the sun sparkled on the sea, bright but morning-cool, he came out and stretched his cramped muscles.

The hour was early, and the few persons on the boardwalk were elderly and poor. Later it would fill up with servicemen, sun-worshippers, and amusement pier patrons, but now it was those who lived nearby, mostly retirees who had come west to die in the sun and who lived on in its warmth. For nearly three decades from the turn of the century, the Venice area had been a fashionable playground at the sea. The planners had even dug canals nearby to mime the Italian city it was named after, and on the banks were cottages used as vacation homes. But decay and disfavor came together as other parts of the coast were developed, and the canals became weed-clogged ditches breeding mosquitoes, and the hotels were turned into third-rate apartments. The war brought a temporary resurgence to the amusement pier and boardwalk, but a block away the children of the poor played in alleys and on a streetcar right-of-way.

Alex found a group of children near his age playing in an overgrown vacant lot. Divided into *armies,* they split the territory and lined up on the borders, facing each other at thirty feet. They tore up clods of packed earth with tall clumps of grass. The grass served as a stabilizer and gave visual grace to the hand-launched missiles. Being hit put the target out of the game. It was simple, wild fun to the children. Alex watched for a while, and when a boy quit, Alex offered to take his place to make the sides even.

For the next hour he forgot that he was an escapee from a mental institution and an orphan. He even forgot that he'd shot a man.

When two brothers and a sister had to leave the vacant lot, the contest ended. Some drifted off, but a handful remained, and Alex was no longer an outsider. They were curious, and when he mentioned he was hungry, a tow-headed girl of ten who lived on the block went home to return with peanut butter and jelly sandwiches and a Thermos of milk.

The group was down to the girl, Janey, and the two eleven-year-old boys, Billy Bob and Rusty, who were cousins and lived in the same apartment building. They went to the amusement pier, where one boy's mother worked the fun-house ticket booth. She gave Billy Bob, called "B.B.," thirty-five cents for the matinee at one of the three movie theaters on the boardwalk. All three boys wanted to see a double feature of war movies; next to Warner Brothers gangster movies Alex liked these best. When they got to the ticket booth he found his pocket lined with dirt instead of coins; the letdown and frustration brought instant tears of anger. He wanted to go and felt responsible because he'd promised Rusty. He said he would steal what they needed. He recalled Red Barzo talking about where people hid things in their homes and decided to commit a burglary. None of them protested, though the girl seemed to lag a little while they walked away from the neighborhood of poor apartments into one of middle-class homes, two- and three-bedroom ranch-styles, just old enough for the landscaping—bushes and trees—to feel comfortable embracing the structures.

"Are you really goin' to do it?" Janey asked when they began ringing doorbells. When someone opened the door, Alex solicited work mowing the lawn, but not right now; he would come back with his tools on a weekday afternoon around twilight. He actually got two customers and dutifully borrowed a pencil from them to write down the address. This was despite the two dollars and fifty cents he asked for, five times the rate for boys then cutting lawns.

He was ringing doorbells to find one that didn't answer. On the fourth try his noise brought only silence at a middle-class version of a hacienda: a recessed doorway of dark wood, wrought-iron bars on the windows, red tile on the roof, the walls a facsimile of adobe. It had a riot of shrubs and trees as did the house next door, which helped to hide the yard and rear windows from neighbors. He led his band boldly down the driveway to the back yard, a postage-stamp-size place ninety-five percent occupied by a kidney-shaped swimming pool.

"Boy, this must be super-rich people here," B.B. said, dipping a dirty bare foot into the immaculate water.

Alex grunted, his stomach now in knots. He would have walked away if he'd been alone. That was impossible with the eyes of his peers upon him. He quickly found what Red had told him to look for, the small bathroom window that most people leave unlatched and a little open to invite the fresh air inside. Using a borrowed pocket knife, he cut a hand-size hole in the screen, unhooked it and lifted the window enough to climb in. Once within, now really hidden, much of his tension deflated. He made one circuit of the house on cat's feet, opening every door before going to the back porch and letting his gang inside. They, too, were nervous until safely inside; then bravado came, along with destructive urges and rebellion against the adult-prescribed neatness. Alex, however, left them to their own devices and went to the bedroom, the place where most valuables were hidden. He was looking for cash and gasoline-ration stamps; even an "A" stamp was worth a dollar. He could sell those, but jewelry wasn't worth anything to him. Even at his age he understood that he couldn't even be seen with expensive jewelry without being grabbed. Yet the plain, stainless-steel watch he immediately found in a top dresser drawer wouldn't cause trouble. He'd never heard of "Rolex." He looked through the pockets of hanging clothes and found a small cluster of one-dollar bills and coins, the change from a purchase, in a pants pocket. He found a flower vase on the nightstand half-full of coins, about ten dollars' worth. He already felt good; the score was already successful; they could go to movies for a week. . . .

The bedroom had no more money, not under the mattress or in boxes on back shelves in the closet, or under the paper lining the drawers.

In another bedroom he found an envelope ready to be mailed to a finance company; it had a thirty-three-dollar car payment. He also found two books of gas-ration stamps, one an "A" book and the other a "C," which meant several times as much gas and would bring three times the price.

While searching these back rooms he was vaguely conscious of the noise the others were making, mostly laughing and talking, the words indecipherable. It irritated him; one of them should be watching out the front window for the owners to drive in. He hadn't thought of it before, but after this he'd never forget.

Having taken what he wanted, he now half-humorously planned to filch a snack from the refrigerator. Then he saw the raw egg splattered on the buffet cabinet mirror, running down it in obscene yellow and white. Sudden anger pumped blood into his cheeks and head. He'd already felt misgivings about stealing from a home, as compared to a store or business, where he had no qualms. With the flush still rising and first thoughts forming, he heard the crash of breaking glass from the kitchen, followed by laughter.

B.B. and Rusty had demolished the kitchen, coating the walls with all the soft food and vegetables they could find. Now they were breaking dishes.

"Stop that!" Alex yelled, his young voice falsetto, making him blush in embarrassment. The boys froze instantly but didn't understand his attitude. He looked around the mangled room and felt sorry for the people who lived here. For a moment he thought of cleaning it up, but that was ridiculous. But the frustration of the situation made his eyes sting.

"Where's the girl . . . Janey?"

"She got scared and went home."

Alex's hunger had gone, and he was suddenly verging on panic as he imagined hearing a car motor in the driveway. That was a false alarm, but it put the others on edge, too. They got out quickly and broke into a wild run when they reached the alley behind the property. Alex had remembered the man on the beach coming home to his store.

The only thing taken by the two boys was a hunting knife in a scabbard for Rusty. They hadn't even looked for loot, so Alex kept what he had. He took them to the double-feature movie, and when they came out the amusement pier lights were getting the darkness they needed to feed upon. The night was chilly, but they ignored the goose pimples as they wandered around, eating cotton candy and playing games in the penny arcade and riding the bump cars.

Both Rusty and B.B. lived in an old, substantial brick apartment building, Rusty with both parents, B.B. with his mother. She had a garage assigned to her but didn't have a car, so it was used for storage by both families. A dismantled bed was one item in the garage. The boys moved the mattress into a corner and opened it; then they moved boxes and crates around to create a hideout. B.B. stole a blanket and a fat candle. *Voilà*, they had a niche where Alex could sleep at night and hide in during school hours. Both police and truant officers would want to see his excuse for not being in school. Using the candle because there was no window, Alex spent the day reading stories from *Colliers, Saturday Evening Post,* and *Reader's Digest;* back issues were stacked along a wall. His friends invariably brought him part of their lunches when they came home from school.

They usually went to a nearby playground until dark, playing softball or half-court basketball. When night came, they took off in search of adventure, sometimes going to the amusement pier where Alex begged change from servicemen, tearfully claiming that he had lost his bus fare home. Sometimes they just explored, walking miles, rifling the glove compartments of cars as they went.

For a week Alex lived in the garage. At his age it was time enough for memories to fade and emotional wounds to heal. The state hospital was yesteryear in his feelings instead of yesterday. Every morning he woke up in a new world, wondering what adventure would come that day, not that he was being hunted and inevitably would be caught.

■

The inevitable came on the eighth morning. Despite his age, the juvenile officers of the Los Angeles Police Department took no chances. "He might only be eleven years old," one said, "but we know he can pull a trigger. He wasn't in the nuthouse for being a good boy." So eight uniformed officers in four cars came as backup the morning of the arrest. The uniformed policemen surrounded the garages; then the two plainclothes officers moved in.

A kick at the mattress opened Alex's eyes. Morning sunlight from the open door sparkled on the drawn revolvers pointed at him.

"Freeze, kid . . . keep your hands in sight."

Alex was startled, too surprised to move. He could see the pistols but not the faces beneath the wide hat brims. For the first time in his young life he knew the fear of death. "Put the guns away," he said. "I won't run."

A kick was his answer. Aimed blind at the blanket it hit his kneecap, making him wince.

"Get up on your knees, hands behind your back."

As he followed the order, the same policeman who had kicked him now grabbed his hair and shoved his head down. "Keep 'em behind you," the man said.

The handcuffs were snapped on, and he was pulled to his feet and pushed toward the door. When he stepped out, blinking in the sunlight, he was surprised to find a small crowd gathered at the back door of the apartment building, and the uniformed officers coming from their positions. Even Alex could read the surprise on the faces in the crowd when an eleven-year-old appeared. A voice rang clear in the quiet: "It's a little boy."

Things moved too swiftly for deep feelings to seep into Alex, but he felt a mild, bizarre satisfaction at being the center of attention. He met the curious stares with a defiant sweep of his eyes.

Two uniformed officers drove him to the fringe of downtown Los Angeles, to a two-story yellow building that was an emergency receiving hospital and the Georgia Street Juvenile Jail. The jail occupied the second floor; it was for the temporary detention of juveniles. The law allowed police to hold suspects seventy-two hours for investigation, during which a complaint had to be filed or the person released. A writ of habeas corpus could set bail before that, of course, but the poor can seldom afford the lawyer and the bail bondsman, especially for two or three days. Adults were held in local precincts or the city jail in Lincoln Heights, but juveniles were kept separately. Because it was temporary the facilities were spartan, one vast room filled with barred cages in rows. Everything but the floor was bars—even the rear of each cage, where a lidless aluminum toilet and washbasin were attached. There was a double bunk along the side bars, and a prisoner lying down in one cell was intimately face to face with anyone doing the same in the adjacent cell. Bars, walls, bunks—everything—were enameled a brownish-yellow, and that was defaced by jailhouse graffiti, some fresh and other names gouged so deep into the underlying concrete that they showed through layer on layer of paint. Pervading everything was the odor of Lysol; it hid whatever other smells there were.

In the early afternoon when Alex was ushered through the gate, just a few cells were occupied: one by a young Mexican from across the border, and three by blacks (they were in a row) arrested together for killing an elderly transient during a mugging. Alex was across the room and didn't speak to them, but their voices were loud and he listened, thinking that their English was more slurred and syrupy than that of most blacks he knew. He wondered if it was because of fear. All were obviously terrified, two of them shrill as they blamed the third, telling him that they weren't going to the electric chair " 'cause a stupid-ass niggah hadda use a rock." The rock user raged back, but his voice was more than shrill; it broke and quaked with terror. Somehow Alex got the information that they were fresh from Alabama, that their sharecropping parents had gotten together to make the exodus to the promised land away from lynchings, where they could work in defense plants for decent wages. They were so dumb that he felt truly sorry for them. He called out that they didn't have to worry about the electric chair, that they were too young to get the death penalty. His attempt to help turned fear-filled fury on him. He was a "stupid Paddy" who "damn sure didn't know what the po-leese knowed . . . an' the po-leese said they was gonna burn if they didn't tell everything they'd been doin' here in Los Angeles."

Red-faced, Alex pressed his lips together and wouldn't answer even when they called, which brought yelled curses and threats.

During the afternoon the jail began to fill up, mostly with teenaged blacks and Chicanos. They weren't showered or given denims; they were frisked, their shoes taken, and then they were locked in a cage. Each race had a virtual uniform: the Chicanos in pomaded ducktails, "draped" slacks or khakis, and maroon shirts buttoned to the top; blacks had "conked" or "processed" hair, jeans and tennis shoes, and loud sport shirts; whites had Levi's and leather jackets with fur collars, though they were in a severe minority. Alex was younger than most, the average age being about fifteen, so the deputy sheriff left him in a cell by himself. The juveniles came from barrio, ghetto, and slum. Middle-class and rich kids were turned over to their parents. They came for curfew violations (if a burglary had been reported in the area and they wouldn't confess), for carrying switchblades, for burglaries and car thefts and all the other felonies in the penal code that poor juveniles could commit. They came alone, in pairs, and groups. Seven Chicanos had been pinched cruising in a stolen Cadillac Coupe de Ville. Worse than that, an ounce of mari-juana in a Prince Albert can had been found under the seat. Most were familiar with this place or others like it. Some fell on the thin, sweat-stained mattresses and went to sleep; others yelled from cell to cell, in-creasing volume to compete with each other until a deputy came in, banging a large key on a pipe and screaming for them to hold it down. Those who were familiar with jail hated it utterly, but they were not afraid, and *fear* was society's cudgel. Conditions made the person worse. Fear of imprisonment, not imprisonment, was what kept law and order.

About six-thirty, adult trusties pushed a cart into the cage area. A deputy followed with a clipboard. As he called off a name, the name called his cell number, and a trusty passed through an aluminum bowl— they looked like small hubcaps, actually—of boiled pinto beans, a slice of bologna, and two slices of bread. Not everyone was fed, only those at the jail when the "count" was called to the kitchen at four P.M. Alex was given a bowl of ugly food that he normally would have disdained, but he hadn't eaten since the night before, and he wolfed it down. When voices began screaming in protest at not being fed, he stopped with half the bowl eaten. He wrapped the bologna and bread in toilet paper for a later snack and asked the unfed Chicano in the next cell if he wanted the bowl.

"Do people in hell want ice water?" the Chicano quipped. He had to eat with a spoon through the bars because there was no way to pass the bowl without spilling the beans.

Sharing the ill-tasting ration had a compensation. The Chicano, a slight fifteen-year-old nicknamed Mousey, had smuggled two cigarettes in his sock through the booking desk frisk. Discolored from sweat and misshapen, they nevertheless made Alex's mouth water with desire.

"You can have one, or we can fire 'em up one at a time and pass 'em back and forth . . . save one for *mañana* after breakfast."

"Whatever you think, man. They're yours. You don't owe me nuthin'."

"I know, *ese*. But you did me right. . . . What're you busted for?"

Alex hesitated. "Escape."

"Oh yeah! Where'd you split from?"

Again the hesitation, a fearful anticipation of Mousey's expression if "nuthouse" was mentioned. "Reform school," he said.

"Wasn't Preston. You're too young. Gotta be Whittier. My *carnal* is there. Ernie Obregon?"

Alex was shaking his head, his face hot as the lie got bigger. He couldn't claim Whittier because Mousey might well know things that he, Alex, didn't. "No, I split from reform school in . . . Arizona."

"Are you from over there?"

"Uh-huh. I just stole a car and got busted over there."

"Is that right, and they put you in reform school there?"

"Yeah."

"They gonna send you back?"

"I dunno. . . . Say, how are we gonna light that cigarette? No matches."

"Look at that," Mousey said, pointing at the bare hundred-fifty-watt light bulb in the ceiling above the bars. It was within arm's reach. It was over Alex's cell, so he followed Mousey's instructions, putting a sock over his hand before unscrewing the hot bulb. Mousey meanwhile made a string by shredding the corner of a blanket and then dug a hunk of cotton from the mattress, fluffing it out. He fastened the cotton to the bulb by wrapping the string around both.

"Screw it in," he said.

While they waited, he told Alex of another way to "hit" the lights if the bulb was too small. Get a pencil or paper clip and wrap the cotton around that. Unscrew the light and stick it up there. Bang! "The sparks light the cotton, but sometimes it blows all the lights out. It ain't what they teach in the Boy Scouts, but. . . ." He shrugged.

A thin tendril of smoke started in two minutes. Another two went by and the smoke increased.

"Blow on it," Mousey said.

Alex stood on the top bunk, tilting his head to the overhead bars and blowing as hard as he could. Suddenly the cotton, which had already darkened, smoldered orange. Alex pulled it away without unscrewing the bulb. Moments later they were puffing on the cigarette, passing it back and forth.

The smell wafted through the large room. Delinquent, caged youths began calling out. "Hey, somebody's smoking. Hey, gimme one!"

"Damn assholes," Mousey said. "The deputy is sitting right outside. He hears everything. I've been in here and heard guys confess without knowing it . . . just yelling to their partners."

The first smoke he inhaled made Alex dizzy for half a minute, a pleasurable dizziness, cousin to when he huffed and puffed and held his breath. Then it was really good, and even in jail he was momentarily happy.

The cell on the other side of Alex's had two sixteen-year-old blacks, one with a heavily blood-spattered shirt. Usually just the jailer deputy came in to lock up new arrivals, the delivering deputies waiting beyond two sets of steel gates. But four burly deputies, two to each youth, had brought in this pair—and they didn't remove the handcuffs until after the gate was closed. From sentence fragments he overheard from the deputies, Alex had learned that the pair had fought in the substation. "If they weren't juveniles they'd get an issue," one deputy said while leaving.

The blacks, feeling their bruises, had lain down until now.

"Hey, Paddy boy," one of them said, standing at the bars, "let us have a cigarette."

"I haven't got any cigarettes," Alex said.

"Whaa! What's that—you punk motherfucker! Lyin' junior redneck."

The words felt like slaps. Alex enjoyed being generous, would have shared even the butt if it had been his. But at insults, and especially at threats, something short-circuited in his brain and throbbed hot in his skull. "Your mother's a lyin' punk motherfucker," he said.

"Wha . . . ?" The second black rose into sight from the bunk, standing beside his partner. Both of their faces were lumpy with rage. "Little *white punk!* I'd put this black dick in your ass if I was over there."

"You'd suck a dick," Alex retorted, but into the momentarily mind-blotting temper came some reasoning. And fear. Either of the older, muscular youths would mangle him without difficulty. Not that he would ever back down. "I really don't have any cigarettes," he said in a conciliatory voice, thinking the situation senseless and unnecessary.

"Naw, white boy, you can't clean it up. You been talkin' 'bout my mama." To his partner. "Look at this jive punk motherfucker tryin' to clean it up. Talk all that shit behind bars. He'd scream like a bitch if I got at his ass."

"Well, fuck you in your black ass."

"Better hope they don't open our gates at the same time."

"If they do, do what you're big enough to do." He turned away to Mousey, who had been a silent spectator, boldly puffing the last of the first cigarette in hope that they would say something to him. "Most of 'em are bluffs," he said. "I live in the projects in Hazard with lots of 'em. Some are cool, but most ain't shit. They talk bad, bad, but mostly it's a fake."

Alex grinned. "I don't think these cats are bluffing."

"Forget it."

"Yeah, ain't nuthin' gonna happen."

At ten-thirty the main lights went out, those over the cells, but jails are always lighted twenty-four hours a day, the many sets of bars slicing and reslicing the light in squares, rectangles, and parallels. Slowly the youths quieted, and the conversations of those still up became softer, soothing murmurs rather than discordant roars. Everyone had troubles, but most wore them more lightly than an adult would. Most would be released in a day or two; some would be charged but allowed to go home during court proceedings. Others would go to Juvenile Hall, and a few from there to a California Youth Authority institution, AKA reform school.

Mousey and Alex talked through the bars late into the night. He'd been in Juvenile Hall five times already, for burglary and car theft ("just joyriding, *ese*"), and had already served six months in a county juvenile camp, the last stop before reform school. "I'm a cinch for Whittier this time, burglary *and* car theft, and smashed the car into a fireplug when they chased me. I'm okay. Except it's gonna kill my mom. I've got five brothers. The oldest one is a dope fiend. The next one is straightened up. He's in the Eighty-second Airborne . . . but he was a fuckup. The rest are okay except the one in Whittier. I'm the baby, and it hurts my mother worse when—"

"Then why do you fuck up?"

"I dunno. I just . . . wanna, I guess."

They told each other stories until Alex dozed off while listening. He hadn't thought about the altercation with the blacks for two hours.

Mousey saw his friend asleep, shrugged, and pulled the blanket up to his chin.

The blacks had been waiting for both of them to close their eyes. Now the blacks threw the paper cup of piss and spit at him through the bars. The vile mess landed on his chest and splattered on his face, bringing him out of sleep, aware both of the sticky wetness and the laughter. It took just a few seconds for realization to come, rudely slapping grogginess away. He came off the bunk with tears of fury in his eyes. He spat at them through the bars, but it was powdery saliva. Emotions had his mouth dry.

"You dirty, fuckin' . . . cocksucker!" He wanted to scream "niggers," but it was a word he couldn't call a black, not even these.

"Shaddup, white punk!"

His fury was so great that he couldn't find adequate words; the most vulgar curses were insufficient. Though he couldn't call them "niggers," if he'd had a pistol he would have opened up point-blank and without concern for the consequences. He looked around the barren cell, his eyes glazed with madness, but there was no weapon. Then he felt the fullness in his bowels. He knew what he'd do—if he could. He lowered his pants and sat on the toilet, straining. He'd pick it out with his bare hands and let it fly through the bars.

"Hey, what're you doin'?" one black asked. "What's that crazy motherfucker doin'?"

"Okay, motherfucker!" Alex said.

"*Hey, deputy!*" the other black called. "We got a crazy motherfucker in here!"

"*Jailer!*" screamed the other. "*Jailer. Get in here!*"

The rattling keys, the clank of one going into a big lock, heralded the jailer's entry. "What's wrong? Who called?"

Alex was straining, his face contorted. He needed just another minute.

"Right over here, deputy."

The jailer came, his flashlight's beam swaying and bouncing along the cells. "What's wrong?"

"This crazy sonofabitch is trying to throw shit on us."

The flashlight illuminated the dark face, the pointing finger swiveled over to Alex on the toilet. "Oh, you! The nuthouse kid. Get off that toilet. What're you doin!?"

A little bit was loose, but not enough, and it was hard when he wanted it splattery soft.

The deputy saw Alex's reaching hand. "Better not or I'll kick your ass up to your throat. . . . You'll spit out shit instead of throwing it."

"Get him outa here. He's been callin' us *niggers,* too."

"*You snitchin' cocksuckers,*" somebody yelled. "Tell 'em what you did."

"What'd you do?" the deputy asked. "What'd they do?" he asked Alex.

Alex was so young that the "code" wasn't yet imprinted indelibly on his values, much less down to his essence as the ultimate commandment and value; his reflexive desire was to tell what they had done, about the cup of piss. What stopped him was the previous yelling voice calling them snitches. He said nothing.

"Okay, Bogart," the deputy said. "I've got a place for you."

Ten minutes later Alex was escorted by the jailer and another deputy to the "hole," a carbon of the hole he'd been in at the first substation, narrow and dark with a hole in the floor for body waste—a hole exuding a stench that nearly made Alex retch. It was absolute darkness, without even a peephole or a crack beneath the door. He was drained of tears of rage, of indignation, of pain—sapped of emotions and utterly exhausted. He slept deep on the dirty concrete.

■

Late the next afternoon, the door opened and two white-clad hospital attendants accompanied the jailer inside. They had leather restraints and put them on Alex. He couldn't remember seeing them at Camarillo, and as they crossed the parking lot to the car, he asked what ward they worked on. "We're not from Camarillo. We're from Pacific Colony. It's got security, and we can handle escapees."

"And troublemakers, too," the other said. "We heard about your starting trouble with those colored kids back there."

Pacific Colony was near Pomona, the city farthest east in Los Angeles County, fifty miles from City Hall. The drive was start-and-stop in the rush hour traffic, giving time for Alex to think while looking out at the passing city. What was happening to him? Where was he going?

One husky attendant rode in the back seat with Alex, covertly glancing at him from time to time. The boy understood the logic but thought it was exaggerated and silly because he was in leather restraints and the inside door handles had been removed. Moreover, if security at Pacific was even faintly like Camarillo (and he had no reason to think otherwise), anyone could escape whenever they wanted.

While still in the heavy city traffic, the attendants watched him closely, as if he would suddenly become a demon of some kind, but Alex ignored them and sat staring out at freedom. When the car reached the open highway the attendants seemed to forget their passenger, or at least talked as if they were alone. It was gossip from small minds: whose wife or girlfriend they wanted to lay, which ones could be laid—and this somehow became comments on how bad the food was at the employees' cafeteria. One of them was planning to go home for lunch; he lived just five minutes away. "Eat a little and eat a little," he said, laughing snidely. The other, younger attendant, was newly married. His wife "can't boil water." "Yeah, I saw her at the employees' dance. With her legs, who cares if she can cook. I'll trade you my ace cook for her." He slapped the now blushing younger man on the shoulder, leaning from the back seat to do so.

Alex listened to them, and something in how they talked seemed simplistic, even stupid, to him. He was still unfamiliar with words such as "banal" or "inane," which fit more precisely with what he thought. He didn't, however, think about their destination; it was their conversation that caught him. When their voices became a background hum, he conjured recollections of when things had been happier—his few interludes of freedom. So it was almost a surprise when the car braked and turned into the grounds of Pacific Colony. Spread over a hundred acres, the one-story buildings were gleaming white with red tile roofs—much like Camarillo except that they were separated, each ward at a distance from the next, each with its own paved, fenced yard. Most yards were now empty, and those that were occupied were too far away to see more than figures. Alex was nervously curious, until they turned a corner near the rear of the grounds and the narrow road was ten feet from a fenced yard. What he saw brought fear and revulsion, fear of the unusual, revulsion at semi-human monstrosities. He didn't know that Pacific Colony was almost entirely a state hospital for the feeble-minded. In that category was what was hidden in maternity wards, not displayed in cradles beyond glass. These were hidden shames rather than children. And these represented the tiny minority that survived infancy, though few would mature. The vacant, round faces of extreme mongoloids looked beautiful compared to skulls without eyes, or with eyes next to deformed ears, or bloated heads and pinheads too small for a brain. These were far more horrifying to Alex than the wildly insane at Camarillo had been.

Still traveling slowly, the car turned another corner, heading for a sprawling ward building at the farthest reach of the institution. This one's yard fence had a ten-foot extension of wire mesh, too thin for a grip. Nobody was going to climb out of this yard, not even standing on someone else's shoulders. All the wards had barred windows, but these were also covered with the mesh, nearly doubling their effectiveness.

As they exited the car, someone inside who was expecting them opened the door. Alex struggled with his fear, vividly recollecting the creatures. The attendant escorting him saw his fear, or at least that he was keyed up, and firmly gripped the leather so he couldn't bolt for freedom.

Two more men in white were inside a small, bare room. An inner door had a tiny window with a man peering out at them. He unlocked that door when the outer door was locked.

The delivering attendants had papers and a receipt for the ward attendants to sign. When they were gone he was ordered to strip naked. Then they instructed him to go through the ritual of the skin search for the first (but not the last) time in his life. His thin eleven-year-old arms were raised overhead; then he wriggled his fingers and ran them through his hair. He raised his penis, then his testicles, then turned his back to them and raised one foot at a time. Finally, he bent forward and pulled the cheeks of his butt apart. In years to come, he would do it without thought, and when in a playful mood, he would anticipate each ensuing order and carry it out ahead of the words. He could maintain dignity thereby and hoped for his arrogance to show, though this first time he was awkward and apprehensive. This was increased by the obvious hostility of the attendants. He knew this world was a nightmare compared to Camarillo.

They searched his clothes, squeezing every inch. But instead of returning them, they gave him a zip-front denim jumpsuit, freshly washed but never pressed. Instead of shoes they gave him canvas slippers.

Through an inner door was the ward office; it had glass walls overlooking the long dayroom—a dayroom as different from Camarillo's as was everything else. Instead of the soft chairs there were hard benches in a line around the walls. Alex got a glance while a side door was being opened. Instead of the movement of Camarillo's dayroom, everyone was seated. He noticed that the deep-red floor had a bright gloss, as if the hundred slipper-shod patients left no mark or never moved.

An attendant walked him down a hallway to a shower area and clothing room. He showered, was given a clean bedsheet to use as a towel, and was then issued ill-fitting denim pants and a chambray shirt. It had two missing buttons. When he pointed this out to the patient in charge of the clothing room, a young man going prematurely bald, he was told, "This ain't no fuckin' department store." The tone used was even harsher than the words. Alex was so nonplussed that he barely heard the added statement, that he could check out needle and thread and sew buttons on in the morning. What he heard vaguely he quickly forgot. Through his mind ran a chant: Oh God, it's awful here . . . awful . . . awful . . . awful.

When Alex first came in, the charge attendant, a middle-aged man with close-cropped steel-gray hair, had been off the ward at lunch, but now he was in the office. He ordered the escorting attendant to close the dayroom door, which made Alex even more anxiously conscious of the eyes beyond the glass. Indeed, he was so intensely aware of being scrutinized that he had to concentrate on the words so they didn't dissolve into a nonsensical drone.

"I'm Mr. Whitehorn," the man said. "I'm the big boss around here. We heard a little about you—how you shot a man and all that, then raised hell in Camarillo and finally escaped. Well, this ain't Camarillo. You're a few years younger than most of 'em around here . . . and you look a lot less tough. If you cause any trouble here, you'll think you ran into a shitstorm. Most of 'em here are judged feeble-minded, though this is a 'high-grade' ward. It's also *the* high-security ward. We've got some mean people here . . . some dangerous people. But we handle 'em. We can handle you too! Now you're just here for observation. The staff at Camarillo said you were a borderline psychotic—know what it means?"

Alex shook his head. He'd heard the term "neurotic," but not what Mr. Whitehorn said.

"It means nuts. They also said you were a psychopathic delinquent . . . and even I don't know exactly what that means except that there's no hope for you. Anyway, the court wanted another report, so that's what you're doing here. So we'll not only keep you in line if you cause trouble, we'll send a report that'll bury you. . . ."

While the charge attendant stared challengingly at the boy, there came a loud crash from beyond the glass. A bench had toppled over backwards as a fight was in progress. A Chicano and a black were rolling on the floor and punching. Both were nearly grown men in body, though the black was heavier and more muscular. Attendants were pulling them apart even before Mr. Whitehorn could tear through the door out of the office. Alex watched through the glass, unable to hear the words, though they were unnecessary to understand what was happening. Mr. Whitehorn spoke to each of them, and each nodded vehemently. Benches were pushed aside as the combatants took off their shirts and kicked off their slippers. The charge attendant said something, and the hundred patients rushed from their seats to form a human ring. Half a dozen attendants were in the forefront.

Mr. Whitehorn stood in the center, a referee. He used both hands to motion the combatants to come together, and then stepped back to the side. For perhaps ten seconds the battlers circled each other, hands raised in a facsimile of boxing. When they finally lunged together the facsimile ended. They weren't allowed to wrestle or hold. They stood toe to toe and punched as hard and fast as they could. Though the black was bigger and stronger, it seemed that his hands were a fraction of a second slower, or perhaps his rhythm of battle was wrong, for the Mexican's fists landed an instant sooner, hence with more force because they sucked power from the black's. Yet the black was forcing the Chicano back, step by step. When he came to the human ring, an attendant put hands on his back, signaling the end of retreat. The hands didn't shove, for the intention was not to give advantage, but nonetheless they upset his balance. He tried to duck and circle to his left, but he ran into a looping right hand. It hit him above the eye and blood sprayed out instantly. He stiffened for a moment but kept circling. Now he was in the center again, but he was already defeated. He still punched but defensively now, thinking of the other's fists, ducking from feints, tiring himself. The black's fists found solid flesh more often. He stalked, his whole body exuding confidence. He lashed out with a left jab that hit the Chicano's mouth, splitting lips against teeth. The Chicano's head snapped back, and his hands dropped. The black punched a powerful right. It landed on the chin, and the Chicano dropped to the seat of his pants. An attendant pulled the black away. Mr. Whitehorn helped the Chicano to get up, said something to him, shrugged, and stepped back, waving for them to continue.

Now the Chicano was standing on pride alone. The black faked a left, crouched, and sunk his right to the solar plexus, sending the Chicano's hands up in a jerk. The ensuing gasp could be heard throughout the large room. The Chicano started to double over. A clubbing right hand sent him on down, his legs twisted awkwardly beneath him. He was fighting for breath, spraying flecks of blood from his torn lips.

The black's right eye was swollen and discolored, and his dark flesh had red lines where skin had been raked off. He'd been hurt, and his fury was not sated. The attendant was holding him lightly. The black jerked free, stepped around Mr. Whitehorn, and kicked the Chicano in the side of the head. Even barefooted, it elicited a yelp of pain.

"Bastard!" Mr. Whitehorn said, letting go a backhand that knocked snot from the black's nose. He flinched, but instead of giving up he lowered his head to ram through to the Chicano. Before the black could launch himself, Mr. Whitehorn had a headlock on him. Other attendants piled in. Instead of just restraining him, they began punching and kicking. Their fists landed mainly on his kidneys, though some were in his face until Mr. Whitehorn, grazed by a punch, commanded: "Easy . . . easy. . . ." The kicks were at his knees and ankles—until he went down. Then they were everywhere except his head, and they missed that only because his arms covered it. They reviled him while kicking.

Fear had begun in Alex at the beginning, a nervousness of identification mingled with excitement. But the excitement disappeared when the attendants rushed in. Even in Camarillo an attendant sometimes lost his temper and hit a violently objectionable patient. But what Alex watched now was four attendants methodically stomping a human being senseless. Alex was trembling as he stared through the glass. It was arbitrary and unjust, but fear outweighed his indignation.

The Chicano was brought into the office. He had to be driven to the infirmary for sutures, and Mr. Whitehorn was going with him. From the man's expression it was obvious that he'd forgotten Alex. "Mr. Hunter," he said to a short, older man with muscular wrists, "get this new punk a seat . . . and put that nigger on the cement block for eight hours. See how much he wants to keep swinging when it's time to stop." Whitehorn was rubbing his right hand. "Fuckin' niggers have heads like granite."

"Can't take it down in the breadbasket though," another said.

The attendants all had an excited levity following the incident, as if they felt both good and a bit ashamed. Their faces were flushed and their laughter was nervous.

Alex was given a seat on a bench near a corner. His name was inked on adhesive tape fastened to the bench. He was told to sit without talking when everyone else did so.

So now he sat, conscious of his heartbeat, wondering if his feelings showed to the many eyes that seemed to be studying him. He was afraid to meet any gaze because his moving glances told him that nearly everyone was older; some were even young men. Nor did he see any of the horrible distortions of the fenced yard, nor even the disarray of Camarillo's deranged minds. In the coming weeks, he would learn that nearly all of these (except for three or four like himself, who were observation cases) had gotten into trouble with the law and had scored below 65 on I.Q. tests, which got them committed as feeble-minded. However, all functioned at least adequately in the world of institutions. But when Alex tried to explain something abstract, even something simple like "light years," he failed to get through no matter how he tried. Some, however, had apparently just not tried to perform on the tests. It was a way to keep them out of society for long periods.

But these things were in the future, and now he was conscious of being younger and smaller. Though someone sat at his right, the person didn't try to speak. The seat on his left was empty. Everyone was silent, and attendants walked quietly in a space behind the benches. If someone was caught talking during silent periods, they were knocked off the bench. Alex saw it happen before he was seated ten minutes.

An attendant banged a key on a door. "Yard and recreation," he yelled. The room erupted in movement. About half of the men gathered around the door to the yard; others dragged two large tables and benches to the center of the room. Blankets were stretched over the tables, and there was a scurry for seats in the two poker games, one for higher stakes than the other. An attendant turned a radio in a wall cabinet to a rhythm and blues station, then locked the cabinet.

Alex sat watching. Nobody spoke to him. He could see down one of the two corridors. From the foot traffic in and out of a door he was certain it was the latrine. His bladder ached with fullness.

When Alex entered, several youths were lounging next to a barred window, smoking and talking. None spoke to him, but he could feel their eyes as he relieved himself. On the way out, as he reached for the door, someone called:

"Hey, you! New guy!"

Alex half turned.

"You were in Juvenile Hall last year, huh?"

Alex nodded.

"Shot a guy, didn't you?"

"Yeah."

"Kill him?"

"No." Alex waited, but the questioner turned away, speaking to his friends. Alex couldn't hear. Slightly embarrassed, conscious of his face warming up, he pushed out into the corridor, feeling simultaneously stupid and yet gratified. What he'd done in the darkness of the grocery store on the beach gave him some status in the topsy-turvy world of institutions and outlawry. He'd felt it way back in Juvenile Hall, but his pain and remorse and despair had overwhelmed any shred of gratification. Now it was so long ago that remorse was gone, and his spirits lifted mildly at the recognition.

Thus, looking inward, he stumbled over a weird contraption. He didn't fall but almost lost his balance. Then he froze and stared at it in disbelief. A hundred-pound block of concrete was sewn into several layers of old blanket. A twelve-foot canvas harness stretched from it and was wrapped around the waist of the black who'd been fighting. His dark face was puffed and discolored. Thick wax had been put on the floor. He pulled the device up and down the corridor, turning the wax into a sheen. His face was expressionless as he looked at the younger boy. The dread and gloom that had lessened in the latrine now rushed back more intensely than ever. It was horror.

It's *torture*, he thought while walking back to the dayroom, fighting tears of despair while wondering how such things could be.

The dayroom was noisy now with music on the radio and voices from the poker game, which had a crowd of spectators. He, too, stopped at the rear of the crowd, but just momentarily, his mind not on it, except to note the stakes (nickel ante, fifty-cent limit), and that two attendants were playing. Poker was apparently a big thing here. For the first time he had no desire to play. And as he went back to his place on the bench, he vowed also, for the first time in his life, to stay out of trouble.

Patients going by looked at the new arrival, but nobody said anything to him, which was fine with him. He hungered for friendship and acceptance, but he wanted nothing in this place except to be left alone—and to get away. Why had he been such a fool to go with Scabs?

At three-thirty in the afternoon, those in the exercise yard came inside. The poker game broke up and everyone went to their places. At a signal the noise became silence. Half a dozen patients swept the floor and then ran steaming, wrung-dry mops over it; then they had to push wooden polishers up and down to restore the shine. An attendant came along the benches with a clipboard, taking count by checking off each name.

For the next hour they sat in silence. Some whispered or made faces when no attendant was watching. One young attendant, a clean-cut young giant in his early twenties, tiptoed behind the benches. He came upon two whispering patients and smashed their heads together. It brought titters of laughter from most of the others, and the young attendant grinned. Alex didn't laugh; into his fear came hatred.

At five o'clock they lined up in the corridor, double-file against the wall, and trudged into the mess hall. They passed the black still hauling the concrete block, his swollen face stoic.

An attendant supervised the mess-hall seating, filling each eight-man table, letting each start eating when the table was full. A cafeteria-style serving table wasn't used. The food was already on stainless steel trays and already many minutes cold. If hot it would have been unpalatable even by institutional standards. Alex gagged, forcing down a few bites of something resembling stew, though the nearest thing to meat was grayish lumps of grease. Alex hadn't eaten in a dozen hours and had an institution-strengthened palate, but his stomach threatened to throw this back up. He saw that others were managing to nibble down bits and pieces picked out. They all wolfed down the two slices of bread; it was the main thing they ate.

Hunger's hollowness was still with Alex when he followed the others out. In coming weeks he would manage to eat a little more of the swill and crave much less as his stomach shriveled. The awful food was a small problem in the sea of torments.

As the patients crowded the hallway another fight suddenly erupted ahead. To Alex, it was as if the whole press of bodies became agitated. He could hear grunts, curses, and blows and see the movement, but all he really saw of the fight was two Chicanos being dragged away in choke-holds and arm-locks. The next day he saw them in leather restraints, the punishment for an unauthorized fight.

The ward had a second long corridor, and this one had sleeping rooms. A low cot was the only furnishing in each room. Most patients slept in a dormitory. Younger patients and observation cases were given the rooms, where they couldn't be raped. At nine o'clock, Alex and the others were called. He did what they did, taking off his clothes and piling them neatly at the mouth of the hallway. They walked naked past an attendant while another one let them into their rooms. The locks clicked behind. Soon the room lights were turned off from outside. Alex was already in his bunk, but he got up to look out. The grounds were lighted. On the outside roof above him were lights. He could see myriad insects rushing and whirling toward the lights, battering out their brief lives. A big gray moth bounced its life away on the screen, finally fluttering out of sight below the window ledge. Alex remembered the lights coming through the dormitory window in Juvenile Hall. Every institution seemed afraid of darkness. All of them had lighted grounds at night, even when nobody was moving around. He could see one ward about a hundred yards away, most of its windows glowing squares. He'd soon learn that it was the high-security ward for females, confining the same category females as the males on his ward. It was easier for the females to get released, however; they could go whenever they agreed to sterilization.

Now, however, the day's tension had enervated him. His body

yearned for sleep, both to rejuvenate and because sleep was an escape. He was gone to Morpheus half a minute after he closed his eyes. He didn't remember dreaming, but he came awake suddenly in the middle of the night. An attendant had a flashlight trained on his eyes through the small window in the door and was banging on it. The bed was soaked with sweat.

"Knock off that yelling!" the man behind the light said, "or I'll come in there and give you something to yell about."

This time Alex cried himself to sleep but muffled the sound in the pillow.

though not hostile to friendly overtures, Alex had already learned suspicion of them when he was a newcomer in an institution. Despite loneliness and a yearning for acceptance, he was blank-faced and cold-eyed when someone spoke to him, an unusual facade for an eleven-year-old. Moreover, despite being afraid of the attendants and among the youngest on the ward, Alex was keyed up to fight instantly if challenged. In the first week he saw six fist fights, including three where the benches were pulled back. This happened when the match seemed even and both were willing. No punishment was inflicted if the fight was good. The black had been made to pull the concrete "block" on that first day because he'd kicked the Chicano, who happened to be one of Whitehorn's favorites, a flunky who cleaned the office, made coffee for the attendants, and shined shoes.

Two Chicanos in their early twenties were brought in from an open ward. They were well-known to both patients and attendants, having been in and out of Pacific Colony for several years. They were brought in for gathering a huge dose of phenobarbital that got them goofy, and because phenobarbital acts very slowly, they were goofy for three days. Although Whitehorn laughed at them and apparently liked them, he still put them on the concrete block for thirty-six hours spread over three days.

One was given a seat across the room, the other the empty place next to Alex. The returnee's name was Toyo, and in a slurred voice he began talking to Alex. It was impossible to ignore someone so high. Toyo was skinny and swarthy, with high cheekbones and a hooked nose. Despite his size, he was one of the "dukes"—one of the best fighters in a world where nothing else mattered in deciding status. He always won in a long fight when the benches were moved back because he never got tired. He was fairly fast, his bony fists cut, and he could go full-speed for half an hour without rest. Most others were winded and energy drained in five or ten minutes.

Considering Toyo's proximity and garrulous condition, very much akin to that of a happy drunk, to put him off would be outright insult-

ing. Alex wasn't ready to insult—nor to refuse the cigarettes that Toyo
had and shared generously. Hence, when Toyo finally got off the concrete polisher and sobered up, he was Alex's only friend. Through Toyo,
Alex began talking to others on the ward, among whom Chicanos were
a majority. He never got close to anyone for several reasons: he was already interested in other things, such as books; he didn't want to admit
that he might stay here very long; he was among the youngest, and those
his age were obviously feeble-minded, not just uneducated or with language problems. One Saturday, he found Toyo in a corner during recreation period, the Chicano struggling to write his sister, who would read
the letter to his mother, translating it into Spanish, for she spoke no
English. Toyo hadn't finished the fifth grade and spoke no English at all
when he started school. Now his brow was furrowed as he tried to make
his handwriting less obscure. Alex began answering how to spell words
exceeding one syllable, but it was easier to take over, more or less, and
write what was dictated. Next a Chicano nicknamed PeeWee, a friend of
Toyo's, enlisted Alex's help to compose a love letter to a girl on the ward
across the road. After that Alex was asked several times a day to write a
letter for someone. It gave him acceptance, though not status. The stu-
pidest cared the least for intelligence. When there was no real fight, they
"bodypunched." That was the same as fighting except that no punches
were aimed at the face. It was a boxing match sans clinches, from the
neck down. Sometimes it got heated and turned into a fight, but usually
it was both practice and a test. Toyo and Alex bodypunched several times
in the exercise yard, the Chicano augmenting the lessons given by First
Choice Floyd in Camarillo. Alex's boyish gawkiness was diminishing so
he could better control his body. He'd only been able heretofore to practice Floyd's teachings in the air; now it was almost for real. At first he
couldn't let fly at Toyo, both from fear and because he was his friend, but
when Toyo tagged him sharply, the pulse of competition took over. He
began blocking punches without flinching or closing his eyes, snapping
his own back fluidly. He could punch nearly as hard as Toyo, though he
was unable to put together swift combinations like the Chicano. Sometimes he would land a clean, hard blow and Toyo would retaliate swiftly.
Once or twice Alex's wind was ripped from him, but Toyo wouldn't let
him quit. Sometimes he ached, and sometimes at night in the small
room he shadow-boxed, practicing feints and footwork, blocking and
slipping imagined blows, counterpunching wickedly. He was learning
how to fight with unusual skill for his age, notwithstanding a lack of special physical abilities.

He also began playing poker, using what Red Barzo had taught him and winning regularly. Actually, most games played here lacked any re-semblance to real poker. They were offshoots, with many wild cards and odd rules. Alex remembered Red and simply threw in his hand until he had something special. The others played every hand, so he took their small money and cigarettes; he was happy to share it with Toyo, who had backed him in the first place.

Thus the terror of the first day diminished, though it never disap-peared entirely. He never relaxed completely or felt comfortable or stopped hating this place. Tension was constant, and he was always glad when the door of the sleeping room locked behind him at night.

After a month, a young female clinical psychologist came to the ward and spent two afternoons in an interview room administering a battery of tests to him. He recognized the first as the Wechsler-Bellevue intelligence test, and he concentrated intently, wanting no mistake that would keep him here. The other tests were new to him. She put out pic-tures of faces, asking him which he liked the best and which he dis-liked. He was shown other pictures of people doing things and asked to tell a story of what he saw. These took one afternoon; the next afternoon he had to answer five hundred questions "yes" or "no." It was all he saw of professional staff. The ward doctor was observed talking to Mr. White-horn in the office once or twice a week. He had five wards and never saw a patient unless there was a special problem. Pacific Colony's function was custodial, the care and feeding of morons, not futile attempts at teaching them. What could be done for cretins and halfwits?

The psychologist told Alex that he'd be appearing before "staff" in a few weeks. This was a meeting where the court report and recommen-dation would be decided. He wouldn't be returned to Pacific Colony; he definitely wasn't feeble-minded. But if he was designated a "psycho-pathic delinquent" he could be committed indefinitely and sent to Men-docino, the hospital for the criminally insane. Pacific Colony was a playpen compared to Mendocino, so the grapevine said. Alex couldn't imagine anything much worse than this. At least several times a week, someone was beaten up severely by the attendants. The evening crew was worse, as was the night charge attendant, a choleric little man in his fifties who had, by legend, been a featherweight boxer in his youth. Whitehorn had a sense of humor, but Mr. Hunter never smiled—except while watching patients fight among themselves or while attendants were whipping one of them. Any infraction, no matter how trivial, brought an ass-kicking during the evening. Talking in the mess hall or during silent periods brought a punch or a kick. Alex learned to stay ex-pressionless while watching three or four attendants thrash a patient, though his heart always raced in dread and he smoldered in silent, raging indignation. Juvenile Hall's lesser brutalities had somewhat prepared him for this, teaching him that violence went on everywhere that men had power over each other. He had his first layer of callousness. But fear outweighed indignation, and he managed to mask his rage.

Routine helped the days go by. Because he was an observation case, he was confined to the ward. Committed patients went out on crews, cutting the lawns, digging ditches, and other labors of brawn and no brains. He swept and mopped the kitchen hallway after breakfast, then lounged in the dayroom for the rest of the morning. In the afternoon he went into the yard. It was paved with asphalt, and the high fence was topped with concertina wire.

A week before "staff," the trouble happened. It was night, and he'd gone naked into his room and folded back the bedsheet and single blanket. He could hear the benches being moved in the dayroom as the late cleanup crew went to work. Soon the lights would go out and he would stare into darkness, feeling pangs of longing—an inarticulate pain.

A mop slopped against the bottom of his door as someone did the corridor. Alex went to the lidless toilet to urinate. While standing there, he heard someone yelling from the nearby mop-room window to the women's ward: *"Marsha! Mash, mi vida!"* Without thinking about it, Alex turned from the toilet to the window, seeing a figure in the distant window, faintly hearing the answering yell. For a few more seconds Alex stared out, now at the stars thick in the night sky. He heard a sound from the door behind and turned. A face was in the small window. A moment later the key turned in the lock and the door started to open. The rule required any patient in a room to stand up when an employee entered, but Alex was already up, so he simply turned. It was Charge Attendant Hunter, nicknamed "The Jabber," and his eyes were hidden behind his glasses catching the wan light. The Jabber always moved in a rolling gait on the balls of his feet, but now he moved more swiftly, so Alex sensed something amiss. He experienced a flash of fear before The Jabber lashed out with a backhand and his knuckles rapped wickedly across the boy's nose, hurting even more than a punch would have, bringing instant blood from his nostrils and water (not tears) from his eyes. He ducked away reflexively, too surprised and hurt to think. The other hand flashed at his face, this one a closed fist that flashed lights in his brain and snapped his head back.

What the . . . ? his mind asked, totally confused as he covered his face. The man snatched the boy's hair with one hand and punched his face with the other. This time Alex went down, sitting with his legs doubled under him.

"Get up, you punk!" The Jabber snapped, kicking the boy in the ribs. Alex rolled over and braced his hands on the floor, preparatory to rising, but a volley of slaps sat him down again. "Caught your little ass, didn't I?" The Jabber said, kicking him in the side. "Yellin' to those simpleminded sluts, eh? See if you do it again!"

Alex shook his head and started to deny his guilt, but before he could issue the words, a vicious slap knocked his teeth together; he could feel chips of them on his tongue.

"Get up, you punk!" The Jabber said. "Stand when I'm in the room." He stepped back, one leg forward, head arched in a deliberate pose of haughty cruelty. Alex peeked out and understood; the man was deriving pleasure from this. Tears of stifled fury welled in Alex's eyes. The man came forward and Alex's hands rose to cover his face; he cowered back in the corner. Mr. Hunter's bald head gleamed, and so did the gold crown on a tooth as he sneered. His gold-rimmed glasses enlarged his blue eyes and made them bulge. He feinted, snickering as Alex flinched, deriving enjoyment from the boy's fear. "Make your bed," he said, turning and going out.

When the key turned, Alex let the tears flow. It wasn't pain that made him cry but the humiliation of being beaten when innocent and not fighting back. He hated his own fear more than the cuffs and kicks.

Somehow the cot had become disheveled. Alex pulled it away from the wall to get behind, sobbing and trembling while he tightened and tucked the covers. With each passing minute his fury increased, totally filling his consciousness; he'd cowered when innocent, accepting an undeserved and cruel punishment. So it was that he didn't notice the door being unlocked for the second time. His first awareness was the three sets of shoes below white pants. He looked up. The Jabber and the two other burly attendants were inside, while behind them in the doorway was the adult patient who ran the clothing room. The Jabber was twirling his heavy keychain with blurring speed.

"This is the asshole who's been yelling," The Jabber said, ending with several grunts of emphasis.

The pale blue eyes doused Alex's rage. He froze behind the bunk. He was already on his feet so he didn't have to stand. The Jabber came to the boy, who was nearly in the corner. The man's hand flew out, quick as a striking snake, burning the boy's cheek, bouncing his head against the wall. Flashing lights from the blow blinded Alex, but something else exploded, too: his own brain. His fist struck back, his position too cramped for full leverage, but it was stiff and straight and the man didn't expect it. Eyeglasses crumpled, shards of glass cutting cheek and nose. The blow froze Mr. Hunter. His mouth gaped open. Alex punched again, using the other hand, adding power. It hit The Jabber in the mouth and drove him back—but he had nowhere to go. The bunk tripped him and he fell on it. Alex lunged forward going for the kill. He tried to get around the man's drawn up legs. He managed to grab a handful of white shirt-front with his left hand, cocking his right to punch again.

The two attendants, paralyzed by surprise for seconds, now leaped in. A heavy forearm circled his neck from behind, cutting his wind and crushing his larynx. His punch stopped as he was jerked back, but his clutching fingers still held The Jabber's shirt; it ripped from neck to waist, leaving the black necktie dangling on a disengaged collar.

Alex clawed futilely at the forearm choking him. The Jabber was up, his face blotchy, spots of blood seeping from the glass cuts on his nose. He was still in front of Alex, raising a fist, teeth exposed in a snarl. Alex kicked him in the testicles, erasing the snarl, eliciting a cry of pain and doubling him over.

Alex never saw the fist that smashed into his eye, instantly swelling it to three times its size and closing it for a week. All he saw was a flashing light accompanying pain. Another blow crushed the wind from him. Someone grabbed his thrashing feet and lifted him. An attendant still had the choke hold. The terror of choking mixed with his pains, and he writhed maniacally but futilely. An attendant held his legs, and the patient was standing on the bunk, kicking him in the stomach. He screamed, knowing it was futile but unable to do anything else.

The Jabber, too, was recuperating, spitting blood and curses as he came around and repeatedly smashed his fist into the boy's unprotected face. Alex wanted to scream and plead for mercy, but only gasps came from his mouth. He could barely breathe. He was going to die. When he fell limp and unconscious the blows continued, but he couldn't feel them.

He awoke in the night choking on his own blood. It covered the sheets. It had dried and his cheek was stuck to the mattress. He tore loose in agony and felt the right side of his face. It was grotesquely swollen; his hand seemed to touch a huge grapefruit. His whole body throbbed in pain, every heartbeat pulsing it. He wondered if his jaw was broken or if teeth were gone; it hurt too much to touch and find out. He was in too much pain to cry.

Thus he lay unmoving in the darkness, occasionally drifting into a few minutes' sleep. And he was utterly terrified of them. Thus when the key turned and the door opened, framing in the corridor light the bulk of the graveyard-shift attendant, he struggled to his feet, moaning as he tried to stand erect.

One of the midnight-to-eight-shift attendants played football at nearby Claremont College. Young and huge, tonight his breath smelled of alcohol. Alex caught the odor instantly, a second before the football player lurched forward and swung. Alex dropped to the floor, the punch missing him. "Oh, please," he said, trying to clutch the young man's leg, feeling the big muscles bunching for the kick. Alex rolled once and began crawling under the low cot, whimpering in torment and terror. The shoe caught him in the thigh; then he was far underneath.

"Punch an old man, huh?" the attendant said, voice slurred, puffing from drink, exertion, and emotion. His flashlight beam played about his feet. He began to kneel, muttering maledictions. Alex slipped as far back as possible, his heartbeat racing. The man's head tilted down low, issuing the smell of bourbon. The flashlight blazed into Alex's eyes. He let out a scream of terror, more that of an animal than a human being.

"Shaddup, punk!" the attendant said.

But other footsteps sounded in the doorway. "Fields," the voice said. "What's goin' on here?"

"Teachin' this sonofabitch a lesson. He swung on Hunter, broke his glasses."

"You're just supposed to be counting. Get up and get outa here. You know that room doors aren't unlocked this late without calling the O.D."

"Yeah, but—"

"But, my ass. Get outa here."

Fields got up grunting and went out muttering. The other attendant hunkered down. "C'mon, Hammond, get up in the bunk. He won't come back in here."

Alex stayed partly under the bunk, ready to retreat instantly until the door was securely locked.

■

Mr. Whitehorn and the ward doctor never made rounds before ten A.M., but this morning they were at Alex's door at eight-fifteen. He hadn't been let out for breakfast. A tray had been delivered, though he couldn't chew and had to nourish himself on semi-liquid gruel, faintly resembling corn meal mush. Whitehorn frightened him, but hope surged on sight of the doctor. Alex's fingers had hinted at how his face looked, and he expected the doctor furiously to demand explanation. A physician was inherently against such brutal inhumanity, and this one was a refugee from a Central European country, hence a victim of sorts. He brushed the ashes from his vest and, with a heavy accent, asked Alex to move his jaw; he then tugged the boy's nose and poked his ribs. When finished he announced that nothing was broken. Alex waited futilely to be asked what had happened. It finally sank through that this doctor didn't care that three adult attendants had kicked and punched him into this condition. He was on their side.

Despite his years, Alex had learned stoicism, though the words were different: "Don't snivel. . . . Don't show any weakness. . . . Hold your mud. . . . Never give them motherfuckers the satisfaction of knowing they hurt you. . . ." Other admonitions meant the same thing, and he had taken them sufficiently to heart that he managed to clench his teeth and not accuse anyone, although the doctor's attitude instilled more hate in the boy than the brutality of the attendants. Alex looked coldly at the round, olive-complexioned face throughout the brief examination. The doctor had been prepared for a diatribe, and he became nervous (perhaps with guilt) when all he got was an unblinking stare from the boy's unusually cold eyes.

"Now you learn maybe, huh?" he said. "When you attack somevone, you can expect retribution in kind, vhat?"

Now Alex's staring silence was as much consternation as stoicism. He couldn't believe what he was hearing, that instead of victim he was culprit.

"Bet you don't swing on any more attendants," Mr. Whitehorn said. "You got away lucky. If you broke my glasses you wouldn't have any teeth. Who's gonna pay for Mr. Hunter's glasses?"

Lacking an answer, Alex felt tears of hatred stinging his eyes. The others were brutal swine, but these men were supposed to be responsible.

"Brave bastards! Aren't you? All of you bastards!" The terse accusations were punctuated with gasps, but the words were nonetheless clear, and Alex was immediately horrified that they'd spilled from his mouth. He'd seen one patient speak rebelliously to Whitehorn, and snot and blood had flown from his nose as the knuckles silenced him. Alex was in too much pain to withstand even a few blows. Even probing fingers brought a groan. "I'm sorry!" he said. "Please . . ."

The man with the steel-gray hair had flushed, jaws knotted, and he would have struck from reflex except for the doctor's presence. His eyes went back and forth (the doctor was grinning, as if the outbreak was humorous), and the quick apology gave him a way out. "You must be crazy . . . not know what you're saying. But don't go too far and swing on another one of my attendants. Isn't that right, doctor?"

The physician nodded. "Vhen seffen attendants control one hundred and thirty patients, all who are criminals and not intelligent, sometimes it takes harsh measures."

At the door, Whitehorn paused. "We're leaving you in this room for now . . . until staff decides something. . . ."

When the lock bolt slipped into its niche, Whitehorn then testing the door with a shake, Alex stood mulling his situation for a long time. Some things made him feel better, while others put the corrosive acid of anxiety into him. Meanwhile, with each heartbeat his awesomely battered, swollen face gave a throb. He was actually glad to be confined to the room. He would have been painfully embarrassed to show himself like this, especially with the adult patient who had helped the attendants out there. He would have to attack the man, and he didn't have a chance. Alex felt dizzy with murderous thoughts, remembering the traitor. Locked up here, though, he could escape the constant tension of the madhouse. In the room he could rest, masturbate, and dream. If only he had reading matter—but, come to think of it, he'd never seen a book anywhere on the ward. An occasional magazine, yes; books, never. Yet with a supply of books he might prefer this to the ward indefinitely. Indeed, he would have glorious moments when something especially thrilled him. It was magic the way words could make worlds. Some books he liked more than others, but he thought this was just himself rather than a difference in quality in them. Alas, it seemed he would have to go without. Assuming he stayed locked up until he went back to court, it meant a month with nothing to do.

It was the thought of court feeding the roots of his anxiety. The staff here would recommend his destiny, and the judge would simply ratify the recommendation. The fight with the attendants wouldn't help him. He'd assaulted The Jabber, so it was written on the reports, and to the world the reports were gospel. Nevertheless, he was proud of what he'd done. No matter how he examined the maiming nightmare, he was right. He'd been a fool, true, but wrong—never. . . . Even if he'd yelled at the women's ward, it was wrong for grown men to punch and kick him. This he knew absolutely, despite his age. No doubt the institution staff would want to hurt him for it, just as the ward doctor and Mr. Whitehorn were against him. It would hurt most if they recommended a permanent commitment to mental hygiene, if he went to Mendocino. . . . Toyo said that patients in Mendocino were given electric-shock treatments for fighting. Electric-shock therapy wasn't used here in Pacific Colony, but Alex had seen it administered in Camarillo, and just thinking of it terrified him. If he was committed, sent to Mendocino, he would kill himself. He'd read where the ancient Romans took their own lives when things became unbearable, and it was considered a noble act. It would be better than becoming a vegetable. His decision, made fiercely, was followed with immediate fear that he would lack the courage to do it. "I won't think about it," he said aloud, with the same ferocity. Hearing his voice so angry made him laugh; the tension eased away. He began looking at birds on the lawn outside the barred window.

In the later afternoon he was napping when someone banged on the door. He came awake and sat up just as something was slid under the door—a *Saturday Evening Post* magazine with a small bulge in the middle. When he opened the magazine he found five cigarettes, several loose matches (themselves total contraband on the ward), and the piece of a striker. He knew it was from Toyo; he had no other friend on the ward, at least none who would do him a favor. His gratitude was an ache bordering wet eyes. Whoever swept the hallway had delivered the magazine, probably threatened with an ass-kicking if he refused. No doubt more would be arriving tomorrow, and for as long as he was locked up. He ripped a small hole in the mattress and hid the smoking material; he'd ration himself to make them last. But it was the magazine that thrilled him. No matter that it was a year old. He would escape for the evening with it. Not knowing if it would be confiscated if seen but assuming the worst, he raised his legs beneath the blanket to hide the magazine as he read. The first article was about the new two-hundred-inch telescope planned for Mount Palomar.

■

By the following week, Alex's right eye was open enough to see through, but his face was still puffed and discolored. Forever after he would have a small lump beneath his right cheekbone, unseen but easy to locate with a finger. On the morning of "staff," Mr. Whitehorn informed him that he wasn't going in person. The staff would decide without him. Alex was frightened. He'd counted on seeing the other doctors and convincing them—sobbing and begging on his knees if necessary—that it would be wrong to recommend committing him to a hospital. Now they would have just the reports, and he was afraid. God, he was afraid.

A long time later he would realize that the doctor and Whitehorn hadn't wanted the staff to see his face because nothing on paper could justify battering a child to such condition. But now while it happened his guts crawled, and he felt hollow with fear. Even a new *Reader's Digest* failed to exceed a blur. Then in the afternoon, just before shift change, Mr. Whitehorn was due to come around, already wearing his coat preparatory to going home. He never opened the door but peered through the window. He had to sign a log on Alex's condition before turning things over. Whitehorn had sat in on "staff" and knew the recommendation. So Alex was waiting at the glass, his cheek pressed to it so he could see the man coming. When the man approached the door, Alex put his lips to the crack and called out, "Mr. Whitehorn. Lemme talk to you!" He shifted back to the glass.

"What's up?"

"Can you tell me what happened today?"

"At staff?"

"Yessir. What'd . . . what's the recommendation?"

"You'll know pretty soon."

"Please . . ." But Whitehorn was already moving away and out of sight.

"Dirty . . . rotten bastard motherfucker!" Alex spat between clenched teeth, turning away and kicking backward on the door, a hard kick. The door jumped in its frame, making a loud bang. Alex expected the noise to bring the attendants down on him, but in his anger he had no fear. When he thought about the beating, he was afraid, but in rage he was less afraid than before.

He flopped down on the bunk and folded his arms across his chest, staring at the ceiling and burning with anger. God, he hated *them*. . . .

13

on monday morning, without advance notice, an attendant brought Alex's clothes in a bundle and threw them on the cot: not the ward denims but the clothes he'd worn in the garage near the beach when arrested. Two months of being rolled up unwashed had made them stink, but the odor was insignificant compared to his upsurge of joy. He was leaving this place—not to freedom, of course, but even freedom wouldn't have made him happier. He was so keyed up that he fumbled tying his shoelaces, and then he had to be told to button his pants.

The ward was on work call and cleanup period, twenty minutes in the morning when they didn't have to sit on the benches. Word was out that Alex was leaving, so Toyo and two others were waiting when he was escorted across the dayroom.

Toyo started to shake hands, but the attendant got between them. "Say good-bye, but no contact."

"They think you'll give me a gun, I guess," Alex said with a sneer, words and attitude that would have brought a backhand not long before but not when he was leaving. Toyo and the others trailed to the side.

"Where you going, *carnal?* To court?"

"Yeah, I think so. Where else?"

"You won't come back here, will you?"

"Jesus, I hope not. This fuckin'—"

"It ain't so bad." But Toyo made an ugly face behind the attendant's back. "Take it easy, *carnalito*. Learn to duck those right hands . . . and hook off the jab." Toyo ended with a grin and wink, giving Churchill's "V" for victory sign, so popular in those days.

They were at the office door and it closed behind him, ending the good-byes and turning the friendship into memory. Alex never saw Toyo again or met anyone in his later travels who knew the skinny Chicano and what had happened to him.

In the room beyond the office a uniformed deputy sheriff was waiting with handcuffs. Several inches over six feet and many pounds over two hundred, his cheeks flushed with embarrassed surprise on sight of his prisoner. He chuckled and, almost shamefacedly, put the handcuffs back on his belt.

"How old are you?" he asked Alex.

"Nearly twelve," Alex replied, wondering why the man was shaking his head in disbelief.

Attendants and deputy performed the rite of signing receipts for his body, etcetera. When that was done, the deputy signaled he was ready and the door was unlocked solemnly. "C'mon, slugger," the deputy said. "We're late already, so let's get rolling."

Stepping into the bright sunlight, Alex froze, temporarily blinded. It was his first time outdoors in two months. The deputy led him by the arm, firmly but not roughly. "They said you were mean, but they didn't say you were eleven years old. 'Mean.' How the fuck can an eleven-year-old be mean?"

The car was plain white, without markings or special lights, although the inevitable police radio was inside, giving constant static-punctuated directions to misery, pain, and violence. The deputy shut it off as they left the grounds. Alex bubbled seeing freedom after seeing nothing except a manicured lawn from a window for so long. Scenery-watching was a habit he developed young and never lost.

The deputy was supposed to deliver him to court by ten A.M., but it was nine-thirty when they left Pacific Colony in heavy traffic, and fifteen minutes later they were still thirty miles away from downtown, stopped at a railroad crossing while a train jockeyed back and forth at five miles an hour, the freight cars banging in ragged sequence time and again. When automobile traffic finally got under way, it was ten-twenty. The deputy pulled to a phone booth in the corner of a gas station.

When he came back to the car, he grinned. "Okay, Slugger, it's put off until one. I can run you right in and leave you in the bullpen at the courthouse, or we can stop for a cheeseburger and milk shake. You probably haven't had anything like that lately."

"No, sir, not for a while." Alex restrained his urge to show joyous anticipation.

"Okay, kid, just one thing. I don't want to have to watch you like a hawk every second. And I'm not going to handcuff you to a table and have everybody think I'm a monster. So give me your word that you won't try to run and we'll make it look like we're pals. Okay?"

"You'll believe me?"

"If you give me your word . . . sure I will."

"You've got it. I don't have anywhere to go anyway."

In San Gabriel, a picturesque suburb highlighted by one of California's old missions, directly east of downtown Los Angeles, the deputy parked behind a restaurant. Large and gleaming—because it was glass, chrome, formica, and stainless steel—it was the kind of short-order restaurant peculiarly endemic to southern California. The lunch-hour trade had persons waiting for booths.

The hostess said: "There's room at the counter, if you and the boy. . . ."

"How 'bout it?" the deputy asked, ruffling the boy's hair.

Alex shrugged. "It's cool with me," he said, then followed the big man, conscious that he was inches from the butt of his revolver. It would be so easy to jerk it out. The thought passed quickly through his mind—pointless speculation—and disappeared as they slid onto stools.

"How's cheeseburger, fries, and a vanilla shake sound? My wife doesn't let me carry too much money."

"That sounds good . . . really good."

Thus was the order given to the waitress without using the menus she brought. When she turned away, the deputy leaned close. "I have to use the restroom. You stay here. Remember you gave your word. Don't get us both in trouble."

When the man was gone, Alex's sensibilities were swarmed over by the flux of bodies, by the cacophony of voices and dishes. Everything was so sharp, so crystalline as to seem unreal and confusing. In the mirror facing him he could see street images behind him, scurrying pedestrians, hurtling automobiles, all of it alternating from drab to brilliant under scudding clouds. It took Alex's breath away, and a nameless, keening hunger went through him. Without being able to articulate the yearning specifically, he sensed a fierce call to freedom. It would be so easy to get up and walk out; the deputy would never see him, much less catch him. "Free" meant more than not being in an institution. He already knew absolute freedom, being able to go wherever he wanted whenever he wanted, following his nose over the next hill. A child never had freedom unless he had lived as Alex did as a runaway.

As the longing peaked, recollection of his promise braked the thoughts. He'd given his *word*. His struggle against that truth lasted just a few seconds. He was munching his cheeseburger when the deputy sheriff returned.

■

The windowless room where juvenile prisoners were held waiting for court had been painted since Alex's last appearance. It was already liberally marked with fresh graffiti. The bailiff had given Alex a sack lunch, the standard slice of bologna slapped dry in stale bread and an orange spotted greenish-gray. With a full belly, Alex had taken the sack, because youths from Juvenile Hall were always hungry and would take a second sack lunch. But nearly all cases had already been heard on the morning docket, so just two others were waiting when Alex came in, and they didn't seem concerned with food. They hadn't even opened their own bags. They glanced up when the door opened and went back to their conversation when they saw it was another boy. Both were white and about Alex's age. Alex sat on a bench and leaned forward with his elbows on his knees, looking down at the concrete floor, pointedly ignoring the two youths. He couldn't, however, turn off his ears.

"Man, whaddya mean, *you can't?*"

"I just can't, that's all."

"Ow, wow!" He threw his hands up in exasperation with such sudden force that the other boy flinched away in panic, afraid that he was being attacked. "Dammit, Bobby! If you just say it wasn't me with you, they'll cut me loose." The speaker stopped, shook his head, and rubbed his hand hard across his face and eyes, meanwhile staring and showing venom in his expression. The other boy kept his eyes averted, frequently glancing at the door.

"Bobby, listen here. I haven't said anything, man—but I know you snitched on me."

"I didn't—"

"Shut the fuck up!" The words were unleashed fury, seething with threat. They silenced Bobby. "You did. You had to. How else could they have come for me so fast?"

"Yeah, Max, you said it was cool . . . no night watchman."

"There shouldn't be in a fuckin' secondhand thrift store."

"There was."

"So he snatched you for the cops. I wasn't back at the playground fifteen minutes when they came looking for me . . . asked the coach for me *by name.* 'Where's Max Dembo?' You got busted cold duck, but the watchman can't identify me. They got you. But if you say it wasn't me with you they'll let me go. Bobby, man, you don't wanna be known as a snitch, do you? A stool pigeon. Do you want that?"

Bobby shook his head. "But I don't wanna be locked up either. You've been there before. You can take it."

Now Alex was watching intently. Max had a sharp-boned face, making it unusually expressive and adult. Now it personified contempt, so open a sneer that Alex had seen such an expression only in the movies. Bobby seemed to cave inside under the glare; he cowered without moving, refusing to turn his eyes upward even momentarily.

Alex could see the gears turning in Max's mind, the tightening resolve to smash the weakling. It was so obvious that Alex's stomach knotted in anticipation. He felt no sympathy for the snitch.

The key turning the lock froze everyone except for turning heads. The uniformed bailiff hooked his finger and motioned to the two of them. The weakling moved instantly, as if the bailiff was a rescuer (which he was), while the other boy moved slowly, head down as he passed the man waiting to relock the door. The boy, who was barely in his teens, managed to radiate an arrogant indifference to both the waiting officer and the situation.

When the door was locked, Alex looked around at the ugly concrete walls, remembering with sudden clarity how he'd felt here nearly a year ago. He'd been afraid of the unknown, and that included nearly everything about this world. Still stunned by his father's death and his own predicament, he'd been insulated from too intense feelings. He couldn't feel. Now he was able to feel everything, and fear was there, an awful, specific fear of going back to a place similar to but more horrible than Pacific Colony, for he'd be committed as a psychopathic delinquent, not as feeble-minded, and that meant Mendocino, not Pacific Colony. Now, however he knew this world, understood it, and the world of freedom beyond walls and bars and locked doors had faded to the vague and unreal. True, it was the promised, fabled land, the one of dreams, but it was as hard to visualize as are dreams in the morning. The heaven of freedom was as nebulous to him as the heaven of God.

Now he had minutes to waste alone in the bullpen. He shadowboxed for a minute, practicing what First Choice Floyd and Toyo had shown him, and then his bladder ached for release. The lidless toilet was in the corner.

While buttoning his pants, he saw a paper clip on the floor. Someone had straightened it out and dropped it. Alex picked it up and scratched his name into the paint. He couldn't match the curlicues and fanciness of the Chicanos, who'd had lots of practice in defacing walls, so below his name Alex added something he'd heard Red Barzo say several times: "If you can't do time, don't fuck with crime." Below that he put: "Whittier, 1944 to ?" He was sure that was where he was going; he knew he wasn't crazy. . . .

Then he began shadowboxing again, stabbing out jabs and sliding forward to turn them into short hooks followed by right uppercuts, punching in combinations at imaginary opponents. He pivoted on the balls of his feet, slipping and counterpunching, loosening up.

He was leaning forward, simulating a flurry of short body punches, when the door opened. The bailiff chuckled. "Don't hurt nobody, kid!"

Alex stopped, flushed with embarrassment. "Er . . . uh . . ."

"You wanna be a boxer?" the bailiff asked, seeing the boy's embarrassment and trying to assuage it.

"Yeah," Alex said spontaneously, though not insincerely. It was the first time he'd conjured the possibility. "I'd like to do that . . . if I've got the talent."

"It's a tough game. Say, I came to find out if your parents are here to go to court with you?"

Alex shook his head.

"Is anybody else? An aunt? A guardian?"

"Naw. Nobody. I haven't got anyone."

The grin on the bailiff's face lessened, as if he shouldn't grin at an orphan. "Okay. You'll be going in a few minutes." He locked the door.

When the door opened again two bailiffs were wrestling the cursing, kicking figure of Max Dembo. One bailiff had the boy's arm twisted up behind his back, while the other had a headlock on him. They half-entered the room and threw the youth forward. "You're goin' to the hole when you get back tonight," one said.

"Fuck the hole, fuck you, and fuck that snitchin' punk you sent home to his mama!"

The men hesitated, obviously wanting to slap the foul-mouthed boy into respect. One of them tensed to do so. The boy didn't flinch, but the other man grabbed his partner. "Fuck this punk. Imagine . . . jumped on that other boy right in the judge's chambers. Picked up a brass ashtray and busted his head wide open."

Alex was awed, all his sympathy and respect going out to the defiant youth still glaring balefully at the men.

"Did His Honor swallow his teeth?" the other bailiff said, chuckling, his anger suddenly dissipated.

"Naw. He started yelling, 'Get him outa here! Get him outa here!' " Then to Max Dembo: "You're a tough punk, but where you're goin' there's lots of toughies . . . Okies, niggers, and bean bandits who been fightin' all their lives . . ."

"I just don't like finks," the boy said. "And I'm already in the hole in Juvenile Hall or I'd have beat his ass before this."

"I don't like finks either, kid. Why don't you cool down? Don't raise no more hell, and we won't report what happened to the people back at the Hall."

While they backed out and locked the door, Alex wondered what

kind of hell the boy could raise in this bare room? Perhaps kick up a
ruckus by kicking the door, or start a fight, or flood the toilet.

The boy began wiggling his shoulders, as one does to get rid of a
kink of pain. Although his face was flushed, he didn't appear otherwise
discomfited.

"What happened, man?" Alex asked.

"Ah . . . fuck! What I figured would happen. That punk spilled his
soul. The judge asked him if I was *involved*. Damn near told him that
he'd go home if he said it was me. Sheeit! After that they damn near had
to choke him to stop his snitching! They put him on a year probation.
So when it was time to go, and his fat-ass mama was huggin' him, I
busted him upside the head with the ashtray. He started screaming like
a bitch. Weak-assed motherfucker." The word "motherfucker" seemed
particularly gross in this boy's mouth. Unlike the blacks, who used it as
noun, verb, and adjective, flavoring every sentence and slurring it to virtual unrecognizability, this boy enunciated it precisely, each syllable
clear; it was more vulgar by how it was said. Indeed, his entire manner
of speech was unusually harsh.

"What about you?" Max asked.

"I dunno. Haven't been into court yet. But I think I'm goin' to Whittier. Fuck it!" He tossed a shoulder; reform school didn't matter.

"Yeah, fuck it! I'm goin' back there. I just did eighteen months and
stayed out ninety-four chickenshit days. Ain't that a bitch?"

"Sure is. I've been busted for a year."

"Yeah. What for?" The first real interest was aroused. Max raised his
head to listen.

"I shot a guy. He caught me busting in his store."

"Kill him?"

"Uh-uh . . . no. Just wounded him . . . I've been in the nuthouse for
observation."

"Yeah, they do that when something's serious. See if you're crazy.
And you damn sure are goin' to Whittier. I'll see you there. My name is
Max Dembo."

"Alex Hammond."

"Good luck."

"Good luck to you."

"Yeah, I need it." The hard-faced boy, whose whole manner spat defiance at the world, curved his mouth in a grin; his eyes sparkled, and for
that moment everything about him was warm.

They shook hands, Alex feeling somewhat foolish in performing
such an adult gesture with someone his own age, and before more words

could be exchanged they heard the sound of the turning key. The bailiff stuck his head inside and summoned Alex.

"Good luck again, man," Max said.

"Thanks, man."

This time the large courtroom was empty because the bullpen was likewise empty. The dozens of families were not there because the bullpen didn't have dozens of boys waiting to be called into the hearing rooms.

The combination office and tiny courtroom was the same as a year ago, the same nondescript clerks, recorders, and probation officer flanking the judge behind the polished darkwood table. The bailiff pointed Alex to a chair across from and below the judge. Alex couldn't remember the previous judge's name, or anything of what he looked like, but he knew this was a different judge simply because he was a Negro, albeit light-skinned, with his graying hair greased and pressed down to tight waves close to his skull. He wore owlish glasses of great thickness, making his dark amber eyes appear huge, yet he lacked the dour visage that Alex recalled from the last one. There was a kindly emanation from his face. He was studying a file and Alex knew it was his. The judge studied it for less than a minute, but that was long enough for Alex's imagination to create a mental hospital worse than Pacific Colony. Utter terror arrived with the creation, nor did the judge allay the fear when he looked up; his big eyes were staring unsympathetically.

"You don't seem to get along anywhere, do you? It goes way back— runaway, runaway, temper tantrums, and finally breaking into a store and almost killing the owner. I'm sure it wasn't in your plan, but you *did* pull the trigger. An adult would be in prison a long, long time for that." The judge paused, and Alex felt the man was waiting for some comment, but Alex could think of nothing to say. The judge turned to the probation officer. "Are you sure he doesn't have *any* family? None whatsoever?" The voice had a note of incredulousness.

"None that we can determine. And there's a file from social service agencies going back to age four, even prior to the court becoming involved."

The judge shook his head and grunted; then he spoke to Alex. "Well, you're not crazy. At least not in the way we usually think about crazy. You seem sane, you talk more than just reasonably sane for your age, but some of the things you've done"—the judge shook his head—"can only be described as insane behavior."

What was he saying? What was going to happen? The dread of Pacific Colony or someplace worse swelled malignantly through his brain. It nearly drove out reason and made him scream his terror. For a few seconds he lost track of the judge's conversation. The lips moved, teeth and tongue showed, but Alex couldn't untangle sound and give it coherence. He was afraid to interrupt and show his confusion; it might tip the balance if the judge was weighing mental hospital against reform school.

"Well?" the judge said, his eyeglass-swollen eyes staring. "What do you think?"

"I . . . I dunno, sir." Alex twitched a shoulder as children do in confusion.

"You don't know how you *feel* about what you've done?" The rising note of incredulousness cut through fear as cleanly as a boning knife through beef.

"Oh, I know I'm sorry," he said hastily. "But I didn't mean to do it, not shoot him. I'd give anything not to have done it. But I didn't mean to . . . I was scared and it just went off."

"Mmmmm." Some judicial rigidity faded. To all present, most of whom were disinterested, thinking about lunch and a distant siren, the judge said, "This is one of the tragic cases where we don't have the means to do what is right. It's a classic institutional treadmill: the broken home and now no family whatsoever, the foster homes and military schools, chronic runaway but not criminal, not yet, eventually committing a crime and coming into the criminal-justice system. And what can we do? Our options won't protect society in the long run. The best protection would be to make this boy a member of society, a citizen. We don't know how. We don't know what will come out of the other end of the system, someone better or someone worse. Statistics say he'll probably be worse. But what can I decide? Society demands he be punished. He shot a man. But if they didn't, where could I send him? To another foster home, boys' home? He'd run away."

"No I wouldn't," Alex interrupted. "I wouldn't."

"I believe you're sincere. But, yes, you'd run away. I'm sure you would. But how else can I help you?"

Alex's mind screamed silently, Let me go home, which didn't mean home, for he had none, but was the euphemism of the imprisoned for going free. But that was equally impossible. At his age society didn't allow freedom, even without such a crime as shooting a man during a burglary. Not knowing what to reply, Alex shrugged. His circuits were overloaded.

"Do you think going back to a hospital would help?"

"No! Please! Please don't . . . back there." The choked fervency was heard, and the jurist frowned, lowered his head so he could peer over his eyeglasses, his eyes suddenly small and myopic—and very, very human.

"Is it *that* bad? I've heard different stories."

Alex was suddenly afraid; it shot through him. He knew it was dangerous to criticize one authority to another. They were all together when it came right down to it. "I just . . . not for me. I hated it and . . ."

"Don't worry. Everyone agrees that you need treatment for emotional problems, but you're not mentally ill. I'm going to commit you to the California Youth Authority. The commitment is until you're twenty-one. You'll probably go to the state school out in Whittier because of your age. They could keep you until you're twenty-one, but that *never* happens." The judge stopped for a wan smile. "Those who need confinement until they reach twenty-one usually manage to get into enough trouble so that San Quentin gets them at eighteen or nineteen. Most boys are released in a year to eighteen months. You might get out even sooner, considering the time you have already been in custody. I'm going to order them to consider it.

"I'm not certain that sending you to the Youth Authority is the best thing. I'm *never* sure, or even half-sure, except when . . ." He trailed off, paused, shook his head. "Off the record, I somehow feel like Pontius Pilate in this case."

Somehow, the judge's tone made Alex feel momentarily sorry for the man across the table. Then the judge threw off his personal involvement. "So that's the Order of the Court. Commitment to the California Youth Authority. They will make the decisions of what to do with you. I hope you manage to make something of your life. I'd hate to see your good mind go to waste."

■

When Alex followed the bailiff back to the bullpen, he felt relieved that he wasn't going to the hospital, but he also felt tension. Whittier State School was the end of the line for boys between ten and fifteen. The toughest kids from the entire state were there. He would have to measure up or get walked on—or get sodomized and become a "punk," which was the absolute degradation. Punks suffered every sadism that young rage could conceive. Whittier wouldn't be so savagely brutal as what he'd seen, at least not where punishments were concerned, but he knew there would be more conflicts among the boys. He would be younger than most, and he vowed to prove his mettle. If most were bigger and tougher, nobody would have any more guts. That he promised himself as the bailiff opened the heavy door and locked it behind him.

Max Dembo was stretched on his back on a bench bolted to the wall. He swung his feet to the floor at the sound of Alex coming in. He jerked his head, silently asking, What happened?

"C.Y.A. How long before we go?"

"I'll go quick because they already have my records and stuff. You'll stay in Juvie for a month or so while the papers get processed in Sacramento. I'll wave hello when you get there." He grinned, the wizened face turning boyish. "It's gonna make you tough or break you."

"Well, it's not gonna break me."

Max grinned even wider, then winked. "I think you'll make it."

"Can't do nothing else." It was another philosophic phrase he'd heard from First Choice Floyd.

14

alex hammond spent the next six weeks in Juvenile Hall while the wheels of the unseen bureaucracy turned, processing his commitment to the California Youth Authority. This time he got along better because he'd learned how to fight. Rather, he'd learned how to *cop a Sunday*—strike a sneak, full-force punch and follow the advantage with a volley of feet and fists. The black monitor had kicked him in the rump for whispering while in line en route to supper. It was his second day back. The counselor was watching so Alex took it silently, though his brain reddened with fury and he could barely choke his food down. After the meal, the company went outdoors for recreation. The huge yard had an area for each company; mixing wasn't allowed. This company had the basketball court.

During the meal and the march out, Alex's eyes had met the black monitor's several times. When the company was dismissed, Alex met the eyes again. The black was slender and tall, with a grace of movement indicating muscular coordination. He had to be a good fighter to be a monitor. Alex's stomach mixed anger and apprehensiveness. He couldn't let the kick pass, but he didn't know exactly what to do.

The decision was taken from him. The black youth sidled over, his manner tense and ready. "Say, suckah," the black said. "You cuttin' yo' eyes at me like you got somepin' on your mind. You wanna get it on or somepin'?" He was leaning forward, hands partly up, coiled to fight.

"Man, I don't want no trouble," Alex said, spreading his hands with the palms up.

The tension went out of the black. Alex could see it ooze away, the eyes becoming milder. That was the moment Alex swung as hard as he could punch—left and right, using his shoulders and body weight the way First Choice Floyd had taught him. Both blows landed full-force, making loud "splat, splat" sounds, and Alex could feel the shock run up his arms.

The black dropped instantly, flat on his back, blood gushing from his mouth where his teeth were driven through his lip. He was out cold. It was the first time Alex had ever knocked someone unconscious. And from the encounter he learned the value of surprise. He was certain the black could whip him in a fair fight.

The fight cost him five days in "seclusion." He didn't mind because a prior occupant had stashed half a dozen books under the bunk. Two were Zane Grey Westerns, which he always enjoyed, and three were from the Hardy Boys series, which he'd once loved but now found too simple. Still, he read them. The last book didn't have a title that meant anything to him—*Native Son*—and he put it aside until nothing else remained. It was a little hard to read at first, but soon he forgot the words he sometimes missed and was lost in its world of ghettos and blackness and *life*. He was too young to know why it was affecting him so much, why it was so different from everything else he'd read. It was as if the brutalized and hate-filled young Negro reflected an unbelievable amount of what Alex had seen and experienced and felt. Alex still had the last few chapters to read when a counselor told him to get ready for the main population. He wasn't supposed to have books in seclusion, so he couldn't carry it out. Feeling a pang of guilt, he nevertheless tore out the remaining chapters and stuffed them down the front of his denims. He *had* to finish this book. He did so that night seated on a toilet in the small dormitory restroom under a wan light after the regular lights were turned off.

The black monitor still had strands of catgut jutting from his drooping lower lip. But when his glance met Alex's, the black looked away, and the white boy recognized his own victory. He'd expected another challenge and was ready to fight without bothering to talk. The monitor's nickname was T-Bone, and whenever the counselor brought out the boxing gloves, T-Bone put them on with anyone who dared. After seeing T-Bone, Alex was even more certain that the black could beat him up. But T-Bone didn't know it, nor did anyone else in the company. Thereafter Alex had far less trouble than during the first sojourn in Juvenile Hall. On Sunday afternoons, following the visiting hours, the boys got the packages of candy and magazines brought by their families. Alex got no visitors, but he always was offered lots of candy and the first chance at the magazines. He had gained status in a pecking order built entirely on violence. He was too young to question its values, where a cretin could be the most highly respected if he was the toughest, but nonetheless his intelligence gave him an advantage. He had beaten the black by thinking fast, and now he had an upper hand because he'd been smarter.

During the weeks of waiting for delivery to reform school, Alex kept pretty much to himself, his demeanor aloof, discouraging any attempts at friendship. Even the fact that he was going to reform school, the worst punishment the state possessed, gave him added status in Juvenile Hall.

■

During a long rainstorm, the worst to strike southern California since 1933, a counselor came to the classroom to fetch him. If it had been someone in Juvenile Hall calling him for an interview, a monitor would have come with the pass; the counselor meant that transportation to Whittier was waiting.

A pair of men in cheap business suits were waiting for him and two others. The men were from Whittier. The other two boys were Chicano; they were brothers who had inflicted multiple slices on a youth from a different street gang. These two brothers were from "White Fence," a barrio with a block-long white fence in it. They were also afraid of Whittier; White Fence was a gang at war with nearly all other Chicano gangs. It was without allies. And its members, unless unusually tough, were given a rough time in the youth institutions. They'd been pointed out to Alex by another Chicano, a friend of Lulu's from Temple Street. Lulu was already in Whittier.

The Chicano brothers were already in civilian clothes and being handcuffed together when Alex entered; one of them was holding a shoebox of letters and snapshots. A rain-pelted tree was wind-lashed so it scratched a window; it was the loudest sound as Alex changed into his own clothes, now musty from hanging unwashed for so long. The men from the reform school watched him, and when he was through one of them patted him down and brought out another pair of handcuffs.

"Should we put this one in the middle?" he asked his partner. "He's the jackrabbit in the bunch."

"Naw, he'll be okay on the outside."

The steel was fastened around Alex's right wrist, binding it to the left wrist of one Chicano. The trio was shepherded through the electronically controlled doors and hurried with heads down through the rain gusts—one man leading, the other following—to a station wagon with State of California on its side.

The drive took an hour. Whittier was a suburban community east of Los Angeles, and at first Alex had a terrifying thought that they were really going back to Pacific Colony, which was also east. Whittier, however, was ten miles to the south.

Elsewhere the storm was hitting the southern California coast with wicked backhand slaps, and causing canyon houses to slide off their perches; but here it was merely shivering trees and overflowing gutters and empty sidewalks. Once the driver had to slam a heel into the brake pedal to avoid plowing into a stalled car. Everyone in the station wagon lurched forward. Alex was shot through with a moment's fear as the car slid on the wet street, but as it straightened out and they gained momentum, he wished that they'd been wrecked—a bad wreck in which the prisoners had a chance to run. In later years, whenever he was transported anywhere he would beg fate for such an accident. This was just the first time.

The tires hissed on the wet asphalt as they passed beyond the barrios of East Los Angeles to the stucco suburbs and citrus groves. Trees leaned and writhed. The few vehicles moving around traveled slowly, their headlights turned on.

Whittier State School had its name on the front gate. The gate was open and no fence ran along the front. It faced a busy boulevard. The rear, however, had tall fences with rolled concertina. The buildings spread were brick Tudor. The grounds were twenty acres of manicured lawns and trim lodges. It looked more like a small college than a reform school. It took close inspection to see the chains welded across the windowframes, making sure they wouldn't open wide enough for a body.

Receiving Company was what its name indicated, a place where newcomers were processed and indoctrinated. The first day was spent at the institution hospital; he was examined, vaccinated, inoculated, and, because of his history, interviewed by a psychologist. Half of the next day was spent with a social worker, who had the court records but wanted to know what schools and institutions he'd been in, what social service agencies had handled him. Whittier would write for more information about him. Such things were immaterial to Alex; he was concerned solely with learning the reform school routine, the mores and styles, in learning his role and being accepted. The routine was basically military school discipline, enforced by civilians. The main civilian in each company was called a housefather; he and his wife lived in the cottage with the boys. Two other men worked the morning and graveyard shifts; they were counselors. Aiding the civilians were "officers," three boys, one of each race; they called the cadence, gave orders, and were quick to kick the slow-witted in the buttocks for dozens of infractions.

Mr. Morris, the Receiving Company housefather, still had traces of an English accent. In his fifties, he was a balding physical-fitness zealot. So was his petite-framed wife. In addition to the perforated paddle ("Bend over and grab your ankles"), Mr. Morris enforced discipline by liberal calisthenics. Minor infractions, such as audibly cutting wind in the dayroom or whispering in line, brought thirty-five situps or twenty pushups. Serious matters could bring an ear-ringing cuff on the head, a kick in the rump, or swats with the paddle, depending on circumstances and mood. Then, in the evening, the miscreants (there were several every day) did one hundred pushups in five sets of twenty, fifty deep knee bends, and fifty situps, which Mr. Morris did with them. Often his wife did them too. Despite being forty years old, she'd kept a taut figure, and the boys watched her brown legs and tried to sneak glances up her dress. The most adventuresome attached tiny bits of mirror to their shoes, then stood close to her, swearing later that they saw hair via the mirror.

Three hours a day were spent learning how to march. Alex already knew how from his sojourns in military schools, but he was a rarity. For the first three days, a newcomer was taught by a boy officer away from the rest of the company. After that, he was put with the others to learn or suffer. Being out of step brought a boot in the butt, as did any other drilling error. At the end of each drill period, the company did half an hour of strenuous exercises; they also did them before breakfast. When they went to a regular company they were in top condition, the thin arms of boyhood growing a ridge of muscle at the tricep, an unusual thing in young boys; and instead of boyhood's usual tummy, they developed rippling stomach muscles. Mr. Morris worked hard to create healthy bodies; he didn't think they had minds, so he didn't bother with that. In weeks they marched like a military drill team.

Because Alex knew how to march and had had the experience of other institutions, he avoided conflict with the officers. But he had a small, hard nugget of resentment for what they did, meanwhile recognizing that any of them could make mincemeat of him. Nevertheless, he knew that any kick or punch on the shoulder would make him fight whoever did it. He must have radiated his preparedness, for he wasn't kicked when he whispered during silent periods. The officers just signaled him to be quiet. They were obviously picked first because they were among the toughest in the company, and secondly because they would do so for extra prerogatives; few thirteen- and fourteen-year-olds understood the underworld "code" to the extent where this behavior violated it. They did know that outright "snitching" was *wrong*, but doing the Man's work of enforcing order was different. Alex seemed to be the only one who had misgivings when an officer beat up another boy for breaking the rules. A big, tough white officer (he weighed one seventy and shaved regularly at fifteen) nicknamed Skull kicked a smaller Mexican for horseplay in the shower line. The Mexican was snatching a towel from the waist of another Mexican in front of him. When kicked, he turned and punched—and the fight was on. The Mexican lost, but it was a hard, vicious brawl where the two boys stood toe to toe and the much larger Skull had a black eye and bumps on his face. When the Mexican officer went to a regular company, the fighting Mexican was promoted to the vacated position. He began kicking those who started the horseplay in line, those who talked, those who did anything, and joyfully pummelled any who fought back. A few boys were immune from the officers because they were too tough; they, themselves, would have been promoted except that they were just too much trouble—too rebellious. Mr. Morris took care of them. Another category received kicks, but "pulled," delivered at half-force with the flat side of the shoe; the culprit could arch his back and take it painlessly. The majority, however, learned to march and follow the rules by bruising kicks. They learned quickly, too; and any sign of protest brought a fist in the mouth.

Receiving Company was especially strict. Everything was done in silence. Every process, from wakeup, through washup, breakfast, drill and even showers, was done by the numbers. For example, they filed into their narrow lockers preparatory to showers. The officer gave them a left face, so they stood at attention facing each locker. At the command of "one" they put their hands on the locker; at "two" they opened it; at "three" they took out the towel and put their shoes inside. . . .

So it went for months and months. Alex knew he'd been marked as a troublemaker from things Mr. Morris said. Word had come from the front office, based on the files. "We'll break you," Mr. Morris said once. "You're not so tough," he said another time. But Alex didn't get into any trouble; the extreme discipline somehow made him patient and watchful. It was a challenge. He didn't know anyone in this company, which was newcomers from the whole state of California. Receiving wasn't allowed to mingle with other companies, but Alex saw faces he knew in church. Everyone had to attend either Catholic Mass or Protestant services. He went for the Mass because many boys wore the rosary as jewelry; he liked how it looked, and he got one from the priest. At Mass he saw Lulu, who grinned and nodded a greeting. It made Alex warm inside. He also saw Max Dembo, who waved a greeting. A few others from Juvenile Hall waved recognition and greeting. Some newcomers knew nobody, but others, especially blacks and Chicanos, saw a score or more of friends from their neighborhoods. It was old-home week to them.

The youngest boys at Whittier, from eight to ten years old, were in Wrigley Cottage; their "dress" clothes were Cub Scout uniforms. Wrigley Cottage was famous for its marches. Wrigley not only won close-order drill competition from the rest of Whittier, it had also beaten the U.S. Marine drill team from Camp Pendleton. Hoover Cottage was for slightly older boys, eleven or even twelve. Then came Scouts and Washington. The oldest and toughest boys were in Roosevelt and Lincoln. Most were fifteen and some were sixteen.

Alex was later transferred to Scouts, and he had mixed feelings about it. By comparison to the other cottages, Scouts was less regimented. It was the only cottage with private rooms instead of dormitories. On Sundays, it provided escorts for visitors from the front gate to the picnic area or auditorium; the weather dictated which. The boys thus had a chance to ask the visitors for cigarettes, the most valuable commodity in the institution. Running a distant second was Dixie Peach hair pomade; it was also contraband, as were all pomade and hair oil, because the boys drenched themselves and grossly stained the bedding. Their intricate hairdos, all with fancy ducktails, required lots of grease to stay in place. Access to the visitors allowed boys from Scouts to smuggle in cigarettes and pomade for others. The boys were searched, but the escorts could hide things in bushes en route here and there. They were too young, at least in this era, for marijuana, though a few had experience with it, and many claimed experience.

Scouts Cottage also went on more "town trips" than the others: the Boy Scout jamborees, parades, and an occasional movie. Such things were all to the good. To the bad—what caused Alex's misgivings—was that boys too soft for Washington, Lincoln, or Roosevelt were also sent to Scouts. Not all were thus. Most were average delinquents and a few were "crazier" than average. But the twenty percent in Scouts because of being weak gave a stigma to the others; the question was always raised if a newcomer was assigned there—until he proved himself, anyway. So, despite the comparatively easier living—and it was entirely by comparison—it rankled Alex that anyone might assume him too weak for a different cottage. He was ready to fight a grizzly to prove himself.

Scouts had faces that Alex recalled from Juvenile Hall, but he couldn't put names to them and didn't know them. The white boy officer got him bedding and linen and showed him the room he was assigned on the second floor. All the rooms were there, down two hallways at right angles. Where the hallways joined was the stairwell and a heavy door, the only exit. Here sat the night man's desk, too.

The room was nicer than any Alex had had in a foster home or military school. The small space was used efficiently. The bunk was built in against a wall, and its bottom had large drawers for extra clothes and property. A tiny wardrobe cabinet was fitted at the foot of the bed to the wall beside the door. The room door was never locked because the showers, washroom, and toilets were down the corridor. Writing desk and chair faced the room's small window, which had curtains and no bars. But he couldn't climb out because a short chain had been welded to the windowframe so it wouldn't open far enough.

Alex noted these things while making the bed. The white boy with the English-style officer's bars on his collar waited in the doorway.

"Tomorrow's Saturday," the officer said. "We have a room inspection before lunch. You gotta get the dust even from the corners of the bed-frame *under* the mattress, for example."

Alex wanted to reply sarcastically but held back. He didn't resent the information but how it was given. The tone wasn't friendly advice; it was an order with an implicit threat. Moreover, Alex had previously noted this boy and disliked him. His last name was Constantine (everyone used last names almost exclusively, as in the army), and he conveyed (at least to Alex) a snobbish, superior attitude, as if he thought himself better than the others. Where nearly all the boys, including Alex, combed their hair in ducktails, Constantine parted his and had a small pompadour. Where the style was to pull pants far down and roll them up at the bottom (this was the "hep" look), Constantine wore his conventionally. The man often used him as an example. He was the housefather's pet, and yet he had to be able to fight or he wouldn't have been an officer.

Thinking about Constantine occupied Alex while he "squared" the corners of the bed in the neatest manner.

"Do the rest later," Constantine said, meaning the rest of the cleaning of the room. Somehow this simple instruction likewise grated on Alex. Saying nothing, he knew that he and Constantine would eventually collide. Alex doubted that he could whip Constantine in a fair fight; he would have to obtain, and maintain, some kind of an advantage. . . .

■

Whittier's youngest boys, those in Wrigley and Hoover cottages, attended school all day. Their classrooms were in the cottages. They were kept away from the corrupting influence of the older boys, who attended school for half a day in the education building, then worked the other half. Some were assigned to vocational shoe shop, print shop, paint shop, sheet metal, and so forth; they learned to put heels on institutional brogans and slop whitewash on institutional dayrooms. Others took care of the hundreds of chickens and the herd of milk cows, or irrigated the alfalfa. A handful were on the Extra Squad, a crew that labored wherever needed. Sometimes they raked leaves or swept a road—but a broken pipe beneath the road had them digging through asphalt, dirt, and clay. Alex found himself doing the work of a grown man. For the first week his back and legs ached in the morning, but his body adjusted and toughened. Although he vilified the assignment and listened to boys ridiculing it (a shovel was one of the "idiot sticks" of the world), deep inside he derived pleasure from the work. It validated him as a man, and he got a gut pleasure from the bite of the shovel into the earth and the bunching of his shoulder muscles as he hoisted it. He didn't drive himself to special effort, but he did enough to avoid yells from the man, usually a relief counselor from one of the cottages who had nothing to do while the boys were at school. The housemother, the wife of the housefather, who had the afternoon and evening shift, kept a few boys for "housecats." They cleaned and polished the cottage. But the day counselor had other duties, supervising a work crew or helping to watch Jefferson Cottage, the disciplinary company. Jefferson really worked hard.

Alex had been on the Extra Squad for two weeks (he attended afternoon school) when the regular man called in sick. The day counselor from Lincoln filled in. He was younger than most, barely thirty, and he was nicknamed "Topo" (Gopher) because of his protuberant front teeth. Nobody called him Topo to his face, but disguised voices often called to his back: *"Topo es puto,"* or "Topo sucks dicks." He reacted with rage. His real name was Mr. Lavalino, and the boys thought he was tough. They respected toughness but not cruelty. Mr. Lavalino was also cruel occasionally; he used the boys under his control to vent a variety of frustrations. Alex knew him only by sight when he took the Extra Squad one bleak, rain-threatened morning. The dozen boys were digging up a leaky pipe near the front of the institution. They'd reached the pipe the day before, but the actual leak wasn't precisely where they'd excavated. They were enlarging the ditch by following the pipe. The earth was soft, but the work was sloppy. It had rained during the night and turned things to mud.

The boys had divided themselves into shifts because everyone couldn't work simultaneously. Some loosened the earth with mattocks; others shoveled out what had been loosened. Alex was half-leaning on his shovel, watching the other shift do their stint, when the dirt clod hit him behind the ear and shattered. It didn't hurt, but it stunned him momentarily, the surprise of it. When he turned, confused with shock, his face commencing to draw up in anger, he expected to see another boy. Whether it was a joke or an insult, he was ready to issue a challenge.

No boys were looking at him. But Mr. Lavalino was. The man was standing beside a fifty-gallon drum with a fire in it. He wasn't warming his hands. He was glaring at Alex.

"Get your ass in gear," he said. "Quit lollygagging and leaning on that shovel with your finger up your ass."

Every word was like an unexpected slap. He didn't even want to explain how the work was divided; he was trying to fight the redness growing in his eyes and brain; it made any long, explanatory sentence impossible. "Did you . . . throw that?" he choked out; even those few words were difficult.

"Yeah, yeah," Mr. Lavalino said, nodding his head for emphasis, voice rising, "I threw it. You don't like it or something . . . punk?"

Alex couldn't reply, not in words. "Punk" was the ultimate insult. He was beginning to pant, his breathing loud and strained, the excessive oxygen further dizzying his brain. All peripheral sights disappeared. In the reddening world he could only see the grotesque face of Mr. Lavalino grinning with malicious challenge.

The fury that erases thought took over. With a gasping scream he raised the shovel like a baseball bat and ran at the man—he meant to erase the grin with gore. He would bash in *that* face. . . .

But Mr. Lavalino no longer grinned. In seconds he blanched, seeing the truth. He flinched back one step and then turned and ran, yelling out, "Help! Help!"

The original distance between them was fifteen feet, but it was across the ditch and the mound of soft, damp earth. Alex stumbled, nearly falling, but found his balance and veered around the ditch.

Within moments the violent drama turned to comedy. Mr. Lavalino ran around the ditch, keeping it between himself and the enraged youth. The boy chased him around it once, sinking into the soft dirt, unable to get close enough to swing the shovel.

The other boys on the crew had stood dumfounded. Boys fought boys, not the Man, especially not a man such as Topo, who was notorious for kicking around anyone who showed the slightest rebelliousness. And this newcomer brandishing the shovel while sobbing in rage was obviously crazy. Nobody but a crazy kid would do this.

After the second time around the ditch, both of them panting, Alex stopped. So did Mr. Lavalino, keeping the ditch between them like a moat. Using a shred of reason, Alex feinted continuation of the chase, and then he started to charge directly over the ditch. He could leap it and cut off his prey. But first he had to go over the pile of soft dirt dug from the ditch. It was too soft. He sank in, stumbled, and fell to his knees, the shovel out of control.

At that instant, a fat black boy, compelled by a loathing of violence he would never admit (scarcely even to himself), took three quick steps and tackled Alex from behind. It was a high tackle, the black boy's shoulder slamming into Alex's back. The shovel jumped from Alex's hands, and he went face-down into the dirt, the weight of the heavy boy pinning him.

"Motherfucker!" Alex yelled reflexively, keeping his mouth from the earth and trying to struggle.

Other boys saw the madman disarmed and came forward to subdue him. The front office, and maybe the parole board, would look favorably on this humanitarian behavior. Young they were; naïve they were not. "Settle down, settle down," one of them said, meanwhile putting a headlock on Alex.

Alex twisted his head away from the soft dirt so he could breathe. Struggle was useless, but he muttered curses, for now into his mind jumped the certainty of punishment. To threaten their power was the worst behavior imaginable. They went half crazy over being attacked. And the worst part was that the punishment would come without his having had the satisfaction of smacking Topo with the shovel.

"Lemme up," he said.

"Take it easy, pal," the fat black said. "You'll just get in bad trouble."

Mr. Lavalino came around the trench as the fat black and two others helped Alex rise, meanwhile still holding him securely. Two hands pinned each arm, and resistance was useless. Alex watched the man approach, anticipating blows and planning to duck his head as much as possible, the memory of the terrible beating in Pacific Colony flashing into clear focus. Maybe he could tuck his chin next to his shoulder and take the punishment on the forehead. That was better than taking fists in the mouth and nose. It might even hurt the motherfucker. Hands often broke on foreheads.

Mr. Lavalino was pale with fright, not florid with rage. His hands were raised with open palms. "Easy, Hammond, easy." Every other time he'd asserted his authority—these were tough punks who only understood and respected force—it ended there. It never got to the administration building about a kick or a cuff. This one would go to the disciplinary company for the attempted assault, no matter what the provocation, but throwing the dirt clod could cause repercussions—at least a reprimand in the personnel file; it would be seen during promotion hearings.

Alex was still being held by two boys, and Mr. Lavalino was still frowning his indecision, when the institution patrol car pulled up. The supervising counselor, who cruised the reformatory checking on things, had seen the boys standing around instead of working. He didn't get out of the automobile, merely rolled down the window as Lavalino came over.

"Anything wrong?" the supervisor asked.

"Naw, not really. Just some bullshit friction I can handle okay."

The supervisor looked at Alex; he had been told about him in a staff meeting just last week, as were many newcomers over the course of time. "That's Hammond, isn't it? He's supposed to be wild . . . borderline psychopath with real problems about authority. So keep your eye on him."

"Oh, I can handle him," Lavalino said, smiling in a way that added to the claim.

"I know you can."

"What's on the menu? It's almost lunch."

"Boys' mess hall or staff's?"

"Both. I eat where it's best."

"Chili mac for the gunsels. Salisbury steak for us."

"Both lousy. But the chili's free."

The supervisor chuckled, said good-bye, and drove off. Lavalino clenched his teeth and turned to deal with Alex. The man's shoulders were round in unconscious body language supplication, and his hands were extended palms up, showing he was hiding nothing. "Easy does it, young'un. You don't have to be upset."

The tone more than the words jolted Alex, surprising him, for he'd expected a raging adult who would curse and threaten at the very least, and very possibly might lose control. The conciliatory tone stopped Alex cold, yet he sensed that this wasn't the man's real nature. The man who'd thrown the dirt clod was the true Lavalino, not this phony with a soothing voice.

The adrenaline was gone from Alex, so instead of continued rage there was thought, and even a moment's reflection said that pacifying the situation was the right thing to do. He had *won;* the man with power was now calming him. How different from three minutes ago—the dirt clod and the arrogant challenge.

"Let him go," Lavalino said, having made sure the shovel was at a safe distance. "Are you cooled off?"

"Yes, I'm okay." Actually, he was trembling from nervous exhaustion.

"C'mon," Lavalino said, then glanced at the dozen boys standing around, all of them watching intently. "Take a break," he said to them.

Warily, Alex followed the man's beckoning gesture and fell in beside him.

"I'm not going to report this. If I did, you'd be in the disciplinary company for at least thirty days . . . and that's no picnic. And it'd probably mean an extra few months before parole, too. But it's partly my fault. I didn't mean to hit you in the head with that chunk of dirt. Bounce it off a leg or something . . . just get your attention so you'd work."

"I *was* working . . . hard as anybody. The mattocks were loosening it up for the shovels to dig."

"Okay, okay, let's not argue about it. Anyway, you're not getting a disciplinary report . . . but keep it quiet, 'cause my Italian ass would be in a sling, too, for not reporting something this serious."

"Don't worry. I'm not a fink."

"And lemme give you some advice, kid . . . rein in that temper. It's gonna bring you lots of misery if you don't." Lavalino punctuated the advice with a big brotherly squeeze of Alex's shoulder. The man's solicitude, real or faked, short-circuited the undercurrent of anger still in Alex. The lonely boy within washed over the tough kid. Momentarily his eyes were wet, and he turned his face away, stifling the telltale sniffle. Lavalino was still talking, but Alex didn't hear. He was asking inwardly: Why do I always have to fight? Why is it so ugly? God, I'd just like to be like everyone else.

From the institution power plant came the blast of the noon whistle, signaling it was time to return to the detail grounds for lunch. The whistle also exploded flocks of sparrows from roofs and trees. After lunch Alex went to school. He and Lavalino turned back to where the youths were gathering the tools and lining up. The incident of violence was over.

But not forgotten. The boys on the crew were from various cottages, and by evening all had told the story of "some crazy motherfucker in Scouts, a white guy named Hammond, tried to knock Topo in the head with a shovel . . . had the dirty bastard running with his tail between his legs." Boys fought each other without thought, but what Alex had done was the ultimate "craziness." During the next couple of days he was pointed out on the detail grounds, and the storytellers embellished what they'd seen so that some boys thought Alex was a "maniac," which wasn't a pejorative, and some boys thought him a "ding," which was definitely pejorative.

Distorted word of the assault got to most of the counselors, too, despite the lack of a report. A boy officer in Roosevelt Cottage gossiped to the night man (who smuggled cigarettes in at a dollar a pack when they cost fifteen cents), and the night man told his morning relief, who told others at lunch. When Lavalino was approached, he disparaged the seriousness; he couldn't admit running scared from a twelve-year-old. The counselors never got the whole story, but they got enough to recognize that Alex, although certainly no match in a fight against many of Whittier's youths, was one of the more unpredictably explosive. Some men would simply watch him closer, others would be cautious, and a few would take it as a personal challenge and decide to come down hard if he showed any temper toward them.

Thus, within a few weeks of leaving the receiving cottage, Alex Hammond had gained high visibility—was known by the majority of the boys and counselors. He noticed it on the detail grounds. The cottages marched there at work call twice a day. They were dismissed to go to specified areas according to their assignment. For a few minutes all could mingle. The only other time it was allowed was at church. Otherwise the inhabitants of one cottage were kept away from those in different cottages. After the shovel chase, Alex got occasional nods of recognition at work call. Boys he didn't know would nod or wink on meeting his eyes and say, "All right, Hammond." Or, "Easy does it, Hammond." It happened four times in two weeks. It made him feel good.

It also got him in a brief fight. While joining the school line one afternoon (the largest single group, some hundred and fifty boys), the officer ordered: "Right dress!" The arm that came up didn't just extend for spacing; it shoved him violently.

"Hey, man!" he said, regaining balance, looking at the boy who had shoved him. He was smaller than Alex but he was in Lincoln, the toughest cottage, where his size made him stand out. Alex had noticed him before. His name was Fargo.

"You don't like it?" The challenge was thrown.

"Naw, I don't like it from a fuck. Don't shove."

"Aww, you might tell Topo what to do, but you're just another punk from Scouts, so don't tell me nuthin'."

Punk! Punk! The word of words in the reform-school lexicon. A fight was inevitable. That thought was in Alex's mind when Fargo kicked him in the ankle; a hard kick with steel-capped toes. While the pain shot through Alex, his fist shot out into Fargo's nose. Blood poured instantly and profusely. Alex stepped back and out of line to get room to fight. The ranks broke up for the combatants.

Fargo, however, was leaning forward, holding his head extended so the blood wouldn't drip on his clothes. He was muttering obscenities.

The teacher supervising the march to classes saw the bleeding boy and called a halt. He ordered Fargo aside and had them form into ranks. Alex watched Fargo being led toward the hospital by a counselor, and then he was marching on to school. Throughout the afternoon, Alex couldn't concentrate—not that anyone else even tried to concentrate, or any teacher cared. Reform-school youths have no concern about education, and teachers who wanted to teach resigned to work elsewhere. Whittier had school classes because the state law required it. Everyone did what they wanted short of rebellion and riot. But where most others drew pictures, played games, or leafed through magazines and cut out lingerie ads, Alex tried to learn some things because they interested him: history, geography, social studies. He refused even to try to learn mathematics or science, but the teacher was happy to have a boy desirous of learning anything—most couldn't read and didn't care to learn how—so she let him decide, helping him. It really came down to reading; he liked what he could learn simply by reading.

This afternoon, however, the printed pages became sheets of squiggles. At evening recall on the detail grounds he would have to continue the fight. He wasn't afraid. Rather, the fear was controlled and he was ready to fight—but the wait had his mind running repeatedly over the situation. His brain was stuck like a gramophone record. Once more he wondered why he had to fight continually. Other people didn't have to; he knew that from books. Momentarily, he considered "turning the other cheek," but it made him chuckle. If he turned the other cheek they'd have him bent over spreading *both* cheeks of his ass while making a toy-girl of him—a punk. . . .

Alex was quickly out of the classroom door when the whistle sounded. He waited on the walk while the line of classrooms emptied. He knew an aggressive demeanor might give him an advantage, especially if he started swinging first.

Fargo wasn't at school. He hadn't returned following the bloody nose.

When the school formation marched onto the detail grounds and was dismissed, Alex didn't go to the area where Scouts formed. Instead he stayed in the center, visible and available, while work crews and shop crews arrived and dispersed to the various cottage formation areas.

Fargo was still absent. Was it fear? That was hard to believe, both from how he'd acted and because he lived in Lincoln, the toughest cottage. The smallest guy in Lincoln, too. Yet where was he?

Alex could wait no longer. Cottages were forming ranks. He started toward his own and saw Lulu Cisneros, his first acquaintance in Juvenile Hall, coming toward him. Weeks before, when Alex had gotten out of Receiving, Lulu had given him half a pack of Camels. (Lulu's visitors made him reform-school rich by smuggling him two packs every Sunday; Alex carried them in from the visiting grounds for five cigarettes.) Later, from the shoe shop, Alex pilfered him a pair of capped-toe brogans, a shoe much favored by the boys. Having a pair was a status symbol.

"I was lookin' for you—where you line up?" Lulu said.

"I've been waitin' here for another guy."

"Little Fargo?"

The surprise on Alex's face was sufficient reply.

"He's at the cottage," Lulu continued, "and maybe has a broken nose. It's swollen up and both eyes are black. That's why I'm here. Do you wanna forget it?"

"He fucked with me. I didn't fuck with him."

"Man, man, fuck all that. We ain't got all day. We gotta line up . . . remember."

"Yeah, okay. What's happenin'?"

"I talked to Fargo and he copped out that he started it. He's salty about his nose, but he can laugh at it, too. He didn't expect it. Somebody told him you were a punk or something. But he'll let it drop if you will . . . unless you start talking shit and bragging."

"Afraid of getting his ass kicked." Alex said it without reflection; it was the standard conclusion by the routine values of the reformatory. Anyone who avoided any fight by so much as "excuse me" or one step backward was deemed afraid.

"Naw, uh-uh, that little cat ain't afraid of a grizzly bear. He's a fightin' motherfucker . . . an' probably can kick your ass. In fact, 'cause he is a tough little cat and everybody knows it, he can let it slide without anybody thinkin' he punked out. He knows he was dead wrong and respects you for having guts."

The detail grounds was now virtually empty. A few stragglers were running toward their formations. Cottages were straightening ranks while a counselor took a head count.

A supervising counselor was bearing down on Alex and Lulu, waving an arm for them to move on. They started to move, angling away from each other while going in the same general direction.

"So what'll I tell him?" Lulu called from ten feet away.

"It's over as far as I'm concerned. I'll shake his hand when I see him."

"Man, don't get fuckin' sickening." Lulu turned and began sprinting for Lincoln, which was the farthest formation. Alex half-walked, half-trotted toward where he belonged, a sudden elation filling him. He'd been ready to fight but was happy that it was unnecessary. It was the sudden removal of the tension, however, that made him glow inwardly.

"Where the fuck have you been?" Constantine snapped when Alex reached the cottage and slipped into his position.

"Just late, man, just late." The smile went, the elation died. As he marched in step, able to do so without thinking about it, he rankled at the way Constantine had spoken. Sooner or later I'm gonna have trouble with him, Alex thought. Then he remembered the cigarette hidden in his pants cuff. The cottage would fall out at the recreation area for half an hour, then wash up and march to supper. It was summer, with long evenings, so after supper there'd be a softball game. He would be the center of three or four boys because of the cigarette. He'd have to share it to get a match, but he didn't mind. He liked sharing. They would lie on the grass as far away from the counselor as possible and pass the butt around surreptitiously. He felt good looking forward to it. . . .

■

The houseparents were a couple in their early fifties named Hoffman. They had twin daughters who were married, and a third in the WACs. Although one counselor worked from midnight to eight A.M., and a second counselor worked from eight A.M. to five P.M., the Hoffmans were in charge. Living in a small apartment in the cottage, they were nearly as available as real parents. Any boy could knock on their door except, infrequently, when a DO NOT DISTURB sign dangled from the doorknob. When it was there the boys speculated on what was happening within. Roosevelt and Lincoln cottages, with older boys, didn't have housemothers, but all the others had the same staff setup as Scouts. The Hoffmans, however, were more involved with their boys, and did all they could to make institutional living as homelike as possible. They used their own money for a record player, and to have ice-cream-and-cake birthday parties once a week for every boy having a birthday in that period. The Hoffmans tried to break down the "codes" of the underworld that these teenagers were making their personal ethics. When it became obvious that a boy was no longer malleable, he was transferred to another cottage, unless he was under the care of the institution psychiatrist, who was also the only physician. Scouts Cottage was deliberately more lax than the other cottages. Alex sometimes felt that he didn't belong there, but he was nonetheless grateful—except for Constantine.

Two boys were assigned to the cottage as a work assignment. Called "housecats," they cleaned and did light maintenance. Every boy had some small cleanup duty in addition to his own room, for Mrs. Hoffman kept the cottage immaculate, despite fifty delinquents, many of whom knew nothing except slovenliness and dirt, which go with poverty.

The Hoffmans showed a special interest in Alex. They were interested in all the boys, but even real parents have favorites, albeit secretly, and the Hoffmans were more interested in some boys than others. When a housecat went home, Mrs. Hoffman offered Alex the job. It was better than digging ditches, raking leaves, or pushing a lawnmower, and Alex had no desire to learn a trade—shoe shop, paint shop, sheet metal. . . .

Constantine, without doubt, was Mr. Hoffman's most favored boy. Tall, well-built, and good-looking, with curly black hair and a seductive smile, it was easy to see why he was a monitor, especially when so many others were unattractive—unattractive in both looks and manner. Many were grossly ignorant and angry, illiterate black boys from the rural South, brought to Watts as sharecropping diminished in favor of mechanized farming; their parents searched for factory work and they took to the streets of the city. The Chicanos, many of them, had similar stories, except that their parents came across the border. And Okie accents were common among the whites, children of the Dust Bowl—or of broken homes and alcoholics. Youths of all races unable to respond to affection except with suspicion, unable to handle any problem except with rage, children disturbed by an endless list of family and social ills. Scouts Cottage had more boys with severe emotional problems than did the other cottages. Though the Hoffmans were fair, or tried to be, it was impossible not to prefer one who seemed near the All-American ideal. Constantine knew the value of his handsomeness. He hid his rage better than the others, and he also hid his background; his mother was a call girl, and he was a mistake. *Nobody* knew who his father was.

From the beginning Constantine saw Alex as a potential rival with the Hoffmans. The newcomer's education also rankled Constantine, for Alex occasionally, and unintentionally, used some word that the ill-educated boys didn't know. The second day that Alex was in the cottage, Constantine chalked an announcement on the bulletin board. Without thinking, Alex spoke up to correct a misspelling. The correction flushed Constantine's cheeks and planted the seed of hostility.

Many of the authority-hating boys disliked Constantine, whispering, "He's just a kiss-ass snitch." But they were also afraid of him. When they saw how he felt about Alex, they kept their distance from the latter. It wasn't "silence," and he could always find someone to help him smoke the cigarettes Lulu gave him, but he couldn't make any close friendships, and oftentimes he ached with loneliness, although he didn't see anyone in Scouts whom he really liked and wanted for a buddy. He doubted that he could whip Constantine, though he wasn't afraid to try—except he knew that it would turn Mr. Hoffman against him. He was careful to give Constantine no excuse to start anything. Getting out of step, making a marching mistake, or talking in ranks would bring a foot in the ass, the standard summary punishment approved by Mr. Hoffman and the superintendent. Alex was among those, and they were many, who never accepted a kick without a fight. That would bring Mr. Hoffman down on him, win or lose. Ergo, he made no mistakes. His quarters were immaculate. The anxiety would have been too great, and he would have gone at Constantine no matter what, except that he could relax completely in the mornings when he worked for Mrs. Hoffman. All the boys were gone in the mornings except for the other housecat, a thin Chicano nicknamed Hava. They usually worked for an hour or two, waxing the dayroom, pruning weeds from the shrubbery outside the cottage, washing windows. . . . Even then his mind could relax. Then, invariably, Mrs. Hoffman would call them into the apartment for donuts or cake or some other sweet delicacy. Whenever he thought of Mrs. Hoffman in the later years, he always thought of brownies; she gave him the first one he could ever remember. He dreaded noon when he and Hava joined the rest of the cottage on the grounds detail. Even though he didn't see Constantine at school in the afternoon, he had to stay ready. Seldom did an afternoon pass without at least one fist fight.

■

A month after becoming a housecat, Alex made a bushel of Chicano enemies, adding to his dilemma of feeling he didn't belong. It was Sunday morning and he'd gone to Mass, so he could talk to Lulu afterward—find out if the Mexican was getting a visit in the afternoon. If so, Alex would pay the black monitor two cigarettes to make sure he was assigned to escort Lulu's visitors to the visiting grounds. En route he'd pick up two packs of Lucky Strikes and hide them under a brick beside the recreational area for later pickup. Following visiting hours, everyone in Scouts was searched, and everyone who got a visit was skin-searched before returning to their cottages. Tomorrow, during school recess, he'd retrieve the cigarettes, take twelve and deliver the rest.

Mass was over. The boys had to file out one aisle at a time. Even then there was horseplay. Just beyond the door, where the priest stood and smiled good mornings, a grab-assing youth jumped backward to avoid retaliation and crashed into Alex, knocking him backward into someone else. "Excuse me, man," he said. "I'm sorry." But the boy ahead, who'd knocked Alex back, merely glanced at what he'd done and ignored the situation. Alex thought he saw contempt flicker on the boy's face.

"Hey, man!" Alex called, his face hot. "Can't you say 'excuse me'?" His voice was loud and challenging. It froze the youth, called "Chango," a *huero* Chicano with bright green eyes, low forehead, and hair that stood up like porcupine quills.

"What . . . ?" he snapped, eyes glassy. "What the fuck did you say?"

A fight was at hand. More words would make no difference to that certainty. So while the Chicano's mouth was still open, Alex put his fist in it, then followed the clean punch with a swarming volley. The first two punches caught the Chicano flush, knocking him backward. He clutched at Alex, ducking his head under the swings. They grappled, seeking a hold or a clean knee to the testicles.

The priest came running at the first sound of violence. He was still wearing the vestments of the Mass. He grabbed Alex by the collar from the rear and hurled him back. Alex couldn't keep his feet under him and fell on his rump, hands extended behind him to take some of the force and to scrape the skin. Meanwhile, the priest had grabbed the furious Mexican and was holding him. The Chicano was spitting blood and cursing Alex—who gave him the finger in return.

Two counselors pushed through the milling boys, yelling: "Clear it out! Get to your cottages! Get on there! Break it up!"

As Alex got up, waiting for whatever was next, a dark Chicano from Roosevelt Cottage who looked like an Indian (and was nicknamed "Indio") passed close by and paused for a moment, his dark eyes glittering. His face was a mask of fury. "You fucked up, white boy," he snarled. "You shouldn't have punched my homeboy. You're gonna get fucked up."

"Fuck you and your greasy mother, too."

"Okay, punk, okay!"

"Okay my ass, sissy!"

A counselor was bearing down, hand outstretched to grab Alex as a culprit. Indio turned away, going with the flow of movement to join his cottage. He stopped to look back and nod affirmation of his threat.

The man vised Alex's arms, digging in until the boy flinched.

"I'm sorry," the man said. It was obvious that he, too, was a little nonplussed.

The antagonists were kept apart and escorted to the supervising counselor. He was in charge of the institution on Sunday mornings. He grabbed the Chicano's nose to make sure it wasn't broken. He asked no questions because he didn't want to hear any lies. "You're in different cottages so you can't try a rematch. Can't you find plenty of fights? . . ." He looked at the blank faces and knew how useless was any advice, even sardonic. "You've both got three hours of extra duty tonight. The next time you start fighting at church, I'm gonna finish it . . . and then drag your asses to the disciplinary cottage. They'll have to pull my size twelve outa your butts." To the men, he said: "Take 'em back to their cottages. Don't bother with an incident report."

■

That sunny afternoon, with the visiting grounds full of boys and their families, so it looked like a picnic area in a park, Alex looked for Lulu and his family. He had walked Lulu's sister and her husband in earlier, picked up the cigarettes, and now he was back to see his friend. Lulu saw him coming and got up to meet him, beyond hearing range. Usually he motioned Alex over. Now his face was stern. "Man, how come you copped a Sunday punch on Chango?"

"Because the motherfucker crashed into me . . . and he was gonna Sunday me."

Lulu shook his head. "Watch yourself, man. A whole bunch of beans are mad."

"Let 'em scratch their asses and get glad." The bravado hid the knot of worry. It wasn't overpowering fear, but it was serious. It would have been worse in nearly any other cottage, for Chicanos were fifty percent of the institution's population, but of fifty boys in Scouts, just seven were Mexican, and none were troublemakers. In fact, they were there because they were too Americanized and didn't even speak Spanish, which made them semi-outcasts among other Chicanos. Except for Hava. He was well-liked, or so it seemed to Alex. Hava always had plenty of friends from other cottages to talk to him on the grounds detail and whenever else the cottages mingled. Lulu said that Hava's brother was a bigshot narcotics peddler in East Los Angeles. Alex hoped Hava wouldn't turn against him; not that he was afraid of the Chicano. Alex could handle him with ease, but he liked Hava. He also liked Lulu. "What about you, man?" Alex asked; he was just learning about race. He'd never thought that anyone but white persons could be prejudiced, and he'd never been so.

"I won't jump you . . . but I'm a Mexican . . . and I can't go against my people to help you."

"Yeah, I know, man."

One of the counselors who watched over the visiting grounds had been eyeing the talking boys. It was against the rules, and he'd let them have enough leeway. He started to move in. They saw him and said good-bye, shaking hands. It was an unusual gesture, gauged by the predicament.

Alex continued to the restroom, and while he urinated an ache of loneliness rose inside him. It seemed as if he was at war with the whole world without having anyone on his side.

"Fuck 'em," he muttered as he buttoned his pants.

Because it was summer and twilights were long, the cottages went to the outdoor recreation yards following supper. A big, mainly dirt athletic field was divided in half by a line. Scouts Cottage had one half; Washington Cottage the other. Hoover Cottage had an area visible in the distance, and the other cottages were elsewhere on the state property, near the buildings housing them.

When the ranks disintegrated, most of the boys gathered around Mr. Hoffman and Constantine—and the cardboard boxes filled with brown bags, the goodies left by visitors earlier in the day. Mr. Hoffman called out each name, and as each boy got his bag and turned away he was joined by his friends. They flopped on the lawn and gorged on whatever the family had left, predominantly cookies and candy.

Ignoring the crowd, Alex strolled with his head down to the trees beside the road, which was the boundary line. He sat down with a tree trunk as a back brace. Pretty soon he would be picked up to do the extra duty for the fight—wash the high, vaulted windows in the mess hall. Meanwhile, he'd light up a cigarette. Probably one or two of the few boys he talked to would come over, mouths salivating for nicotine. He'd share with them because it made him feel good, even thought he had no close friends in this cottage—not even one partner, which nearly everyone had unless they were finks or dingalings.

Two boys whom he didn't expect approached him. One was Watkins, a skinny Okie with a loud mouth. Hearing his voice without seeing him, anyone would expect a huge brute, not a fourteen-year-old with a wizened countenance and a jagged scar down his cheek.

The second boy was a newcomer, but Alex had seen him over a year earlier in Juvenile Hall. Joe Altabella by name, he was called JoJo. An already husky lad, he would fatten on pasta with passing years. Now he was good-looking, with curly dark hair tumbling down his forehead. He wore a ducktail, as did everyone. Because he was Italian, and could also pretty much understand Spanish, he got along with the Mexicans. He wasn't considered a "white boy," per se. He'd had a visit today, his parents (the mother cried) and two sisters. One was a skinny ten-year-old, but the other had many boys looking. Precociously developed at thirteen, she had full breasts and hips to go along with luxuriant dark hair and big hazel eyes—and the tint of olive in lovely skin. Alex flashed these thoughts in the half minute as the two boys approached. He shaded his eyes with his hand to look up. The dying sun was behind them.

"What's happening?" he asked.

"Ain't much," Watkins said. "Thought you might wanna smoke one of JoJo's fags with us—but you're fired up already."

"I saw that scene at Mass this morning," JoJo said. "Chango is a troublemaker. He tried to get me jumped in Juvenile Hall . . . said I was trying to be a Mexican 'cause I was speaking Spanish. He's a real nutty guy."

"Yeah, man, you gots troubles," Watkins commented.

The statement touched a nerve, seemed a challenge. "I got trouble," Alex said, "but he's got two black eyes. You guys come over to offer help?"

"No, no!" Watkins said. "I ain't fightin' all the Mexicans for no California boy." His voice was shrill, nearly a parody. It made Alex smile. Watkins was a clown in his way.

"We wanna get outa here," JoJo said. "Split."

Watkins turned his head and glared. "We decided *I'd* tell him, huh, man?" He waited for JoJo's nod, then said to Alex, "Would you like to make it outa here?"

"I haven't thought about it . . . not seriously anyway. *Everybody* thinks about it some."

"Well, man, put some serious thought on it and let us know."

"I couldn't think seriously on it without knowing what you've got in mind. Right?"

The duo looked at each other; then JoJo touched Watkins' sleeve and made a head gesture. They would talk it over alone.

■

No sooner had the pair turned away when the supervisor's state car came down the road, braking when it got to Scouts' recreation area. Alex got up and hand-brushed the seat of his pants. It was time for the extra duty. He was ten feet from the car before the man got out. The supervisor waved to Mr. Hoffman and gestured that he was taking Alex.

Fifteen minutes later, Alex was on an eighteen-foot ladder with rags, Bon Ami, and water. A couple of free cooks and helpers were still in the kitchen, but the vast mess hall was empty and silent, an atmosphere conducive to reflection while working. Maybe the trouble with the Chicanos (it wasn't all of them, just Chango's friends and those who put *La Raza* over everything) would go away if he played it soft and watched himself. They might cool off, go on to other conflicts and enemies. What the fuck, it was just a chickenshit fight and Chango was in the wrong.

Escape! It was harder than it looked. True, the front lacked even a fence (but the sides and rear, which had fields and orange groves outside, had fences and rolled concertina wire), but it was a heavily trafficked boulevard in a business neighborhood, and every citizen knew the reform-school clothes. Blacks and Mexicans really stood out; the town of Whittier was lily-white. No escapee would last long walking down the sidewalk in broad daylight. At night they were locked in the cottages. When they marched around after dark, to the auditorium or gymnasium, there was a chance to bolt for it. This was done sometimes, but Alex knew he didn't run fast enough. The boys in Greenleaf Cottage, who wore all-white uniforms and were close to parole, were sent after those who ran. Several of them sometimes walked along with a cottage just in case. A capture of a runaway and the "close to parole" became "immediate release." And a cottage that had no runaways for thirty days got a picnic or movie. Then, too, the men of Whittier State School knew the terrain. Unable to walk the streets, the runaways had to follow riverbeds and railroad tracks. The men knew these routes and sat watching them when boys were missing.

After getting away, what then? Alex had nowhere to go, nobody to help him. Without such things he would surely be caught sooner or later. It was far past the era when a young boy could live on his own. Still, the vision of a few weeks or months of freedom, just wandering the streets where every new dawn was the possibility of an adventure, was dizzying to imagine.

He made no decision that night, and by morning he had forgotten, at least on the conscious level, the offer of a hunted freedom. Other things intervened; nothing of serious consequence, but enough to snatch his attention. On the detail grounds he saw Indio point him out to another Chicano. Alex's stomach knotted and turned queasy, part fear and part anger. That afternoon he kept watch between classes and on the crowded detail grounds, keyed up to start fighting if anyone made an aggressive move. Nobody, not Chango, Indio, or their friends, came within twenty feet of Alex.

After recall and count he could relax. Or mostly so. In the cottage was Constantine. Thus the day and early evening were dominated by acting tough—or actually being tough, for he was ready for trouble. But in the privacy of his room at night, the pain of it all, of being other than what he wanted to be, geysered up and put tears in his eyes. What kind of a life was this? In institutions, fighting all the time, being ruled by men who used authority for whim and caprice? It was shitty. That's what. Plain shitty.

The pain and wet eyes soon hardened into deep, defiant anger.

15

the next friday afternoon, during class recess, Alex went to the latrine at the end of the corridor. As he stood at one of the half-dozen urinals, he instinctively glanced over as someone came to the next one. He didn't know the name, but the face was one of Chango's clique. The boy's facial muscles were twitching, giving it away that it was a trap.

Alex spun, frightened. Chango was sneaking up behind him. Indio was coming through the door.

"Okay, you Paddy punk motherfucker. You got it coming."

Alex retreated along the wall toward a corner. He had no chance to win. He had to get past them out the door. In another three steps he'd be cornered. They were waiting for that. He sensed it somehow.

Suddenly, he lowered his head, partially raised his hands, and lunged forward.

The unnamed Chicano snatched at his arm, but Alex jerked it loose and spun like a football player. Chango kicked at him, trying for the testicles but hitting his thigh. Alex shoved him, taking the force from a blow Chango was also throwing.

Indio was blocking the door, but instead of tackling Alex with a shoulder, bringing him down for the others, Indio sidestepped and grabbed a sleeve with one hand, swinging with the other.

The sleeve ripped, and the swing glanced off the top of Alex's head.

Alex hit the latrine door with both hands and exploded into the corridor. Behind him the trio screamed challenges. "Come back, you scared punk!" and, "We'll get your ass, you sissy!"

Ten steps later, Alex stopped. The entire episode had taken a few seconds, yet he was breathing hard from excitement and exertion. He was neither afraid nor hurt, but emotional pain made him want to cry. He suppressed that feeling with anger, meanwhile fumbling with his torn sleeve, trying to make it less visible but unable to concentrate on this simple act because his thoughts were tumbling and incoherent.

He was still breathing faster than normal, still collecting himself, when the bell rang and he went back to his seat. That afternoon he did no work; he didn't even read. He looked at pages and thought about what to do. . . .

■

"So what's your idea?" Alex asked. He was between Joe Altabella and Watkins while they paced back and forth down the right-field line of the softball diamond. It was after the evening meal.

"It's like this," Watkins said. "You're a housecat. During the day you've got a chance to get the chain off the locker-room window downstairs. Right?"

Alex nodded.

"On Wednesday night you stay down to separate the laundry. We sneak downstairs and go out the window—"

"Here's the best part," JoJo interjected.

"—out the window and over to the landscape building, not over the fence. There's a furnace underground with a little room. I loosened some boards and stashed water and candy bars and two packs of smokes. We hide there until the next night and walk off. They just look for a few hours."

"Anybody else know about it?"

Watkins shook his head.

"Sure? You know someone'll snitch if they know."

"I'm tellin' ya . . . ain't nobody knows nuthin' 'bout nuthin'."

"You wanna go, man?" JoJo asked.

"Lemme think about it."

"How long?" Watkins pressed.

"I'll tell you . . . at breakfast. Is that cool?"

"Cool enough."

The conversation with JoJo and Watkins had been impulsive. During supper, Alex had poked at his food with the spoon (the only utensil allowed) and brooded, his thoughts mixing anguish and anger. When the cottage marched afterward to the recreation field, he'd seen the two boys, and escape seemed the answer. The streets were far away from his troubles—the troubles for which he had no answer.

But during the talk he'd imagined what some would think: that he'd escaped because he feared Chango and friends. That would be a taint in this world, and he would be back, eventually. Return was inevitable, sooner or later. And it *was* fear—in a way. Not physical fear not exactly. He might get ganged up on and beat up, but he would survive and had no real dread thereof. His fear was of living constantly with tension and incipient violence. That's what he wanted to run from, just so he could lie

down somewhere in the grass and relax, without Constantine, and
Chango, and other youths wanting to be "bad" more than they wanted
anything. Thus he'd approached the duet. Yet while they talked he visualized Constantine gloating, maybe even saying: "He ran 'cause some
beans were after him. He's probably a punk." Imagining that made Alex's
face burn; he would fight all of them. Fuck 'em. If only *that* would end the
necessity of being perpetually on guard, an animal with risen hackles.

When the whistle blew for the boys to line up to march to the cottage, Alex was still undecided. It was dusk, the reddish twilight blanket-
ing a hush on the world. An early evening breeze stirred the trees,
making the leaves rustle and sometimes fall. As Alex marched, he looked
at the sun-reddened cumulus clouds in the sky. A formation of birds
were black clots too high to determine what kind they were. A longing
coursed through the boy, a bittersweet pain that had elements of loneliness but was really beyond articulation. He had nowhere to go even if he
got away; nowhere and nobody, so in the end he would be caught.
Nonetheless, he suddenly decided to go. An escape would also be a
search for something. Whatever *that* was, he would never find it locked
up. Out there every dawn would offer a new challenge and adventure.
Anything might happen. Fuck 'em if they thought he'd run from fear.

When the boys took off their shoes outside the cottage (they went on
stockinged feet indoors), Alex was gleefully excited. As soon as they filed
into the locker room, each boy depositing his shoes in a numbered box,
Alex touched JoJo's arm, winked, and whispered, "I'm going with you."

"Cool, man, cool."

■

The locker-room windows had twin frames that opened outward. A short
chain connected the twin windows in the middle, keeping them from
opening enough for anyone to climb out. On Monday, Watkins stole a
pipe wrench from the plumbing shop. On Tuesday morning, while Mrs.
Hoffman was upstairs with the other housecat, Alex used the wrench on
the hasp where the chain was attached, working it back and forth until,
with a loud *pop*, it snapped free. He froze, waiting to see if the noise got
anyone's attention. When nobody came he attached the chain with a
piece of wire, hoping that nobody would look for the next thirty hours.

That afternoon, Alex saw Indio in the education building hallway.
The Chicano was going the other way and didn't see Alex, who was
wrestling with his rage, tempted to use this chance to attack with surprise. He could tap Indio's shoulder, and when Indio started to turn . . .
But the satisfaction would get him sent to Jefferson Cottage, the pun-

ishment unit, and ruin the chance for immediate freedom. Still . . . His indecision lasted long enough for Indio to turn into a classroom, erasing the chance for revenge. It was just as well, he decided.

Following supper, at recreation, the trio of escapees walked off by themselves the moment they were dismissed.

"It's ready," Alex said. "All ready for tomorrow night." Welling up in him was happy pride. He spontaneously draped an arm around Watkins' shoulder and hugged him.

Instantly, in reflex, Watkins jerked and threw off the hand. The gesture was so sudden and intense that Alex blushed, startled by his reaction. He'd forgotten how tangled were such matters in reform school, where freshly pubescent boys were without girls, and where there was an obsessional dread of being thought a *punk*—a punk being one who was buggered. Any touching of buttocks was cause for an immediate fight, and the paranoia extended sometimes to any touching whatsoever, especially where affection was conveyed. It was a weird world where trivialities caused brawls, and if a boy didn't follow the standard, his manhood was suspect. Watkins was obviously more confused than most.

Silently they went to the pepper tree near the road. Alex sat down, his back against the trunk. JoJo sat in front of Alex, shielding him from the Man while Alex took out two cigarettes wrapped in toilet paper. He split a paper match in half and lighted one cigarette. They passed it around, keeping it hidden in a cupped palm, shaking it to stop smoke from being visible—and they watched Mr. Hoffman thirty yards away.

"Was it easy?" JoJo asked. "Bustin' the chain?"

"Yeah . . . but the fucker sounded like a gunshot when it broke . . . if only nobody notices." While speaking, Alex eyed Watkins, but there seemed no residual hostility from the indignation of minutes ago. Alex wouldn't make the same mistake.

"So now what?" Alex asked, deliberately deferring to Watkins.

"Tomorrow night . . . half an hour after we go upstairs. You'll be downstairs, won't you?"

"Yeah. Counting dirty shorts and socks."

"Hoffman's off. The relief man will be upstairs. We get someone to call him down a hallway away from the stairs. We go down, grab our clothes and shoes, and go out the window."

"Are we gonna dress there?" JoJo asked.

"We should put on shoes, at least," Alex said. "Might step on something."

"You can be dressed," Watkins said. "We'll see how it is then."

"Sure sounds easy," JoJo said.

"It is . . . that part anyway," Alex said.

"I told you about the water and stuff down there, didn't I?"

"Yeah," Alex said. "I got some smokes, too."

"I wish we had some money," JoJo said. "It's a thirty-mile walk into L.A. We could catch a bus when we get to another town."

"Maybe we'll hotwire a car," Watkins said. "Tomorrow night when it's dark . . . so the cops won't see it's a kid driving."

"Can you hotwire a car?" Alex asked.

"Sure, man! Me and my brother done it fifteen, twenty times. He usually drove 'cause he's older."

"I can drive," Alex said.

"Good, man, good."

The conversation became boyish fantasies of what they would do in the free world. JoJo's family—actually, his pretty teenaged sister—would hide them. The Altabellas owned a big, old frame house in the Italian section of San Pedro. A rear cottage was rented out. Besides two garages and a pigeon coop, there was a shed with a cot and sofa. An alley behind the property would let them come and go pretty much unseen by neighbors. Their "plan" was to stay at JoJo's for a while. When they got some money they'd buy an old pickup truck and go to northeast Oklahoma, in the hill country near the Missouri border. "Yeah, man," Watkins promised. "My uncle's got a cabin out in the boondocks. We can live there as long as we want, do some huntin' and fishin'. We can even get work around the farms. And there's lots of cabins around that nobody uses except a couple weeks a year. They all got food in 'em, so we ain't gonna get hungry. . . ."

The boys' minds embellished reality. Alex saw the plan as within possibility. It might be possible to stay away forever. After a couple of years the California Youth Authority would forget them—and when he turned twenty-one they couldn't keep him anyway.

Elated expectation enthralled them when Mr. Hoffman split the air with his whistle. The fifty youths began moving toward the road and forming ranks. Alex's group was farther away than most and straggled a little. They weren't late, but they were last—and they were still talking and laughing.

"Hurry the fuck up," Constantine yelled. "You guys are holding up the works."

As always, Constantine grated on Alex, causing him to clench his teeth until his jaw muscles were rocks. But tonight it was easier to pass it off, because after tomorrow night nobody would be yelling at him, or giving him orders. He even smiled at Constantine while going by.

Seven evenings a week the boys were allowed to shower if they so desired, but on Wednesday and Saturday it was mandatory. They exchanged bed linen, underwear, socks, and towels, and were checked off a list. By nine P.M. it was finished. Wearing nightgowns, wet hair shining and pressed down, they lined up and marched upstairs to their rooms. It was another hour until lights-out.

Alex remained downstairs, confronted by piles of dirty laundry. He still wore his clothes, except for his shoes, because he was expected to sort out, count, and bundle the dirty laundry. Although the boys were supposed to sort their own, it was inevitable that socks and jeans got in with sheets and towels. Despite the escape half an hour away, Alex did his work, counting out sheets (the laundry would return *just* that many) and stuffing things into laundry bags. He did it mainly to keep his mind off the main event. Yet he heard noises from upstairs, some of them making his heartbeat race. He heard muffled voices and footsteps, and occasionally a raised voice.

He did enough work so that the relief man would think everything was normal (in case Watkins and JoJo didn't show up); then he got Watkins' and JoJo's clothes and brogans from their lockers and put them in rolls next to the window. Only eighteen minutes had gone by, but to Alex it seemed several hours. Every small sound stiffened him. Several times he thought he heard someone coming down the stairs, but it was his imagination—and when they really came he heard nothing until they appeared in the doorway. They were so close together that JoJo stumbled into Watkins when the latter stopped.

"Nobody see you?" Alex asked.

"Nobody," JoJo answered. "We had two guys start raising hell on the end of the hall."

"There's your clothes," Alex said, pointing. He then went near the doorway to hear any possible pursuit.

"Let's get dressed," JoJo said. "I don't dig runnin' around in a fuckin' nightgown."

"Yeah, yeah," Watkins said.

They stripped their nightgowns over their heads and began throwing on clothes, ignoring the underwear and socks.

"Put 'em in your pocket," Watkins said to JoJo. "You can wear 'em later."

JoJo nodded, breathing audibly from excitement. Both boys were frantic, fumbling with metal buttons on pants.

Alex waited near the doorway, watching them and glancing out. Now they were on the floor, pulling on their heavy shoes. Footsteps sounded on the stairway outside.

"Shhh!" Alex said, gesturing with raised hands for emphasis. They froze, looking at the door.

Constantine came in, wearing nightgown and slippers. "What's happening here?" he asked, but his face registered that he knew.

Nobody answered. The two lacing their shoes sat motionless. If Constantine summoned the Man, they would spend the night naked in a stripped cell and the next few months doing road-gang work in Thomas Jefferson Cottage. Alex, too, was near panic—for a few moments. But when Constantine looked at him, he'd realized that a yell wouldn't be heard upstairs, and Constantine wasn't leaving this room. Maybe Alex would have trouble alone, but three of them could surely overpower him.

Constantine read Alex's eyes, and the confident smile dissolved. He started to edge backward, but Alex took a long stride, grabbed Constantine's nightgown front with both hands, and swung him around, deeper into the room, so now he was more or less surrounded.

"Hey! What the fuck!"

"What the fuck! Your ass."

Watkins and JoJo had scrambled up, shoes on but untied.

"We should stomp your ass," Alex said, his pleasure at this power making him forget momentarily freedom's imminence.

"Why, man? What'd I do?"

"You're a fuckin' fink, that's why."

"I'm no fink, man."

"Whaa! What the fuck are you, then?"

"It's my job. I wanna go home as quick as I can."

"So you fuck over other people."

"Easy, Alex . . . cool it," Watkins said, gently touching Alex's shoulder. "I know Constantine. He's okay." He patted Constantine's shoulder; only Alex could see the wink.

Despite the wink, Alex wanted to plant his fist in Constantine's eye. The codes of the underworld were becoming Alex's own, written on his forming personality by his experience. By the code, Constantine was a stool pigeon, even if some thought otherwise because of his *job*. . . . He couldn't interfere with them, or get out to sound an alarm— so fuck him. . . .

"Look here, Connie," Watkins said. "We've got an extra pack of Luckies. No use takin' 'em. We can get plenty out there—"

Now the blood was pounding in Alex's head. The Luckies were in his pocket.

JoJo had finished lacing his shoes and was tucking in his shirt. He was conscious of his appearance no matter what the situation. "Hey, man, you won't give us up to the Man after we're gone, will you?"

"He's not gonna do that," Watkins said. "That wouldn't be right after we give him the smokes."

"I wouldn't anyway," Constantine said. "I do what I do 'cause the Man's watching."

"Here, man," Watkins said, extending his hand to Alex for the cigarettes. Alex realized that the hillbilly wasn't stupid. Watkins had seen that the danger from Constantine was *after* they were out the window. There was no way to stop that by force short of murder. Alex handed the cigarettes to Watkins, who gave them to Constantine.

JoJo was by the window. "Man, let's go," he said, unfastening the wire, the chain clattering as it fell free.

"I better get back upstairs," Constantine said, but he didn't move until Watkins nodded approval. As he went out one way, JoJo was in the window to go out the other.

As with all institutions, the grounds had many bright lights, making pools of brightness, many overlapping. Where there were shadows, they were deep black.

The escapees came out behind shrubbery next to the cottage. The greenery was already damp with night dew. It sprayed on them as they crept along the side of the building, bending limbs that sprang back. At the end of the building they couldn't be seen from the upstairs windows when they took off across a lawn toward an institution road, through floodlit brightness to darkness beyond. This was the shortest route.

"We'll circle around the recreation fields to get to horticulture," Watkins said. "It'll take a few minutes longer, but it's away from the buildings. Some fool might look out and yell: 'Check this!'"

"Yeah, yeah," Alex said, having acknowledged silently that Watkins was the leader, at least for now.

"Go," Watkins said. They crashed from the bushes together, running low across the wet lawn, throwing elongated shadows in the bright lights. In half a dozen seconds they were in the safety of darkness. Again they were in bushes. These were next to the fence around the superintendent's house. They could see it, a two-storeyed brick cottage. To Alex it was a mansion. The lights were on downstairs, and a night breeze wafted the sound of music to the fugitives.

Watkins led them around the outside of the back yard, and across a patch of dark lawn between the rear of the hospital and the fence. Then they were on the recreation fields, three in a row, all slightly larger than a softball field. Beyond the last was a storm fence. The vocational landscaping area was on the other side, separated from the farm. Here was half an acre of canned infant shrubs and trees and flowers. A greenhouse was attached to a small office and, on the other end, to a wooden double door a few feet aboveground. The door went down to the underground furnace.

They scrambled over the fence, the sound racing along it as the fence rippled. It seemed loud and goaded them into action.

Alex dropped first, one foot crashing into a small plant, the stick snapping. "Shit!" he said, crouching and trying to fluff it up.

"C'mon, man," Watkins said.

At the door into the ground, Watkins pulled a pin and lifted the door from the wrong side. The padlock was still closed. The space was about eighteen inches wide, but that was enough for three boys to slide in on their stomachs, swinging their legs down to the ladder. The firelight from the furnace cut the darkness enough to see silhouettes and shapes. It was hot down in this hole. The furnace took most of the space, but Alex found room to lie down on the concrete. The others did the same next to him.

"You sure they won't look here?" JoJo asked.

"They didn't the last time somebody was missing. I left a thread across the door for a month and checked it when those two Mexicans from Roosevelt beat it. The lock's outside. They probably look at it."

"Where's those cigarettes?" Alex asked. "You gave mine to that . . . fink rat bastard."

"Yeah, yeah, I know you didn't dig it—but what the fuck could I do? We had to stop him from snitchin' the minute we were gone. When we had him jammed, we could kick his ass to keep him quiet, but after that . . . My brother, he's in Leavenworth, said somethin', 'You gotta kill a stool pigeon or kiss his ass. Ain't no way to get around 'em.' Me, I didn't wanna kill Constantine, so I bribed him. It seemed to work. Wasn't nobody out chasin' us. Right?"

"Yeah, right," Alex said grudgingly, thinking that this semiliterate Okie was older than everyone else in Whittier. Watkins didn't think like a kid. Nevertheless, Alex couldn't decide whether or not he liked Watkins.

The cigarettes came over while Watkins talked. JoJo also lighted one.

"There's water and candy bars," Watkins said.

"Any Snickers?" JoJo asked.

"Yeah, but you're not hungry now, are you?"

"I want a candy bar."

"Okay . . . but when they're gone, they're gone. We got a dozen, and that's what we eat at least until tomorrow night."

"Shhh," Alex said. "Voices carry at night. We don't know when they're up there."

"Right," Watkins said. Thereafter they talked in whispers. But conversation was meager. They lay side by side, heads resting against the concrete wall, feet toward the furnace. Alex had misgivings when he faced that he had nowhere and nobody to go to—not alone. Without their connections he could only wander around for a few days, until he was too dirty and too hungry, and then the police would swallow him. He'd learned that much from his prepubescent runaways. Even with money he couldn't rent a hotel room, not a young boy. At some future time he might be a successful fugitive in an intense manhunt, but not now. Not without the help JoJo and Watkins had.

Yet it would be worth it if he got a few months of freedom, especially if they were really *free;* then he could take the punishment and extra incarceration. Despite the tension, or perhaps because of it, he dozed off amid these thoughts. The furnace's proximity made him dream of sunbathing and sweating on a beach—sea, sun, sand, and water.

A hand was over his mouth. Another shook his shoulder. He jerked his head and came awake, instinctively struggling to breathe freely— until his mind registered the circumstances.

"Shhh," JoJo whispered, lips almost touching Alex's ear, jerking a thumb upward.

Voices of indecipherable words drifted down. Then came the clanging sound of a gate being opened. Seconds later the padlock rattled.

All three boys held their breaths, waiting, but after the padlock everything was silent. Moments later the gate clanged again. It was obvious the searchers were gone, but the boys remained quiet just in case.

Three hours and half a dozen cigarettes later, all of them sweating profusely from the heat, JoJo said: "Fuck this, you guys. Let's make a move now. By tomorrow night I'll be shriveled up—dehydrated."

Alex, too, had been fretting with impatience.

"Whaddya think?" Watkins asked.

"Fuck, man," Alex said. "It's gotta be three or four in the morning.

They're probably done looking already. I ain't got no eyes to stay here all day. And the man *might* come down here."

"Okay, let's try it. We'll stay off the roads if we can . . . and duck when we see headlights. By morning we'll be a few miles away."

"Let's have another smoke and put the show on the road," JoJo said.

Which is what they did. They squeezed out the way they had entered, the sweat turning to goosebumps in the night breeze. Alex fought down shivers while waiting for the others to emerge.

Bending low at the waist to minimize visibility, they trudged through the reform-school's fields—first the beets, then next a cornfield, where they had to protect their faces from the crackling, dry stalks. At the end of the cornfield was a dirt road just inside the fence. The fence had rolled concertina wire along its top, except at the rear gate. There it was just three strands of barbed wire sticking straight up. On the other side was a privately owned orange grove—and freedom.

The boys crouched in the cornfield, watching the gate.

"Let's go," Watkins said.

"Hold it," Alex said. "We oughta wait here awhile, I think."

"Why?"

" 'Cause they ain't damn fools, and it's obvious this is the easiest place to climb out. They could be watching."

"Man, make up your mind. You wanted to get going instead of waiting. Now you wanna wait."

Alex tossed a shoulder. "Fuck it. Do what you want."

"You guys wait."

Alex hesitated, feeling it was a challenge to his courage. The moonlit night seemed peaceful and unthreatening. Crickets serenaded.

"We'll be right behind you if it's cool," he said.

Watkins moved farther back into the cornfield and urinated. He moved away from them to a more direct run at the fence. He sprinted out and leaped. The fence began rattling instantly, a loud sound in the still night.

"HOLD IT!" screamed a voice. Two men burst from the cornfield only twenty yards away, flashlight beams bouncing as they ran.

Watkins had his hands at the top, one leg up. But he didn't get the other leg above their grasp. They tore him down. A flashlight beam whipped through the darkness as it was used to club the struggling boy.

JoJo turned to run, but Alex grabbed his shirt collar and jerked, sitting him on his rump. Alex wanted to help Watkins, but he knew it was hopeless without a weapon, and none was within reach.

The men bent Watkins' arms behind his back, doubling him over, cuffing him on the back of the head, demanding: "Where's your pals . . . where's your pals?" Meanwhile they dragged him down the road.

When they were a hundred yards away but still visible, Alex patted JoJo's back. "Now we go. C'mon!" Without waiting for a response, he leaped up and ran to the gate, springing high, his fingers curling over the top, but below the barbed wire. JoJo hit the fence a moment later.

"There they are!" one man yelled. "Goddammit! Stop!" They were too far away for anything more than yells.

Alex's pants cuff caught on the wire. He tore it loose. A barb raked his calf, but he ignored it. He poised on top, gathered himself, and leaped, landing in plowed dirt. JoJo grunted as he landed a moment later. Alex was already running into the trees. "Run, motherfucker, run!" he said, now enveloped by the darkness of overhanging foliage.

The dirt was soft and loose and seemed to grab at their feet. Alex's leg muscles quickly began aching. JoJo was falling behind.

A dirt road ran through the orange grove. Alex turned down it, now able to run faster. Hot knives cut into his lungs when he sucked in air. Soon, however, he stopped, ducking back into the trees. JoJo caught up and stood bent over at the waist because it was easier to breathe. Alex knew that speed wasn't the answer. The men would sound an alarm, and no matter how fast they ran, the institution's automobiles were faster and could cut them off. In minutes those who'd caught Watkins would send pursuers, and they would know the terrain, whereas Alex had no idea what was beyond the orange grove. He knew they had to keep moving yet avoid what the hunters would expect.

When they had partially regained their wind, Alex started down the dirt road, alternately trotting and walking fast. JoJo was a few paces behind. After a quarter of a mile, they turned back into the trees, angling back toward the institution. A highway, Alex recalled, ran beside the east end of the reform school and this orange grove. The hunters would expect them to be much farther away. If they could cross that highway right next to the institution, the land on the other side was undeveloped, a rolling landscape of sandy earth, some cactus, and dry bushes—a home for jackrabbits.

Ten minutes later they knelt in the tall, wild grass on the reform-school side of the road. The sweat of their exertions met the predawn chill and turned to goose pimples and shivering. They waited ten minutes for a break in traffic big enough where nobody would see them cross, but the rumbling diesel trucks and whippeting automobiles kept coming. The boys moved to the shoulder and dashed across, momentarily illuminated in headlight beams. It wasn't the authorities, because the car kept going.

On the other side, they slid down the embankment into a drainage ditch, where ankle-high water was hidden by greenery. The mud sucked at their shoes, and when they stepped out they were soaked and filthy halfway to the knees.

Fifty yards later Alex felt safe. They stopped to rest and think. Looking back, he could see the line of orange on the horizon, heralding the new day. It had been a long night, and ahead was a long walk, but by dusk they would be at JoJo's—if they carefully stuck to railroad tracks and riverbeds. They were already so dirty that they would raise eyebrows trekking through suburban streets.

"C'mon, JoJo, ol' pal," Alex said. "We got a long hike, so we might as well start." He offered a hand to the seated JoJo, helping him to his feet. It was an effective gesture; it perked up the Italian youth.

16

the reform-*school* escapees reached the sanctuary of JoJo's home as the street lights came on. The boys moved cautiously down the rutted alley behind the house, slipped through a latched gate on a rickety wooden fence, and then crouched behind steel trash barrels next to the pigeon coop. They watched the back door. JoJo had wanted to strut up and surprise them flamboyantly, but Alex's caution prevailed. Although two teenaged boys wouldn't warrant a police stakeout, they were worth detectives asking a neighbor to call in if they were seen. Alex recalled it happening to other boys.

The wait in the back yard was brief. Teresa Altabella, the pretty older sister, came out to empty the garbage. The family dog (a mix of German shepherd and beagle) accompanied her. He sensed the boys and began barking and jumping from side to side. Teresa dumped the sack and called the dog. She was reaching for his collar when JoJo called her name. She jerked, startled, uncomprehending until JoJo called the dog's name, "Hey, Kilo!" and the dog recognized the family member and went into joyous paroxysms of barking and jumping.

Teresa came into the darkness, calling her brother's name.

"Is it safe? No cops around?" JoJo asked.

"No, nobody's here but me."

"Where'd they go?"

"To the movies . . . *Dragon Seed*."

They entered the house and went directly upstairs to JoJo's room, which had one window overlooking the street. They stripped off the soiled reform-school clothes for things in the closet. When Alex had begun his institutional odyssey he was too young to care about style in clothes, but pubescence was changing that. Now the right plumage was important, both for looking good to girls and being correct in his milieu. This was essentially a poor, inner-city milieu, and although the particular block was Italian, the neighborhood was mostly Chicano, and to be "sharp" a youth had to follow their styles. It was just toward the end of World War II, when the boys in white suburbia wore Levi's and leather flight jackets, but in the barrios of Los Angeles, youths wore khakis or surplus marine fatigue pants with giant patch pockets down the thighs. Sometimes they were dyed black, and often they were topped with surplus "Eisenhower" jackets, with patches removed and also dyed black. The shoes had a plain capped toe and extra soles, and horseshoe taps on the heels. They could not run in such shoes, but they could kick. . . . The extreme zoot suit had gone, but slacks were "semis," loose at the knee and narrow at the cuff, and jackets had large shoulder pads.

JoJo had a full wardrobe, and although he was huskier than Alex, some of the girth had come since he went to Juvenile Hall, and Alex could wear most of his clothes. After a quick rinse in the shower, Alex dressed and looked in the mirror on the bedroom door while combing his hair. He massaged in a heavy dose of Dixie Peach pomade, which partially came out in his comb as he fashioned an upswept ducktail and flipped curls down over his forehead. He liked what he saw. It was a far different image from that of the eleven-year-old who had run away from the Valley Home for Boys some two years ago. All he needed was a tattoo or two—a cross with three dots in the flesh between thumb and forefinger, and maybe a beauty mark on a cheekbone beneath an eye. Some guys put a cross on their foreheads, but that was too extreme.

JoJo took a longer shower after Alex and dressed himself much the same way. Alex, propped on the bed, watched his confederate comb the curly hair and thought how good-looking he was. It was obvious that Teresa adored her brother. She made them tuna salad sandwiches and brought them up with a quart of milk. They were gulping them down when the headlights of the family car sprayed across the front of the house, flaring momentarily in the window. The horn honked, unnecessarily announcing the arrival of the family, and then the motor went silent. Teresa started for the door.

"Don't tell 'em we're here," JoJo said.

Teresa stopped, hand on the knob. "Why?"

"Well . . ."

"Lisa's going to come up here, so—"

"Tell her . . . and we gotta tell Mama pretty quick, but the old man—he don't need to know. No tellin' what he'll do."

"Mom got the call from the reformatory this morning, but she wasn't going to tell him—at least not till they went out to the movie. She knew he'd use it as an excuse not to take her."

"What difference would that make?" Alex asked.

"*Anything* might make a difference," Teresa answered, moving from the door to gather the pile of dirty clothes. "I'll burn these."

When she went out, Alex was both sorry and glad. Whenever she looked at him with more than a glance, his face got hot and his tongue thick and unwieldy. This was the first girl he'd talked to since puberty, which had changed his fantasies and hungers. Teresa Altabella was pretty and prematurely enticing, with full breasts, a tiny waist, and full hips and thighs. It was enough to discomfit many adult males, much less a thirteen-year-old who had seen no girls for a long, long time. He knew that she was thirteen from JoJo, and, when asked, he'd told her that he was freshly fifteen, blushing even more hotly at the lie.

When she was gone, JoJo explained that his parents weren't happy, not that there was any chance of their separating. They didn't do such things. But Joe, Sr. was from the old country, and didn't care about anything but making money and babies. He owned a dozen small apartment buildings in the slums. He'd put three thousand dollars into a unit in 1934, and when he had enough equity, he borrowed against it to buy another; the peasant understands the value of property more than the middle class does. Nevertheless, he kept working as a meat-cutter for a supermarket, taking all the overtime they offered. His wife, born in Brooklyn, thought they should enjoy life, that he should buy her nice things and take her out. At thirty-eight Lorraine was young enough to want some fun. She didn't want to bear more children, whereas babies were also wealth to him.

Even at thirteen Alex knew enough, had read enough, to know that the Altabella family was somewhat bizarre. Despite that, he felt the underlying warmth between them. It felt good, the belonging. It felt even better when he thought of Teresa—she with the soft brown eyes and quick smile and breasts uptilted in an off-the-shoulder peasant blouse. He stared at her compulsively when her gaze was elsewhere, but the moment their eyes touched, his dropped to his shoes.

The older Altabellas slept in the large downstairs bedroom at the rear of the house, while the three children had two small bedrooms upstairs. The house roof slanted to a peak, making it much smaller upstairs. There was a small bathroom and the two bedrooms, nothing else. In fact one had to go through the girls' room to reach JoJo's.

Teresa went downstairs and returned with her eleven-year-old sister, Lisa, for whom no genes of beauty had been left. With eyes set too close, teeth needing braces, and a nose both big and hooked, she caused her mother to worry that she wouldn't find a husband. Lisa was still too young to feel much pain about her homely face. Now, when she burst into the room, she was visibly afire with joyous excitement. She leaped up and hooked her arms around her brother's neck, and he swung her around several times while she screeched and kissed him.

Never had Alex been told that men rise to their feet as courtesy when women enter a room, so he hadn't moved from the bed, back against the headboard, legs extended. He was moved by the love flowing between the handsome older brother and homely little sister.

"Alex, meet my baby sister, Lisa."

He nodded, still on the bed. "I met you on the visiting grounds a couple of weeks ago."

"Oh yes, I remember! You had a Boy Scout uniform." She turned to JoJo. "When I saw *you* in a Boy Scout uniform I nearly started laughing."

"Yeah," JoJo said, grinning and shaking his head. "And the old man was fuckin' *proud* of me in it. It didn't matter that I was in reform school . . . I was a Boy Scout."

"Lisa," said Teresa, "you're Daddy's favorite, so maybe you should tell him about JoJo."

"Why tell him?" JoJo asked. "Mom has to know, but he's gone all day, and he never comes up here or goes out back. He goes from the dinner table to the bedroom—in a straight line."

Teresa shrugged her indifference, and it was thus decided. At least for now, Joe Altabella Senior would be kept unaware that his son was more or less at home. The way the house was arranged, with the master bedroom at the rear downstairs and the stairs at the front, JoJo and Alex could come and go, even with Joe, Sr. home, without being seen. During the day, when Joe was gone, they would exit by the kitchen door into the back yard and through the gate into the alley, emerging on a busy boulevard a block away. This route made it unlikely that neighbors would see, just in case the police had someone watching. At night, when Joe was home, the darkness would protect them from possible eyes as they went out the front door.

On the second day, a pair of juvenile detectives came to ask the mother if JoJo had contacted his home. (She shook her head no, silently saying a Hail Mary to expiate the lie.) They also asked her to call them if he did. They promised not to hurt him if she turned him in.

But on the first night, totally exhausted from the tension of the escape and the thirty miles of trekking, Alex unintentionally fell asleep fully dressed on the bare mattress of JoJo's bed. It was around midnight, and they had turned the radio on, tuning in a popular music disc jockey who broadcast from a South L.A. drive-in, and who took dedications over the phone. Alex's interest in the love songs of popular music had risen almost simultaneously with puberty. The real music to him, however, was the mellifluous voice of Teresa. She was telling JoJo about mutual friends and about his girlfriend, Connie Gianetta, who kept asking when he was coming home. Alex was a listener, entranced because such talk was totally new to him. He failed to see the banality because of his age. He listened while lying comfortably on the bed, totally comfortable, even though he was dressed and the mattress was bare. Sleep clubbed him down without him asking for it. He dreamed of Teresa. It was the first time dreaming of a girl—or at least the first time he remembered in the morning. It was a flash of a dream: she was lying beside him, fully clothed, though he could feel her body arousing him. Her mouth was on his face, so warm, so very warm, and he moaned with longing for the open mouth and hot, sweet breath. Those were the fragments he recalled in the morning.

■

Also in the morning, JoJo had two twenty-dollar bills. He'd crept downstairs in the wee hours and took them from his father's wallet.

"Man, I've been gettin' him since I was nine years old. It's the only way to get a nickel from him—steal it. Shit! He don't even give Mom grocery money. He does the shopping."

"You don't have to convince me, JoJo," Alex said, sensing from the tone that his approval was important.

"And he's fuckin' rich," JoJo said. "We live in this fucked-up neighborhood when we could be somewhere nice. Ah, man! I'd do anything to meet some of those chicks from Hollywood High and Beverly Hills High, even if they are mostly Jewish chicks . . . who don't fuck around. Lana Turner went to Hollywood High. Did you know that?"

Alex shook his head, and chuckled. "That don't mean they all look like Lana Turner."

"Naw, but they are fine, fine, fine . . ."

"So what're we gonna do today?"

"Whatever we do, it's gotta be better than what we were doing. Right?"

"No bullshit!"

A light knock on the door preceded Teresa's entrance. A tight, white turtleneck sweater accented her breasts, and a tight gabardine skirt did the same for her derriere and thighs. She also wore the mandatory white and brown saddle shoes and bobby socks. "Daddy's gone to work. We'll tell Mom you're here now."

"Okay," JoJo said.

"What're you dressed up for?" Alex said impulsively, then blushed. The blush worsened when she replied, "I go to school. Remember?"

"We'll be down in a few minutes," JoJo said.

"Not me, man," Alex said. "This is a heavy scene and I'll just get in the way."

"I want you to meet her."

"Yeah, sure, but not right now this morning. We've got time." Alex gently but firmly pushed JoJo toward the door. "Go on, see your mom."

Teresa had left the door ajar moments before. She was visible through it in her bedroom, leaning slightly forward while drawing her mouth in the heavy red lipstick of the time. While passing her to reach the stairs, JoJo slapped her backside, not hard enough to hurt but enough to make her arch perceptibly forward. JoJo's footsteps clattered on the narrow stairwell while Alex stood in the doorway between the two bedrooms, watching Teresa and wondering what to say when she turned from the mirror.

She pressed her lips together, joined the lipstick tube together, and her eyes met his via the mirror.

"You're sure pretty," he said, half tentative, half blurting.

She smiled and glowed with it. "Thank you."

"I'll bet you've got tons of boyfriends." He cursed the comment the moment it was in the air. His feeling of stupidity grew when she continued to smile without replying.

"Do you?" He pressed because the silence was worse.

"I guess boys like me. I wouldn't say *tons* though."

"Anyone special?"

"Mmm, yes, I guess so . . . sort of."

"Oh . . ."

"I haven't heard from him in a couple of days. Which is kinda weird. He comes by nearly every day, and calls once or twice." She was obviously musing aloud; then she pointedly added: "He's half Chicano and half Irish. His name is Wedo. Wedo Murphy. He'll be seventeen next week. A real sharp guy."

The information wilted sprouting fantasies. He'd known that any girl this pretty and developed would have boyfriends, but a seventeen-year-old was virtually an adult. A thirteen-year-old, even one passing as fifteen, was no competition.

"Oh, oh, wow!" she said suddenly. "I gotta go. I'm already going to be late—again. God! I wish I could quit."

She was an explosion of energy, grabbing books and things, pausing for a last long look around to see if anything was forgotten. Then she was gone, leaving a smile and a "see you later." Her scent and her presence lingered, at least Alex thought so. The pleasurable nervousness and the sort of ache was something new—and he recognized what he felt. He went into JoJo's bedroom and looked through the window as she appeared below, went through the gate and down the sidewalk, finally moving beyond his angle of vision. He remained looking long after she was gone. Everything was bright and clean in the sunlight. The neighborhood was a poor working-class one, but there were postage-stamp lawns and occasional palm trees, jutting high and tilted. Somewhere a carpenter was already pounding nails, the sound of the hammer carrying clearly in the morning air. Alex suddenly longed to go out into the sunlight and see the city. He wanted to look for experience.

Sometime later JoJo came rushing upstairs. Alex was on the unmade bed, reading an old *Esquire* he'd found. JoJo was obviously happy.

"It went good, huh?" Alex asked, putting down the magazine and sitting up.

"Oh yeah . . . but she's all fucked up . . . happy to see me, scared to death 'cause I'm on the run. She wants to meet you—and you're welcome here forever as far as she's concerned."

"You'll have to tell your old man, too."

"Who? He doesn't have to know."

"What happens when he goes to Whittier to visit?"

JoJo's grin turned blank. He hadn't thought of the visits. Two Sundays a month the family went to Whittier. After a ticking silence, he threw off the problem. "So we tell him. He ain't gonna turn me in, that I know. So fuck it, why worry? Let's go out somewhere. I'll show you San Pedro. It's a beautiful day."

"That sounds real good to me. What've you got in mind?"

"Well, man, I thought we might check out the neighborhood, get some reefer—I can get some good, fat joints for half a buck apiece. How's that sound?"

"Sounds good to me." Even under torture Alex wouldn't have admitted to never before smoking marijuana, nor that he had fears of it while wanting to be initiated. All the sharpest guys in Whittier talked about getting high on weed and, yes, another thing: breaking open Benzedrine inhalers for the saturated strips inside. He had to try that, too.

"Can you roll?" JoJo asked.

"Roll?"

"Yeah, roll cigarettes, joints." JoJo made a hand gesture to indicate.

"Oh yeah," Alex said, then laughed inwardly, recalling that he'd learned to roll cigarettes by hand in Camarillo. It already seemed a long time ago. For a moment he wondered what had happened to Red Barzo and First Choice Floyd.

"Good," JoJo said. "I gotta learn how. I use a little pipe now when I can't get somebody to roll 'em. It's a lot cheaper to buy it loose instead of joints already rolled. Man, I can get a lid, 'bout fifty joints, for eight bucks, if it's loose."

"So let's get it that way. But let's go. Fuck, I didn't split from that place to look out windows. Maybe we can go downtown to a movie."

"No, no, a flick is risky in the daytime. Truant offiers check 'em out 'cause every kid playin' hooky goes to a flick."

"Yeah, you're right. I didn't think. But there's something we can do."

"We'll go to the pool hall, get that weed. Then sort of play it by ear. You hungry?"

Alex shrugged. "Yeah, sort of. We got used to regular meals in there."

"I know a good Mexican café where they give up *huevos rancheros* for sixty-five cents."

"What's *huevos rancheros?*"

"Mexican-style eggs . . . with chile and refried beans. It's good."

"Yeah, it sounds good."

"Let's get moving before the breakfast hour is over."

■

Fifteen minutes later they slipped out the back way into the alley. High board fences, some sagging, hid them from the adjacent houses and any possibly curious eyes. At the corner they turned onto the sidewalk of a hillside street. The slope was not severe, but the hill overlooked the Los Angeles harbor beginning two miles away and stretching to the distance. The bright morning sunlight turned the calm harbor waters into molten gold. "Man, that's beautiful," Alex said.

"Well, let's go down to Cabrillo Beach when we get that weed and eat."

"Yeah . . . good idea," Alex said, standing another few seconds to look at the panorama, suffused with awe so potent that it ached. The anchored ships were strewn across the water; some still wore the paint of war. Others were drab, long tankers, or bulky cargo ships with booms. One was huge and white, with a giant red cross on its side and across its top. The arc of the shoreline had a conglomeration of structures, the otherworldly silhouettes of an oil refinery next to giant silver oil-storage tanks. Shipyards were there, with drydocks and giant cranes that reminded Alex of prehistoric birds—and in the distance the skyline of Long Beach glinted in the sunlight.

"Let's go, man," JoJo said. "Any cop 'round here knows me."

At the bottom of the hill was the main business street, thick with

pedestrians. Alex looked at the faces, all of them intent and serious on
their own business. He wanted to scream out his happiness at being
free and able to see the world. It was a street primarily of the poor, with
small markets, a day-old bakery, small men's shops, and a Goodwill
store. The pool hall entrance was down an alley off the boulevard. Of the
six tables, two were for snookers, and just one of the six was in use.
Four Chicanos dressed much the same as JoJo and Alex were playing. It
took a minute for the newcomers' eyes to adjust to the dimness after the
outside brightness.

"Eh, JoJo!" one of the quartet said loudly, stopping the game.
"When'd you raise, man?" He shook hands and patted JoJo's back.

"Hey, Rico, baby. I didn't raise. I split. Me and this dude here."

The conversation paused while JoJo introduced Alex to Rico, and
the two shook hands. The other three players watched for half a minute
and then ignored what was going on. It was a lot of protocol for
teenagers, but these youths lived in a harder world than those of the
middle class. Alex felt the dark eyes studying him as he shook hands.
Rico was slender, fighting acne, his age anywhere from fifteen to eighteen.

"Got any grass?" JoJo asked.

"*Quantos?*" Rico asked.

"A lid . . . half a lid. Not joints."

"Go to the Toledo, man," Rico said.

"Got change, man, for a twenty?"

"Hey, brother, you gettin' rich." Rico turned and spoke Spanish to
one of his associates. Then to JoJo: "We got change."

Alex waited while JoJo went to the men's room at the rear, followed
by Rico and the Chicano he'd spoken to in Spanish. The other two ignored Alex, and he ignored them, meanwhile rolling a billiard ball across
the green velvet of an empty table to have something to do.

The trio was gone for one minute. When they came out, Rico came
over with JoJo and spoke to Alex. "I got a cousin in Whittier, man. JoJo
says he's a friend of yours. Lulu Cisneros from Temple Street."

Alex's face lighted up with a grin. "Yeah, man, Lulu's my buddy. He's
a good guy."

"How's he doin'?"

"He's doing all right—all right as you can do there. He did have a
motherfucker of a fight with Spider Contreras from Eastside-Clover.
One of the baddest fights I've ever seen. They punched toe-to-toe for
five minutes—wingin' punches from the shoulder. It was even. But Spider is supposed to be a *duke.*"

Rico listened, grinning, the anecdote of courage and toughness a thing of pride. "When does he raise?"

"He goes to the Youth Authority board in a couple months . . . October, I think. He should be out for Christmas."

"Yeah, man, cool." The Chicano offered his hand, and Alex took it, nodding and winking. "If you need anything," Rico continued, "come on by. If I'm not here, one of these guys will be . . . and they'll know where to find me."

"Thanks, man," Alex said, then glanced to JoJo, who gave a head motion of "Let's go."

As they walked toward the door, Alex felt good at being accepted by Rico, hence Rico's friends.

■

The marijuana was in a paper bag stapled at the top.

"I hope it ain't full of stems and seeds," JoJo said.

"We'll see when we get where we're goin'."

"We're goin' to the beach, remember. Let's get something to drink. Weed makes my mouth dry."

"That's a good idea."

"How's ale sound? It's a lot more potent than beer."

"Yeah, that's cool, too."

They found a wino leaning in the doorway of a flophouse hotel. For half a dollar (he could buy Muscatel) he took their money into a liquor store and came out with two quarts of ale and a bottle opener. Then they took a nearly empty bus two miles to the stop for Cabrillo Beach, where they had to walk down a steep sidewalk.

Part of the beach, to the right, faced the open sea, but on a right angle to the left the beach was behind the giant seawall that created vast Los Angeles Harbor—the largest man-made harbor in the world.

The beach café and small museum of oceanography were at the bottom of the street, near where the breakwater separated sea from harbor. So, too, were most of the people. The beach open to the sea was small because the cliffs came down to the water a few hundred yards northward. But the beach within the harbor was two miles or more in length, several hundred yards wide beneath the cliffs of Fort Douglas McArthur (sic). Nobody trekked very far up this beach, or at least Alex saw nobody, and the sand touched by the tide wasn't marred by recent feet.

Alex removed his shoes and walked barefooted on the hard-packed damp sand. Because it was within the seawall there was no real surf, just softly lapping water at low tide exposing the harbor's flotsam cast upon the shore to the high-water mark. The two boys trudged and drank the ale. Eventually they reached where the beach curved sharply away from the cliffs. Ahead was a fence jutting into the water. Beyond was private property and a yacht marina, a line of floating docks with myriad pleasure craft tied up side by side—everything from a twenty-foot cabin cruiser to a hundred-foot motorsailer, though the largest yachts were anchored offshore. Another man-made breakwater of granite blocks separated the marina from the vastness of the harbor.

Beneath the seventy-five-foot cliffs of the fort they found an empty antiaircraft gun emplacement. The cannon was gone, but the pit, trenches, and sandbags remained, though one already had leaked its contents into the wooden slots of the floor. They went down a ladder and were out of the wind. It was a good place to roll the joints, and an old newspaper was found to do it on.

They dumped the marijuana out, ground it down in their hands, and then shuffled it on the newspaper so the seeds separated from the rest. Alex rolled the joints, using one paper, which made JoJo frown—most persons used two papers, he said. "That's 'cause they can't roll," Alex explained.

When they lighted up, Alex inhaled as he would a regular cigarette.

"Man, are you sure you smoke grass?" JoJo asked.

Alex's face burned. "Whaa? Man, you saw me roll these joints. What the fuck do you think?"

"Yeah, well . . ." JoJo inhaled deeply, sucking the smoke as far into his lungs as possible, making the necessary sucking sound of the deep toke.

And Alex watched, obliquely but intently, so when the joint was handed back he knew what to do. He fought back the cough as the strange smoke burned his throat and lungs. He held the smoke in and handed the joint back.

Three times they passed back and forth, and suddenly Alex could feel the elevation in his mind, in his whole being, in fact. A sudden laughter or chuckle, senseless yet hilarious, started somewhere inside and burst from his mouth. JoJo grinned in sympathetic unison.

"Oh wow, man!" Alex said. "I'm high!" The words seemed to echo and resonate; they seemed almost visible.

"Good weed, man," JoJo said, blowing on the joint so the orange tip glowed brightly.

The statement and gesture looked strange, yet wonderful. Everything, in fact, looked strange, both more real and less real.

JoJo upended the green bottle of ale, some of the liquid leaking from the corner of his mouth as he guzzled. He finished, handed it to Alex, and belched, grossly and happily. Alex drank deeply, came to the end of the bottle and pitched it out of the hole. It would join other bottles and cans on the beach.

Alex was unaccustomed to alcohol and its effects—and in a short time he was *really high* for the first time in his life. He tried to study how he felt, as if a chamber of his mind was watching detachedly, yet struggling not to be sucked down into the vortex. His eyelids were weighted, and his eyeballs needed rest. Yet everything looked cleaner, clearer, new and different. His being seemed to soar, and he couldn't find even private articulation for what he felt. It was true that his lenses of perception were more open, with colors brighter and truer than ever before. Every sound had a unique tone, a musical quality that entranced him. Suddenly, as before, an urge to wild laughter welled from deep in his belly. It carried JoJo along, so both of them sat laughing loudly and privately at nothing on the beach in the waning afternoon sunlight.

"Hey, man, this is *good* pot," JoJo said.

"Yeah, it's pretty good." The understatement seemed hilarious, and there was another gale of laughter.

Time was lost, but soon enough Alex's thoughts began to slur; his head spun and his stomach followed. Nausea was next. He vomited on the wooden slats and the dirt. He tried to kick dirt over the mess, but the earth was too hard.

JoJo watched, eyes blurred, a grin on his mouth.

The vomiting made Alex feel a little better and lessened his inebriation. In fact, he felt good. The earlier fear of the unknown—of what marijuana would do—had gone away. Now he flowed with the high and luxuriated in the sensations. He wanted to go somewhere, but nowhere specific. "C'mon, let's walk."

They climbed the steps and walked along the hard-packed sand toward the populous area around the beach café and the beginning of the breakwater.

The marijuana increased his fascination with looking at things. He stared avidly at everything, registering freshly what usually would have gone unnoticed. "God, look at 'em," he said in awe, watching the soaring beauty of seagulls in flight. "Nothing flies more gracefully."

"Or shits on more things," JoJo said; the high was obviously different for him.

On the breakwater, which stretched for about three miles, a few fishermen watched lines draped into the harbor side. The seawall was made of huge granite blocks. It was wider at its unseen base beneath the water. It rose in steps, and was flat (roughly so) and five feet wide at its top. The waves and tides rose and fell against it.

"Let's take a hike out there," Alex suggested.

"Why? What's there?"

"Just to see."

"Man, I can see everything from here."

Alex made a snorting noise of disgust and shook his head. JoJo had understood from the beginning and now dropped his act. "Okay, I know," he said. "I can understand—but I don't wanna go. So why don't you go, and I'll go over there"—he pointed toward the large, low stucco building containing the small marine museum and café—"and get myself something to eat."

The tide was out, so the first thirty yards of seawall were on the shore. Alex walked gingerly; the granite blocks weren't flush to each other, and sometimes the cracks were large enough for a foot to slip inside. About fifty yards out the waves began crashing against the barrier, throwing foam and spray high above the parapet, then backing up to try again. What really fascinated Alex was how they came at an angle, the explosion of collision starting in the distance and racing down the wall toward him, then going past while another assault began far away. Sounds of roar and hiss jumbled with the raucous cries of countless seagulls.

Alex was suffused with scrambled feelings. He looked up at the scudding clouds, then studied the rolling wild sea on one side and the oily, smooth water on the other. Although he was young, he'd both experienced and read a lot, and he now saw a metaphor for life in sea and harbor and breakwater—and he knew he wanted to live on the wild sea, not the polluted harbor. He also knew that his destiny was to be an outlaw, a criminal. Indeed, it was already branded on him and within him. It was already too late to turn back. Strangely, the recognition made him feel free, and good, deep inside. He began laughing; it was soundless against the sea's roar.

■

When he went back toward shore, JoJo was waiting at the start of the seawall.

"Damn, I thought you fell in and drowned," JoJo said. "You ready to go home?"

"I dunno. When's your sister get there?"

"You got eyes for Teresa, huh?"

"Man, I mean—bong!"

"Yeah, I guess so. Everybody says it. But a guy can't see his sister like that . . . know what I mean?"

"Yeah, I know."

"Oh yeah, I think she got a new boyfriend while I was in Whittier. I heard her talkin' about him to Lisa when they visited me. He's like us, been in trouble, and I think he's sixteen or seventeen."

Alex said nothing. The odd part was that he'd barely met Teresa, and nothing besides her attractiveness had led him to the mild fantasies and speculations.

JoJo took a different route to the house, staying down near the harbor, shortcutting through the yards of canneries and along docks where fishing boats were moored. Across a ship channel was Terminal Island, where many big ships were drydocked. "Man, last year I used to go over there to sell newspapers. One time a big troop transport came in. I was damn near the only one on the dock. A whole division of G.I.'s was hanging on the rails. One guy wanted a paper—so I threw it up and he threw me half a buck. Then they all started throwing money down for papers. I only had thirty-five and wound up with better'n twenty bucks."

They finally turned away from the harbor, heading toward the houses clustered on the sides of hills which rose two miles away. In between was an undeveloped area, the roads sometimes were dirt. The land was mostly vacant lots with high weeds and discarded trash. But when they came over a low rise, ahead was a chain link fence around several acres. Within the fenced acreage were big, gray life rafts knocked together with flotation drums and wood. Every cargo ship and tanker had carried several during the war, augmenting the lifeboats. Now they were surplus.

"This is new. I never seen it before."

"Let's go in and see what's what."

The fence was low for agile youths, and the area was unguarded. Curiosity and zest for adventure had them inside in seconds. The huge rafts were stacked on top of each other. They climbed to the top of one stack to see what was in it. They found storage compartments with waterproofed packages of emergency rations, C-rations, chocolate, and tiny packs of cigarettes and matches. Medicines, flare guns, and other valuables had been removed.

They also found dye markers and three big, gray cans with pins like hand grenades and writing on their sides. They were orange smoke bombs—to be thrown overboard far at sea whenever a ship was anywhere on the horizon. They took two of the cans, simply to do something, and climbed back over the fence.

Half a mile away, in high weeds next to some railroad tracks, Alex put one can down and pulled the pin, jumping back quickly. At first it sputtered inside, and then the unimaginably bright orange smoke issued forth. Initially it came slowly, but it quickly gained force and density. Within thirty seconds it was geysering thirty feet into the air. The can began spinning with the force of whatever was going on inside. As it rocked the smoke came out more thickly. It also stayed thick as it rose—now sixty feet in the air.

"Wow!" JoJo said. "That fucker sure does kick out the smoke."

"And it smells like shit, too." Indeed, a vagrant gust of air had carried the acrid, lung-searing smoke to Alex, making him duck away.

They both heard the siren. The scream of it grew rapidly. They knew it was coming to the orange smoke. Whether it was a police car or fire engine made no difference. Either one would grab them—if they were available. They ran, Alex carrying the other smoke canister tucked under his arm like a football. They went over a rise, around a corner, and now they slowed to walk down an alley. The siren went silent, indicating that the vehicle had reached the cause of the smoke. The boys looked back every few steps, just in case, and also watching the orange smoke still hanging in the air behind them.

"Get rid of that," JoJo said, meaning the canister. "If they cruise around and spot us when you got that . . ."

"They're not gonna do that. I'm keeping it. I've got an idea."

"What idea?"

"Wait until we reach the pad. I'll tell you then."

■

The following morning they found the market they wanted—not too big, but not a mom-and-pop corner grocery either. This one had two cash registers (just one was operating) and four employees on duty. It was a hot, hazy day, and they watched the market until the afternoon, going in twice to buy Dr. Peppers and stand beside the case while drinking them.

Just before the closing hour, they came back with the canister of orange smoke in a paper sack. They stopped around the corner of the building.

"What if they ask what's in the sack?" JoJo queried nervously.

"So what? Show 'em and don't do nothing. Just come back and we'll find another place. It ain't like you had a gun or something. They won't know what's in your *mind*. Right?"

"Yeah, it sounds right, but—"

"But shit . . . Get going before you think too much."

Alex gave him a hug and a shove. JoJo sighed and went around the corner into the market. The girl at the cash register glanced up for a second, then went back to her newspaper. An aproned stock boy putting cans on a shelf didn't even glance up. JoJo went down one aisle; then turned back to the empty aisle closest to the cash registers. He was trembling as he opened the top of the sack and pulled the pin. He put the can down so quickly that he almost dropped it, and then hurried toward the rear. He was at the end of the aisle when the fizzing noise started, followed by spluttering noises—after which the orange smoke belched forth. As the day before, the beginning was small, but each passing second added to the smoke. It was at the ceiling and spreading swiftly when the first voice cried: "Hey! What's that?" And there was fear bordering on panic in the voice.

"Oh my God!" said the girl.

At that moment Alex came in, stepping to the side. Nobody saw him because they were watching the smoke, frightened but not knowing what they confronted.

"GAS!" JoJo bellowed from the rear. "IT'S MUSTARD GAS!"

The scream was the catalyst. They ran for the front door, the young woman going over the counter without dignity but with remarkable agility. They were all galvanized by panic.

In another ten seconds the entire store was filled with orange smoke. It poured out the front door.

Alex had a wet handkerchief over his nose and mouth. He was just a few feet from the cash register. He bumped into the checkout counter, went over it and felt for the cash register. He took a breath; it burned his lungs. He punched the buttons. The cash drawer came open and he stuffed the contents in his pockets, first the paper, then some coins. He had to breathe again; it was worse this time. He dropped to his belly. Some air was within a few inches of the floor.

He stumbled blindly for the front door, knocking over a display of cold cereal. Panic strained to control him, the deep fear of being unable to breathe. Then he saw the patch of light indicating the front door. He stumbled out into the sunlight.

The rapidly increasing crowd was already two dozen persons, both passersby and employees of adjacent shops.

JoJo was in the forefront. He grabbed Alex's arm, pulled him away from a clucking, concerned woman, who kept asking, "Are you okay? Are you okay?"

Alex's lungs still burned, and he kept coughing, but he also kept going, nodding and saying, "I'm all right, all right." He and JoJo were passing people heading toward the smoke. Once they were around the corner, Alex began laughing. He felt wonderful.

Back at JoJo's, they locked themselves in the bedroom and Alex pulled the money from his pocket and dropped it on the bed. It was three hundred and ninety dollars, not a bad score for two young boys.

27

the next day Alex and JoJo went shopping for clothes. JoJo bought one garment, an off-white blazer with flecks of tweedy red in it—and no collar. The cardigan sport jacket was "in" that season, at least in their milieu it was. It had heavy shoulder pads and tapered to a close fit at the fingertips. Alex bought the same jacket in powder blue. He also bought other clothes. Now the packages were spread across JoJo's unmade bed, some opened, others waiting. It made Alex feel good to have new, sharp clothes—and he also still had over seventy dollars of the loot from the smoke-bomb caper. Last night he and JoJo had taken Teresa and one of her girlfriends, half-Chicano, half-Italian, to a movie theater where their crowd hung out in the left balcony. When JoJo began necking with the friend, Teresa allowed Alex to put his arm around her—but she gave no sign that he could go further toward intimacy. So he sat, his muscles beginning to ache after a while—but he still refused to move it. It was the first time he'd been with a girl since puberty made him feel differently about them. From Teresa's softness, from her scent and his half-formed fantasies, he got an erection—but that part of longing he fought down. He was terrified that she'd notice how his pants were bulging. He was sure that she never went that far; a girl worth loving never did, or so he thought at thirteen. His ultimate dream at the moment was to neck with her, something else he'd never done. But she gave him no opening, so he contented himself with the warmth of her shoulder under his hand. He knew that she was being faithful to her steady boyfriend, Wedo—who still hadn't appeared or been heard from. Teresa was obviously angry at him—or worried about him; her attitude changed several times during the day. When they went out for hamburgers and milk shakes after the movie, she obviously had forgotten Wedo for a few minutes. She was a girl who glowed when happy.

Afterward, Alex had trouble going to sleep. Teresa kept jumping into his mind, amplified by the occasional soft sounds from the adjacent bedroom—especially by the music from the all-night disc jockey specializing in romantic ballads of the era: "Sentimental Journey," "For Sentimental Reasons," and "To Each His Own."

Because sleep came late, it lasted late. Teresa was gone to school when Alex awakened. It was JoJo's idea to buy the clothes. Now Alex was unpacking what he'd bought when the unusual noise came up the stairs. They could hear voices, but the words were indecipherable. Once Lorraine's laughter burst forth clearly.

"I think that's Wedo," JoJo said after a couple minutes.

"It ain't the cops or she wouldn't be laughing, would she?"

"I don't think so. Lemme go check."

While JoJo's feet were clumping on the wooden stairs, Alex recognized the painful feeling in himself as jealousy. In his short life he'd been envious of things that other people had, but nothing had this combination of hurt and anger.

He finished unpacking the clothes and stuffed the brown paper in a wastebasket. The clothes he left on the bed in a neat pile. He lighted a cigarette and looked out the window to the street below.

The cigarette was near its end when Alex heard footsteps on the stairs. He turned. Wedo was leading the way, JoJo at his heels.

"Hey, man, you're Alex, *que no?* I'm Wedo." His hand was extended and Alex shook it, surprised by the gesture. Most youths he met merely nodded when introduced.

"So you split from Whittier, eh? That's cool, man. Fuck 'em in the ass." Then to JoJo, "When's my chick gettin' here?"

"She gets outta class at three-fifteen. We'll call the Kit Kat to make sure she doesn't get hung up there."

"Yeah, cool," Wedo said. "Say, you got any c-c-clean socks. My feet are *phew.*" He held his nose to illustrate.

JoJo got socks from a dresser drawer, and while Wedo changed into them, telling his story, Alex watched the newcomer, fascinated. The earlier jealousy was gone. He liked Wedo immediately.

"Yeah," Wedo said, running a finger between his toes before slipping on the socks, "the fuckin' heat stopped us over on Soto and Marengo. Jive motherfuckers! Just 'cause it was five *vatos* in the *ranfla.* They wouldn't've fucked with no rich Paddy-boys in a high-rent district, *verda?* They found eight joints next to the car—not in it. The fuckin' punks couldn't pin 'em on anybody, so they slammed us around, one at a time, three or four to one. Anyway, they didn't have anything to file except a drunk and disorderly. I told those *putos* I was eighteen, so they took me to Municipal Court. The judge gave me five days, and the fuckin' cops left me in the drunk tank at Lincoln Heights . . . full of punk winos with d.t.'s and shit. Some of 'em were cryin'. . . ."

"That's a bummer," JoJo said.

"What if I told 'em my right age—seventeen? Sheeit! I'd be in Juvenile Hall six weeks before seein' the judge." Wedo pulled his shirt away from his torso and put his nose down inside the collar. "Phew!" he said. "I gotta get home and get a bath and some clean clothes."

"You can take a shower here."

"Naw, *ese.* Hank's got his car outside. I know my mother's outa her mind right now." Wedo laughed, as if picturing the hysterical woman. "I gotta let her know I'm okay. I just wanted to see Teresa—but she ain't here. So tell her what happened . . . and all that shit. I'll give her a buzz later . . . or come back."

Alex had listened and watched intently. Wedo talked fast, with an occasional slight stutter and much emotion, and with an occasional word of *pachuco* Mexican thrown in. Did he have trouble with English? He didn't look Mexican. Wedo meant "light-skinned," but Wedo didn't have any Indian features, and all Mexicans had some Indian forebears. Wedo had thin, sharp features on a narrow head. He wore the ubiquitous ducktail, though now his hair jutted out wildly in some places; pomade was unavailable in the jail. His clothes were dirty and he had the stubble of a developing beard. He bordered on being skinny, but it was a muscular skinniness.

An automobile horn bleated from in front of the house.

"That's Hank . . . with his balls in an uproar. I gotta split. Why don't you *vatos* come on? We'll cruise and fuck around. . . ."

JoJo shook his head. "Naw, man. I gotta stay and do somethin'."

"What about you, Alex?" Wedo asked. "You wanna fuck around?"

The invitation was total surprise, and he replied with total impulse. "Yeah, I'm game—for anything."

"Well, let's split, man. We might get back here later."

■

Following Wedo down the sidewalk to the car, Alex was filled with anticipation of adventure. The car was a black '39 Ford convertible customized according to the fashion. Both the windshield and the canvas top had been "chopped," so the roof was very low. Nobody mentioned the decreased visibility—how it looked was what mattered. This was a really sharp car, Alex thought, the black bodywork gleaming from many coats of paint and wax. The wheels had chrome spinners. It was the first time Alex had ridden in a peer's automobile, and it made him feel good. It was a sign of getting older, the way to greater freedom of choice and experience.

Hank was husky and swarthy. He nodded at the introduction as Alex slid in beside him and Wedo took the outside.

"Where to, man?" Hank asked. "I can't fuck around too long right now. I gotta be at work, you know. Payin' this car off keeps me on the ball."

"Well . . . fuck . . . cruise by Metropolitan. I know some fine chicks there from the west side. And I gotta check in."

Alex didn't care where they went. He felt gloriously adult. He leaned back and devoured the city scenery. The dingy streets of East Central Los Angeles seemed beautiful. Unlike the slums of other cities, where the poor were stacked in tenements like sardines, in Los Angeles they were just as likely to be in a bungalow or duplex—and no matter how ramshackle, it was in the sun with a palm tree on the street in front.

Alex liked how teenaged girls ogled the car. Wedo flirted with two waiting for a bus, offering them a ride. They giggled but declined. Hank didn't even look, and when the traffic light turned green, he released the clutch and pushed the gas. He spoke very little, and Alex wondered about him. He looked to be eighteen and had a dark shadow of a heavy beard. He drove fast, accelerating hard from each stop, braking equally hard on every red light. It kept Alex keyed up, but he also enjoyed the excitement.

As they crossed the city, Alex learned that Metropolitan was a special high school. Its students attended as little as four hours a week and had permits to hold jobs the rest of the time usually spent in school. Wedo had a permit but no job. He was supposed to attend school six hours a week, but it was rare that he attended six hours a month. In fact, he hadn't been in a real class for half a semester—and under the circumstances the Board of Education had no way to force him. His mother couldn't even understand the papers they sent.

"Wedo, man," Hank said as they turned down the last block, "I'm gonna have to leave you here. I gotta get to work."

"Where do you work?" Alex asked.

"At the *Examiner,*" Wedo answered. "He takes proofs around to the department stores—proofs of their ads—to get them okayed."

"That sounds like a good job," Alex said, and he meant it. For a moment he imagined himself having a car like this and a job like this; it was all he wanted to change his whole life.

"Usually I don't make the run until later, but this is for the Sunday paper and they run it early."

"Okay, man," Wedo said. "I don't wanna hang you up, *ese*. We can come by later on, *que no?*"

"Sure . . . you been there before."

"Yeah." Wedo turned to Alex. "Hank here got me a way-out picture of John Dillinger, a big, glossy thing." He shaped his hands to show a ten-by-twelve photo. "He sure looked square, Dillinger, I mean. His hair was short and parted . . . and he wore a square suit with a necktie."

"It was a different time," Alex said. "You know, man, styles change. A couple years ago everybody was wearing full drapes, now it's semi's."

"Yeah, right. I didn't think of that."

Hank pulled to the curb in front of the brick administration building. Alex and Wedo got out and the customized Ford pulled away, tires screeching.

"Wait here," Wedo said. "I'll be about ten minutes. Then we can go to my pad so I can change my rags. Is that cool?"

"Okay, fine."

Wedo disappeared through the tall doors and Alex loitered on the sidewalk. He really liked Wedo, who seemed so smart and confident— and he also liked Hank. It was so good to be free, away from institutions and able to do precisely what he wanted. Moreover, he was being accepted by youths several years older. They were almost grown men. He would never let them know his real age, not by word or action. He would make them respect him by their own standards.

The fifteen minutes became half an hour, and still Wedo failed to reappear. Alex began to fret. He felt conspicuous standing on the empty sidewalk, and he got scared when a black-and-white police car cruised past, the uniformed passenger eyeing him. He felt sure they would have stopped and asked why he wasn't in school, except that he was standing in front of one. Policemen were suspicious of youths with long, duck-tailed hair.

A minute later, however, the bell rang, and within seconds the doors flew wide and a multitude spilled out, hiding him in the crowd. Cars went by filled with students. Metropolitan was the only school of its kind in the Los Angeles School District. Its students came from everywhere, a polyglot collection. Nobody more than glanced at the boy lounging against a wall. Wedo exited as one of the multitude. He was shaking his head in apology as he came over.

"*Carnal*, I'm sorry. That fuckin' *ruka* made me go to class."

Alex moved away from the wall, preparatory to departing. Wedo held up a hand in a gesture of restraint. "Hang on, man. There's a fine *gabacha* chick comin' out in few minutes. I wanna shoot on her."

So they waited, Alex copying Wedo's pose of propping one leg up on the wall, meanwhile flourishing a cigarette and commenting on the girls going by.

"Where you from?" Wedo asked.

"Here . . . L.A."

"What neighborhood?"

"I dunno. Fuck . . . all over in foster homes and military schools. Mostly in the Valley and Hollywood."

"Your people got money or somethin'?"

"Uh uh. I'm an . . . orphan." It was the first time he'd formed the word consciously—and doing so meant something painful that he rejected instantly. To Wedo it had no special significance. He just nodded. "How long you been busted?"

"'Bout two years."

Wedo whistled silently.

"I shot a guy in a burglary."

Now Wedo's eyes were wide, his head cocked. His was the world that admired violence. Alex had proven himself really violent by that world's standards. "You kill him?"

"No, just fucked him up."

Wedo nodded slowly, savoring the information, planning to ask JoJo if it was true. So many punks bullshitted about how tough they were. "I asked you if you were from a neighborhood 'cause you could go in the wrong one and get hurt. *Vatos* from Maravilla are after White Fence, Temple Street is at war with Alpine and Third Street."

Alex nodded, although he already knew the facts from reform school. Suddenly Wedo was moving toward a pale girl in ponytail, bobby socks, and saddle shoes. She blushed as he cornered her, some distance down. Her back was against the wall and Wedo leaned over her, one hand against the wall, his face close to hers. It was a position of capture and domination. The girl was husky; she would be fat at thirty. She had precociously large breasts encased in an uplift bra within a tight blue sweater. Alex imagined how they would look (his vision didn't match what would have been the sag of reality) and how they would feel against his chest. It dizzied him.

He watched avidly, wondering if he would ever be half so confident and relaxed with girls. Finally Wedo nuzzled the girl on the ear, whispered something, and touched her breast. She pushed him away, raising a hand in feigned readiness to slap. He turned away, laughing, and she was smiling, too. He had a street-hip walk, exaggerated by a slightly pigeon-toed right foot. It added bounce to his stride.

"Sorry, man, but her tits are—" He grunted in punctuation. "Besides, she fucks . . . she likes it. We might go by her pad tonight. Her folks go out a lot." He had started down the sidewalk with Alex beside him. "I live about six blocks away. We can wait for the bus or walk."

"Let's walk."

The neighborhood was mostly brick warehouses and garment factories, or other light industry. Occasionally a faded-gray frame house sat between the business buildings—a house with a sagging board fence, a dirt yard, and plants in gallon cans on the porch railing. In the window of one such house were three small flags with stars. One flag had a blue star. The others each had a gold star. Wedo pointed them out. "That's where a *camarada* of mine lived. His older brother got killed at Guadalcanal, so Ralphie lied and enlisted. They got him at Iwo Jima. Their mama went crazy. I was thinking 'bout joinin' the Eighty-second Airborne, but—" He stopped.

"But what? Your family won't sign?"

"I just got my mother—and she'd sign anything I gave her. I just don't read too well." The end of the phrase was very soft.

When they passed the neighborhood Catholic church, Wedo made the sign of the cross. "No use takin' chances."

Where Wedo lived in one room with his mother was a three-story wooden building that appeared never to have been painted. The bare wood was dark brown; it had been jerrybuilt forty years ago. The entranceway reeked of urine and Lysol, and up the stairs the hallways reeked of cooking odors impregnated in the walls.

When Wedo opened the door to the room, a stench assailed Alex and made him queasy. It wouldn't have been so distasteful if it hadn't been so heavy. It came from a homemade altar that covered a dresser and half a wall. Dominated by a crucifix, the tableau was jammed with icons, plaster saints, pictures of the Madonna, and dozens of candles. The stink came from years of incense and candles. Alex nearly gagged, but Wedo didn't notice.

"Where's the toilet?" Alex asked, wanting a chance to open a window to prepare himself for this ordeal.

"Down the hall to the right," Wedo said. "The last door. Here." He took a key from a nightstand table and handed it over. "We gotta lock it or the winos sneak in and sleep."

Alex took his time in the bathroom. When he came back, Wedo had changed clothes. The style was the same, but these were clean. More than clean, they were pressed faultlessly. His shirts hadn't been folded in drawers; they were on hangers and had military creases down the back.

He buttoned a maroon sport shirt to the very top, yet wore no necktie. Over that he put on a surplus Eisenhower jacket, patches removed, dyed black, and also faultlessly pressed.

"Say, man, look here," Wedo said. "My mom is worried like a motherfucker. I know her. She's out to church now—goes three times a day to *her Jesus*. I expected her to be here, but I gotta leave her a note. I ain't been around for a week. I don't write too good. Do it for me, *carnal.*"

"Gimme a pencil and paper."

The stub of a pencil was sharpened with a used razor blade. The paper was the back of an advertising handbill. The note neglected any mention of jail; it simply said that he was okay, would be home later, and she was not to worry. "It's silly to tell her not to worry," Alex said.

"I know it, but what the fuck . . . I gotta say it . . . just like she's gotta do it." Wedo took the pencil to sign his own name, doing so with filigree and curlicue. It was more than a bare signature. While it had letters, its origins were the specialized "mark."

Darkness reigned in the lower canyons between the buildings, though the parapets still reflected the sliding sun.

"So whaddya wanna do?" Wedo asked. They were on the sidewalk.

"I dunno. I'm with you."

"Got any *hondo?*"

"What's that?"

"Money, scratch, lace, bread, all that shit."

"Yeah, about seventy bucks."

"Damn, you rob a bank or somethin'?"

"Uh-uh, a market." Alex told the story of the canister of orange smoke. They walked while he talked. As he finished, he noticed that the buildings were taller. "Where we going?"

"To see if Hank's busy. We might borrow his car anyway. Drink some white port, smoke some *yeska*, and pick up a couple of sisters I know— fine young Chicanas with fat legs. Actually they're half-breeds. Their old man trains fighters."

The sprawling building housing Hearst's *Examiner* and *Herald-Express* was nearby, and they started walking there. En route, Wedo pointed out a furniture warehouse he'd burglarized by going through the skylight. He'd shot a flashlight beam down into an office; then he'd hung over the open skylight and dropped down. However, he hadn't seen that the office was glass-enclosed. He'd smashed through, landing terrified amidst a rain of glass. A shard had sliced something in his leg. He'd managed to get away, but the result was the slightly twisted right foot that gave him a pigeon-toed gait.

Wedo knew his way through the back stairways of the newspaper building. Alex waited in a stairwell until Wedo came back, shaking his head. Hank was out on his job for the next hour or so.

"Fuck it," Wedo said. "Let's go fuck around Main Street for a couple of hours. Check out the fruiters and hustling broads. We can come back later."

"That sounds okay, man."

Fifteen minutes later they were at Sixth and Main, where the neon was most garish and music spilled from the opened doors of sawdust-floored cocktail lounges. Some music was Mexican, heavy with guitars, raucous voices, and sadness; some was rhythm and blues; some was country and western, and some was the popular music of the era—Jo Stafford and Frankie Laine. The sidewalks were crowded with servicemen, whores, and homosexuals—and with those who preyed on all of them. The pungent odors from hot-dog stands mingled with the music. Alex inhaled the sights and sounds of raw life beneath the miltihued, flashing signs. He wanted to look at the photographs of strippers outside the Burbank Theater, L.A.'s burlesque house, but Wedo kept moving and Alex followed. An apron-garbed Negro at a shoeshine stand greeted Wedo by name, grinning to show a solid-gold front tooth. His own shoes were obviously very expensive, and a moment later Alex saw why. The shoeshine man slipped something into Wedo's palm, and then Wedo asked Alex for five dollars. "I copped some joints and a roll of bennies. Ever take any bennies?"

"Just once," Alex lied, certain that Wedo meant Benzedrine.

At the next hot-dog stand they shared an orange drink and washed down the flat, white tablets with the X on them. Alex hid his mild trepidation while waiting to feel whatever was coming.

"I know what we can do," Wedo said. "See a *camarada* of mine. He's an old *vato* about forty. He's been in the joint twice. Him and his old lady stay in a hotel over near Angel's Flight. Wanna do that?"

As with everything concerning Wedo so far, Alex agreed without a hesitant thought. They trudged more blocks, out of the bawdy area, through a darkness-abandoned financial district, and then up a sloping alley in a zone of seedy resident hotels. Wedo led them through a side door and up the rear stairs. The hallway's carpeting was worn beyond threadbare; one of the two bare light bulbs was burned out. Wedo moved silently despite the metal taps on his shoes. He scratched softly rather than knocked. Alex knew a hard knock would upset those within. He expected a man in a shoulder holster to crack the door, but when it was opened, it was by a haggard woman in her thirties. She wore a cheap cotton dress, and a dirty-faced toddler was holding the hem. In the corner a baby gurgled with its bottle in a dresser drawer converted to a crib. Through an open door the bathroom was visible; next to the door was a table with bread, eggs, canned food, and an electric hot plate.

"Hi, pretty Alice," Wedo said, giving the woman a hug and a peck on her cheek. "Where's your old man?"

"Charlie? God knows," she said, a note of bitterness in her voice. "He cut out two hours ago . . . said he'd be right back. He's probably waiting for the connection."

"Oh, Alice, is he fuckin' around with that shit again?"

She nodded and snickered. "We're in this goddamn bustout hotel with two kids, I go out hustling my ass, and he's fuckin' around with that needle again. I swear—"

"But he's your old man, baby."

"I don't wanna talk about it, especially around strangers. Who's this kid?"

"My pal Alex. You don't mind if we wait, do you?"

"No, find some room and get comfortable. Sit on the bed if you want." She started toward the bathroom, gathering an outfit of clothes from the bed, obviously intending to put them on. "There's just some wine, if you want a drink. Over there."

They poured one glass (they found just one glass) of unchilled white wine to share and sat on the edge of the pulldown bed, waiting for Charlie. During the wait, the Benzedrine tablets exploded, sending nearly electrical energy through Alex's body and brain. It wasn't like being drunk or on marijuana, but it was definitely "high." He felt more alive than ever before in his life. Thoughts raced through him pell-mell, but cleanly and precisely. He wanted to chatter like a magpie, but Wedo obviously felt the some way, and he got the floor first. The occasional stutter and the street Mexican inserts fell away for the most part. In slums, barrios, and ghettos, and even more so in reform school, there was a high premium on being able to fight, to "kick ass and take names." Conversation often revolved around violence. Alex now had his own tales of brawls and sneak punches to tell—but he'd never listened to anyone like Wedo, who apparently was the "baddest motherfucker" around, according to his stories. Now he was apparently incensed at someone named Don but neglected to say why. He got more fired up while talking, as if his own voice and the Benzedrine added to his fury. "I'll kick that punk motherfucker's ass . . . cocksucking punk!" He compared what he was going to do with other exploits in the past, describing in detail and with great relish how he'd punched this guy or stomped that one. Initially Alex listened without question, but twenty minutes later, when Wedo's mouth had foam at the corners, Alex felt that the talk was too extreme. Alex lacked an interpretation, but he wondered if something was wrong with his friend in this particular area. Wedo seemed obsessed with convincing the world how tough he was. Alex found his attention wandering to the dirty-faced toddler, who was playing with a toy truck on the carpet.

The knock on the door was nearly the same as Wedo's, a soft scratching. Charlie's voice followed, calling, "Alice."

Wedo opened the door and Charlie came in quickly, followed by a light-skinned, tall black man in a raincoat and processed hair. Charlie was small-boned, with a hooked nose and shifty eyes. His voice was slurred and husky as he was introduced to Alex. Wedo caught Alex's eye and winked.

Now the hotel room was crowded. The black man, introduced as "Dog" Collins, perched on a hard-backed chair near the door—and moments later his head sank on his chest. The cigarette in his hand dropped to the floor. Charlie picked it up and put it out.

"Hey, baby, I'm back," Charlie said, knocking on the bathroom door. The woman answered, but the words were muffled.

"So whaddya been up to?" Charlie asked.

"Fuckin' around. How you doing?"

"Same old shit, tryin' to make a buck. But the heat's on and we can't work the bus station."

"Charlie's one of the best short con men on the West Coast," Wedo explained. "He plays The Match and The Strap."

Alex nodded as if he knew what they were. "I know a couple colored guys who play con games. They were in the joint, too." When nobody said anything, Alex added: "Red Barzo and First Choice Floyd."

At those names, the nodding black man raised his head. "You know them suckers, huh?" ("Suckers" was said fondly.) "Where'd you meet them?"

"In Camarillo. They were takin' a cure."

"What were you doin' there?"

"Seein' if I was nuts. I shot some guy and the judge wanted to see what was wrong with me."

The Negro junkie grinned. "After fuckin' with them fools you probably went crazy."

"Alex split from reform school," Wedo offered. "Him and my chick's brother."

"Say, Wedo," Charlie said, "you said you wanted to learn to play short con. What happened?"

"Ah, Charlie, man—you know that ain't me. I can use force, but I ain't got the right kind of nerves for playin' no con game."

"What's 'short con'?" Alex asked.

"It's any con game that takes place all at once. I mean, you knock the mark in for whatever he's got in his pocket. We work the *sheds*, the train station and bus depot. People traveling usually have cash in their pockets. Ain't many of 'em come back across half a dozen states to testify. They don't get any money back. What's wrong now is that the bunco squad's got everybody's picture. The motherfuckers know us on sight so we can't work the *sheds*. I wanted to school Wedo so he could steer the suckers out to us."

Alex smiled and nodded as if thoroughly understanding; actually he had a mere glimmer of what Charlie was saying.

"I'd like to learn that shit—how to play bunco."

"No bullshit?"

"Sure. I'm interested in learning everything."

"Once you qualify a sucker, make sure he's right, it's like a script. You say something, your partner says something, you say the next line, and so on. Want me to run it to you?"

"Damn right—but I couldn't learn it this fast. We ain't got time right now. Can you write it down for me?"

"Yeah, in a day or two."

Alice came out of the bathroom and poured herself a glass of white wine. Alex ignored what Wedo and Charlie were saying, for he was glancing at the woman. She'd metamorphosed from drab slattern to brazen hussy. Clothes and makeup did it. Close inspection showed a pot belly pressing the satin dress, but she was still sexually attractive. Her body was good, her ass round, and the line of her panties showed. Alex trembled between his legs.

Finishing the wine, Alice put on a long coat, kissed Charlie on the cheek, and headed for the door. When she was gone, Wedo said, "Hey, Charlie, how come you stick that shit in your arm? It's killin' you. You could be drivin' around in a Caddy and livin' in a choice pad. Instead you're in this flophouse and your old lady's out turning tricks."

"Hey, hey!" Charlie said. "Get off my back, man."

"I know I got better sense than to fuck with that shit."

"You ever take a fix?"

"No."

"So how can you judge what it is?"

"I ain't been dead yet either—but I can dig when I see the maggots eating somebody's body. I don't like it. And I can see what happens to everybody who gets hooked on heroin."

Charlie made a flatulent noise with his lips, making Wedo blush. For several minutes they sat in silence, watching the Negro "nod."

"We gotta split," Wedo said finally.

As they approached the door, Charlie said, "Alex, man, if you really wanna learn to play The Strap, short con, get in touch. Like I said, we need somebody to catch the suckers and steer them outdoors."

"Yeah, man, that sounds like something I'd wanna learn."

Going down the stairs Alex asked, "What's she cost?"

"Who's that? Oh . . . Charlie's old lady? Alice? She's ten and two. Ten for her and two for the room."

"Man, she's worth *that*. She's got a fine body for an old chick."

Wedo stopped, grabbed his arm. "Hey, *carnal,* back off. We don't do things like that. He's a partner."

"But she's a whore, ain't she? She sells herself."

"Right—but we still don't do that shit. Tricks are that—*tricks*. Not friends, or friends of her old man. Buyin' pussy is okay, there's plenty of young, fine whores around—if you wanna be a trick. But you don't trick with a friend. No sirree, *carnal*. Bad scene."

Alex understood about Charlie's woman, but about being a trick, he again remembered Red Barzo saying, "I'm laying to be rich enough to pay a hundred dollars for pussy."

Wedo missed the implication. "A trick's a trick."

"I just want to fuck—anybody."

"You act like you've never had any pussy before."

Night and neon hid Alex's fiery blush. "Sure, man, whaddya think? But I've been busted for almost two years." Alex thought his own voice had a croak of confession. Wedo's gust of laughter made him feel even more stupid and embarrassed. It was so bad that he started to become angry.

"I forgot," Wedo said, snapping his fingers in inspiration, laughing more. "Yeah, *ese,* I got an idea to get you some fine pussy for free."

"Where, man?"

"Down the road. It's a hustling chick, young and tender . . . if you don't mind burning some coal."

"What's that? I don't want some scag."

"She's a nigger—but just a little. Coffee with lots of cream in it. We're gonna tell her you are a cherry, a full cherry, plus you just split from reform school. I'll bet she gives you a play, *carnal!*" With that, Wedo tugged Alex's sleeve to change their direction, ducking through the increasingly seedy crowd of pedestrians as they went east on Fifth Street toward Central Avenue.

Every block was a seedier world than the last. Garish transvestites with their boisterous mannerisms seemed to be everywhere on one block, overflowing the fag bars to make little groups on the sidewalk. Their rouge and lipstick and affected movements created grotesque parodies of women—and for some reason Alex remembered a short story, maybe by Poe, where there was a masked bacchanal during a plague— maybe it was smallpox—and when the masks were removed all the people were really dead. Exactly how the macabre tale related to drag queens in downtown L.A. was beyond Alex, but it was what came to mind. He would never admit it, but he had a sneaking respect for some faggots he'd met, not any as flamboyant as these but still very obvious ones. He'd found them better-educated and more intelligent than most of the others he met in cages. So far he hadn't found a partner who ever read a book; when he mentioned books, their faces looked as if he'd said cod-liver oil.

On the next block, the faces were nearly all black. The music spewing from the open doorways was rhythm and blues, raising Alex's mood, so he popped his fingers and bounced while he walked.

"It's on the next corner," Wedo said.

Although the block showed rampant black poverty, it also had a form of conspicuous consumption: pimps sat in the new, fin-tailed Cadillacs, dark hands with diamond pinky rings resting on the steering wheels. The flash of the street pimp, crude as it seems to those preferring understatement, has the same function as the fanning feathers of the male peacock: it attracts a certain kind of female, telling her that she can share the Cadillac and have pretty clothes.

It was an issue of pride in stables of streetwalkers that their old man had the longest, prettiest Cadillac, the biggest sapphire or diamond (or several), the brightest plumage. The pimps sat and watched their turn, trying to out-floorshow their brethren.

A block from Central Avenue, amid the wine-devoured minds and the hopelessness of impoverished old age, was a nightclub, grossly out of place. Cadillacs filled the parking lot beside it, and a canopy extended from the entrance to the curb. A uniformed doorman was on duty, assisted by youths to provide valet parking.

"It's a hangout for high-rolling pimps, gamblers, and dope dealers," Wedo said. "Most of 'em are niggers, but a few white boys and Chicanos fall in. They have good jazz groups sometimes."

"I wonder how a guy gets chicks to sell their pussy and give them the money."

"*Quien sabe, ese?*" Wedo said. "I guess they make it good to 'em."

Alex grunted, dissatisfied. The answer was oversimplified—but this wasn't the time to speculate.

When they were thirty yards away, a prewar, silver Rolls-Royce pulled up. It was the first Rolls-Royce Alex had ever seen. Exiting first from the right-hand drive side was a tall, slender man who would be classified Negro only in the United States. His skin was olive, and his hair had tight curls, not kinks. His beautifully tailored clothes seemed conservative compared to those worn by the others. What really impressed Alex, however, was his two women; one black, one white, yet they were a matched pair. He watched the white girl, who had gleaming raven hair spilling around her bare shoulders. She wore a simply cut dress of red silk, its hemline falling nearly to her ankles in the "new look" style of the postwar era. Her figure was outlined by the clinging material.

Alex and Wedo walked by while the girls stood waiting for the man to explain something about the car to the attendant. Alex could smell the girl (she wasn't much older than himself), and for a moment their eyes met.

"Those hookers don't walk the street, what you bet?" Wedo said. "Those is call girls, *ese.*"

"In a whorehouse?"

Wedo's face registered disbelief. "You're jivin' me. You don't know the difference between whores and call girls? They're all whores, but call girls make appointments by phone. They live in classy pads out on the Strip. They make big money . . . keep that *vato* pushin' a Rolls-Royce and eatin' filets."

Alex glanced back while Wedo talked and saw the raven-haired girl take the pimp's arm. Alex felt a sharp pang of envy and desire. For a long time he would remember her image as an ideal of beauty, and she would be the focus of longings and fantasies.

"Where are we going?" Alex asked; they were beyond the canopy.

"Just follow me."

Wedo led them around the side and through the parking lot to an alley, dark and foul-smelling with a row of big garbage cans against the opposite brick wall. Alex heard a bustle of noise and scurrying, the inevitable rats of the slums.

Ahead was a sheet-metal door with a small light bulb over it. The rear entrance was less ostentatious than the front. Two men were in the shadows near it, passing a cigarette back and forth. Alex could tell it was marijuana from the smell. The sound of music came faintly through the closed door.

Suddenly Alex stopped. He realized that he didn't want to go inside. He didn't want to be in a room with an experienced whore and not know exactly what to do. Even if she withheld her laughter, he would know his own ridiculousness. During the walk he'd become so interested in the life he saw that his tingling sexual desire had gone away. He hadn't even been aware of it.

"What's happenin'?" Wedo asked, disconcerted. "Somethin' wrong?"

"Let's split. I don't wanna go in there."

"What, man? Are you crazy?"

"Forget it. Come on." He started walking away, and Wedo had to follow. Alex wouldn't have explained everything no matter where they were, but in the alley's quietness the men by the door would hear every word: they kept him from talking, and Wedo from asking, until they were back on the street.

"What happened to you?"

"Too many niggers around," Alex lied, deliberately making his voice hard to shut off Wedo's probes. It was easier than trying to explain a complex truth he didn't understand. As much as anything else in the world (or almost), he wanted to fuck a girl. Even the imagining of it got his prick hard. He knew what fucking was, the thing itself, but he was also certain there was more to it than that; he'd read as much via allusion and euphemism. It didn't tell him enough to help, just enough to establish his ignorance. What he needed was a girl near his own age, as inexperienced as himself, so she wouldn't know he was learning.

Without discussion they had automatically turned back toward Main Street.

"Well, whaddya wanna do?" Wedo asked.

"I'm following you."

"Let's go check Hank out, see if he's through, maybe cruise around. Say, you ever roll any fruiters?"

Alex shook his head.

"We can make some bread strong-arming them. Me and Hank have done it before. We pick 'em up in a couple of public toilets—one in Pershing Square, the other one in the P.E. depot on Sixth and Main. One of us goes down and stands at the pisser, fakin' like he's pissing. Just look around, and some pervert'll give you the eye. They just wanna suck a dick . . . anywhere. So whoever gets one takes him to an alley, or up on

Angel's Flight, and whoever is waitin' follows until the spot is right. We kick the motherfucker's ass and take his bread. You for that?"

Ashamed of backing out at the nightclub, Alex was anxious to show his guts. "Sure, man, that sounds all right." He answered without thinking, not that reflection would have changed his answer; it might have instilled some misgivings, however.

■

Hank wasn't enthusiastic, at least not for that night. He had a girl to meet and enough money for the moment.

It was nearly midnight when Wedo and Alex came out of the *Examiner* building.

"What now?" Wedo said. "I'm tired."

"Me, too. I don't have anywhere to go."

"I could go . . . home," Wedo said, but then patted Alex's back in comradeship. "If you could call the nasty motherfucker that." He choked the words out with false levity. "But I don't feel like it. Lots of times I don't."

"So where do you sleep?"

Wedo shrugged. "Here and there. At Hank's sometimes. His mother likes me. Sometimes at Teresa's . . . sneak by her father and go upstairs . . . and sometimes in an all-night flick on Main Street. Wanna try that?"

"Sure, man."

Thus was it decided, and in ensuing weeks they would spend several nights in one triple-feature movie theater or another, always sitting adjacent to an exit in case the cops who scanned the place from the door started down the aisles. The all-night theaters closed about six-thirty, dumping their creatures into the daylight and the rising city, where they were lost amid the swarm.

On the morning following that first night, they also established another pattern they would repeat. They took an old yellow streetcar to JoJo's and Teresa's, waiting with hands jammed in their pockets and vapor coming from their mouths until old man Altabella drove off to work. Alex's new clothes were in the house. He bathed and changed while Wedo walked Teresa to school.

JoJo was still snoring when his buddies showed up, but when Wedo returned from the walk, JoJo was perfecting his ducktail and was ready to go.

Both Alex and JoJo had money left from the smoke-bomb caper, so they paid for the marijuana, wine, and the gasoline for Hank's car. The quartet drove to the beach, but it was off-season and bleak and empty. Even the hot-dog stands were shut down. Alex felt good just riding around in the back seat, looking at things. JoJo was beside him, while Wedo rode in front with Hank. The wine and weed opened shutters in Alex's mind, making him think and feel with unusual intensity. Colors could be felt, music seen, each piano note hanging individually before his mind's eye. He knew he would get busted sooner or later and would have to go back to jail. The awareness of that always lurked on the fringe of his consciousness. He also knew what most people thought when they looked at four youths with greasy ducktails and thick-soled shoes: distaste laced with apprehensiveness. It wasn't ideal, but it was better that than the way they fucked him around. He really liked his new buddy, Wedo; Hank, too, except that the latter was taciturn by nature and hadn't opened up yet, though a wink and a grin told Alex he was accepted.

On the drive back to the city, they took winding Sunset Boulevard. For much of its length it was lined with large, beautiful homes. They had various architectural styles, but white was the prevalent color, and they were all nestled in greenery. All four youths were awed, and when they neared the turnoff through the Bel Air gates, Wedo wanted to turn in and cruise around.

"It's a free country, ain't it? That's a public street, *que no?*"

"Let's keep going," Alex said. "We stand out too much to be cruisin' around in there. We'll get pulled over, sure as shit. Me and JoJo are wanted."

"We stand out here, too," Wedo argued.

"Yeah, but this is a big main drag. That ain't the same as up there. First one of those rich people sees us out the window, they'll call the police about the zoot-suiters or something. And the cops work for them."

Wedo finally nodded. "Yeah, you're right."

Being thus validated, Alex felt even better. He leaned back and scanned the mansions of Beverly Hills, wondering what the odds were for him to ever have such a place; how did people get so rich? It was beyond his dreams, which ended at a new convertible and sharp clothes— a double-breasted one-button roll in sharkskin.

■

That night Wedo borrowed Hank's car. They went to a Billy Eckstine concert at the Million-Dollar Theatre. JoJo had a girl to take, and Wedo had Teresa. Alex didn't want to go, but on Wedo's urging, he dressed up and went along. Eckstine was the favorite singer in the barrios and ghettos of Los Angeles.

Afterward they went cruising, stopping at a drive-in for hamburgers, then up into the Hollywood Hills to follow Mulholland Drive along the winding crest. They could see the city spread out to the far horizon. Everyone but Teresa smoked marijuana and drank beer. Alex was high, and as sometimes happened, he suddenly got serious. He wanted to talk about books and ideas, but he knew before he spoke that nobody was interested. They wanted a good time and wouldn't know what he was talking about; they'd think *he* was a *fool*. He felt very lonely as he watched the girls snuggling up to Wedo and JoJo. He vowed that this situation wouldn't happen again.

The situation had no chance to happen again: JoJo was arrested the next day. He went to a malt shop across from the high school to wait for the girl he'd taken to the concert. The malt shop was nearly empty, which was usual until classes were over. Two juvenile detectives from the local precinct came to see the owner about a recent burglary at the dry cleaner's next door. There sat JoJo on a stool. Both detectives knew him well enough to call his nickname; both also knew he was an escapee.

"JoJo Altabella, as I live and breathe!" one of them exclaimed cheerily.

When Teresa came in after school, the malt shop owner told her what had happened. She immediately called home and warned Alex. He was out the back door and gone through the rear alley five minutes before the detectives came looking for him. He and Wedo spent that night in a flophouse hotel on Sixteenth and Main streets. It was the first time Alex had rented a hotel room, and he really expected the clerk to refuse a thirteen-year-old, or at least to have questions. But when he eyed them, Wedo gave him an extra two dollars, and his suspicion became a wink.

Alex became enamored with roaming the city streets. Within a few days his uncertainty was washed away by the constant challenge and excitement. Each day opened with the possibility of new adventures. Wedo was seventeen and, notwithstanding his illiteracy, extremely street-smart. He'd grown up virtually without supervision, fending for himself in tough neighborhoods. He had no cognizance of abstract values, or analysis, or of anything else except how to function on the mean streets. Because of his age and experience he was the leader, but without his realizing it, Alex was the more violent of the pair. Wedo talked about violence constantly, and Alex took the word for the reality; he didn't know that Wedo's constant talk was unconscious compensation for the Catholic religion he overtly rejected but which his mother had deeply instilled in him while he was still a toddler.

Alex and Wedo committed a variety of crimes, averaging nearly a felony a day—not counting smoking marijuana—if anyone wanted to make a tally. They jackrolled homosexuals the way Wedo had described, enticing them from public restrooms to some dark alley and jumping them. The scores were meager, never more than thirty dollars, so after four such robberies they quit that and devised a way to steal the coin box on streetcars, at least those streetcars with a single motorman-conductor. The youths would get on separately a stop apart. One stayed near the front; the other went to the rear. The one in the rear would reach out and disengage the rod connecting to the overhead electric wires. The streetcar lost power and stopped. The conductor would go to the rear to deal with the problem. The boy in front snatched the coin box, leaped out the front and ran. They did this three times and were smart enough to stop, assuming that pretty soon someone would be waiting for them if they kept it up. Actually, they needed relatively little money. It was plenty if they had ten dollars apiece, a few joints, and a bottle of wine—especially if they were cruising in Hank's car, looking tough. When that car was unavailable they hotwired one and joyrided around, never keeping it more than eight hours, for Wedo knew that license numbers didn't go on the "hot sheet" until the shifts changed. In six weeks they stole eight automobiles.

Their adventures were not always pleasurable. One night Wedo bought the ticket for an all-night movie on Main Street while Alex waited in the alley to be let in through an emergency exit. The exit was in the lobby of the men's restroom. Alex heard noises inside, became impatient, and knocked. The door opened, but instead of Wedo it was a uniformed policeman with a raised nightstick. Alex whirled and ran as the club crashed on his right shoulder near his neck, a pain so great that he scarcely felt the hard kick to the tip of his spine. He sprawled on his hands and knees and could have been caught if the policeman hadn't been satisfied. The next day Alex could hardly move his arm, and the entire shoulder area was purple. It was months before he could lift his arm straight over his head without pain. Everything in his life showed him the primacy of violence.

In this postwar time, only the first waves of the human sea had come to Los Angeles, and the San Fernando Valley was just a few communities surrounded by citrus groves and alfalfa. But the city was already an immense sprawl. Its poorer citizens already inhabited the older and seamier central and east side areas. Circumstances pretty much kept Alex in these poorer environs. He didn't truly appreciate the different worlds as divided by money. If anything, he found the poor quarters to be where he was less affected and more willing to accept things—or maybe it was because Wedo knew people who thought nothing amiss in a pair of youths running loose, and those were the people Alex met. Every day was an adventure, and Alex enjoyed just seeing things. One evening at dusk they abandoned a stolen car near Alameda Street, in the middle of a vast scrap yard. Everything was old, impregnated with grime and rust, all the colors dull and gray, a world of monochrome. Alex followed Wedo over a board fence. It was a shortcut to Wedo's neighborhood to cross this immense yard of scrap metal. The hush of dusk was upon the place. Alex was awed and fascinated by the mountainous piles of castoff automobiles; they loomed to create a skyline. He got the same feeling in the railroad yards, seeing one hundred pairs of tracks filled for miles by dusty boxcars. It was a sense of something for which words were inadequate. It was akin to the awe most persons feel at the grandeur of nature. It was not the same feeling but a maimed cousin thereto.

A night finally came where Wedo had to go home and they had no money for the cheap hotel room. The hour was past midnight. Earlier it had rained, and there was the kind of wind that usually precedes more.

"No jive," Wedo said. "I got the runny shits and I'm weak." Though the night was cool, beads of sweat were on his forehead.

"You don't look good," Alex said.

"If Hank had been there, he coulda drove you to San Pedro. Teresa said it was cool."

"What about a streetcar?"

"They stopped running at midnight."

"Don't worry about me, man. I'll be okay."

"It might start raining. You gotta get in somewhere. If the fuzz sees you—bam! You're dusted."

"Maybe I should find some fruiter to take me home," Alex said, half joking.

A wrinkled mask of disgust was Wedo's response.

"I know," Alex said. "Besides, we got 'em terrorized. The word's gone around. I can see some of 'em lookin' at us funny. They heard a description, I'll bet."

"You don't wanna do that anyway."

"It's better than pneumonia . . . or getting busted. Anything is better than that. I just wanna get in somewhere."

Wedo snapped his fingers, "I know a spot . . . close to my pad, too. C'mon."

They left fifteen cents for the two coffees and started walking. The place Wedo knew of was the basement of an apartment building. "There's some old couches and shit stashed down there. You can make it one night."

The building was two stories high and spread along half a block. It was two blocks from Wedo's home. It was a building for the poor, as was everything in this neighborhood.

"Around back," Wedo said.

They turned into the total darkness of an alley. Behind the apartment house was an unpaved parking lot. It was very dark, totally black against the building, though someone there could see movement and some shape looking out. They kept silent, Wedo leading him by touch.

The building jutted out in wings, creating a "U" shape. The basement door was at the base of the "U." As they reached it, the loudest sound they heard was their breathing. In the stillness they could clearly hear passing cars half a block away. Wedo tugged Alex close and whispered, his mouth an inch from Alex's ear. "Light a match. It's loose on the frame and a catch lock. It'll take one second."

Alex leaned close, shielding the glow. Wedo had his pocket knife ready. The moment the match flashed so he could see exactly where the catch was, he jabbed in the knife point, pried, and tugged. Indeed, it was faster than turning a key.

The door squeaked and Wedo hissed between his teeth. Now they were in absolute darkness. Alex lighted several matches before they went down the creaky stairs. More matches showed a room fifteen-feet square.

"Nothing here but cobwebs," Alex said softly.

"Oh, man, I was down here three months ago and they had it over there."

A padlocked door was at one end; breaking through it was out of the question.

"Let's split," Alex said. "Fuck this place."

"We'll think of something."

On thieves' feet they ascended the wooden stairs, Wedo in front.

They pushed the door partially open. Ten feet ahead to the left was a wooden stoop outside a screen door. The screen door squeaked. It sounded to them like a scream. A bulky figure started out, his white undershirt a lighter shadow. Wedo bolted instantly and wordlessly. He had to run in front of the man to get out of the "U." Alex was still hidden and unseen in the doorway's blackness.

The figure stepped on the porch. His hand came up as Wedo went by. "Freeze, goddammit!" he bellowed.

Alex spurted out, lunged three steps, and hit the revolver before the man could shoot.

"Run, Alex!" Wedo yelled, his voice already distant.

It was useless, for a grip too strong held him, and there was the terrifying sound of a revolver cocking next to his head.

"Don't move or you're dead," the man said.

A moment later his wife was in the screen door with a flashlight.

"I called 'em," she said. "You got one . . . my god, he's just a kid."

"He's a punk."

"Your mother's a punk," Alex snarled, tears of frustration and pain forming. It almost felt good when the man backhanded him. The strong blow made him think of physical pain, not the worse kind that had been rising.

■

Twenty minutes later he was handcuffed in the back seat of a prowl car, fighting back tears as he stared out at the city—the lights, the night, the people, freedom—all gone again. The only sound was the chronic crackle of the radio and the monotoned voices calling out. "Eight twelve to fourteen twelve East Beverly. See the man and keep the peace . . ." Police radio calls would always thereafter wrench his stomach.

He could tell by the sights that he was being taken to Georgia Street. They would try to get him to "clean the books" on burglaries in the area. He would say nothing—and even if he did, they could do nothing. He was already in the worst place they could send him. They would call Whittier. Tomorrow he would be picked up and taken back.

28

alex expected someone from Whittier to pick him up the day after his arrest, but it took four days, and the men who signed him out were from the Los Angeles office. Sacramento had ordered him transferred to the Preston School of Industry, the reformatory for older, tougher youths. Its age bracket was fifteen to seventeen. Alex was thirteen, and his stomach felt hollow when they told him the destination. Nobody in Whittier had ever been in Preston, but there were legends of how tough it was.

When he signed for his property envelope, which the transportation officers took possession of, he asked if he could get cigarettes from a machine in the corner. One of them took twenty cents from the envelope and got a pack of Luckies for him.

Then came handcuffs. From now on whenever he was transported there would be restraints. He was a known rabbit.

Night's dark coolness was still on the city when they took him out to the parking lot. While they unlocked the station wagon, the back seat of which was screened off, Alex sucked in the fresh predawn air and stared with longing at the dismal old buildings. The coolness felt especially good after the stale odors of the jail. A hundred youths had passed through during his four days, seven of them in his cell. Despite the momentary twinge of fear when he heard about Preston, his mood was jovial. Without being conscious of it, he'd learned to derive pleasure from what was available, and at the moment it was his first ride up the California coast, or at least partly up the coast before turning inland. He didn't probe or try to dissect his unlikely good mood. If asked, he would have replied that it came from getting out of the dirty jail.

"Did they feed you back there?" one of the men asked.

"Naw," Alex lied. At four A.M. the jailers passed out compartment trays with nothing on them but mush. It was so rubbery that they slid the trays through the bars sideways, for the mush stuck to the tray. Then a jailer came with two slices of bread for each boy. Very few stayed in Georgia Street more than a night, so swill for food hardly mattered.

"We'll feed you later," the man said. "We want to get out of the city before the morning rush."

"How come we're going up the coast route? It's not the shortest, is it?"

"We have to pick up two more in Santa Barbara."

A few minutes later the car passed the lighted *Examiner* building. Trucks with the morning edition were pulling out. The familiar streets put a pang of longing in Alex. Then he saw Hank's car at the curb, and his ache turned to damp eyes; he cursed the tears silently and fought them down.

As they drove west toward the coast highway, Alex stared at everything, imprinting on his memory all that he could of freedom. Everything had an unusual clarity. Even the red and green of traffic lights had unusual intensity.

It grew light while they were following the curves of the coast highway. The blackness of the sea turned into an oily dark green under the solid gray blanket of clouds.

They pulled off into a truck stop café. Several big rigs and half a dozen cars were parked in the lot, and through the misted glass Alex could see it was crowded.

"You ready to eat, son?" one of the men asked.

"Are you going to take these off?" He extended his handcuffed wrists.

"Oh, no, no, no," the man said with a pleasant grin. "We don't have any weapons with us, and you're too young . . . no doubt you can outrun us."

"Yeah, okay," Alex said. "Let's go." A protective anger surged through him, so that he swaggered, and inside the café he met the looks of customers and waitresses with burning eyes and lips trembling near the snarl of an animal. Most of them met his eyes only for a second, then looked away nervously—at least those who noticed him in the first place did so. It was only a handful; the vast majority were too involved in their own affairs to pay any attention.

The men with him, however, did notice. They exchanged glances and made mental notes to document the boy's streak of hostility and viciousness.

In Santa Barbara the driver waited at the car with Alex while the other man went inside. Fifteen minutes later he came down the walk with two youths handcuffed together, one white, one black. Alex began grinning and chuckling. The black was Chester Nelson, he of the light, freckled skin whom Alex had met his first morning in Juvenile Hall. Chester, however, was no longer a skinny kid. His chest, shoulders, and arms filled out his shirt, and he obviously needed to shave twice a week. He leaned forward to get in first, saw Alex, and froze momentarily; then he shook his head and grinned, showing another change: he'd lost his two front teeth.

"Hey, baby," he said. "It's the same old faces in the same old places. I know you well, 'member when we met makin' the bed in Juvie, but your name I forgot."

"Hammond—"

"Yeah, Alex Hammond," Chester interrupted. Now he was inside, next to Alex. He awkwardly extended his left hand to shake; his right was cuffed to the other youth.

"How'd you get busted up here?" Alex asked. "You're outa Watts, aren't you?"

"Not Watts, sucker. Them's country niggers. I'm from the west side."

"How'd you get here?"

"In a hot car. How else."

"That's what they got you for, car theft?"

"That and some burglaries."

"That'll hold you."

"Damn sure will. You goin' to Preston, too?"

"Uh-huh."

The man on the passenger side squirmed around. "Okay, listen up," he said. "We got an all-day ride. We can do it easy or hard. You can smoke, but crack a window and use the ashtrays. Talk all you want, but don't start yelling out the windows. Look at the pretty girls, but keep your mouths shut. In about ten minutes we're gonna stop at a gas station. You better take a leak then. It'll be your last chance. If you're all right, don't give us any trouble, we'll get you cheeseburgers and Cokes for lunch. If you do give us trouble, you'll get to Preston about five this evening—hungry. Any questions?"

"Yeah, man," Chester said.

"What?"

"We get french fries too?"

Everyone grinned.

■

It was five past five when they pulled up to the gatehouse. While the driver showed the papers to the guard, the boys leaned forward and looked up the road to the administration building, the only one they could see. Constructed of brick, it was old for California. It sat on a hilltop (Preston was built on low, rolling hills) and had a fifty-foot bell tower.

"That's the Castle," Chester Nelson said.

The gate slid open electrically and they drove to the ad building, where a man waited at the top of the stairs. In a hallway of dark wood and waxed floors, the escorts removed the handcuffs, exchanged the inevitable paperwork, and turned the trio over, wishing them good luck.

Still wearing their street clothes, which were wrinkled and dirty from the jail, the newcomers followed the man out a back door to a paved square with a small office. Several youths wearing sharply creased black uniforms were lounging outside the door. They stopped talking and stared at the newcomers, their faces cold, their eyes hard. Alex stared back but not at any particular one, so as to avoid a personal challenge.

"Hey, Kennedy," the man said, "run these fish down to the mess hall. Bring 'em back here after they eat so we can dress 'em in."

A burly youth with acne-pitted cheeks came away from the wall. Without a word, he started toward an open gate, signaling the new arrivals to follow. They went along the side of a road, passing other two-story brick buildings that reminded Alex of Whittier, except these were older. The road went over a low hill; at the bottom a company of about fifty boys was forming in marching ranks outside the mess hall. They wore blue khakis, not the black of their escort. They marched up as the newcomers came down. Alex noted that the marching was much looser and more lackadaisical than allowed in Whittier.

"Say, man," Kennedy said to Alex, "those are pretty nice kicks you're wearin'." He was looking at Alex's shoes. "You oughta let me have 'em."

"Oh yeah." The mental hackles rose instantly in Alex. Kennedy was three or four years older and twenty pounds heavier, plus being much more muscular, but Alex now had had experience in institutional jungles and refused to be taken advantage of. "Why should I give 'em to you?"

"You're gonna lose 'em anyway. They'll take 'em away when you get dressed in."

It seemed reasonable. In Whittier the shoes went like everything else. He didn't mind giving them away under the circumstances.

"I'll give you half a pack, too," the detail boy said.

"I'll need something to put on my feet."

"I'll go get you something while you're in eating."

"Yeah, okay."

Talking was forbidden in the dining room. The boys communicated by signals or learned to whisper from the sides of their mouths without moving their lips. The rule failed in quieting the mess hall because the inmates ate from stainless-steel trays using stainless-steel spoons. Four hundred of them scraping together made a nerve-grating cacophony.

When they had gone through the serving line, the fish sat down with their trays in an empty area near the door. Kennedy leaned over Alex and promised to return in ten minutes. Alex nodded and tried to force down the meat loaf, which he usually liked. Being on display, which was what he felt like, made his stomach too nervous for food. Sweat began making his shirt damp under the arms.

What had been called "cottages" in Whittier were "companies" in Preston. The companies now began filing out, one table at a time, passing close to where the fish sat. Alex watched them go by, his first thought being how much older they seemed than the boys of Whittier. Then he began seeing familiar faces here and there, boys he'd seen leave Whittier during the first few months, and a couple of faces he recognized from even earlier, from Juvenile Hall. A few gave him a nod, though he couldn't recall their names. They had been acquaintances, not friends.

Chester Nelson was getting the same greetings, perhaps even more, from blacks.

Then Alex saw Watkins, his Okie escape partner who'd gotten pulled from the fence. Moments later he got another wave; he saluted back with a clenched fist, even though he couldn't put a name with the familiar face. It was the youth whom he'd met in the bullpen next to the juvenile court.

When Kennedy came back with an old pair of low-cut brogans, the mess hall was empty except for the three fish—and the mess hall workers wiping off the tables and mopping the floor.

The brogans were too big, but Kennedy assured Alex that a new pair would be issued, so Alex took off his pretty, almost new shoes and handed them over. It was better than giving them to the institution.

Back on the detail grounds, the man, who was a supervisor, took them around the outside of "the Castle" to a door with a "Receiving and Release" sign on it. The man had a key.

Inside were long shelves of blue khakis, supposedly arranged by size. These were used clothes, though laundered and halfway pressed.

"Pick yourself some and don't make no mess," the man said. "When you get done there find some shoes over there." He pointed to a screened-off area that apparently served as a shoe repair shop. It had bins marked by size, and in each bin were state-issue brogans, high-top and low-cut, all old but with new heels and half-soles.

"What about my own shoes?" Chester Nelson asked. "Can I send 'em home?"

"You can keep 'em. You're entitled to one pair of personal shoes and—"

Alex missed the last clause of the dialogue, because as the truth of the first hit him, the pounding red blood in his brain erased everything else. Kennedy had snookered him, conned him out of his shoes. Preston was tougher than Whittier, its inmates older and more violent; they were also sophisticated—not that Kennedy's "story" was especially slick. It had been simple, and it was told simply and with matter-of-fact sincerity. It fit the circumstances. That superficial analysis, that momentary reasoning, sapped Alex completely—left him nearly gasping. It was night when they came out of Receiving and Release. They had sheets, blankets, a towel, and a pillow case, with toothbrush, comb, safety razor, and blades. Also half a yellow pencil, already sharpened, and paper and an envelope. It was the standard "fish kit." The man told them to write home and tell their families they were okay. He said that the institution disliked parents worrying, calling the superintendent or Sacramento, so their letters were censored and nothing upsetting was allowed to go out.

Alex barely listened; it wasn't relevant to him—he was thinking of Kennedy and the shoes. He was younger than nearly everyone in Preston, and although he was as tall as many, he wasn't as developed. His brain pulsed with indignant rage. It almost blinded his thoughts. Even without the emotions screaming in his mind, he knew that he couldn't let Kennedy get away with it. Whittier had taught him what would happen to anyone who showed weakness. In a world with violence at its pinnacle, to let something like this go would mark him. Others wanting to establish their toughness would prey on him, and inevitably someone would try to fuck him. So when the first, literally blind rage dissipated, he was left with an implacable determination.

They assigned him to "B" Company, the one company housed in the old Castle. A few of these fifty youths he'd seen in Whittier or Juvenile Hall, and one or two he knew. He exchanged nods, but they were at assigned tables in the dayroom so there was no chance to talk that night.

His bunk was next to a window. Bright lights outside reminded him of his first night in Juvenile Hall. It seemed so long ago, yet it was from the same moment of panic. By raising up on an elbow, he could see over the window ledge down across part of the grounds. The fence with barbed wire on top was nearby—and beyond it he saw a dozen deer grazing blissfully, a couple of fawns moving between them. For some reason beyond his capacity to analyze, a terrible ache and longing surged through him. Tears swelled in his eyes, and he jammed his face in the pillow, struggling against sobs.

■

As in Whittier, the companies came to the detail grounds for work call. Alex had been told to wait until all the crews were gone, but he saw Kennedy lounging with the other black-clad detail boys next to the office, and when the ranks of companies dissolved to report to work supervisors, he went over to Kennedy, who saw him coming and took a step forward.

"Hey, man," Alex said, "I gotta have my kicks back."

"Whaddya mean?"

"You gave me a bullshit story. I could have kept them."

"Could you? I didn't know that." The way Kennedy spoke, however, was edged with arrogance.

"I want those shoes back."

"I ain't got your shoes."

"You took 'em. I want the motherfuckers back, man."

"You *want!* Who the fuck are you?"

"I don't want no trouble, but—"

"If you don't want trouble, get outa my face before I put the foot in your ass." Kennedy was swollen up, ready to fight, his whole being coiled for violence. He outweighed Alex by twenty-five pounds, and there was no doubt he could easily handle Alex in a fight. His arrogant confidence became contempt. "Look, punk, get outa my face before you get hurt."

For a moment Alex was actually dizzy as the blood pounded through his brain, his rage magnified because of his helplessness. Yet he'd known he was no match for Kennedy, and that previous awareness jerked him back to a semblance of rationality. He dropped his head and wound his way through the shifting crowd. Boys were going to specified areas according to assignment. Work supervisors waited with clipboards.

Watkins and a slender Indian youth were at the "B" Company formation area when Alex got back. He'd seen the Indian in Whittier but didn't know his name. He was with Watkins.

"Where you been?" Watkins asked as they shook hands.

I had to see a guy 'bout something."

"We gotta go in a minute. Do you know Miller?"

"In Lincoln, weren't you?" Alex said, shaking hands.

"Right," Miller said.

"Here," Watkins said, openly giving Alex a pack of Chesterfields, grinning when Alex looked around. "They don't bother you about cigarettes here. It's kind of fucked up, though. They don't let you buy 'em, but you can have 'em. They have a 'smoke line' after meals."

"Where do they come from?"

"Mostly visits. Some guys from Sacramento and San Francisco get visits every week—and bring in two cartons apiece."

"The fuzz lets 'em?"

"Yeah, man. In a lot of ways this is better'n Whittier. Shit, I do all right. I work in the butcher shop. I've got three cops bringin' me cigarettes for meat . . . a pound of choice steak for a pack. Another one brings me a Benzedrine inhaler for two filets. That's where they come from." He indicated the pack of cigarettes in Alex's pocket.

"Hey, you!" a counselor yelled at them, starting to come over. "Where are you supposed to be?"

The detail grounds had nearly emptied, and the boys who remained were in groups under the watchful eye of a foreman.

"We gotta go," Watkins said, he and Miller turning their backs to the man, faking that they hadn't heard him as they walked away. Suddenly Watkins snapped his fingers and called back. "What happened to Altabella?"

"Fuck, they got him two months ago. Sent him back to Whittier."

"Okay. I'll see you after work."

When "work call" was over, a supervising counselor gathered the three newcomers and drove them to the institution hospital for a cursory physical examination. It was in the waiting room that he found what he'd been looking for: a weapon. He hadn't wanted to ask anyone because it could conceivably have gotten back to Kennedy. What he found was the heavy brass nozzle of a firehose. He unscrewed it from the hose while Chester Nelson was in the examination room. Stuck in his waistband beneath his shirt and jacket, it pulled his pants down on one side. It was so blatant that he expected some man to ask him what he had hidden there—but none of them really looked at him, much less noticed the sag. He had misgivings because it was so heavy. He had no desire to kill Kennedy, yet if the equation was reduced to forgetting what had happened or killing, he would kill. During the remainder of the morning, which he spent leafing through tattered magazines in "B" Company dayroom, he kept looking futilely for something more appropriate. He simultaneously had to lock his mind, refuse to look at anything beyond the act he planned. Whenever any image of consequence came up, he ruthlessly pushed it out of his mind . . . and deliberately remembered Kennedy's contemptuous arrogance until his fear was replaced by the pounding blood of fury in his brain.

He planned to wait until afternoon work call, following lunch. But at eleven-thirty A.M., the whistle blew for recall. Everyone returned to their companies for noon count and lunch. The detail grounds again filled with the seven hundred reform-school inmates.

Kennedy was easy to spot in his black uniform. He was with two other detail boys, forming a conversational circle outside the door of the detail office. Alex held his breath, clenched his teeth, and ran on tiptoe the last three strides. Kennedy's back was to him, but one of the others saw the heavy brass nozzle glint in the sunlight. His eyes widened in reflex, and he yelped, "Look—" as it arched down.

At the last fraction of a second, even while striking, Alex pulled the blow, snapping it with his wrist instead of smashing it with arm and shoulder. Nonetheless, the heavy nozzle made a loud "plop!"—a hollow sound like a giant egg breaking. Blood jumped from Kennedy's head. His legs buckled, but he didn't go down. His companions blanched and fell back, aghast. Kennedy stumbled forward two steps and whirled around. He now faced Alex. His face had two huge streams of blood running down his cheekbones—bright red tears. He wiped his palm across his face, smearing the gore and covering his his hand.

"You fuckin' punk," he snarled.

Alex had been stunned, hypnotized, but he heard the words and thought he saw the body tense to attack—so he swung the heavy nozzle again, this time without hesitation. It was the horizontal blow of a frightened youth. It caved in Kennedy's cheekbone and dropped him as if he'd been shot in the brain.

Many dozen eyes had turned at the first sound of violence. The second made them gasp collectively, and those who were close backed up reflexively. Some thought they'd just seen a boy murdered.

Then Kennedy began slowly pumping his legs, as if he were riding a bicycle. A hand came up to clutch his cheek, blood seeping between his fingers. Alex stood unmoving, the nozzle dangling by his side, the image being cooked into his brain. Misgivings flickered for one moment, and then were snuffed out by indignation; the bullyin' motherfucker had it coming.

Several freemen had turned in time to see the second blow. Seconds passed with everyone on the detail grounds frozen motionless and silent. Then a foreman who was behind Alex ran on tiptoe and crashed into him with a high blind-side tackle. Alex went down, the nozzle flying

from his hand. Even before he hit the asphalt, others were piling on top
of him. One of them, driven by fear, grabbed his hair and began slamming his face into the pavement.

■

Every institution that confines people has a "hole." It may be called anything—Isolation, Segregation, Seclusion, Meditation, The Cooler, The
Shelf, The Adjustment Unit, etcetera—but it is still "the hole," a jail
within a jail, and often there's a special hole inside the hole. In Preston
the hole was called "G" Company, and was in a secluded part of the institution. Alex was handcuffed and driven to "G" Company by three supervising counselors.

The men on duty in "G" Company had been telephoned and were
waiting when he was brought to the door. They seemed indifferent,
maybe even bored, as they took custody of him. Later he'd learn that
two, the Neiman brothers, were from Alcatraz; a kid, no matter how violent, wasn't going to upset them in the least.

"G" Company was newer than most of Preston, and it was actually
a prison cellhouse in design, with two tiers or galleries instead of floors.
The center of the building did have a solid floor. Around it were rooms
used for necessary functions: an office, a shower, a clothing room, and
a closet that served as a library. The mess hall was down a corridor off
the center; it extended out from the rectangular shape of the building.
Each tier had seventy-five cells. The doors were solid except for a barred
observation window. Light came into the building from high, barred
windows at each end. The sunbeams were dissected into patterns,
spilling down on the highly waxed tile floor and giving a sepulchral
mood to the place. Everything was spotless, and everything was silent,
except for their footsteps. A few faces appeared at cell doors to see the
newcomer.

Alex's clothes were taken and he was given a strip-search. He'd been
locked in cells before, but never in a place so much like a prison.

He was given an unpressed, zipup jumpsuit without pockets and a
pair of cloth slippers. One man motioned for him to follow along the
bottom tier, while the other opened a box and pulled a lever. It raised a
security bar that dropped into a slot over the door. As long as it was
down no cell door could be opened.

The man escorting Alex opened a huge spike key to unlock the cell
door. Alex immediately saw that someone had slept in the bunk since it
was made up. It had sheets and blankets, but they were turned back

and rumpled. Dirty socks and a towel were on the floor under a push-button sink, below which was the toilet.

"Go on in," the man said. Then, when he'd relocked the door and his partner had dropped the bar, he added, "We'll send you down some bedding later. The kid who was in here went to the hospital last night—appendicitis. Anyway, the rules are simple. No talking in here at any time. It's a silent system. We catch you yelling out the window and we've got a place without a window—or anything else except concrete and a hole in the floor to shit in."

Alex nodded.

"We've got some other rules, too. You get up at the morning bell—seven A.M.—and make your bunk. You don't get back on it until after supper. Other than that, keep your eyes open and your lip buttoned and you'll catch on to the routine." The man spoke laconically, a speech made to every newcomer. He waited to see if Alex had any response—Alex was thinking how pale the man's eyes looked—and then turned away.

When Alex was satisfied that the receding footsteps were real, he began examining his new domicile. Besides the bunk bolted to the floor, there was an aluminum washbowl and toilet. They were one unit, with the washbowl with pushbuttons on top. Its drain ran down into the toilet bowl. It was aluminum instead of porcelain, and the inside of the toilet was permanently stained. In the corner between the fixture and the wall was a small bag and some dirty rags. The bag contained cleanser.

Alex tore the dirty sheets from the mattress. When he lifted the mattress to turn it over, he saw a sheet of steel where springs should have been. He also found a partial bag of Bull Durham tobacco and many loose book matches and a striker. The matches had been split in half, so each gave two lights instead of one. He had enough smokes for several days.

His greatest discovery, however, was on the floor in the corner behind the bunk: a stack of old magazines and nearly a dozen books. The covers were torn off the books. It was before the era of paperbacks, and apparently the hard covers were a security threat, although Alex was unable to imagine how. The tension and violence had drained him, leaving an incipient depression and a hollowness, but seeing the books elevated his mood considerably. He began flipping the pages to find the titles: *The Iron Hell* by Jack London was one, *The Foxes of Harrow* by Frank Yerby, *Saratoga Trunk* by Edna Ferber, *Main Street* by Sinclair Lewis. Alex remembered Lewis from *Arrowsmith*. He'd read that one first. As long as he had books he would be okay. In fact, as long as he had good books he preferred to live in their worlds than the ugliness of his own real world. So far he didn't mind this hole at all.

■

Around noon he heard noises and stood up to the door to see. Across from him on the bottom the inhabitants were being let out of their cells. They wore shoes and regular uniforms instead of the jumpsuits and slippers.

Then security bars went up elsewhere that he couldn't see. He heard doors nearby being unlocked. A minute later a man unlocked Alex's door and pulled it open. A boy appeared carrying two compartmented food trays. He passed one of them to Alex and told him to slide it out under the door when he was through. The space was too small if the tray had food, but it was enough when the tray was empty, although residues of earlier trays already marred the door's bottom.

The food was cold, but Alex's two years in institutions had made him indifferent to such things. He finished eating and went back to his book.

When sounds of activity again broke the silence and brought him to the door, a score of youths were lining up in twos. They wore regular clothes and shoes. A minute later he saw them again, this time trekking up the hill outside his window with short-handled hoes on their shoulders. At the top they began chopping weeds, working down. Obviously there was more than one status in "G" Company.

During the day nobody talked in the building. It was silent as a cathedral. Three counselors were on duty until five P.M. At night it was different. One man was in charge, although he couldn't open a cell door by himself; he didn't even have a key to exit the building. When anything happened he used the telephone to summon assistance. Also, he couldn't be surprised by his superiors, so he simply sat in the office, drinking coffee, listening to a radio, reading magazines he got from the boys, and sometimes dozing. The office door was visible from several cell doors, and if the man came out, the youths in those cells passed a warning. The man couldn't hear them from the office because they talked through the windows, calling out along the outside of the building.

The first night Alex kept out of the conversations, but by listening and using inference he learned that "G" Company had two sections. One was for punishment, per se, where the boy stayed anywhere from ten to sixty days. Some of those went out to work, but Alex was unable to learn what decided if it was work or cell. The second section of "G" Company was the half of the building beyond the office-administrative area. Apparently the other section was for boys permanently assigned to "G" Company—troublemakers the staff didn't want in a regular company, such as "dings," "fruiters," the chronically assaultive, and whoever else might disrupt the institution. It wasn't punishment, so the officials said; it was just segregation. They had full privileges except for attending the weekend movie. They worked around the building, passing out the food and then washing the trays, keeping the floor of red tile buffed to a sheen, performing make-work; or else they went on a special crew that did hard labor, their tools being mattocks, shovels, and hoes, for the most part.

That much Alex gleaned from listening for several hours to at least five different voices. One reviled the disciplinary committee for permanently assigning him to "grade B" in "G" Company. The others made fun of him: what did he expect after three escapes. He was lucky they weren't transferring him to San Quentin for security. San Quentin was the next step up the institutional ladder.

■

Around ten A.M. the next morning, Alex was lying on the concrete floor, but his mind was living in the Oklahoma Territory of the late nineteenth century, carried there by the novel resting on his stomach. He was really enjoying the story and missed the sound of the approaching man until the key hit the lock.

"C'mon, Hammond. The disciplinary committee wants to see you."

The disciplinary committee used the building office for a hearing room. Each youth waiting to be heard sat on a bench outside the office. One "G" Company counselor stood next to the door, watching the boy and waiting to usher him in when the last one came out. A second counselor brought another boy when he took one back to his cell. A youth was just going in when Alex arrived and was pointed to the bench.

The man beside the door eyed Alex for a long time. It was unabashed scrutiny, and thirty seconds of that is long. Finally the man asked, "How old are you, Hammond?"

"Fourteen," he lied glibly, adding three months.

"That's pretty young for Preston. There's a few your age, but eighty percent of our boys are sixteen or seventeen. You must be a fuckup."

Alex didn't know what—or if—he should answer, so he shrugged, but he was careful to avoid flippancy in the gesture.

"I know you fucked Kennedy up. He almost lost his eye . . . won't ever see right out of it again."

Once more Alex was silent; he couldn't very well say he was glad and that in the jungle culture it would give him status. Nobody else would try to take anything from him.

The door behind the man opened and a face with a goatee appeared. "Hammond?"

The man waved Alex in.

Three persons sat around the desk. It had been cleared except for a pile of manila folders. Each one contained a boy's file. Some were skinny, with just a few sheets of paper; others were thicker. Alex's was among the thickest. The man in the chair behind the desk (the other two were on each end) had a graying crewcut and a nameplate pinned to his jacket: J.N. KEPPEL, ASST. SUPT. He had a long, thin face and a sharp-bridged nose. His necktie was too tight, and it exaggerated his Adam's apple. The other two men were Reverend Flowers, the Protestant chaplain, and Mr. Hill, the institution's consulting psychologist. Keppel was obviously the power. He had the center position and his visage was stern, his eyes penetrating and cold. "It didn't take you long, did it, Hammond? You nearly killed that boy."

Alex looked down at the floor between his legs.

"What was it about, Alex?" the psychologist asked.

Alex shook his head without looking up.

"Christ almighty!" Keppel said, huffing and puffing. "We've got another *punk* with the *code*. Let me see his file." As he took the file, he added, "You don't like being called a *punk*, do you? That's bad, isn't it? Well, that's what you are—a *punk!*"

A punk submitted to sodomy, and to be called that was a bad insult. But Alex restrained a retort.

While Keppel leafed through the file, which he then handed to Reverend Flowers, Mr. Hill commented, "Kennedy says he doesn't know why you attacked him. Was he trying to fuck you?"

"Nobody's tryin' to fuck me," Alex said, raising up to snap angrily at the bait.

"Well, you must've had a reason."

"I've got nothing to say."

The chaplain, meanwhile, had brought out a letter stapled to a hand-addressed envelope. Letter and envelope had been loose in the folder, not holed and spindled. "Did you see this?" he asked his associates.

The psychologist shook his head and took the letter. Alex was halfway watching them, curious about what it was. It wasn't a regular report from an official.

"You're not a child and you aren't going to get kid gloves around here," Keppel was saying. "We have fist fights around here . . . but we don't have punks doing this. You've got a lot of violence on your record. Don't you ever want to get out of these places?"

"Sure I do . . . but . . ."

"But what?"

"Nothing."

"Say, Alex," the chaplain interrupted after reading the letter. "Your aunt is looking for you."

"Aunt. What aunt?"

"Your father's sister. She and her husband just moved to Los Angeles and tried to find her brother. She found out that . . . about him . . . and that you were in Whittier. She wrote this"—he held up the letter—"but you were gone, *sic transit gloria*, from Whittier. You had escaped."

Alex was frowning, head spinning. He vaguely recalled his father mentioning a sister; she had a husband Clem disliked, or so it seemed. Alex didn't even know her name. It didn't really matter what he remembered of yesterday; the future was what counted. An aunt!

"Can I write her?"

"I'm sure we can arrange that," said the chaplain expansively.

"Hold that up, Mr. Flowers," interrupted the assistant superintendent. "You can talk to him tomorrow. This is a disciplinary hearing." To Alex he said, "You're here on a *serious* charge—attempted murder of that boy." Now Keppel's voice had the wrath of righteousness. Gone was the false fatherliness most of them used talking to him. The harsh tone was a bony finger of accusation, an accusation that demanded an accounting and responsibility. It surprised Alex. He was already spinning about this new aunt, his father's sister. Did it mean he had a home somewhere?

"You sneaked up on him like a coward and hit him when he wasn't looking. And you're old enough to know just what you were doing."

"Yeah, I knew . . . and I wish I'd killed the motherfucker!" The words flew forth unbidden, unexpected. In a way he meant them, at least figuratively; Kennedy had started it by taking the shoes. Whether or not he meant it literally he would have to think about when he wasn't upset.

The sentence upset them instantly. They all sat up straighter, and their eyes came to life. Mr. Keppel turned ashen and then red, and then even redder with white spots in the red, while his jaw muscles pulsed. He looked back and forth at his associates with the jerky motions of a chicken moving its head.

Alex expected him to yell, but when he spoke it was almost a whisper, albeit a furious whisper:

"Can we send this . . . this . . . to San Quentin? Is he old enough? What's the law?"

Alex was sorry he'd flared up. Now he hurt, and they would *never* forget. It would be an immutable fact documented in his file forevermore. Whenever someone looked in the file they would see that he was unremorsefully homicidal. He already knew about files; whatever was in them became the gospel. Who knew how long people would be deciding his worth and destiny by the file? He wanted to say he was sorry, but he couldn't—so he sat with a burning, unrepentant face while Keppel learned that only seventeen-year-olds could be moved to San Quentin, and then only in unusual cases.

"I'd say it's unusual enough—he's already shot a man, too. But he's only—" He looked at the age on the file and decided not to say it aloud.

Being unable to transfer a thirteen-year-old to San Quentin, the disciplinary committee ordered him assigned permanently to "G" Company, with review of the order in six months. On the report of their decision, which also went in the file, it was their conclusion that he'd committed an unprovoked armed assault on another boy, that he showed no remorse whatsoever, and he was too unpredictably explosive to be trusted in the general population.

That night they moved him to the other side of "G" Company.

■

From the beginning Alex knew he would remain in "G" Company until he went to "Broadway," the nickname for freedom. How long that would be was unknown, but until whenever happened he would be in a "G" Company cell.

The routine was monastic, and Alex adjusted to it quickly. The daily schedule was simple and seldom deviated from. He ate in the building's small mess hall with the rest of "G" Company's permanent residents. After breakfast, he went out on one of the three crews, carrying hoe, shovel, rake, or mattock, depending on the job to be done. Sometimes it was chopping weeds on hillsides or removing them from roadside drainage ditches so the water would flow better. They dug up leaky pipes or loaded piles of rotting lumber on trucks. In autumn they raked leaves all over the institution, and for two months they cut off the side of a small hill to widen a road. When it rained, they sat indoors shucking peas from their pods. Most of the work was hard labor in the sun, although it was just for six hours a day. When his muscles adjusted, Alex didn't mind the work. He actually sometimes took joy in it. At eleven A.M.

they came in to eat lunch and were locked up until one. They worked again until four, when they showered and ate again. If the weather was good they were let into a small, fenced yard next to the building until it got dark. In the winter they went directly to their cells after supper. Twice a week a teacher came down at night for an hour, using the mess hall as a classroom, thereby satisfying the state law about every adolescent attending school. The teacher had no curriculum. He donated magazines they could read and take back to their cells; or else he gave them pencils and paper and coaxed them into writing letters home, which was the only place they were allowed to write to. The teacher also had workbook courses in English and mathematics that the boys could do in their cells, but few bothered to take them, nor did Alex. He disliked any structure and hated math anyway. He fed his yearning for knowledge by voracious reading. A utility closet had been converted into a makeshift library holding a couple hundred of the coverless, donated books. He managed to get one of the men to let him into the bookroom for a few minutes once or twice a week. He always grabbed half a dozen books without bothering to open their pages to read the titles. That took too much time with the man waiting, his key inserted in the lock. Nobody else was interested in the bookroom, so Alex devised a procedure where he put the books he'd read on their backs on a shelf, and then taking the next batch in order so he wouldn't get what he'd already read. The collection was eclectic and middlebrow, from Book-of-the-Month Club best-sellers to nonfiction leaning toward history and psychology. At night he always read, from the time he went into the cell until lights-out, and sometimes when he was particularly engrossed he read long after that. A floodlight outside the building threw enough light through the window to read by if he sat on the edge of the bunk with his back to the window. It took him eight months to read every book in the room, even those on uninteresting topics, like religion. After that he got the teacher to bring him books. They were fewer in number but of better overall quality. He would've talked to the teacher about books if the eyes of the others weren't always present.

As for religion, Alex got his fair share from his aunt's letters. Every month or so they wrote each other. Along with five dollars, she never failed to admonish him to accept Our Lord, to turn to Him for the way. . . . Her letters were short and uneasily formal and repetitive, the letters of someone unaccustomed to writing. If he snickered at the religious parts, he did so with gentle thoughts, imagining her as a kindly woman he would like—and be able to manipulate. It was understood very near the start that he would come to stay with her and her husband whenever he was paroled. They'd opened a small café in Los Angeles. Her husband cooked and she worked as a waitress.

Alex turned fourteen in "G" Company. The hard labor conditioned him as he filled out. He was still growing, but now he stood five-seven and weighed one thirty-nine, not a mature man but not a bony eleven-year-old either. He got to know the names of everyone in "G" Company, but of the thirty boys permanently assigned, he never spoke to half except when absolutely necessary. Others he kept aloof from, and only a handful did he associate with at all. And just two were friends. Both were fuckups. One was Allen, known as Twig because he was tall, thin and gawky. Twig had been in Whittier with Alex. He was in permanent segregation because a black cadet officer in "N" Company had kicked him for horseplay and then knocked out his two front teeth when Twig fought back. Twig melted down a toothbrush handle and inserted a razor blade in it while it was soft. When it hardened he was ready. Twig waited until the other youth was bent shirtless over a sink. Twig walked up behind him and stroked once all the way down his back with the razor blade held in the handle. It took a hundred and fourteen sutures to sew up the cut—and Twig was assigned permanently to "G" Company. In later years, after prison and bouts with electric-shock therapy in state hospitals, Twig would become the West Coast leader of the American Nazi party.

Alex's other friend was Marsh, a burly seventeen-year-old who'd killed a man who was fighting with his father over a traffic dispute. They were rolling on the ground and Marsh came to his father's aid with a tire iron. He was fresh from Oklahoma and had a heavy accent that caused him trouble sometimes. The city boys ridiculed him, while the blacks assumed from his voice that he was a bigot. Not that it really bothered him; he was a junior-sized grizzly. He wasn't allowed to bring in cartons of cigarettes as were those on the mainline, but the Man usually let him bring two or three packs. He couldn't keep them in his cell, but he could get a few after each meal and when they went out into the yard. Marsh, Twig, and Alex didn't have to roll the Bull Durham when the sack was passed down the mess hall table. They hated Bull Durham, although it was fine when they could get hands on a bag and smuggle it into the cells where they weren't supposed to smoke.

He got to talk to Lulu when the Mexican came down for thirty days. Lulu had gotten drunk on home brew and put a turd in the shoe-shop foreman's lunchpail. Alex saw Watkins by going to the hospital on sick call or to see the dentist, for Watkins was a hospital orderly. Since the failure of the escape, Watkins had been working his way out of the reformatory. He went home three weeks before Alex got word that his own application for parole was being granted. It had taken two months after the caseworker put in the papers. His aunt had written the Youth Authority via the caseworker; so had her Baptist minister in her church. He hadn't been in any trouble in the quiet routine of "G" Company. Mainly, however, he had served a total of more than three years when they added the time spent in state hospitals and Whittier. The average stay was eleven months. When the caseworker brought him word that he was going home, he added that there was one special condition: the parole officer in L.A. was instructed to arrange a psychotherapy program for him. The Youth Authority members were worried about his temper and potential for violence.

"As soon as he sends us a teletype on that, you'll be on your way."

"How long'll that be?"

"We have to send your files first. I'd say two, three weeks at the most."

Three weeks!

As the days passed, Alex swelled with expectations, dreams, and ideas. Often he couldn't sleep until early morning as he thought about being free, legitimately free. Would the last morning finally arrive?

It did, of course.

fear of freedom, an emotion known to everyone imprisoned for very long and repressed by everyone else, came upon Alex the night before his parole. Until that moment he'd handled the situation by not really thinking about it. He performed the behavior of release—talking to social workers, getting measured for clothes, taking a "dressout" photo— without dwelling on what these things meant, detached from *feeling*. When he couldn't ignore it any longer, he broke out in a heavy sweat and felt nauseated. The fear had nothing specific to focus on, nothing to overcome. Indeed, it was the lack of specifics, the lack of knowledge, that engendered the fear. It was going into the unknown. That was the world outside, the unknown. What did he know of freedom? The episodes of escape, when he'd been a fugitive, weren't preparation for real freedom and its demands. The fear came upon him when the garrulous bedtime dialogues were cut off by lights-out. The darkness triggered the previously suppressed fear; it had been kept hidden by talk and horseplay. As the release date neared, sleep became harder. It was most unusual, because he always slept easily, no matter how tough the circumstances. In fact, he usually slept to avoid tension. . . .

Alex's eyes were open when the cell lights came on for the last time. His mouth was cottony and he had stomach cramps. Alex swiftly stripped the bedding from the mattress. Days ago his locker had been cleaned out, so now there was one set of new underwear that he'd wear to freedom and the ragged shirt and jeans that he'd discard in Receiving and Release. He'd finished dressing and brushing his teeth when the night counselor unlocked his door.

"C'mon, Hammond," he said. "I'll escort you to Receiving and Release when my relief gets here."

Outdoors was bright with a lingering night coolness, the weather that raises hopes and spirits. Later it would be hot, but now it was perfect. As Alex crossed the detail grounds, heading toward R&R in the basement of the Castle, exultant anticipation swept away the night's doubts. He was finally going to be legitimately free, and there were infinite possibilities in everything. So good was his mood that he was humming aloud, and he stopped momentarily to look at the institution's brick buildings dotting the hills. He felt a tug of affection for the reform school, not that he would ever admit it. Looking back, it hadn't been that tough. Yeah, maybe *tough*, but not *terrible*. According to books he'd read, prep schools were also tough in their way. Here in Preston he'd gotten smarter, and he'd made lifelong friends. He had many addresses and phone numbers in his sock.

Outside the door, the escort shook hands with Alex. "Guess I can leave you here."

The freeman was due any moment. A small-boned, extremely dark black youth appeared, carrying four unframed paintings, two in each hand. He, too, was being paroled this morning, and the paintings were his own work or he wouldn't be allowed to take them. The paintings surprised Alex. He knew nothing of art, but the two he could see (one a slum cityscape, the other a view of the Golden Gate Bridge) looked good. It surprised Alex because the black looked really stupid. He'd seen the black in the white clothes of a kitchen worker, but they'd never spoken and didn't know each other's names. Now the black ignored Alex and leaned the paintings on the wall.

"That bridge is nice," Alex said. "You do it?" Alex knew he had.

The black hesitated, suspicion in his eyes. "Yeah, I done it. I'm takin' it home to Mama . . . that one. Gonna try to sell the others."

"We'll be travelin' together, huh?"

"Nope. My mama and her boyfriend are drivin' from Oakland. They'll be at the gate."

"Yeah, I'm goin' to L.A. anyway, out near Santa Monica. I've got an aunt and uncle came out from Louisville last year. Ain't never seen 'em, but they've—" Alex stopped talking, realizing the black youth wasn't listening. The Receiving and Release man appeared at that moment, his keys jingling.

Twenty minutes later, when they were dressed and given their sealed packages (sealed so nothing could be slipped into them and smuggled out), the man escorted them upstairs in the Castle to the cashier's office. The black boy got the nine dollars in his account; he got nothing else because he was going out to "home and care." Alex got forty-four dollars and a ticket for the train, plus a sheet of travel instructions and the address and phone number of his parole officer. He had to report to the parole officer within forty-eight hours of arrival.

All that remained was to leave, but even that required a wait. The R&R man had Alex sit on a hallway bench outside the administrative offices while he, the man, escorted the black to the front gate. Then he went for a state car to drive Alex to Stockton, twenty miles away.

While the man was gone, the office workers began arriving for work. None of them knew Alex, so none spoke, except one young secretary; she saw from his clothes that he was being released. "Good luck," she said. "Stay out of trouble. This isn't a fun place to grow up."

"Thank you," Alex said, then blushed furiously. He could smell her cologne, and when she walked away he stared at her legs and buttocks, which were the ideal of his sexual fantasies. Every boy in the reform school had masturbated over her, and the memory of doing it caused Alex to blush. That and the fact that he hadn't talked to any female (except the old nurse in the hospital) for more than a year. When she was gone her scent lingered, strong to him because that, too, had been a long time back.

The R&R man was silent while driving through the countryside to Stockton. Alex was glad, for he thrilled at simply looking at the landscape. It wasn't magnificent countryside. Mostly it was alfalfa and grapes, with a few walnut orchards. This was not autumn, and it was dry and dusty. Heat waves shimmered early, prelude to a scorcher. Yet it was beautiful freedom and had infinite possibilities for him.

Stockton was a farm metropolis, serving a vast valley of unsurpassed munificence. Stockton had many tree-shaded streets, not just in the residential neighborhoods but also in part of the business section. It was larger than Alex expected; it took fifteen minutes from the outskirts of town to reach the train depot near the center.

"There's a two-hour wait, kid," the man said as he pulled to the curb and left the motor running. "Don't get in trouble. Last week I left three here. They're in jail down in Fresno. They stole a car instead of waiting for the train. The highway patrol ran 'em down four hours after they was released."

Alex laughed. "Don't worry. I'm not *that* crazy."

"Ain't my worry. Don't bother me none what you do. Good luck."

"Thanks," Alex said.

They completed the ritual of release by shaking hands; then Alex got out, package tucked under his arm, watching the state car until it turned a corner.

With the car's disappearance, freedom crashed on his sensibilities. It was nearly a physical blow, and for a moment it was frightening. Then he recalled that he had to catch a train, and somehow that mollified him. Still, there were two hours to fill. Several blocks away were signs above storefronts, and vehicle and pedestrian traffic was heavier. No doubt there was a place there to obtain a hamburger; his mouth salivated at the thought of relish, mustard, and onions. Hamburgers in Preston were a liberal mix of bread crumbs with ground meat, cooked in an oven so they were hard and dry on the outside and often raw in the center. Ah yes, he definitely wanted a hamburger. And the café would also have a cigarette machine.

He walked with a grin on his face, feeling a giddy hilarity, meanwhile oblivious to the sweat streaming down his forehead and making his shirt stick to him.

Although air-conditioning was a decade away from small cafés, a pivoting fan there created a cooling breeze. The café was nearly deserted; it was after the breakfast crowd and before lunch. Alex savored the hamburger, delighting in the juices and tastes of meat and relish, mustard and onions. He dripped sweat and finished eating. He wanted to walk around sightseeing before getting on the train.

A cigarette machine was next to the front door. He timed his exit so the waitress was at the rear—just in case she should say something. His twenty cents gave him a pack of Chesterfields and two pennies of change inside the cellophane. He'd left the waitress a quarter tip, and she ignored the minor illegally operating the cigarette machine.

Instead of walking a direct route down the boulevard to the train station, Alex zigzagged down shaded residential streets—just to see what was there. It was a habit he would always keep, this curiosity. Now he saw elderly persons on shaded porches of big, old houses; he saw tanned six-year-olds running through a lawn sprinkler. Two teenaged girls in cut-off blue jeans passed him from the opposite direction. As they went by he smelled, momentarily, their sweetness, and saw the hints of breasts pressing out at their shirts. That and imagination brought an immediate erection.

Yes, there was so much to do out here. He shook his head in expectation as he turned the last corner and saw that station half a block away. But a lot of what he did depended on Aunt Ada and her husband. Ray was his name. Alex impressed it in his mind, for he tended to forget it. Aunt Ada seemed good enough in the letters, except for the religious bullshit—but lots of middle-aged women got all involved with God. It was all right if she prayed for him, just as long as she didn't want him to pray. What he wanted was to work in the café, besides going to school (that was depressing), and save five dollars a week for an automobile. He was worth twenty-five dollars a week and room and board. He was old enough for a learner's permit, but certainly they would understand that he was more mature than most fourteen-year-olds, and that when he was fifteen in a few months (he wouldn't be able to save enough money until then anyway), it would be right to say he was sixteen so he could get a license and have some kind of car. It was so important that he couldn't let doubt creep into his mind, at least not into his conscious mind. He had some other ideas and hopes, too, but he'd wait to see how everyone got along before bringing them out. Maybe he'd been wrong when he stood on the San Pedro breakwater and saw himself fated to be an outlaw. Maybe he had a chance for something else.

20

when the train came out of the switchbacks and curves of the mountains into the basin of the San Fernando Valley, now gathering speed for the final twenty-mile run into Los Angeles' Union Station, the sun was a red half-disk being pulled down between the peaks into the unseen Pacific. Alex had stared avidly from the window every minute of the journey. He'd just read *The Grapes of Wrath*, and when the train went through Salinas and Soledad and the other towns of Steinbeck's world, he wondered where the people were. These were sleepy farm villages without enough life for drama; or maybe there were things he was unable to see. Now it was the San Fernando Valley, and it was all orange groves and alfalfa and desert except for a few small communities close to the Hollywood Hills. On their fringes were the white, wood skeletons of tract homes, precursors to the greatest exodus in human history, though Alex Hammond had no awareness of such things as he rode by.

Dusk became darkness as the train entered the city of Los Angeles. Union Station was minutes away. Now the ramshackle houses with sagging fences were jammed close. In the night only their lights, not their meanness, could be seen. A happy excitement was in the boy as the train slowed. He was among the first to enter the domed vault of the station, the most beautiful in America, built less than a decade before passenger trains became obsolete.

This evening the station was nearly deserted in the area where he disembarked. The big blond woman and the husky man almost had to be his father's sister and her husband. Anxiety made his stomach queasy, but he moved toward them, at first slowly, and then when the woman waved, he picked up speed.

"Alex?" she asked when he was close.

"I'm . . . uh . . . he . . . him?"

The woman laughed, releasing some tension of her own. Her eyes, however, studied the nephew without laughter, sizing him up.

"Well, glad to meet you," the man said. "I'm Ray." The barest trace of a Scandinavian accent was discernible. His hand was calloused and his grip firm. "We'd better get the car," he said. "We're in a no parking, and I wouldn't want to get towed away."

They walked silently through the huge train depot. Ava Hammond Olsen indicated the package under Alex's arm. "Is that all you've got?"

"All my worldly goods. Grown-up ex-cons do better."

She turned her face away quickly, affected by the sentence. "Let's hope that's all behind you now," she said reasonably. Everyone knew the message and what had caused it.

"Are you hungry?" Ray asked, filling the vacuum.

"I can't really tell with all the butterflies in my stomach."

"We'll go home," Ava said. "Eat there if we're hungry."

The car was a prewar Plymouth sedan, well cared for. When Ray unlocked it, Alex got in the back seat, feeling the upholstery and looking at the symmetry of the dashboard's dials. He wondered if they would lie about his age so he could get a driver's license. He'd be fifteen in a couple of months, and even if that was technically too young, certainly Ava and Ray would see he was older than his years—see how urgent a car was, and he'd pay for it from working in the café. He wanted forty dollars a week, one dollar an hour, after they'd deducted for room and board. He'd save ten a week for clothes and another ten for the car. It wasn't too much to ask.

In Union Station he'd had no chance to really study the couple, his aunt and her husband. Now they were silent, dark silhouettes lighted momentarily by splashes of street lamps. Did they like him, or were they just doing "the right thing"? Maybe they wanted the Aid to Dependent Children money the state would pay them for his care. That wasn't likely; she'd indicated he had a place to go before she knew the state provided money for him.

The Olsen residence was a rear bungalow on a long, narrow lot. Instead of coming in the driveway past the side of the front house, Ray turned down a rutted alley behind the property. He parked next to the back door.

As Ray turned the key in the door, Ava said, "We've only got one bedroom, but we fixed up the porch." It was where they were stepping, the foot of the bed directly to the right. It was identical with the surplus army cot he'd been sleeping on. But he hadn't had a dresser, even a small, old dresser, with a mirror. If it was small, it was larger than some places he'd been. The window had no bars; it was big and had a screen outside the glass. He could let in the night and keep out the insects. The way it was arranged he had some privacy. Someone going from the kitchen door out the back door would pass by the foot of his bed. It was more privacy than he was used to.

"We thought about a larger place," Ray said, "but"—he shook his head—"but there's a terrible housing shortage since the war started. Now that it's over, they should start building."

"We even considered buying a two-bedroom a couple of blocks from the beach, but they wanted eight thousand. It's better to wait until new construction brings prices down."

While they passed through the kitchen to the tiny living room, Ray asked, "What would you like to eat?"

Alex shrugged.

"How's a bacon and tomato sandwich sound?"

"Great."

"I'd like one, too," Ava said. Then to Alex, "Ray does our cooking, you know. We don't keep much here . . . what with the café just across the way."

Ray had opened the front door and picked up a folded newspaper. The bloated headline read: BUGSY SIEGEL SLAIN. Ray obviously wanted to read the story, but he had to leave to make the sandwiches, so he gave it a cursory scrutiny, commenting, "They all get caught . . . one way or another," and he left for the café.

Alex picked up the newspaper. A photo showed the gangster's body twisted in death, the blood black in the picture, covering the upper part. The room was plush, and Alex noticed the hundred-dollar shoes Bugsy wore. "It paid for a while," the boy muttered.

"What?" his aunt asked. She was putting her coat on a hanger.

"Nothing." He dropped the newspaper, planning to read it later. In Preston the boys talked about the famous criminals—Dillinger, Capone, Luciano. Bugsy Siegel had always interested Alex. Someone, maybe Big Zeke, had told a story that Alex remembered. Bugsy had been in Sing-Sing on Death Row, two weeks from meeting the electric chair for gangland killings. It was part of "Murder Incorporated," a press name. Anyway, Governor Dewey had gone to see Bugsy, offering him a commutation if he'd turn state's evidence and cooperate. Bugsy replied, "I've been icing stool pigeons all my life. I ain't changin' now." Dewey went away red-faced. Before the execution (Lepke and others burned), an appeals court reversed Bugsy's conviction. The state was unable to convict him in a retrial. Alex had believed the story, and for him it had as much courage as Nathan Hale's famous line when facing the hangman. More, in fact: Bugsy had been offered a reprieve.

The story was untrue, but Alex didn't know that yet.

Ava returned from the bedroom closet. They sat down, he on a stuffed chair, she on the sofa, and there was an empty moment of the kind that must be filled.

"Tomorrow morning you'll go sign up for school. It's four blocks right up the street." She gestured to indicate which direction.

School! He'd refused to think about it before, though he knew it was demanded by law. He loved learning but had always loathed attending school. And it had been so long since he'd gone. Reformatory classrooms weren't the same thing. "Tomorrow's Friday, Aunt Ava. Can't I wait until Monday?"

"Yes, I suppose it wouldn't hurt. It might be good for you to have a few leisurely days right now."

"Another thing. I want to go part-time . . . with a work permit . . . and work for you and Ray in the café." The last words were softer and less vigorous, for the wrinkles had perceptibly deepened on her forehead, and her mouth wasn't responding favorably either. "We'll talk about it later," he finished, but his stomach was knotted with worry.

Ray had the sandwiches and small bags of potato chips in a sack.

"I'll put them on dishes," Aunt Ava said, taking the sack and disappearing into the kitchen. "Alex . . . milk or coffee?"

"Milk, please."

Ray eased the slight tension by making a face—distended cheeks and rolling eyes. Then he shrugged as Alex smiled and picked up the newspaper. "I have to know what's going on in the world—as if I could do anything about anything."

The sandwiches had been halved and stuck with toothpicks. "Watch for crumbs," she said. "We usually eat in the kitchen."

"No, honey," Ray said, "we usually eat across the street. We have morning coffee here, sometimes."

"But when we do, we eat in the kitchen?"

"Okay."

Alex would have eaten carefully, conscious of it, even without the admonition. Institutions developed the habit of wolfing down food with slight concern for amenities (more than once he'd spat some terrible concoction on the mess-hall floor, napkins not being provided), so now he had to watch himself. When he was through, he relaxed, and without thinking he fired up a cigarette. Indeed, he failed to look around for an ashtray until the match had nowhere to go except the plate. He dropped it there; then his gaze came up to meet theirs. Their blank faces and flat eyes made him color.

"Do that outside, please," Ava said. "We don't smoke, and that foul smell stays in the house. Don't you know they're coffin nails?"

"Yeah, sure," Alex replied, now standing up, deciding. "I'll go without this time," he said, then went into the kitchen, doused the cigarette in the sink, and deposited it in the garbage can. The kitchen, like everything else, was obsessively clean. Even the bottles of Windex, bleach, soap, and polishes were arranged precisely in a floor-high cupboard. Everything was so neat that he was apprehensive about touching anything. He was already feeling boxed in and uncomfortable. About them, so far he had no feeling of like or dislike.

The serious talk about specifics was put off that night. The Olsens went to bed virtually at sundown, especially in midsummer. Ray was up at four-thirty A.M. to prepare the café for a six A.M. opening. Ava rose an hour later. She worked both the breakfast and luncheon rush, plus did the bookkeeping and paperwork. The café employed one full-time waitress and one part-time; also a dishwasher.

In his porch-bedroom Alex opened the window. Insects scratched on the windowscreen, seeking admittance. But only the night air, laden with the ocean scent, came in. Alex dropped trousers and shirt on the floor and lay down on the cool sheets, planning to mull over his situation, to make decisions. It was obvious that their reality was different from his. What did they expect of him?

Before he could do much thinking, he fell asleep. It had been a subtly exhausting day.

■

The bungalow was empty when Alex woke up at eight-thirty. After a quick shower (he carefully wiped up splattered water) he dressed in the clothes of yesterday.

I gotta get some more, he thought. His wardrobe consisted of what he wore—slacks, shirt, windbreaker—and one extra set of underwear and socks. He had enough for a pair of Levi's and tennis shoes; he'd go today. He also had to see his parole officer within the week.

When he went out, he saw even more clearly how small and jerry-built the bungalow was. If it hadn't been so well-arranged and immaculate it would have been another slum shack. The café across the street was also smaller than he'd expected. What he wanted wouldn't be a financial burden. Ava and Ray would surely understand.

The sunlight was already so bright on the sidewalk that he narrowed his eyes against the glare. Later the hot, dry air would feel weighted, draining energy and shortening tempers. His stomach called

for food. He went in through the back door, a shed added to the building. Here the dishwasher worked and vegetables were peeled. At the
moment it was empty. Through its door was the kitchen. Ray was there,
a bandanna around his forehead so sweat wouldn't trickle into his eyes.
The kitchen was sweltering. Ray didn't see Alex for a minute, and Alex
watched the smooth, expert motions of spatula and spoon as Ray readied eggs, pancakes, bacon. . . . Ray had a spare tire of fat around his
waist, and Alex was as tall, but beneath the fat the man was powerful,
much more so than Clem had been. His white T-shirt was soaked
through and stuck to his torso. He was pushing plates of food through
the slot so Ava and the waitress could deliver them.

"Hey, kid," Ray said. "Hungry?"

"Sure am."

"We don't have much, but you never have to worry about having
plenty to eat. How's steak and eggs sound?"

"I'd rather have a waffle and ham."

"So be it. Go out front."

The café had thirty stools in a horseshoe shape, half of which were
occupied, as were three of the four booths along the front windows.
Most of the patrons were local workingmen, men with calluses and
grease embedded in their hands. They came from two machine shops,
and two new-car dealerships down the block.

Alex perched on the end seat of the counter, next to the passage behind it and to the kitchen. The waitress, who had very large breasts that
popped one button on her uniform, obviously knew of him—her wide
smile and wink of greeting told him so. Ava stopped for a moment.
"What do you want to eat?"

"I told Ray already."

"Then what are you going to do?"

"I dunno . . . not exactly."

"I think you should go sign up for school. Ray does too."

Her tone nicked his suspicions. Sure the two of them talked about
him. That was to be expected. But something told him to be careful; the
reference to Ray had vague implications, as if they intended to make the
decisions governing his life. They wanted to perform the role of parents; he wanted them simply to supply room and board—for work and
state money—and let him go his way. It had been so long since he'd had
parents, for ten years. He was used to doing what he wanted when outside institutions. It would come out badly if they tried to take over as
parents according to standards followed by most fourteen-year-olds—or
even fifteen-year-olds, which was just around the corner.

"Where is it?"

"Not too far. Go down to Sixteenth Street, that's two blocks, then turn left and it's about four blocks."

"Okay."

Two men in shirtsleeves and neckties came in the front door. As soon as they were in a booth, Ava had glasses of water and menus in front of them. Before she could return to Alex, three men in overalls came in and took another booth.

The waitress brought Alex his breakfast. It was delicious. For three years he hadn't eaten a waffle, since before he ran away from the Valley Home for Boys. Institutions never served real syrup, or else diluted it grossly with water. Now Alex gulped down the waffles, syrup, and ham; it was too good to savor slowly. When he was through, the café was busy. Aunt Ava was too rushed to talk for more than a quick good-bye. He promised to be back before dark.

When he stood in the sunlight on the sidewalk he nearly skipped with joy. Without thinking about it, he'd started toward the high school, but before covering the first two blocks he decided that he would postpone that ugliness. The day was too beautiful; he felt too good. He'd tell Ava and Ray that they wanted him to come back on Monday. Today he'd enjoy himself, visit Teresa and JoJo, find out how to locate Wedo, maybe even look up Miss Coupe de Ville after dark; he'd never find her during the daylight hours. His stride had a bounce as he headed for the streetcar line. He felt glorious as he rode for fifty minutes on the big red trolley. The ride itself was a joyful excursion past an exciting sight—the bizarre but beautiful Watts Towers. The sun was behind the towers, fringing them orange. Plaster curlicues with bottoms of Coca-Cola bottles implanted glistened in the sunlight, while arabesques of steel gave the towers great strength. They somehow reminded Alex of pictures of Angkor Wat in Indochina. Engineers, he remembered reading, had examined Roda's towers and declared them safe. Dozens of times he'd ridden by on the streetcar, often thinking he'd someday visit them. It could not be this day; he had serious matters waiting for him.

His destination was ten minutes away when the streetcar rattled past the oil refinery—a gigantic tangle of pipes, valves, wisps of steam, and giant tanks. Next were the shipyards, now nearly deserted compared to his memory of them. Finally, he smelled the stench of fishing boat docks and canneries, an odor that could nauseate but which now excited him. In minutes he'd be walking up the hill to the house.

He got off the big red streetcar. Front Street's denizens kept holed up during daylight. The neon signs were out; for all their brilliance they couldn't compete with sunlight. The hot-dog stands still had their graffiti-emblazoned shutters down; the box offices of burlesque theaters and triple-feature movie houses were closed; the latter had dumped their bleary-eyed lost souls on the sidewalk about seven A.M., and they had scurried for cover. Shanghai Red's, the Top Hat, and most of the other bars were open, but nobody was in them except a bartender and janitor, one rinsing glasses, the other mopping the floor. Alex strolled along with a bounce, looking into the dark doorways, feeling wonderful.

But he knew it was too early. Those he might want to see came out closer to twelve midnight than twelve noon. Even the pool hall was empty, the manager counting the change in the cash register. He was new—or at least newer than the eighteen months that Alex had been gone. Alex wanted to stop and ask him about JoJo, but the house was just a few minutes away. Someone there would tell him all he wanted to know. Teresa would be in school, but JoJo himself might be there if he'd gotten out, and if nothing else, Lorraine would know. He would take her something to drink; just some beer would be okay. Lorraine would like that.

Alex circled through the side streets and alleys, and found whom he was seeking—actually three of them together—sucking wine from a bottle in a paper bag. For fifty cents one of them got him the bottle he wanted.

He headed toward the house, a stupid grin on his face as he went up the front steps and rang the bell. Immediately the family dog barked. Moments later the curtain moved, exposing the flash of a face—and then the door opened wide. It took some blinking moments to recognize Lisa: the eleven-year-old was now thirteen, and her metamorphosis into a young woman was nearly complete. Curves had replaced bony angularity. She had breasts instead of flatness.

"Alex!"

"Is that you—Lisa?"

She laughed to cover her blush. "Don't stare . . . come in!" She turned and yelled, "Mama! It's Alex!"

The reply was muffled, but Lisa led him into the kitchen. As usual, the unwashed dishes filled sink and counter. Lorraine was in a housecoat at the kitchen table, drinking coffee. She rose to hug him with real affection, apologized for her garb and the condition of the house—as if the dirt and clutter were unusual. "Sit down . . . down. My goodness you've filled out," she gushed, feeling his biceps like a little girl. It made her daughter blush.

"I've filled out—but not as much as Lisa."

The girl colored even more.

Lorraine made a twisted face, saying silently that Lisa caused her worry because of her blossoming. "I thought Teresa hypnotized the boys—but this one . . ."

"Mama . . . please."

"Get Alex some coffee."

As Alex put in the cream and sugar, he told them about getting paroled yesterday and that he was living with an aunt and her husband. He also realized that this unkempt house enfolded him in more human warmth than did the house of his relatives. There was something cold about Ava and Ray. Their sternness (he knew they were holding some of it back) was unmollified by warmth and love.

"Oh Alex," Lisa said, "I have to go to school. I really would like to stay and talk."

"You have to see the eye doctor, too," Lorraine said. Then to Alex, "She might need glasses."

"I'll *never* wear them."

"Yes you will."

Alex laughed. Even this trivial family argument warmed him. It was so utterly different from the world he was accustomed to. His laughter brought a truce between Lisa and her mother. The girl kissed his cheek and departed.

Two cups of coffee later, he learned of events during his absence. JoJo had been paroled from Whittier six months ago and was now living with a maternal uncle in King City, a farm town an hour southeast of San Francisco; he was working in a gas station. Lorraine would give Alex the phone number if he promised not to give it to Wedo.

"How come? You always liked Wedo."

Lorraine's eyes dropped, and either sadness or hardness masked her features. Instead of speaking, she silently made a gesture of pumping her right hand toward the inner aspect of her left elbow. It took a few puzzled seconds before Alex realized she was depicting that Wedo was "shooting" with heroin. It stunned Alex, and then, very clearly, he thought: *That isn't the end of the world. I know junkies and they aren't zombies.*

"What about Teresa? What's with her and Wedo?"

"Her father will call the police if he tries to see her."

"What does she say about that?"

"What can she say? She just cried."

One reason Alex had come here was to locate Wedo. This was where he could pick up the trail. Or so he'd thought before. Now he didn't know—and didn't know if he wanted to see Wedo.

"Are you sure it's heroin? What about pills and pot—or booze?"

"No, no, it's—that! He used our bathroom and didn't come out. When we finally went in—Teresa first and she screamed—he was out on the floor with dried blood on his arm. The kit—"

"Outfit," Alex corrected.

"Okay, the outfit—was right there on the floor. He was out cold and gasping like he was dying. My husband called an ambulance, but before it got here Wedo woke up—sort of. He was still woozy and goofy, but he wouldn't wait for the ambulance. He got out the back door. When he called the next afternoon, my husband told him to never show his face or we'd call the police."

"That's too bad," Alex said, having learned a little guile, wondering how he'd locate Wedo. Teresa might still have contact without her parents knowing. It was probable, knowing her, for loyalty was one of her strong traits. But it was just noon, and she wasn't expected until after four P.M. That was too long to wait, not if he had to just sit with Lorraine doing nothing. Freedom was still too new. It was unlikely Wedo, now nineteen, still lived in the smelly room with his mother, but she still might be there, and wherever Wedo was and whatever he was doing, he would be in touch with his mother. Even a junkie could be a loving and dutiful son.

■

Alex hitchhiked to half a mile from the decrepit firetrap of a rooming house. Both rides took him in immediately after he raised a thumb, but it was still nearly three hours until he was walking the last few blocks of the journey. Los Angeles was already the sprawling *bête noir* of public transportation, and traveling this route would have taken yet another hour and four transfers; the miracle of the freeways was still in the future. Thus he trudged the last half mile under the mellow hues of afternoon sun, wishing he had an automobile. It was still warm enough to make him sweat, but he bought a Pepsi, drank it on the move, and had the quiet affection of familiarity with the area, which was blighted for living in while blooming for business. He enjoyed passing the clusters of people around vending trucks outside the garment factories—so many old women with seamed, strong faces of several colors; children and the old had no race other than human. In the empty lots littered with wine bottles and beer cans played mostly olive-skinned, dark-eyed children with dirty faces. Toward them Alex felt like an adult. He passed two Chicanos about his own age. They wore the khaki pants and perfectly pressed Pendleton shirts that had become the newest uniform of East Los Angeles barrios and gangs. They looked hard at him, a Paddy in a non-Paddy neighborhood, and he looked away—not because he was afraid, although locked stares would have led to words, and from there to a fight, but because his mood was too good to spoil with anger and violence. He knew it wasn't their turf; theirs was two blocks away, around Clanton Street. This lacked enough dwellings to spawn a gang claiming it.

When he reached the dismal second-floor corridor of the rooming house, nobody answered his knock, nor did he see anyone to ask if Wedo's mother still lived there. Knocking on a neighbor's door to ask questions wasn't done here. At best he would find a woman who spoke no English, or someone who would glare suspiciously from behind a door chain.

At a liquor store on the corner, he bought gum, a newspaper, and another Pepsi, and then felt justified in asking to use a pencil and a piece of paper. He left a note with Aunt Ava's phone number under the door.

As he walked away, looking at everything with the same open hunger as a tourist, he felt something entirely new. It was the first consciousness of his own strength. Always before he'd been a frightened boy, helpless before the whims of any adult. This had been especially true in those hours after midnight when children didn't roam the city's streets, and anyone who saw him would know something was amiss; any adult might play concerned citizen and grab him or call the police. In the last year he'd grown and filled out. He would grow even bigger and stronger, but he was already beyond where just anyone could grab his arm and take him along. Although he would turn fifteen in six weeks, he could claim eighteen, albeit a young-looking eighteen. He felt a surge of manhood as he walked through the mellowing afternoon sun. It warmed his back. He bounced on the balls of his feet, feeling the thigh muscles flex and harden. He rolled his shoulders and twisted his torso. He felt good, really good, strong and quick.

21

as the bus whooshed to a stop, he saw it was packed, standees bumping into each other with the sway. He hesitated while others boarded. He loathed being pressed in like a sardine. Then he suddenly realized that the jam meant the rush hour. It was an hour later than he'd thought, and he already expected words from Aunt Ava for being late. He swung up and on; the fare had risen a nickel during his last incarceration.

While he held on and the bus crawled across the sprawling city, the night came. Neon and street lights grew to brightness as they had more darkness to feed upon. Although Alex disliked the press of bodies and their inevitable smells, he enjoyed watching the faces and hearing snatches of conversation. It was as different from what he was accustomed to as a bus in Peking would be to the average citizen.

When he got off there was a warm wind, endemic to southern California and called a Santa Ana. It rustled the palm trees as he trudged the last block to his aunt's house. He knew the late hour would require a story. He would say that after signing up for school he'd gone looking for a job. He would become indignant if they pressed to have specifics. The bungalow's lights were on when he turned in. Through a partly raised window he could hear the radio and recognized the voice of radio commentator H. V. Kaltenborn, who was analyzing why the country was in a postwar inflation and recession.

The front door was unlocked, so Alex went in. The front room was empty, but the radio voice and other noises came from the kitchen. Alex went in and found his aunt with green ledgers, receipts, the cash register tape, and a metal box of cash.

He rapped on the door frame. "Hi," he said.

"Oh!" She jerked upright; then a narrower look came to her face, reflecting a new thought. "Where have you been?"

"Looking for a part-time job."

"Did you sign up for school?"

"I went there and they told me to wait. So I sat for a couple of hours, and then they said somebody was sick and it'd be better if I came back on Monday." His eyes told him that his words weren't having the desired mollifying effect. Her expression was even more sour, and a knot of dread in his belly became a balloon. Although something was obviously wrong, he had to play out the hand as he'd started until he knew what was going on. "I'm hungry," he said. "Anything to eat around here?"

"You should've been here when the café was open, instead of gallivanting around everywhere." But she paused in her accounts long enough to fix him a fat peanut-butter-and-jelly sandwich and a big glass of milk with Ovaltine. It tasted good, or maybe it seemed so because he was hungry. Institutions fed three times a day, but the food was nearly inedible, so now this was especially good, if simple. Moreover, today he'd eaten nothing since breakfast, and his body was accustomed to a routine of eating something three times a day. As he ate, he forgot his aunt's attitude when he came in.

The last of the sandwich was in Alex's mouth when the front door opened. Ava was already in the living room.

"Did he show up?" Ray's voice asked.

"In the kitchen."

"What'd he say about school?"

Ava's reply dropped below Alex's ability to hear the words, but moments later Ray's footsteps sounded louder and the boy readied himself for confrontation.

"So you went to the school?" the man asked.

"Yes. I told Aunt Ava."

"You're a dirty little liar!" Ray spat it out, dripping contempt, his face flushing with his outrage. The fervency was like a physical blow, and although Alex had had premonitions, he was still thrown into a temporary blankness of emotions and thought, staring at the shirtfront of the husky man looming over him.

"Your parole officer came by just after you left . . . not ten minutes. We sent him to the school. He went to find you and came back two hours later. He didn't find you, and they didn't know a goddamn thing about you. He wants you at his office tomorrow morning."

Ava was in the doorway behind her husband. "We were so embarrassed."

"You made fools and liars of us," Ray continued.

The first accusation had stunned Alex and brought pangs of guilt. But when Ray kept standing over him with implied threats and actual accusations, the guilt turned into a small flame of angry rebelliousness that they inadvertently kept fanning.

"If it wasn't for your aunt," Ray said, "you'd still be in Preston Reform School."

"I know that—"

"Shut up!" The man jerked forward at the command, a move that made Alex flinch reflexively and then resent the man even more. He smoldered because he'd flinched. His values already equated fear with weakness and cowardice.

"Your parole officer told us to call him when you don't cooperate. He'll send you back any time . . . for your own good . . . before you get in real trouble again. . . . My wife cried with worry when you didn't come back today. I'm not going to let that happen again. If you wanna stay out here you're gonna play by the rules. You're going to school every day. You'll stay home on school nights, and be in by midnight on weekends. You'll work in the café on Saturday—"

"Remember church," interjected Ava.

"Right!" said Ray. "You'll attend services with us on Sunday. It will do you good to hear the Lord's word. You'll do what we tell you, and if I catch you in another lie I'm gonna take a belt to you." The man's voice was brittle with fervency if not actual hostility—and the words lost meaning to Alex, became a buzz in his head drowned by his own growing rebellious rage. This asshole uncle was the same as the men in institutions who'd brutalized him. Alex forgot Ray's words as his rage grew, but it was a rage accompanied by fear (the parole office could send him back). Ray was a powerful adult male, thick through the chest, shoulders, and arms, and although Alex was already as tall, he was far less husky and muscular. Also he was seated, jammed down between table and wall. Ray was standing above him. Alex had had enough experience with violence to recognize his futile tactical position. While on the edge of rage, he was half intimidated.

Meanwhile, Ray kept spitting out ultimatums—though now Alex's brain wasn't deciphering the messages. He was on fire within, seeing this as identical with cruel authority in institutions. Ray might just as well have been a guard as an uncle. The different factor was that here he, Alex, could leave, get away, escape. There were no bars, fences, and barbed wire; the police revolvers and handcuffs were vague and unimportant here. So Alex seethed silently, waiting, knowing he'd soon have space to rise and face the powerful man on equal terms—if he had an equalizer.

The chance came within a few minutes. A knock came on the front door. Aunt Ava called into the kitchen that it was the newspaper boy. Ray stepped through the doorway, reaching into his pocket for change. Alex was instantly on his feet, rifling through the drawers under the sink until he found the kitchen knives. He removed two—the biggest and sharpest—one razor-sharp boning knife, the other a butcher knife. He slid the butcher knife to the other end of the sink, letting it lie there on the white tile. He held the boning knife against his thigh, his palm instantly beginning to sweat, his heartbeat racing.

When Ray came back his gaze went to where Alex had been seated. He had to turn all the way around to face the youth, who was standing next to the sink six feet away. The man started to pick up his ultimatum-laden speech where it had been interrupted, but he instantly sensed that something was amiss. Maybe it was Alex's burning and unblinking eyes.

"Come sit down," Ray said, instinctively trying to establish dominance.

Alex remained motionless, except for a twitch of lip and cheek—and the narrowing of the blazing eyes.

"Did you hear me?" Ray said.

"I heard you. Fuck you!" As Alex spoke, he blushed, for the words had an inadvertent croak.

"Whaa . . . ?"

"I said fuck you!" Now the rage took over, wiping off indecision. "Fuck you, motherfucker—and your mother—and the horse both of you rode in on." He clenched the boning knife harder. It was still hidden. As he saw Ray's face register uncertainty, his brain sang with joyous rage—with the glorious feeling of rebellion and revenge. The man who had been omnipotent minutes ago was identical with Lavalino, The Jabber, and all the others. But they'd had immediate numbers, clubs and tear gas and dark, solitary confinement cells. Ray was alone, help too far away to really help until it was over. Tears of fury came to Alex's eyes.

"See that knife," Alex said, indicating the butcher knife. "Pick it up and let's see how fuckin' *bad* you are . . . dirty motherfucker! You're too fuckin' big for me to fight—but we can get it on—and I'll cut your motherfuckin' heart out and feed it to you." Even in the middle of rage, Alex was following a script some convict had told him—of offering the enemy a knife while issuing a challenge. It was the behavior either of ultimate *machismo* (a word still unheard of then) or of a madman.

When the truth seeped into the man, that this slender juvenile delinquent was honestly ready to fight with a knife to the death, the adult blanched. It was outside the realm of his understanding.

Alex wasn't bluffing. His mind had locked in, amputating any images of consequences or tomorrow.

"You're crazy," Ray said, and the declaration wasn't a full thought but a reflex, the initial reaction. It dripped fear. He had no doubts that Alex was real.

"If I'm crazy . . . it's motherfuckers like you made me crazy."

"You don't know what you're doing."

The red rage flashed up, nearly blinding Alex. *"Get it, punk!"* he snarled, meaning the butcher knife. "See if you can back up that shit you're talkin'! I'll cut your motherfuckin' heart out and feed it to you." He punctuated the maniacal threat by raising the razor-sharp knife and edging forward. Ray flinched, put his hands up with palms forward, his eyes wide. "Don't, Alex, don't. God . . ."

"You weren't saying that a minute ago. Where's all that shit you were talkin'? See if you can walk that walk."

At that moment, Ava entered the kitchen, oblivious to what had been going on.

"Get out of here," Ray said.

"What's going on?"

"I'm leaving," Alex said. "I'm getting out of this garbage can with this fuckin' asshole."

"What's wrong?" she nearly wailed.

"I said get outa here," Ray said.

"You can stay," Alex said. "This man of yours is a punk. If he was pretty I'd fuck him in the ass."

"Alex!" she cried.

"He's crazy," Ray said. "Okay, okay," he said to Alex. "Just leave."

"I'm goin', I'm goin', motherfucker! Get outa the way." He gestured with the wicked knife, indicating that Ray should move away from the door.

Aunt Ava broke into tears. They came in sudden, racking sobs. Her husband reached for her hand, pulling her away from the doorway.

Alex moved in a slight circle toward the arch while they kept edging away from him. "Motherfuckers like you fucked me over bad," Alex said, his escape route now clear. "I should—but fuck it. You talk all that shit, but you ain't got no guts when it gets tough. Call the motherfuckin' police. I'll be long gone." He backed from the kitchen door into the living room, pausing for a moment to look around. He saw nothing to hold him back, nothing he wanted to take with him. He pulled open the front door and stepped out into the night.

"On the fuckin' run *again*," he muttered as he reached the sidewalk and began to run. He laughed at his predicament. Destiny seemed to be either incarceration or the threat of it. "Fuck it! I'd rather be a fugitive than a captive. I don't belong with those people." He saw a dark alley and turned into it, looking for a place to hole up for a few hours, knowing that Ray and Ava would call the police, who would be looking for him in the area. When things cooled down he'd get away and find his friends in the underworld where he belonged.

22

Teresa's voice had a lilt of affection that warmed Alex even over the telephone, though he did feel a momentary pang when she said she hoped he'd learned how to stay out of jail. "Things are so much better out here. Just be patient and willing to work and you'll have what you want." He didn't deflate her optimistic advice by saying he was already a fugitive—or would be tomorrow when a parole violation warrant was issued.

"How can I see Wedo?" he asked.

"Did my mom tell you . . . ?"

"She told me what's happening. He still's my partner."

"I know . . . I still see him . . . when he has time. That stuff takes every minute of his life. He can't even *think* about anything else. When he isn't chasing it, he's half asleep on the nod."

"What about his phone number?"

"He doesn't have a regular place to live. He's here, there, with a friend, in a motel or hotel. He calls me."

"You don't have any place to reach him?"

"In a way. On Temple Street near downtown there's a place called 'The Traveler's.' He goes in there a lot, I guess. He said they'd take messages for him."

"What is it . . . a bar?"

"I think it's a café and a pool hall, but I've never been there. The number's upstairs—"

"No, I'll get it from the book—or find it."

"When're you coming by to see me? Lisa says you look really good, tanned and everything."

"Sheeit! Lisa *really* looks good. I'll come by in a few days, maybe on the weekend."

Alex replaced the receiver. The telephone booth was in a gas station. He walked out—and out of the circle of light—and down half a block to the car he'd hotwired and stolen a mile from his aunt's bungalow. By daylight he would have to abandon it. The owner would find it gone in the morning and report its theft. For that the license plates could be changed. He would have done that if it was an older car, the kind a teenager might drive; but he would be in the city's poorer neighborhoods, and it was a gleaming new Packard.

Driving the huge automobile through the night, the dashboard radio giving forth sentimental songs, Alex's earlier rage pendulumed to a mixture of melancholy, loneliness, and an inchoate longing. The feelings were not unalloyed agony; they were bittersweet. It was the ache of yearning, not of despair. At the particular time and under the particular circumstances, he was weary of his perpetual war with the whole world—a war he'd been fighting since before he had words to articulate such an idea—a war that, in the beginning, back in the mist of being four years old, had been an instinctive rebellion against being abandoned to foster homes and military schools. Now he somewhat understood his outcast condition, understood it more than even sympathetic adults would understand. In a few weeks he would have a fifteenth birthday, and he was already an outsider, a leper of the modern era. He had no family, the cold Calvinists he'd run from hours ago were certainly not his family. He already had a long record he could never escape. His choices were already severely truncated. He already belonged to the underworld and was locked out of the other world. What parents would let their nice daughters go out with him? Although he didn't face the reality head-on even in his mind, and although there were other fires and yearnings, the main pain was longing to belong, to love and be loved. That was the irreducible truth. He would find Wedo and team up with him, if Wedo was willing—not because that was his real choice but because he couldn't think of anything else to do. Wedo was a junkie, and Alex had heard enough stories to be leery and prejudiced about junkies, but Wedo was Wedo, whom he knew down to the real truths of loyalty and friendship. No matter if Wedo was flawed, was nearly illiterate, he was a loyal friend. He would gladly accept Alex as a partner. Whatever he was doing to maintain his habit, Wedo would know that Alex was game for it.

Tonight it was too late to continue the hunt. Temple Street was "hot" at any hour, but especially so after midnight. Anyone there at such an hour would either be the law or outside the law.

Alex nevertheless drove toward Temple Street, but a couple of miles away he turned into a closed gas station and parked in the dark at the rear. He left the radio on and climbed to the back seat. He cracked the back door so he could push it open and slide through bushes into a back yard. He had an escape route. He tucked his hands between his legs, curled up, and went to sleep.

When dawn was orange streaks against eastern clouds, Alex left the stolen car and began walking toward Temple Street. Half an hour later the streets were glutted, the sun was morning-bright, and he was on the block where the Traveler's Café & Pool Hall was located. The neighborhood was known to every junkie in sprawling Los Angeles County. When the city was dry everywhere else, Temple Street connections still had heroin for sale. Narcotics officers also knew it, making the neighborhood as "hot" as any; the café was "on fire." Alex first walked by without going in, pausing for just a moment to look through the window, but unable to see much because of vapor fogging it. He circled the block, readying himself, and then opened the door and went in.

The café and pool hall had separate sidewalk entrances, while inside an archway at the rear connected them. The café never closed, but the pool hall did so at midnight, opening again at noon. Alex paused to briefly study the hangout. On the left was the counter with two dozen stools. At the right, until the archway, were high-backed booths. At the rear was the kitchen door, a hallway to restrooms and telephone, and a jukebox (now playing Mexican *ranchero* music). Alex walked toward the restrooms, unobtrusively glancing in each booth on the slim chance of spotting Wedo.

Alex didn't see Wedo, but on the way out of the restroom, now thinking that he'd perch at the counter and wait a while, Alex did see a familiar face. It was very familiar, in fact, yet because of civilian clothes, a free-world haircut, and the gauntness of dissipation, it took several consternated seconds to dredge up the name. He might not have been able to if the name hadn't been unusual: Itchy! Itchy Medina. Always small-boned, he was now really skinny. His nickname came from his constant fidgeting, shaking out an arm, bouncing in a chair, shaking his head as if to ease a neck cramp; it was an obvious pathological condition reduced to a nickname. In fact, the first thing Alex noticed was that Itchy wasn't fidgeting. He hadn't spotted Alex. He was in a booth with a young white man beside him. The young man took money from a shirt pocket and passed it over. The young man saw Alex watching and spoke to Itchy, who turned his head, furrows of puzzlement instantly on his face, his eyes narrow. But recognition came in seconds. Alex knew it by the spreading grin, and he grinned in return.

Itchy finished his business, taking the money out and counting it, then taking something from his mouth and slipping it into the young man's hand. The customer was already starting to depart; he was in a hurry to get to his spoon and needle.

Itchy beckoned Alex, who noticed Itchy's expensive suit even while approaching. Itchy extended a hand as Alex sat down across the table. "*Ese*, Alex, *mi carnal*. What's happening? When did you get out?"

"Two fuckin' days, man . . . and I hung up the parole already." However, Alex was thinking that he and Itchy hadn't been close friends, certainly not brothers. They'd been nodding acquaintances with several mutual partners.

Itchy wrinkled his face in sympathy.

"You look like you're doin' real good," Alex said. "Unless it was gumdrops you were sellin' that guy."

Itchy chuckled. "Yeah, I'm makin' it . . . or maybe a little better than that." He stopped there, offering no details beyond the obvious. Alex recalled hearing that Itchy's uncle was Big Mike Medina, who had moved to Mexico on the eve of the war and who had been the first to recognize the U.S. market for brown Mexican heroin when the war foreclosed access to Turkey and the Golden Triangle of Asia. Big Mike was a multimillionaire "on the other side," the euphemism for across the Mexican border.

"What're you doin' here?" Itchy asked. "You wanna score?"

"Naw. I'm lookin' for a partner who fucks around in here, or at least buys smack in here."

"What's his name?"

"Wedo . . . Wedo Murphy."

"Murphy! That jive-stutterin' motherfucker! He owes me two bills." Then Itchy saw the consternation on Alex's face. "Hold it! I'm half-ass-jivin'. He owes me, but he's good for it. He spends a lot of money with me . . . and gives a lot away. He's been making some decent stings lately."

"Do you know where he lives?"

Itchy shook his head. "He told me that he moves every few days. One motel to another. But you'll find him. He comes in here to cop every day—from me."

Alex listened, felt good, and simultaneously wondered what Wedo was doing to support a big heroin habit and the daily rates of motels and hotels. No matter how curious he was, Alex couldn't ask Itchy. Although he was just turning fifteen, Alex had already incorporated many of the habits and values of the criminal underworld—and strong among these was a ban on curiosity about anyone's "business."

"Hey, man," Itchy said, "how 'bout a fix? A freebie?"

"Naw, man," Alex said, trying to show nonchalance. "I don't dig the high. It makes me puke."

"Just about everybody barfs the first couple of times. It still makes you feel *good*, man, *good!* Even the barfing doesn't ruin it."

"For me it does."

"Okay. You ain't doin' nothin', are you? Got somewhere to go?"

"No, a blank."

"Well, *carnal*—me, I gotta fix pretty soon . . . so like take a walk with me. Tell me what's happenin' at the old reform school alma mater since I got out. . . . What happened to that colored guy they claim killed that cleaning woman in the ad building? The trial was going on when I left."

"They're still in trial—the third one. He's had two hung juries already."

"You think he did it?"

"I got no idea. I know he can run with a football. And he always seemed like a cool guy—didn't fuck with anybody or start trouble."

"Didn't some college wanna help him get out and give him a scholarship?"

"I heard that, but it coulda been bullshit."

While standing at the front door waiting for Itchy to pay his bill, Alex realized that the Chicano was more intelligent than he once would have credited him for. Alex had just assumed ignorance.

Before stepping down the sidewalk, Itchy paused in the doorway to scan both ways. Even without narcotics on him, he was in danger. California law had a vagrancy-addict statute; a couple of fresh needle marks might mean six months in the county jail. "I'm on bail on a mark's beef right now," Itchy explained.

"Adult court?"

"Sure. Kids don't make bail, do they?"

The question was rhetorical, so Alex ignored it and asked another of his own. "How old are you?"

"Nineteen . . . last month. What about you?"

"Seventeen."

"You got another year of being a child in the eyes of the law."

"Unless I do something far out—some heinous crime—where they rule me unfit and transfer it to Superior Court."

At the first corner they turned and began trudging several blocks through the rundown neighborhood. They recalled mutual acquaintances, half-forgotten incidents. Sometimes they reminisced about someone, or asked what had become of this youth or that one. Before they reached their destination, Alex knew how to reach four reform-school buddies, who were now young men. One was a prizefighter ready for his first main event. "He'd be a contender," Itchy explained, "if he'd look out for himself and quick fuckin' around with that needle. It's gonna wash him up." Another friend was "in" with Mickey Cohen, the reigning Los Angeles gangster—but really just a bookmaker with high media visibility. The friend took bets in a Ventura Boulevard cocktail lounge. Others were in San Quentin—while far more were in county jails waiting to go there. One was awaiting trial for a robbery-murder. He'd stayed out two weeks.

Alex's friends were no longer juvenile delinquents, having passed the magical eighteenth birthday to reach legal manhood. The sudden metamorphosis seemed strange to Alex; he'd forgotten how much younger he was than his peers, at least younger in years.

Itchy led the way up a hillside street where the small frame houses were perched and pillared up steep flights of steps. They lacked front yards because they clung to the hillsides.

"I don't live here," Itchy said. "My mom and kid sister stay here." He opened the gate and they went up the stairs. "I've got a choice pad in Hollywood, but this is where I was raised." The bungalow was small and inexpensive, but it was obviously a home that someone cared for.

Mrs. Medina, also small-boned and thin, had seen them through the window and had the door open when they reached the porch. She embraced her son and smiled warmly when Alex was introduced.

"Some calls came for you, Henry," she said. "I took the messages down for you. I'll get them."

"Later, Mom. We're goin' in the bathroom now."

The happy smile dropped, but she said nothing in protest. The fight had been lost long ago.

In the bathroom, Itchy had the practiced dexterity of a surgeon. The "outfit" was wrapped in a filthy bandanna and stuffed up under the sink. Beige powder and water went in the spoon, four matches under the spoon brought a boil and dissolved the dope except for scum on top. A tiny ball of cotton was a strainer, as he drew it up through the eyedropper. Moments later, a belt wrapped around his bicep to distend the vein in the pit of his elbow, he tapped the needle in, knowing it was right when blood streaked the eyedropper. Alex noticed a three-inch line of bluish-black scar tissue along the vein. From institution lore, Alex knew the amount Itchy had used was tremendous, enough to kill two men, yet it had almost no visible effect on the Chicano. His voice got huskier, but that was about all.

"Last chance," Itchy said, readying to put things away.

"Nope. Man, I know I'd like it—so I don't want to try it anymore."

Itchy grunted, scratched his nose, and repackaged the paraphernalia. He made little, semihumming noises of pleasure, as if enjoying what he was feeling within. Something had changed, something sensed rather than defined. It was as if there was a wall between him and intense feelings of any kind.

Alex looked around the neat bathroom. It was immaculate and had bright guest towels and a scale. It was very middle class. "I don't see why you're a fuckup," Alex said. "I mean, man, you seem to be cool at home. Everybody else comes from a broken home, or their old man is a lush, or something is fucked up somehow . . . you know what I mean. *They* have all those theories. I fit 'em but you don't."

"Man, I thought you were a maniac in Preston, the way you fucked up and went to the hole all the time. I still think you're crazy, but you're not stupid, *ese.*" He paused, saw that Alex was waiting for an answer, and continued: "I went to Catholic grammar school. So did my older brother . . . who's graduating from U.S.C. law school this semester. But in this neighborhood, that ain't the way to be *in*. My brother didn't care about the fools on the corner, but I did. I wanted to be a bigshot to them, have some identity in the barrio, an' all that shit. Bein' the smartest in the class is to be a punk to them."

"Yeah, I sure found that out in Whittier."

"Right, *ese!* So I started fucking up to be accepted. The same with fixing. It was the most hep thing in the barrio . . . risky, but you know, eh? Besides, it takes away those nervous shakes of mine, the ones that got me this nickname."

Knowing how important acceptance was, Alex nodded.

"And sellin' dope is as much status as I can get here. It's power, too . . . over junkies anyway. They really kiss your ass if you've got the dope bag."

"What about your family?"

Itchy shrugged and made a discomfited face, obviously not wanting to delve into it. He fell silent, thinking, and without warning a "nod" came over him, a somnolence that drooped his chin to his chest. Alex had seen it before with Red Barzo and First Choice Floyd. A few seconds elapsed until Itchy jerked and came awake.

"What about Wedo?" Alex asked. "You say I can find him?"

"Oh, he'll be around sometime today. I'm the priest he's gotta see for his sacrament." Itchy grinned, winked, and then closed his eyes, luxuriating in his wit and the euphoric ecstasy suffusing him.

■

At dusk Alex and Itchy were in the pool hall of The Traveler's. The throbbing guitars and high-pitched singers of *ranchero* music came loud from the jukebox. Wedo Murphy pushed into the noisy, smoky room. Alex was leaning unobtrusively next to a wall while Itchy had two Chicanos in conversation. Alex had been watching the front door and saw Wedo instantly, watching him move through the crowd. His cheeks were gaunt and his eyes sunken. He was even skinnier than usual. His clothes were in style, as always, but they seemed unusually rumpled for the usually fastidious Wedo, who managed to keep knife-edge creases in pants and shirts even amidst the pervasive dirt and sloppiness of poverty. Now, however, his priorities had changed; the monkey had to be fed before anything else could be thought of.

Wedo's eyes flicked over Alex but without recognition. Wedo's gaze was unrelentingly on one person: Itchy. Alex walked around the spectators of a snooker game and came up on Wedo from the rear, getting his attention by grabbing his sleeve. Wedo turned, his eyes narrowed for a couple of heartbeats, and then they widened with recognition. "Alex!" he said; it was almost a question. "Holy fuckin' mackerel! You fuckin' finally raised."

"Yeah, man," Alex said, grinning so wide his facial muscles ached, meanwhile cuffing Wedo's shoulder while shaking hands. "I'm out again."

"Man, did you escape again—"

"No, they got weak and let me out—finally. I'm on parole . . . after almost four fuckin' years, less those few months on escape. When I went in, I was so young I couldn't get a hard-on, much less be able to come."

Wedo still listened, but the exuberance of the surprise quickly disappeared. Wedo's eyes were over Alex's shoulder, fastened on Itchy. Alex saw this and understood. "He ain't goin' nowhere . . . but you'd better see him to put your mind at ease."

"Yeah, man, gotta make sure he's holdin' the bag. . . . Say, you know Itchy?"

"He got out of Preston last year. I knew him there."

"Yeah, right, I knew he was there—but I just didn't think to ask him how you were doin'." He affectionately patted Alex's back. "I don't think about too many things lately . . . one-track mind."

"Okay, go see him . . . take care of biz. I'll be out on the sidewalk. Tell Itchy I said 'thanks.'"

On the sidewalk, posing with one foot propped on the wall, Alex stood watching the jam of vehicle traffic; the bumper-to-bumper autos inching along in the orange glare of sunset looked like a horde of insects—shiny-backed beetles. Alex felt young and energetic, yearning for adventure and excitement.

Wedo came out and walked by him without speaking, merely gesturing with a hand held low. It was best to get off Temple Street quickly, especially with fresh needle marks on his arms and five capsules of heroin in a cigarette cellophane in his hand, held loosely so the caps wouldn't melt. The narcotics officers, unable to catch big dealers, kept up their arrest reports by hauling in addicts for vagrancy and picayune possessions. Besides, Wedo was in a hurry. Nobody is more single-minded than a junkie going to fix.

In the darkness around the corner was Wedo's car, a ten-year-old coupe with a bashed-in right side. The headlight was out, the fender pulled away from the tire, and the right side door held shut by baling wire.

"Slide in the driver's side," Wedo said. "It runs pretty good, but I went on the nod and scraped a brick wall."

"This sure ain't the Batmobile," Alex said, sliding under the steering wheel and along the seat to the passenger side. "I can see us making a *hot* getaway in this fucker . . . like Laurel and Hardy it'll look. . . . Remember that one chase . . . that cop almost killed me."

Wedo grunted; he remembered but was too preoccupied with his imminent fix to reminisce now.

The silent ride took ten minutes of smaller streets where they were less likely to meet narcotics detectives or a black-and-white car interested in a dark headlight. The detectives knew Wedo's car. He was on bail as a vagrant-addict already. He lived in a third-rate residential hotel near Sixth Street and Alvarado. He parked in the alley behind the brick building, and they went up the rear stairs to the second floor. As soon as the door was closed, Wedo not only locked it but also pulled the dresser in front of it. "Just in case," he said. "They'll bust a foot if they try to kick it open." He nodded to the open door of a cramped bathroom. "Get some water."

Alex brought the water. Wedo was spreading his paraphernalia on the dresser. "At least you've got a toilet," Alex said. Wedo didn't answer; he was too intent on what he was doing. He went through the same ritual as Itchy, except his blood pressure was down and it took half a dozen probes until the blood squirted up into the eyedropper to mix with the heroin, giving notice that the needle was in a vein. He also "jacked it off," first squeezing a bit of fluid into his body, then letting the blood rush back into the eyedropper. He did it twice more, and finally squirted the whole thing into himself. Afterward, he wiped the blood from his arm with toilet paper and ran water through the needle. By then the ecstasy of "the flash" was coursing through him. "Mmmm," he sighed. "Jesus, it's fuckin' good dope. I'd give you a taste, but I've just got a getup for the morning." The heroin, at least this amount, made Wedo more voluble and energetic. His attention was now able to turn outward and really acknowledge the presence of his friend. "Man, I didn't think you were ever gettin' out," he said. "I heard stories about you fuckin' up—had a private war goin' with the greasers."

"Just with a few assholes," Alex said, blushing because Wedo's comment had been respectful. "What about you? How the fuck did you get hooked? You used to knock heroin."

Wedo explained that he'd dated a young woman—but older than him, of course—who was a dope fiend whore. She had left her pimp in Texas and didn't have a connection in L.A. Wedo had bought it for her, on her money, and began taking a fix now and then because she always offered it. The intervals between fixes grew less and less, and finally it was every day. She went back to Texas, and he woke up puking and hooked. "I usually do better than this," he said, meaning the sleazy room. "Not the Beverly Wilshire, *ese*, but spots way better than this. But I got pinched last week for marks and the *puto* bail bondsman and lawyer got whatever I had . . . and connections don't up *shiva* without bread, *que no?* I'll get it together now."

"What're you doin' to get money?"

"Lemme show you." He went to the closet, his back covering what he was doing with his clothes. Suddenly he spun around. "Okay, motherfucker! Freeze! Or I'll blow your fuckin' head off." He had a nickel-plated .32 revolver in his hand.

Despite himself, the aimed pistol frightened Alex. "Turn that thing away," he said, raising his hand for emphasis.

"Your money or your life, asshole!"

"Man, point that the other way." His fear was now tinged with anger. Wedo saw the truth and let the weapon hang along his leg.

"Okay," Wedo said, abashed. "Anyway, that's what I've been doing, pulling heists—two or three a week."

"What've you been hitting?" Forgotten was the momentary fear of the aimed pistol.

"Liquor stores, mostly. They're open late at night, and they're off by themselves."

"Can you get another gun?"

"Already got a sawed-off shotgun . . . just a single shot, though. It's in the car. I pulled my first two with that . . . then I got this thirty-two for five caps of stuff. Itchy can get you a pistol *quick*, man! Sheeit! He just tells those junkies he wants one. It'll be there. Those dope fiends will do anything . . . steal Mama's Kotex for two caps."

Alex laughed and clapped his friend's back.

"Where you stayin'?" Wedo asked. "Got a spot to crash?"

"Nowhere, man, nowhere. I even hung the parole up."

"*Este vato, ese,* you just sprung! . . . You ain't gave yourself a chance."

"Fuck all that preachin', man. Let's go make some money."

■

Half an hour later the battered car was cruising through the fringes of Hollywood, with multihued neon bouncing from the painted metal, giving it an undeserved sheen. Wedo drove, able to stay alert except at a couple of traffic lights; then Alex had to nudge him awake. The shotgun was under the seat; the pistol beneath a shirt on the seat between them. Alex was conscious of the broken headlight, which might get them a flashing red light from a prowl car. His belly was knotted and queasy as they cruised—a crime looking for a place to happen.

23

For any hour Alex was ready to point a shotgun at someone to get some money. His mind was locked in determination, his gaze fierce, his jaw muscles pulsing. They spotted a motel on Sunset Boulevard that looked good. The office could be reached by walking in from pitch darkness at the rear. They could park on a dark side street a block away, then appear and disappear via an alley without being followed. But when they parked and got out to walk back, a black-and-white prowl car appeared, coming toward them slowly. It was just about to go by when its spinning red light burst forth. Alex had been watching the prowl car, and the suddenness of the red light sent a bolt of terror through him. He tensed to run, thinking of the single-barrel shotgun under his jacket, and he even took a step before realizing the car was burning rubber— he wasn't thinking of them but of something else.

After that, however, Alex's composure was shattered. As they drove around, looking for something else to heist, Alex's determination oozed away, especially since he lacked Wedo's enslavement. For Wedo, withdrawals were more frightening a prospect than was arrest. He only *risked* being arrested; the agonies of withdrawals were inevitable if he failed to obtain the money to buy the heroin.

Alex rode silently, but his mind shrilled and keened with fear. He'd been out less than three days; the cage was so vivid that he was almost still in it. Instead of ignoring the fear to concentrate on the robbery, he tried to fight the fear down. The silent scream in his mind grew more piercing and sent tendrils down into his guts. Fear was equivalent to weakness in the unwritten codes—codes he accepted because they were of his milieu. When they stopped for a traffic light and another police car pulled up beside them, one officer glancing over, Alex verged on panic. The crushed headlight was legal cause to pull them over and "run a make." It was, among other things, stupid to be cruising around in such a rattletrap with guns, drug paraphernalia, the marks on Wedo's arms, and a parole-violation warrant on file for Alex.

When the light changed, the black-and-white pulled away. Wedo made a left turn. Alex reviled himself, yet was forced to admit that his nerve was shattered for this night. Unable to admit the truth to Wedo, he lied.

"Wedo, man, I'm fuckin' sick as a dog."

"Huh? What's that mean, *ese?*"

"It means my stomach is burning and has cramps . . . gotta take a shit. It feels like diarrhea."

"*Carnal,*" Wedo said, a note of both pain and petulance in his voice. "You know I gotta get some bread for *shiva* tomorrow."

"I thought you had a getup fix."

"Yeah, one chickenshit geeze . . . that I'll do up in a few hours. I need another one to get through the day . . . and one more for the *noche* so I can caper. I already owe Itchy . . . and I was short four bucks this morning."

"Look, Wedo, I'm sick . . . really! I've got a little over twenty bucks. That should get you fixed until tomorrow night. And I'll be all right tomorrow."

If Wedo had questions, he withdrew indicating them. His terror of the next day rescinded; he shrugged and headed the dilapidated car away from Hollywood toward Temple Street. Alex even maintained his lie by having Wedo stop at a drugstore on Melrose Avenue. Wedo waited outside while Alex went in to buy some Kaopectate. When Alex came back out, he was excited.

"Man, oh man! That's what we should rob." He jerked his thumb toward the drugstore. "Sheeit! There's all kind of dope in there. Ain't that so?"

Wedo took his thumb from the starter button and leaned forward to scan the drugstore's windows. Displays hid the interior; pedestrian traffic was light. "Yeah, there's lots of drugs in a drugstore. No heroin, but morphine, dilaudid, pantapon . . . goofballs and uppers up the ass."

"That's what I'm sayin'. Fuck, man, we could sell what we didn't want, and get some decent bread, too." He stopped and watched Wedo reflect. Wedo nodded agreement.

"Besides," Alex went on, "that pharmacist in there is skinny and scared, and has glasses thick as Coke bottles. He won't give us no trouble. In fact," he continued belatedly, "we better bring him toilet paper in case he shits on himself." Gone was the earlier fear. Alex was caught up in imagining his idea. The excitement erased fear. The wheels of his imagination were spinning madly.

■

Alex slept on the floor of Wedo's hotel room. It was a fortunate choice, for in the morning Wedo had several rows of red marks, hard little knots several inches apart in straight lines.

"Bedbugs," Alex announced, having seen the bites before. No other insect nipped in a straight line.

"Fuck!" Wedo cursed, scratching himself while standing in his shorts preparing his "getup" fix. "This is the last I got."

"I told you I had some dough. A little. We'll see Itchy. Tonight we'll have plenty of dope and money. I know Itchy'll buy some of what we get."

"What a way to live," Wedo said, squirting a line of water through the needle into the air, cleaning it; then he wrapped up all the paraphernalia. "How is it that we're like this and they're like they are? I mean, I don't feel like I'm so different . . . not down inside. I don't feel like I made a *decision* to be what I am." The powerful narcotic so obliterated all pain, physical and emotional, that it was the greatest tranquilizer of all. Euphoria is fertile earth for reflections on existence. "Aw fuck it," he said. "Let's go find that Chicano with the stuff . . . and we can cruise by that drugstore, *que no?* Check it out in the daytime—case the joint like the bigtimers do."

■

Itchy was missing from his pool-table office, but according to a pair of waiting junkies, one of whom was already getting sick, he was due momentarily. When he finally arrived an hour later, seven junkies were waiting. Christ personally dispensing sacraments would not have gotten more homage than did Itchy for his heroin.

When Alex and Wedo left, Wedo demanded to fix again, although he didn't need it. "I just wanna get high once," he said, "instead of fixing just to keep from being sick."

They had checked out of the hotel room, so Wedo used a gas station restroom, Alex leaning on the lockless door to make sure nobody came in.

Afterward, with Wedo nodding, Alex took over the driving. With nothing to do until nightfall, he cruised the city, happy to simply see things. In midafternoon the junkheap car was on the winding, expensively bucolic streets of Bel Air. The palaces of the rich peeked out between trees and over manicured hedges. The only life they saw was an occasional automobile or a gardener rolling up his hose. Alex tried to imagine what living in one of these mansions was like, what it meant in terms of a whole life—but such a world was too far removed from his experiences. To him being rich meant a new car, sharp clothes, and a slick apartment. Such things were hard enough to get—he certainly didn't have them except as a dream—and yet he could see clearly (others from his world couldn't) that his desires were trivial, picayune in this world. Bel Air was another universe.

Next he followed the winding curves of Sunset Boulevard to U.S. Coast Highway No. 1, and then along the seacoast northward for an hour. Wedo rose from his stupor but said little as he, too, became involved in watching the serene landscape of ocean, sky and green hills. It was far from the mean streets and the Sisyphian struggle of their tawdry lives.

At dusk they were back in the city, eating cheeseburgers and french fries at a greasy-spoon café. In fact, Wedo pocketed a cheap teaspoon and Alex asked for a paper cup of water to take with them. They parked in a deserted, still undeveloped spot on the road along the top of the Hollywood Hills. While Wedo used the dashboard glow to prepare his fix, Alex stared out over the endless city, the lights of which seemed like exquisitely bright jewels carpeting the world to infinity. It was so beautiful that he ached. The stars were coming forth as the sky darkened, but from here the city's lights were much brighter and more entrancing.

Wedo pulled Alex from his reverie, asking him to hold the flashlight's beam on the inner elbow so Wedo could see the blood register in the eyedropper. It flashed up, a streamer of red in the liquid, and Wedo squeezed the rubber knob, half-humming and half-sighing as the concoction flashed through his system.

"Well, let's go do it," Wedo said, voice gravelly; he was scratching himself in a variety of places. "Fuck! It's either got a lot of codeine still in it, or they cut it with procaine. They're starting that lately, makes the flash stronger . . . but they cut the dope. That's why I'm scratching. But it'll go away in a few minutes."

As they drove down from the hills and through the streets, the knot of fear was in Alex's gullet, but its fingers didn't probe through the rest of him to create a form of paralysis. Tonight he could control fear, for his greatest dread was not of capture but of showing a lack of courage and nerve.

The drugstore's doorway threw a rectangle of light across the sidewalk. Wedo went by and turned down the next street. They would come out, turn left down the side of the building, turn left again through an alley to the next street, and then to the right would be the car. Nobody would follow them down the alley, certainly no unarmed citizen, so nobody would see the car. And when Alex got out, sliding across the seat just vacated by Wedo to do so, he went to the back, looked at the license plate, and decided that when they came running a few minutes hence he would bend the license plate down. Nobody could even see it that way. After the getaway he would put it back the right way.

They began walking. Ahead was the lighted boulevard with cars flashing past the intersection. The fear cried for attention, but tonight Alex was resolute. He clenched his teeth and kept walking despite feeling a weakness in his legs. He refused to let his imagination conjure pictures of bloody shootouts and screaming police sirens. The single-barrel shotgun, sawed off to about twenty inches overall, was tucked beneath his armpit and under his jacket; his fingers curled around the pistol grip that remained of the stock.

As they reached the lighted doorway, a woman holding a toddler's hand came out, making them stop momentarily. Then they pushed in. Just one customer was inside, a man already paying for something and ready to leave. Alex turned to a magazine stand and acted as if he was looking for something. He would cover Wedo's back and capture anyone who entered at the wrong moment. Wedo went toward the pharmacist but waited until the customer had gone out the door. Then he opened his coat to show the revolver tucked in his waistband.

The bespectacled druggist flinched and nearly fainted as the word "holdup" wafted through the air. Wedo glanced back, got a signal from Alex, and vaulted the counter, pushing the man out of sight to the rear. Alex hadn't planned it before, but now he closed the door and locked it. The moment the robbery commenced the fear dissolved completely.

The danger, however, did a weird thing to his senses. He saw things with greater clarity, and shapes and colors leaped hard into his eyes. He heard with special acuteness—the metal cabinet door of the drug box being opened, the voices with occasional clear words. He could hear traffic outside that he hadn't heard moments before.

After what seemed an hour but was really two minutes, Wedo appeared with a heavily laden shopping bag. At his appearance, Alex ducked outside and went down the building to the alley, stopping just inside the darkness until Wedo's footsteps crunched nearby. They both ran for the car, Alex arriving first and crawling awkwardly past the steering wheel to the passenger side. He was laughing as Wedo flew in and started the car.

■

Two hours later they were in the bedroom of Itchy's Hollywood apartment. Dozens of bottles, in various sizes and colors, were in three piles on the bed—and a wastebasket held the discards, medicines of no illegal value. The three piles were opiates, amphetamines, and barbiturates.

"Three hundred for the uppers and downers," Itchy offered.

"Man, they're worth three or four times that," protested Wedo.

"Right, *ese*, if you wanna get out on the corner and sell 'em one at a time. I'm not doing that. I know somebody'll give me four bills, maybe four fifty . . . and *they*'ll sell 'em to the pillheads."

"What about the morphine, dilaudid, and etcetera?" Alex asked.

"We just wanna sell a little," Wedo said.

"Whatever you guys wanna sell, I'll cough up two bucks for each sixth grain, three bucks for each quarter grain—"

"Don't even mention the dilaudid," Wedo said. "It's too good to sell any of that."

"Yeah," Alex inserted, consciously and deliberately showing off. "That Persian tentmaker Omar Khayyam said he didn't know what wine merchants bought that was half so precious as what they sold." He watched his friends' faces; they were blank. "No dilaudid," he added.

"Then get it off the bed," Itchy said.

When it was over, Alex was nearly four hundred dollars richer; it was by far the most money he'd ever had at one time. Wedo had a little less in cash, but he had enough narcotics for a week, and therefore got a much bigger cut than Alex. It was also Wedo's best score, temporarily removing from his shoulders the awesome burden of pulling a robbery every other day.

As the elevator took them down to street level, Alex draped an arm around Wedo. "Let's go celebrate."

"And do what?"

"Fuck, I dunno. I've been busted since I was eleven. . . . What about the amusement pier in Venice?"

"Yeah, that's cool. But remember I gotta get back in three or four hours to fix."

"How could I forget that? Say, Wedo, doesn't it fuck with you . . . I mean your thoughts . . . knowing you *gotta* fix three, four, five times a day . . . day after fuckin' day. It's like bein' a Moslem in a way; they gotta pray to the east four or five times a day."

"Sure it fucks with me . . . but when I pull that needle out I feel so fuckin' good I can't tell you . . . so good there ain't no words. And if it takes *all* my time . . . fuck it! I'm a dope fiend. That's me from here on out, I guess."

Alex was silenced, stunned by the apparent nihilism. He remembered the other junkies he knew, mainly Red Barzo and First Choice Floyd. They knew what it was to "kick cold turkey" in a dirty city jail, stretched on concrete floors, vomiting for days after everything was up and there was only a sour, green bile. They experienced diarrhea beyond control, dirtying themselves and their underwear without access to a shower more than once a week. Mucus drained constantly from their noses, hot flashes alternated with cold sweats. Everything that touched their skin made their nerves cry and whimper in pain. Nor could they rest; they thrashed about, kicking their legs because some agony in the joints commanded it. Worst of all, these symptoms continued night after long night without respite, for sleep would not come for days—until they sometimes actually hallucinated—or until the body shut off the circuits and they had a few minutes of half-sleep several times a night, snapping from the sleep-stupor wringing wet, perhaps with a spontaneous orgasm. While they were hooked, the craving for sex was diminished, and sometimes eradicated. The torments had been described to Alex more than once, and he couldn't understand why they would immediately start "fixing" again at the first chance—even when they had been clean for months or years. "Nothing could be that good," he said. "Nothing is worth what's inevitably gonna happen. You know it's inevitable when you start. Nothin'—"

"Nothin' but heroin," Waldo interrupted. "That's God's medicine."

"Tonight, when we get back, I'm gonna try a fix. I really gotta know what's so good about it. I can't believe it's worth *all* the pain."

"You'll like it. I just hope you don't dig it too much."

"I gotta see why so many people make it their God. You guys give your lives to it."

"Oh man," Wedo said, laughing, "it ain't that bad."

"No? What is it, then?"

"You'll see, motherfucker, you'll see," he said fondly.

■

During the drive to Venice by the sea, Alex held an open bottle of Chablis between his legs. He was careful to swig when no headlights were close behind. He certainly didn't want them stopped for a trivial misdemeanor, especially when he lacked identification and a parole-violation warrant was out for him. Still, he consumed enough alcohol during the forty-minute drive to feel a pleasurable, warm glow in his belly, and the glow of intoxication in his brain, too.

Wedo parked in a lot a long block from the pier. The scent of the sea struck them the moment they got out. The glow of the pier's lights and the sound of its carnival music could be seen and heard over the intervening buildings. The music, in particular, aroused in Alex memories of the eight days he'd spent hidden out around here. The garage he'd lived in was a single block away. It was just two years ago, not long to an adult, but it was a large percentage of the life of a fourteen-year-old striding through pubescence to adulthood. So much had happened to Alex in the interim, so many changes. He wondered about Rusty and B.B. They had hidden and fed him. Now, had he been alone, Alex would have probably looked for them. But Wedo was with him, and to Wedo they would be "kids," too young to merit his attention.

For an hour, Alex and Wedo wandered aimlessly amid the crowds. They ate hot dogs and cotton candy, stood in the throng listening to the pitch of barkers at various shows—one showed the bullet-riddled car of Clyde Barrow and Bonnie Parker, or claimed it to be, and Wedo wanted to go inside, so Alex shrugged and went along, seeing nothing but an old Ford with numerous holes and a cracked windshield. Wedo got angry when Alex said, "Man, I could've seen this in a junkyard." It wasn't fighting anger, however, so Alex mollified it with humor and lighthearted ridicule.

Down the pier they stopped at the roller coaster, hearing the screech of joyfully terrified passengers getting their money's worth. They had paid to be scared—and they were—while still being safe. Alex would have taken a ride, and so would Wedo, but the latter was worried that the excitement would diminish the heroin in his system, necessitating that he fix out of his regular schedule. Thus they went on a little way, stopping at a penny arcade (it was already ten cents and would inevitably be three times that) to push coins into slots and play games. Mainly, however, they walked around and looked at things and people. The idea of having fun at the amusement pier lost its force once they arrived. Emotions necessary for enjoyment had been debilitated by the tension and adrenaline generated earlier to pull the robbery. It would take rest, perhaps sleep, for their systems to clear and for emotional capacity to be rejuvenated.

When they came off the brightly lighted pier itself, they decided to walk the boardwalk along the beach. It, too, was garish: hot-dog stands, fortune-tellers, movie theaters, the panoply one would anticipate under the circumstances—all of it bathed in colored globes and neon. Normally, Alex thoroughly enjoyed amusement parks, the rides, the games and the sideshows—and especially the shooting galleries. Now, however, he didn't enjoy it, but he didn't want to dampen Wedo's pleasure. Wedo, however, felt the same way: "*Ese,* Alex, let's hang this place up . . . go back to our turf and find a motel and fix. Then go eat something?"

"You're reading my mind."

The motel was on Sunset Boulevard near the invisible line that creates Hollywood in the center of Los Angeles. Wedo had stayed here before. Although the office was at the entrance, there was a rear driveway into an alley, so they could come and go without being seen. It was a nice motel that survived on persons who didn't want to be monitored or questioned.

The moment the door was locked, Wedo had a glass of water on the nightstand and was beginning to lay out the paraphernalia. Jesus, Alex thought, a junkie can't think about anything else . . . fix . . . fix . . . fix . . . fuck that.

"So you want a taste?" Wedo said.

"On second thought—I pass."

"Okay, more for me, *ese.*" He grinned and winked.

As is common among crime partners in the underworld, especially with junkies, the two youths were virtually inseparable. They were together nearly all the time. On the morning following the first armed robbery, Alex bought some clothes, including his first suit—powder-blue sharkskin. He even bought a couple of neckties, which he didn't know how to knot. That evening they picked Teresa up a block from her home and went to a movie. Afterward they cruised around, winding up on Mulholland Drive in the Hollywood Hills. Other cars were parked nearby, the occupants overlooking the endless flat sprawl of Los Angeles. The wide boulevards seemed to be twin streams—one of diamonds, the other of rubies, depending on which way the cars were moving. Wedo and Teresa in the back seat began necking so hotly that the sounds played on Alex's mind, arousing him. He got out and stood on the brink of the precipice, smoking and looking down at the city and at the lights of the few houses that dotted the closer hillsides and canyons. He wondered if he would ever have a house on a hillside with the city at his feet. He didn't know if he wanted one, or even what else he wanted, but he knew he wanted something. Maybe he could find better robberies for himself and Wedo. If he were three years older he could legitimately be on his own. Could he last that long? All he could do was exactly what he was doing—trying to steal or rob for the money he needed to live, trying to avoid arrest as a parole violator, trying to see life and experience as much of it as possible. Circumstances foreclosed him even thinking of long-range plans. His was a primal world of action and reaction, of continual tension and fear. It wasn't how most boys turning fifteen years old lived their lives.

His reverie was broken by the single headlight flashing on and off, summoning him to the car. Teresa had to get home.

After they dropped her off, Wedo fixed in a gas station. Then they cruised around looking for a score. They didn't look too hard. They still had some money, and everything they saw had some flaw.

The next night they stuck up another drugstore, this one in North Hollywood. It went without trouble, except that a customer came in, saw Wedo behind the counter with the pistol, and started to back out—until Alex prodded him from the rear with the shotgun. Customer and manager were left in a washroom. The young robbers got nearly four hundred dollars apiece from the combination of the cash register and what Itchy gave them for the excess drugs. Wedo now had enough dope to last for two weeks, an eternity of freedom of choice to a street junkie. They even abandoned the battered junkheap of a car when it wouldn't start, and each put up a hundred and fifty to buy a '41 Buick convertible in pretty good shape.

Wedo preferred to do nothing until they again ran short of money or dope. He preferred to spend his time fixing and nodding in the hotel or motel, going out to eat once or twice a day, usually quick-fried foods at some dingy café. Although much of Alex's young life had been spent lying around cells, which should have prepared him for sedentary living, he fretted about it. Even books failed to provide an escape from the forces grumbling around inside—a chafing irritant, an unfocused yearning, a rage for something. Sometimes he left Wedo dozing and went out to walk the neighborhood or go to a movie, although movies, like books, failed to provide a refuge for the nebulous dissatisfaction. In Preston, his thoughts were that everything would be good, even wonderful, once he resurrected. It hadn't proven true. The reality was dreary and lonely. When he smoked marijuana it failed to elate him, only increasing his sadness and fretfulness. Because in action and danger he could forget his depression, or anxiety, or whatever it was, he prodded Wedo to pull more robberies. Wedo would take the risk only when the wolf was at the door, so to speak, only when he lacked money for a roof and for heroin. Alex, in addition to being goaded by inner tangles, was dissatisfied by hand-to-mouth thievery. He wanted an automobile of his own and whatever else struck his fancy. The feeling of money in his pocket was good; it gave him options that alleviated some of the swirling bad feelings. He did not merely want to go out more often; he now felt ready to go after bigger scores than liquor stores, gas stations, and drugstores. Wedo, on the other hand, thought the smaller places were easier and safer.

In two weeks they lived in one downtown hotel and two Sunset Boulevard motels. Alex had two suitcases of clothes and was proud of how sharp he dressed. Wedo, who had always chased girls, was uninterested in that, too. He even pretty much ignored Teresa, which caused mixed feelings in Alex. He had eyes for Teresa, and if Wedo and she really broke up, maybe Alex could move in—but he disliked the expression and worried about being disloyal, whatever the expression. The three of them went out in the newly purchased convertible. Wedo was too full of drugs and kept nodding out and mumbling incoherently. That alone created tension in the car. Teresa finally showed anger when he didn't notice dropping a cigarette on her skirt until the smell of something burning made them look around. They found the smoldering hole, the size of a half-dollar, and put it out—but they didn't put out her fire. She wanted to go home, and she didn't want to see Wedo or talk to him again if he was blotto on dope. When she gave the ultimatum he felt almost nothing. The heroin in him eradicated the capacity for painful feelings. As soon as she was out of the car, Wedo muttered "fuck it" and let his head fall to his chest in the classic "nod," occasionally scratching his nose somnolently while Alex drove across the city at night toward the motel.

The next day, however, Wedo felt some pain. It showed itself in anger. "We'll show her, *carnal*. No bullshit . . . show her what she lost, *que no?* We'll cruise up in a long Coupe de Ville, know what I mean? And be sharp, sharp in a bad motherfuckin' Hickey-Freeman mohair and some alligator shoes."

Alex listened, nodded, and grinned warmly as his partner "talked shit." Alex hoped it wasn't a momentary attitude. He had happened to walk down a nearby alley while a panel truck was being unloaded behind a wholesale drug company outlet. The truck had a burglar alarm and heavy mesh separating the driver's area from the rear compartment. The rear also had special locks with dual keys. Like some safes, the one way to open it was for two keys to be used in sequence. The driver had one key, the outlet manager another. Alex walked out of the alley and around to the front. Horton and Converse was the company name. Prescriptions could be filled over the counter, but the main business was supplying pharmacies and medical clinics. The front window listed outlets in Los Angeles, Santa Monica, Pasadena, and Long Beach. Retail drugstores had been their best scores so far, and the easiest. Legal narcotics were dirt-cheap in comparison to diamonds and other things, and therefore wouldn't be so rigorously guarded. Their value was only in the underworld. Moreover, he couldn't sell diamonds, but he surely had an outlet for morphine and such. A place like this would have several times the quantity of a drugstore. He'd even mentioned it to Wedo several days ago, but Wedo hadn't been interested, especially when Alex added that they would have to look it over for a couple of days, and watch to see what was what. Wedo preferred to just drive around until they saw something, and then go take it. Now, however, Alex painted a picture of enough narcotics to maintain Wedo's habit for several months, plus enough for them to sell for several thousand. This time, Wedo listened, thinking that Teresa would eat her words if he showed up in a really classy car, maybe a three-year-old Caddy convertible, and him wearing a sapphire pinky ring and Italian silk suit.

24

alex took *the* job of casing the Horton and Converse branch because he distrusted Wedo's capacity to stay alert. After two days of
watching the opening and closing, Alex knew there were three employees: two were middle-aged men and the third a nondescript woman.
One of the men was the manager with the keys. He arrived first and
opened the door; he departed last and locked up. He drove a bronze
Chevrolet that he parked at the farthest limits of the lot, the car's nose
nudging the shrubbery next to the wall that divided the property from
the back yard of a house.

On the third evening, as the gray light of an unusual autumn rainy
day darkened toward a black night without stars, Wedo was crouched in
the dripping bushes with his pistol. He had insisted on that part of the
job after Alex had done the preparations. The bushes had room to hide
just one boy. Alex was directly across the street, standing beside a bus
stop bench, facing both the front door and the parking lot. The plan
was simple. When the manager reached his car, Wedo would appear
and capture him at gunpoint. Alex would see what was happening and
meet them at the door. Inside, they would force the man to open the narcotics locker. They would fill the shopping bags each of them carried,
lock the manager in the washroom or tape him up, and then depart. A
getaway car was unnecessary; the motel was too close. They would go
down an alley behind the building, cross a small street into the same
alley on the next block. Halfway down was a rear passage into the motel
area. They'd go up the side stairs and around a corner to the first room.

Alex waited, hands jammed in his windbreaker, the big, long-
barreled .38 police special stuck in his waistband, rubbing uncomfort-
ably on his hipbone. Despite his discomfort, he enjoyed the awareness
of the weapon. It gave him more than mere power. It gave him consciousness of that power.

The door across from Alex opened, throwing a rectangle of yellow
light across the sidewalk onto the wet asphalt. The female and male employee came out, their good-byes wafting across to Alex; then they separated. She went down the sidewalk, and he turned into the parking lot,

where two cars waited: his and the manager's, an old white Nash and the new bronze Chevrolet—about fifteen feet apart. The man's footsteps crunched audibly to Alex's keyed-up hearing. He reached the car door when suddenly there was a flash of movement beyond him. His hands started to go up in reflex and then dropped as the figure of Wedo reached his side. Alex's mouth dropped; he was dumbfounded. Wedo had captured the wrong man. While Alex was still stunned, both figures disappeared into the shadows in front of the car. Some meager shrubbery was there, too.

All was motionless and calm as far as Alex could determine. He'd held his breath without realizing it; it now hissed from between his teeth. Wedo was obviously holding the first man, waiting for the other. Perhaps he'd been spotted and forced to make the move. Now all they could do was wait.

A couple more minutes passed, during which a misty rain began. Alex turned up his jacket collar and backed away from the bench into a doorway. Finally, the front door opened and the manager came out. As he locked up, the burglar alarm sounded for a few seconds until he closed the door. He would shut it off when they went back in.

Alex felt his tension gathering as the man crossed the parking lot to his car.

A truck rumbled down the street, blocking Alex's view for just a second. When he could see again, Alex literally fell back a step. The manager and the employee were running full tilt across the lot in a direct line toward him. One of them yelled "Help! Help! Help!" until they reached the corner of the building. There they crashed into each other as one stopped to look back. Wedo hadn't pursued them. They unlocked the door, the alarm going off, and disappeared inside to call the police while the alarm kept ringing.

Alex had stood frozen, initially because he was stunned, and then because any action might have attracted their attention. The moment the door closed, he bolted across the street and through the parking lot, the alarm ringing in his ears. As he passed the cars, he yelled for Wedo, just in case. No answer. He took the route planned for the successful getaway, running flat-out. He had to slow for a second to get the pistol from his waistband. He carried it until he reached the dark passage of the motel. His breathing was hard from the exertion as he went up the outdoor side stairs two at a time on tiptoe, trying to combine both speed and silence.

The motel room's lights were out, but when he tapped softly on the door it opened instantly. He shut the door and turned on the lights.

Wedo was standing beside the bed. On the bedspread was a wallet and its contents—papers and cards and three one-dollar bills. Alex's burning eyes looked up from this pittance into Wedo's face, where he saw shame and apology. Always Wedo had been the leader. He was older and more experienced, and usually Alex deferred to him. In this precise moment, Alex became the dominant personality. Not consciously, for he was consciously just angry; not violently so, for Wedo was his friend, but furious in tone and demeanor.

"*That* was a *cool* fucking move," he said caustically.

"Oh, man . . ."

"Grabbed the wrong motherfucker. Jesus!"

"How did I know?"

"Because I told you what fuckin' car. Damn!" He shook his head in disgust, and Wedo said nothing. "What happened back there?"

"I grabbed him, took his wallet, and found out he wasn't the right guy—so I had him lay down under his front bumper. I jumped the wall and split."

"Why didn't you just wait for the other guy?"

Wedo shrugged and shook his head. Later he would rationalize his reason, find an excuse, but now he just felt bad.

"That fool just lay there for five minutes—by himself. Jesus!" Alex shook his head in disbelief, then sneered at the wallet and three dollars on the bedspread. "Is that our *score?*" He couldn't restrain a snorting laugh.

Wedo managed a wan smile. "*Carnal,* I'm sorry I fucked up." He spread his arms to emphasize his sincerity.

Alex shook his head and his eyes were wet. "Fuck it . . . wasn't nothin' there anyway."

■

Half an hour later the Buick was still on Sunset Boulevard, but instead of being near downtown Los Angeles, it was in West Hollywood's Sunset Strip. Most of the posh women's shops and antique stores were closed, but the four-star restaurants and big floorshow nightclubs of the era were doing good business. According to newspapers and some ragged movie magazines Alex had seen in "G" Company, this was the playland of movie notables, the stars and those who got rich behind the cameras or in offices. Alex wasn't looking for something to rob—and it didn't seem he would find it on the Sunset Strip. A big liquor store might have been worthwhile, except that it was across the street from Ciro's, a big elegant nightclub with doormen and parking attendants taking and bringing automobiles. Too many eyes could see through the plate-glass windows.

"Let's go down to Santa Monica Boulevard," Wedo suggested when they neared the end of the Strip, beyond which sat the perfection of Beverly Hills, a world that awed Alex.

"Good idea," Alex said without turning his eyes from the sidewalk, wanting to retain his keyed-up determination, a sort of half-anger necessary to pointing a pistol at someone and taking their money. He could not relax and let the tiny ball of inescapable fear grow and spread until it paralyzed him. He'd learned that he couldn't think too much about what *might* happen; if he did the images could become terrors and cripple him.

As they sat in the left-turn lane, a sheriff's car went by, and Alex was glad they weren't still driving Wedo's clunker. It would always get a police stare, and therefore always added to the chance of them being pulled over.

Santa Monica Boulevard was long and wide and lined with a myriad of businesses, everything from an athletic club to a U-Haul truck rental. Alex could see the neon for miles ahead and was certain they would locate a score. Several times Wedo slowed so they could look at something. Once they circled the block to scrutinize a small grocery. It looked perfect until Alex saw the proprietors—they were Orientals. He knew the underworld maxim that Orientals would prefer death to surrendering their money. Alex wanted money, not murder.

LIQUOR pulsed the big red neon sign. On a corner with a dark side street, it was the ideal getaway situation. Businesses on the boulevard were dark and empty. The closest possible witnesses were in a beer joint on the next block. He began adrenaline pumping as he sensed that here was what they sought.

"Turn right," he said. "Make it slow. I wanna look in."

As Wedo made the turn, Alex scanned the interior through the open door. A big man with a shiny pate was behind the counter.

The side street had apartment buildings on both sides. Cars lined the curbs, leaving nowhere to park except in front of a fireplug in the glow of a streetlamp.

"Put it there," he said.

"It's a bad spot," Wedo said.

"Fuck it. We ain't gonna be long . . . and nobody's gonna be followin' us."

Wedo shrugged and parked. He turned the wheels out and left the key in the ignition. The slight risk was worth the gain of a fast getaway.

Both youths began working themselves into the state of nervous anger necessary to pull pistols and take things. It was easy to reach this condition by remembering the mistake of an hour ago. Frustration made good kindling.

"Man, let me take him and you cover this time," Alex said—and even while he spoke Wedo shook his head.

"No, *carnal*. We'll do like we been doin'. You lay back in the door an' cover me. I'll throw down on the guy and get the bread."

Alex clicked his teeth together, cutting off the impulse to argue before the words came out. Wedo had to make up for the earlier blunder. It was weird, Alex thought, but whenever he was committing a crime his faculties were acutely perceptive. He saw things that were usually filtered out. He understood Wedo as if actually looking into his mind. He also perceived such things as the sound of their footsteps on the pavement, the growl of a truck a block away, a barking dog. His eyes caught the flaming eyes of a cat in a driveway. The red and green circles of a traffic light pierced his senses. He said nothing, for to speak would lessen the intense concentration he needed to point a pistol at people and take their money. They weren't real people; he couldn't let them become so in his mind or he would sprout doubts and misgivings. They had to be the enemy, those who condoned caging him, condoned the "holes" he'd been in, condoned the tear gas and beatings. The policemen, attendants, and guards were their surrogates. He owed them nothing and could maintain the rage toward society that allowed him to rob, steal, and hurt people without guilt.

Now they were in the light of the liquor-store window, ten feet from the entrance. Alex patted Wedo on the back and held back a moment so Wedo could enter first.

As with most California liquor stores, this also served as a convenience market. When Alex entered, Wedo was coming from the rear cooler with a quart of milk. The big, balding man was at the cash register halfway down the counter. Nobody else was visible.

A single glanced showed all this. Alex turned his back and faced a magazine rack along the wall beside the door. It was intended to hide his face and make him look busy. He watched the door; it was his responsibility.

Wedo spoke, his voice dripping fervency though the words were indecipherable to Alex.

"Huh?" the manager said, disbelieving.

"You heard me, punk motherfucker!" Wedo said loudly.

Alex glanced over his shoulder, saw them confronting each other,

Wedo's hand under his jacket near his waist. He had his hand on the exposed butt of the pistol. The big man, bald head gleaming with sudden sweat, had both hands visible.

CLICK-CLACK

The sound was loud, whatever it was. Alex frowned, puzzled.

BOOM! BOOM! The deafening blasts of a shotgun loaded with 00 buckshot.

Alex whirled at the first sound, then dropped to a crouch. The second blast tore away Wedo's left shoulder and cheek, spinning him like a child's top while he screamed. Flesh and blood were blasted away, splattered against a wall; it mingled with smashed bottles. Wedo was down, legs thrashing, screams following each other.

Horror and terror filled Alex as he lurched backward. His own pistol was out. He crashed into the magazine rack and wondered momentarily if he was shot without knowing it.

The manager's bald head came up over the counter. "There's two of 'em," he screeched.

Above the box freezer a man rose up, knocking over a SEAGRAM'S 7 sign he'd hidden behind. He was identical to the man behind the counter. He had the shotgun open and was jamming a red cartridge in as Alex came up. The man behind the counter now had a long-barreled revolver. Alex ducked behind a shelf of canned goods. Some fell, rolling along the floor.

Wedo still screamed.

The big freezer faced the two aisles. The man with the shotgun was kicking over display signs to get into position. The man behind the counter was edging along it. "Billy!" he yelled. "We got the bastard. We got him!"

Fear nearing panic overwhelmed Alex's rage. He was still near the front door. For one instant, quick as a flick of light, he envisioned the other, dark market. But that recollection was gone instantly as he confronted the reality of this moment. He had to get out of here, run the gauntlet. He locked his brain on that one truth—and came up shooting, busting one toward the counter, turning two toward the top of the freezer. The man behind the counter fired once, the bullet sizzling next to Alex's ear like an enraged yellowjacket. Alex's bullet did nearly the same, for that man dropped from view. Alex dashed to the door, meanwhile blindly firing across his chest toward the top of the freezer. His bullets pierced the glass doors and shattered bottles inside.

As he reached the door the shotguns went off, the concussion literally shaking the air. Two pieces of large buckshot hit Alex, one just behind the right hipbone, the other in his right thigh. The force of them hurled him through the door and knocked him down for a moment, jerking his right leg from under him. He came down on his right elbow, scraping his skin away as he skidded.

Momentum carried him around the doorframe beyond the direct line of fire. The same momentum brought him back on his feet, running in a crouch past the lighted window, his mind screaming in fear and rage. As yet he felt no pain, nor was he aware of the blood until, halfway down the block, his right leg collapsed and he fell. He reached down and felt the blood pouring out. When he tried to rise the leg buckled.

The men rushed out on the sidewalk, framed from the doorway light. Alex raised his pistol and shot once. The bullet brought a scream. One man sank down; he wasn't dead because he was whining loudly. The other man jumped behind a car and began shooting down the dark sidewalk. Now, however, Alex was also behind a car. He had extra bullets and was trying to reload, but he was too frantic, hands shaking. He got two bullets into the cylinder and dropped most of the others. The car was thirty yards away. He lay on his back and began squirming along under the automobiles, oblivious to whatever dirt or oil was on the asphalt. At first he was goaded by fear and defiance, by his rage against surrender in any form. Soon, however, he realized he was too slow. Already the outcry of police sirens was audible. Moreover, his strength was oozing away, and he was terrified by the weakness creeping through his limbs. For the first time in his life he understood the fear of death. Life was draining away unless the bleeding stopped.

The sirens reached a crescendo, then died to a whimper; red and blue lights throbbed against the buildings. Lights were on; people were coming out.

"Where is he?" a voice yelled.

"Somewhere along here," another answered.

"I quit!" he yelled, the words and accompanying tears torn from him.

"Don't move!"

So he lay in the gutter half under an automobile. The lament of other sirens peaked as they arrived. He could see the dark shapes of onlookers. He was going back to jail. It would be even longer this time. "Jesus!" he muttered, made sick by the thought of the cage.

A spotlight illuminated the car he was under.

"Throw your gun out," someone yelled. "Then come out on your stomach."

Suddenly the automobile he was under was sprayed by a spotlight. The glare blinded him. He was getting dizzy. He managed to toss the pistol clear of the car into the street. He heard the commanding voice again, but now he was spinning and the words were indecipherable. Blackness sucked him down.

When he came back to awareness—or halfway so—legs and shoes were around him. Most were dark blue, those of policemen, but those lifting him were white. He was certain he would live.

Before he slipped away again, he had a thought: If there's life, there's hope. I won't give up. The story isn't over. . . .